Without Fault

The Hale Series

Janiah Benitez

Trigger Warnings

Fatphobia
Eating Disorder (Purging)
Mentions of Childloss
Mentions of Addiction
Alzheimer's

To anyone who has ever looked in a mirror
and felt like they weren't worthy, you are *without fault.*

Chapter One

SAGE

"**I** FEEL LIKE YOU GUYS are just using me." I look around the room. "Am I being used right now?" I cross my arms playfully, and the girls let out a soft laugh.

"Please do mine," Royal starts, and I try not to laugh at how desperate she sounds about having me in her photo shoot.

Our annual contest officially started a few days ago when we all decided on our location and themes, but Vincent freaking *Moore* posted that he was excited to see what we came up with, and now the stakes have been raised. This just went from a friendly competition to a fight for our lives. That's not an exaggeration.

Vincent is the best designer and owns the biggest modeling agency in the world. He's located in Italy—hot accent, by the way—but he's having a show in LA for his new designs and has asked to have *every* Magic Model. A few of us passed out when we got the news, but he's also having a show in New York in a few months, and we all want in on it. Everything leading up to it is simply to impress him.

All of us work with Magic Model, and we're The Core Eight— we're who you think of when you think of Magic Model—and every year, we compete in this friendly photo shoot contest.

It started off when we had a *horrible* photo shoot, and after complaining to Florence, the CEO and founder of Magic, she told us not to be brats. One of us mentioned how we could've done better than the mess she had us in, and to be very fair, that was rude to say because Florence has never made us look bad. She just got scammed and booked with a bad photographer *once*. She was too prideful to admit it and told us we *couldn't* do better, so the competition started, and it's been how we start off the new year ever since.

We're not allowed to use anyone with a professional background in photography. All of our models have to either be baby models who are new to modeling or not models at all. *But* we get cool equipment to make up for it. Everything else has to be on us.

"You won last year. You don't need her!" Quinn brushes Royal off before handing me a chocolate cupcake. "Be in *my* photo shoot."

I tilt my head back with a laugh, and she nudges the sweet bribe closer to me. We're allowed to be in each other's photo shoots, and ever since Vincent made his post, they've been *harassing* me.

"I don't think either of you need me. You all are great–"

"Oh, shut up, Sage!" Coral throws herself onto the couch, lying lazily over Stel and Macey. "You can post a picture of your pinky and get a billion likes. You know the entire damn world loves you."

Royal agrees before snatching *my* cupcake away from Quinn. "Stop making us kiss your ass and just show your pretty face in our projects so we can get the views." She clearly is losing her patience, and I bite back a laugh.

I turn to the couch where my best friend sits on her phone.

"What do you think?" I ask Helena, and as if she can feel my eyes on her, she looks up at me.

"I think you're going to be in *my* photo shoot, of course, since you're my best friend."

They all start yelling about how that's not fair, and I can't stop laughing.

Nin quietly walks over to me, and I smile at how cute she is. "Can I talk to you?"

I fully turn to her, and she crouches down next to my seat to show me her phone. She shows me a few of her ideas for her photo shoot, and I love that she cares about my opinion. Every year, she consults me in great detail about what she should do, and it makes me feel like she's my little sister for some reason.

"I think the lake setting is better since there won't be as many waves as the beach, and you can get this vibe." I swipe through her reference pictures. "You can also make waves if you want this other vibe and control how they look."

She nods to herself before opening her notes app and writing something.

"Hey!"

I glance over at Stel, and she sits up in her seat.

"Are you *helping* her?" Stel quickly stands, and I bite my cheek before putting my hands up in mock surrender.

"Fucking traitor." Macey shakes her head at me, and I can't hold back my laugh anymore.

"We're allowed to help each other!"

They go on about how I always help Nin specifically, and when I turn to her, her cheeks are slightly flushed. I silently nod for her to not worry about it and she sits next to me quietly.

"Okay," I turn back to the girls, and it's clear I have their undivided attention. "I'll work with whoever is most convenient. I love you all, and you know I'll bend backward for you, but I need to give my photo shoot most of my attention."

I agree to help Helena since her's is in our hometown in LA. Royal voices how her's is in Chicago, and since it's technically close to New York, where my photo shoot is, I agree.

I originally wanted to do mine in LA since my theme is sports. I had the idea of working with my brothers since they play for the LA Dodgers, but Helena snagged LA, and we can't work in the same cities, so I'm settling for the Yankees instead.

"Mine is in Vegas, but if you just fly from LA after Lena's, you can do mine."

I think of Quinn's words, and it's not ideal, but since she *did* ask first and offered me a cupcake, I agree.

My alarm goes off before any of them can continue to convince me to join them. "Okay, I need to–"

"Wait! Hear my idea first!" Stel rises from her seat with Macey close behind her.

"I need to get to work, the boys–"

"It'll take two seconds."

I let out a soft laugh as she follows after me. She rambles her idea, and it's honestly really good.

"Damn, why didn't I think of that?"

"So, will you be in it?"

I agree only because I think she has the potential to win, and if my face being in it will give her the views they all think it will, I'll do it.

The rest of the girls trickle out of my room, and I still can't believe they flew all the way to New York to persuade me of this.

"You know," I turn on my heels. "Since I'm in *your* guy's photo shoot and since you're already here, you may as well help me today." I smile over at them, and they all agree.

We order two cars to get us there and make it to the studio pretty fast. A few tinted cars are parked outside, and considering they're all cars from luxury brands, it's safe to say the baseball boys are here.

My eyes land on a motorcycle as I step out of the car, and I nod to myself at their taste. I don't know much about bikes, but my brother has one, and I'm sure he'd kill to ride this.

Their loud voices fill the studio as I walk up the stairs, and I silently pray that they aren't insanely immature because we need to get some work done.

Their team agent agreed to work with me fairly easily. The few who are in my shoot are all getting paid, of course, but I also agreed to do the team's preseason pictures free of charge.

I still wish I could've done this with the Dodgers since, again, my brothers could've been in it, but also because I love their teammates. I decided to stop sulking about not being able to work with them and put on a smile.

We quickly have the boys' attention as we walk in. A few of them go completely still, and a few others whistle at us. I take note of the ones who whistle and make sure to steer clear of them.

"Hello, I'm–"

"I don't think we need the introduction." A surprisingly tall boy walks over before taking my hand and kissing the back of it. "It's a pleasure meeting you, Sage Loana."

I smile up at him before pulling my hand away slowly. "Thank you," I glance at the group. "I have a list of names, but we should still go around and introduce ourselves—oh! Also, share one thing that starts with the letter of your name; it'll help me remember names."

I walk over to the center and the girls stay in the back, waiting for instructions. My group of baby models voice all of their names, and I laugh softly when they thank me immensely for choosing them to work with me.

I check off their names as they share them, nodding to myself when I see all of them are here. The boys introduce themselves next, and I notice we're missing one of them. I glance around the room and see a guy sitting in the corner on his phone. I almost think he isn't in the group, but I ask anyway.

"Liam?"

He looks up slowly, and with the way he looks at me, you'd think I just asked him to leave... although with how miserable he looks, maybe he'd prefer if I asked him to leave.

"Are you Liam Walker?" I asked since he didn't really answer me.

"Yes."

I glance around the room to see what his problem is, but no one voices anything, and when I look back at him, he's on his phone again.

"Okay, thank you so much for sharing, Liam. That was my favorite one yet!" I smile over at him, and he drags his eyes over to me again and just *watches* me. I think he's going to tell me to fuck off, but he only looks back at his phone.

"Don't mind him," Amir, the one who kissed my hand, starts. "It's that time of the month," he whispers loud enough for us all to hear.

I let out a soft laugh, along with the rest of the room, and when I look back over at Liam, it was as if he didn't even hear him. I feel a bit bad that everyone is literally laughing at him, so I tell the group to get to know each other as I walk over to him, and the boys waste no time getting friendly with the girls.

"Hey," I sit next to Liam, and he glances up at me for a second before looking back at his phone. "Are you okay?"

I notice a small crease growing in his brows, and he looks up at me again. He studies me for a beat before his glare is back. "Yes."

"Oh..." I lean back a bit, trying to decipher the mood he's in. "You seem upset."

He studies me again before turning his head to the side. "Is this on your agenda?" He gestures to my iPad. "Interrogate everyone?"

I let out a laugh but cover my smile with my iPad when his glare somehow hardens. "I don't think I'm interrogating you." I uncover my smile. "But since you feel so harassed, I'll leave you alone."

"Great." He looks back at his phone, and I shrug him off before I return to the group. Whatever. I'm not going to let his mood ruin mine, nor am I going to hold it against him. If he's having a bad day, I'll let him have a bad day.

I scroll through my notes for today before getting the box out with the outfits, and when everyone tries them on, I feel my excitement building. The girls have custom jackets with the jersey number and name of their corresponding partner. I designed the jackets so they're way cuter than regular varsity jackets, and it's clear the girls love them, or at least the boy they were partnered up with.

"Okay, let's get started!" My excitement starts to grow as I tell everyone today's agenda.

Chapter Two

LIAM

THIS IS TORTURE. I'VE HAD to be in this suffocating studio all week, and I genuinely thought it'd get better as the days went by. I was wrong. It's been getting worse as the seconds go by.

"Don't look too miserable!"

My eyes follow Sage as she walks past me like today is the best day of her life. This woman laughs and smiles and is just *chipper* all the time. I may start taking her coffee from her because I don't think this is healthy.

I keep telling myself that there are only a few weeks left of this, but I still can't grasp *why* our agent agreed to this. We're getting paid chump change compared to our checks and *free preseason pictures*? I'd pay any amount of money for those pictures if it got me out of this.

It's not even the money that I'm annoyed about; it's the *people* in this place. My teammates are horndogs, following after every girl, and the models are drooling all over them. The number of shitty pickup lines I've heard should be illegal.

"You know..."

I keep my eyes on my phone as that unmistakable voice starts.

"We've been here for five days, and I haven't heard you say more than—" She takes a second, and I think she's counting. "Eleven words."

When I don't respond, Sage sits beside me. She nudges my arm, and I slowly turn to her. "What?"

"Twelve words!" She beams like she just won the lottery. "This is an improvement." She nudges me *again*.

"Don't touch me."

"Fifteen words, wow." She holds her heart. "I think you're warming up to me." She laughs at whatever look is on my face, and when I don't give her a reaction, she tilts her head to the side before turning more serious.

"Okay, seriously, what's up with you? I want this to be fun for everyone, and you look miserable. Tell me what I can do to make it better."

I keep my gaze on her, and when she offers me another beaming smile, I can't understand why she cares so much. Every day, I don't talk to her, and every day, she sits in this corner and asks me if I'm okay. Since when did silence mean I hate my life?

"Don't worry, Sage." Jordan walks over to us, and I roll my eyes at him because I'm sure he simply walked over here to piss me off. "He's in a pissy mood since he was forced to be here against his will."

"What? Who's forcing you to be here?" Concern rings in her voice. I shake my head at her, and when I don't respond, Jordan tells her.

"Coach is punishing him for not keeping his dick in his pants, but also for his bad temper. This is his anger management class."

"Fuck off." I bite out.

Sage laughs and tries to be quiet about it but fails. "Well, you've thankfully kept all your... *parts* in your pants–" She *giggles*. "—and I haven't seen an ounce of anger coming from you. If you give me his number or email, I'll tell him you were on your best behavior, and you can just go."

I look up at her in surprise and expect another joking smile, but she seems sincere.

"And why would you do that?"

She shrugs before standing, hugging her iPad to her chest. I swear that thing is glued to her. "I don't want you to have to suffer any more than you had in the last few days." She tells me to have a good day before walking off, and I stand without hesitation to grab my things.

"Oh, I don't think so." Jordan snatches my helmet, and I try to grab it back, but he takes a step away from me.

"Jordan, don't start because I will actually punch you in the face. Give–"

"Hey, if I have to be here, so do you. Cheer the fuck up, buttercup." He walks off with my *helmet*, so I follow him. "Look, guys! Liam is joining us."

"No, the hell–"

"Really?!" Sage whips around, and her green eyes land on mine. I study her for a beat, trying to figure out if her eyes are really *that* green or if they seem that way against her dark skin.

"No."

Her smile drops, and I turn back to Jordan, but he goes on before I can. "Coach is asking us all to check in that you're here." He shrugs. "What if someone snitches?"

"You mean, what if you decided to be a dickhead and snitch."

Jordan laughs, and when I take a step toward him, he takes several steps back, but it only pisses me off more. I pull in a deep breath, and he must notice I'm about to punch him because he turns serious.

"Okay," He puts a hand up, stepping forward to surrender my helmet, and I snatch it back from him. "You seriously can't leave, though." He tells me Coach has been randomly FaceTiming my teammates to make sure I'm here, and I hate how much of an asshole Coach is.

All I did was sleep with his daughter and beat up her boyfriend, and now I'm being treated like a murderer in a maximum-security prison. I didn't even know she had a damn boyfriend, and *he* swung at me. Coach's daughter is a cheater, and Liam is the bad guy. I shake my head of my thoughts before returning to my usual seat.

After a few minutes, some girl starts crying, and I decide I'm leaving. I'm heading towards Sage to get to the exit when she whips around and bumps right into me.

"Oh!"

I wrap an arm around her waist and quickly catch her as she stumbles backward. "Those heels are going to get you killed."

She takes a step back as she steadies herself. When she looks up at me, she rests her hand on her hip. "I'll have you know I was awarded Best Walk in nine-inch heels."

"Right." I raise my brows, unamused.

"It's true!"

"Right." I try to walk past her, but someone else bumps into me, and I let out an annoyed breath. "Watch where you're going."

"Sorry!" She wipes her tears, her makeup running down her face, and I feel my skin crawling as things clearly start to fall apart in here. I hate mess, and this is getting messy.

"I am so sorry again, babe..." Sage tries to reassure her, and she sounds like she really does feel bad about whatever she did to this girl. "They're not my rules, and if I can have it my way, I'd let you–"

"It's okay." The girl in tears rushes to reassure her, but she does *not* look like it's okay.

Sage tells her she doesn't have to leave, and she looks a bit better, but says she's going to get herself together in the bathroom.

Sage looks up to the ceiling and lets out an exasperated breath before turning back to me. "This is a mess." She shakes her head, looking over at the group.

"Yeah, I can tell."

A relieved smile touches her lips as she looks back over at me. "Thank you for that, Liam. You sure do know how to make a girl feel good." She quickly shakes her head, and I bite my tongue in amusement at how flustered she suddenly looks. "That's not what I meant."

"What's not what you meant?" I cock my head to the side, and she somehow looks more nervous. "Someone has a dirty mind."

"What?" She laughs, but it's clearly forced. "I have no idea what you're talking about, but clearly, *your* mind is the dirty one."

"Mhm."

She ignores me. "My photographer needs to walk since she has two and half years of experience." She shakes her head at something. "It's dumb and my fault for not doing a background check, but now I need a photographer."

She holds the camera out to me, and I glance down at it before looking up at her. She's simply watching me as if I'm supposed to know how this is my problem.

"You have yet to state your point."

She waves the camera around my frame. "You're not in the photo shoot for whatever reason you are against sharing, and you're *supposed* to be helping behind the scenes, but you've been sulking in that corner–"

"I was not *sulking.*"

"Right."

I return her sarcasm with a blank expression.

She only laughs softly before continuing. "I need a photographer, and we're officially a week behind since we need to start over. That leaves no time to find someone." She pushes the camera into my chest.

"Don't–"

"You seem capable of clicking a button."

"Don't cut me off." I keep my arms at my side, and she lets out a defeated sigh, but this still isn't my problem.

"Please? I'll help you get in your coach's good graces."

"*How* are you going to do that?" I don't even care to get in his good graces, but the look on her face makes me curious.

"It's a surprise." She winks at me, conspiringly throwing another blinding smile at me as if she really thought I was going to believe that.

When she tilts her head to the side, my eyes land on those pretty dimples. I shake my head in disbelief and find the words of agreement escaping against my will. *What did I sign up for?*

Chapter Three

LIAM

"WHY ARE WE GOING THIS way?" Jordan doesn't answer me, so I turn to him. "I asked you a question."

"You don't like it, huh?"

I give him a blank stare, although he has his eyes on the road. "Pull over."

He glances at me before asking why.

"I don't feel like getting in an accident, and I'm about to punch you in the face."

He laughs, and I look forward before rolling my eyes. "Don't make me repeat myself, Jordan."

"We're getting Moon."

I let out a sigh and shake my head. He goes on and on for the rest of the drive about how I should be nice to this kid, but out of habit, I tune him out.

"Hello, friends!"

Someone, please shoot me. I close my eyes when he shuts the door harder than necessary, purely out of his constant excitement. I feel two hands on my shoulders, and he squeezes me. He *touches* me.

"Jordan, tell this kid not to touch me."

Jordan relays the message and tries to mimic me, and they both fill the car with their loud laughs.

"Why do you always call me kid?"

I ignore him, and Jordan drives off.

"I'm twenty-one. I'm not a kid, and you're only like— what? Four years older than me?"

"Five, and you're a kid because of how you act, not your age."

He goes on to list examples of how he doesn't act like a child, and even though I'm not listening, he continues.

"Okay, I have a serious question now."

I type out a response to an email, but when he doesn't go on, I assume he's unfortunately talking to me again. He leans forward to catch a glance at me, and I push him back into his seat.

"Put your damn seatbelt on." See what I mean? Child.

"Who wears a seatbelt in the back seat?"

This kid is a disaster waiting to happen.

He mumbles something else under his breath. I look up when I hear the click of the belt and he is back on his phone, his serious question forgotten I guess. I shake my head and reread the message I was writing.

I don't even get two minutes of silence before Moon lets out a very obnoxious sigh. I look up to the ceiling of the car, and from the corner of my eye, I can see Jordan smiling.

"Damn... she's so pretty." He sighs again, and Jordan laughs at him.

"You better not be talking about–"

"Yes, I am. Please leave me alone."

Jordan is dying of laughter, and when I glance in the mirror again, Moon looks like he wants to be put out of his misery.

"This actually brings me back to my question." He looks in the mirror just as I look away. "Liam?" When I don't respond, he taps my shoulder. "Liam?"

"Moon."

"Yes?"

"I'm not deaf. Do not touch me." I hear him laugh quietly as he mumbles an apology.

"This is serious. Can you listen?"

I let out a sigh and turn my phone off. When I glance over in the mirror, he looks way too happy to have my attention.

"How is it working with Sage Loana?"

"This was your serious question?" I shake my head at him before going back to the actual serious email I was writing.

"Yes! I still can't believe you guys are working with her. Do you think you can ask her if I can sit in on one of your shoots? I think she'll say yes. She seems so sweet on social media."

He keeps rambling about her, and I continue to ignore him.

Jordan wanted to get breakfast, so we stopped by a restaurant a few blocks away from the studio. I pick up the menu to keep myself busy but go still when I hear that laugh. It fills the entire room, but it's too deep to be hers.

I glance up at Jordan, and he's already looking at me. I don't turn around, but I hear whispering from behind me. They walk past me and *barely* skim my shoulder. I let out a scoff and look up.

Just as I do, Sire turns back to me. We hold eye contact for a second before he turns back around and shakes his head. August turns to me next and laughs as he turns back around.

I look down at my fist when I hear that I'm cracking my knuckles. These two are worse than the two I drove here with.

They stay a few feet ahead of us, and I give them my back, but I can still hear their conversation.

"It kind of sucks that we can't stay with Sage longer, but I'm glad we were able to see her set up. Her studio is cool."

Sire agrees with his brother before raving about how he thinks their sister is going to win this contest. A part of me is surprised they don't assume I'm a part of this project of hers and warn me to steer clear of her, but I was already planning on it. I can't stand these two, and considering my coach is already punishing me for fighting, I don't need to add the Hale family to my problems.

Moon walks over to me after the brothers go over to order their food, and I don't walk away because he's watching the Hale brothers, and it looks like he wants to tell me something about them.

"Okay..." He unfortunately starts. "After all this time, I'm still not sure why we don't like them, but would it be weird if I asked for their autograph?"

I blink three times. "Get out of my face."

"They don't know we're friends, so–"

"We're not friends. If you want to be a dick rider, then go ahead and ask for their autograph."

Both Hale brothers play for the LA Dodgers, and while Jordan and I play for the Yankees, we're constantly head-to-head with each other, but that's not the reason I can't stand them.

"Oh, okay, I think that was unnecessary to say. I'm not a *dick rider*; I'm a supporter."

"Go and support them then, and find a ride to wherever you're going while you're at it." Moon doesn't even live in New York, but I don't ask why he came here with Jordan.

His eyebrows raise, and I look away from his dumbass.

"Alrighty, you could've just said, yes, 'Moon, it would be weird' that's it. You–"

"Stop talking."

Another echo of laughs fills my ears, and then someone bumps into my shoulder.

"Shit, my bad–" Sire turns to me and genuinely looks like he didn't mean to bump into me, but then a smirk covers his face when he realizes who he bumped into. "Actually, not my bad."

I roll my eyes at his smug smile. "Back up, Griffin." I use his last name out of habit, it's an athlete thing and as the years gone by, it stuck.

He doesn't look fazed by my words, and beside him, August bites back a smile. I focus on him for half a second, and it irritates me that he's Sage's twin because he has her damn eyes and dimples.

"You wouldn't happen to be here for a particular photo shoot with your team?" August voices this time. *There it is.* I knew they couldn't resist asking.

I fake a confused face. "Do I look like I have time to sit in front of a camera?" *No, but you apparently have plenty of time to stand behind one for his twin.* "What is it your business anyway?" I lean against the table behind me casually.

They look like they're thinking of revealing their sister is in charge of the shoot but wisely choose against it, not knowing I'm fully aware. "Stay away from the photo shoot." Sire threatens cooly.

"Don't tell me what to do, Griffin. Get out of my face." I roll my eyes at him as I glance to the side.

"Or what?" Sire takes a step forward, and I feel my fist balling at my side. "Just stay away." He warns.

I raise my brows. "I'm petrified," I reply dryly before pushing off of the table and stepping to him. "If that's a threat, go through with it now, Griffin."

Sire takes another small step towards me, but August tells him I'm not worth it. They walk away, but their presence is still irritating me, so I walk out and sit in Jordan's car.

After a few minutes, Jordan slides into the car with Moon.

"You good?" Jordan steals a glance, and once I nod in response, he doesn't push for more.

"You look mad." Moon voices as he leans forward to get a better look at me. Before I can tell him, again, to put his damn seat belt on, Jordan beats me to it. I'm not mad; I'm annoyed that the Hale brothers think they can tell me what to do and simply throw threats around.

"Why do you hate them so much?" Moon asks again as if he just read my mind.

When I don't respond, Jordan explains to him that the brothers and I have had *bad blood* since college because we went to rival schools, and while that's true, it's not the whole story.

I don't bother correcting him and we go to the studio pretty after dropping Moon off. Jordan warns me not to have a pissy mood in the studio and I tell him to leave me alone, so he does.

The only thing that makes this *punishment* tolerable is the fact that Sage Loana Hale is gorgeous—stunning, actually.

When Coach told us we'd be working with a ton of models and essentially being their boy toys, I considered taking the chance of pissing off my coach even more and simply not participating. I don't like being on camera; the only time I genuinely enjoy it is if a kid comes up to me and asks for pictures. Kids aren't bad.

Naturally, I did some research and looked up the past photo shoots that these girls did for this contest, and some of them were pretty cool. They didn't tell us which girl we were working with, so I had no clue what I was getting myself into, but Jordan was bugging me the minute the idea was brought up.

He kept saying how crazy it'd be if we were working with Sage Hale, of all people, and I'm convinced he jinxed us.

"Okay," Sage breaks her pose before walking over to me. "Can I see how those few came out?"

I turn the camera to her, and she immediately shakes her head at the first one.

"Yes?"

"Do you not see how bad that is?" She gestures to the picture, and I clearly can't see whatever she sees.

"You look flawless. What's the issue?"

She turns to me but shakes her head at whatever is on her tongue before a smile touches her lips. "Flawless? Awe, that's so sweet!" She seems shocked by my words, but she lights up like they just made her whole day.

I don't say anything in response, and her smile only widens as if I complimented her again.

"I think under all this," she waves around me, "is actually a really sweet guy."

My eyes fall on her smile, and I simply can't look away from her. She is too damn pure for this cruel world.

"You keep thinking that, pretty girl." I gesture back to the camera. She tells me I need to tell her when the girl beside her has a hair out of place, and I honestly wasn't looking at her, but I keep that in mind as she goes back. After a few more pictures, someone calls her for help with something.

"Bro."

I don't look at Jordan, but I can see him in my peripheral vision, making his way closer to me.

"*What* are you doing?"

"What does it look like I'm doing, Jordan? Let's not ask dumb questions." I gesture to the camera in my hand before turning to him.

"You're *also* flirting with Sage. Are you crazy?"

"I have no idea what you're talking about." I try to walk off, but he follows me, to no one's surprise.

"Oh fuck off. You know what you're doing. What happened to staying away from her?"

"I can't really take pictures of the woman if she's across the room, can I?"

He gives me a knowing look, which I simply return with an eye roll.

"You can take pictures without the flirty commentary. You *know* she's a Hale, and *you* were the one who said you'd stay away. Considering her brothers just *threatened* you, I figured you'd remember that."

When that laugh fills the room, I turn and there she is, laughing at something one of the girls is showing her.

"Did you expect her to be like that?"

Jordan turns to watch her with me, and when she glances up at us, she waves so damn happily. Jordan waves back as he responds. "Nope. Considering her brothers are Asshole and Asshole Junior, I expected her to be a bit of a bitch, but she's—"

"Perfect." My eyes cast down her frame, and when I look back at Jordan, I see he's giving me a knowing look because I *can't* get involved.

"You need to change your face and stop the flirting before her brothers find out and actually murder you."

I tell him, once again, that I don't give a fuck about her brothers. While I said I'd stay away from her, it wasn't out of *fear* of her damn brothers. I just didn't want the damn stress, but I clearly have that without her.

Sage walks back over, and we get back to taking her pictures. She keeps stopping after every couple of shots. I think she doesn't trust me, but I don't blame her since I barely know how to work this expensive ass camera.

"Okay, *these* are horrible." She laughs softly. "No offense, Liam." She pats my arm. "You're doing great."

"Mhm."

She laughs again, and I sigh in return. "Just tell me what's wrong so we're not here all day again."

She glances up at me with a pretty smile. "You've been very talkative the last few days," she teases. "I think you found your passion." She grabs my arm that's not holding the camera, and shakes it excitedly. I glance down at her hand, and when she pauses her erratic movements, I look back up. Her eyes are wide with surprise. "You're not telling me not to touch you... Does this mean we're friends?"

"Sage."

She tilts her head to the side.

"Tell me what's wrong with the damn pictures."

She *giggles* before telling me there's a shadow, which doesn't seem like a problem to me, but she wants to move *all* the lights.

"Get somebody else to do it." I take a seat, and she looks offended. Before she can voice her complaints, I wave the camera around. "I'm on camera duty. Tell someone else to move them." The lights are a headache, and last time, she made me move them three damn times just to put them exactly how we had it the first time.

"Fine." She shrugs her jacket off, and my eyes land on her chest. I give her a slow sweep and the dress she's in should not fit her so damn perfectly. It's fucking torture that she looks so good.

"I can do it myself." She ties her curls back like she's on a mission.

I keep my gaze on her as she starts moving things around, but then she sees another problem and drags a chair over.

"Do not climb that."

She ignores me and proceeds to get on top of the chair.

"You're going to break your neck, Sage. Get down; it's fine the way you have it." I lean back in my seat as I watch her get on her tippy toes on the chair *in heels.* When she slightly wobbles, I quickly sit up in my seat.

"Seriously, get your ass *down.*"

"It's fine, I just—" She reaches for the light and tries to angle it a certain way. She stumbles again, and I rise from my seat. Without warning, I lift her into my arms and plant her on the ground.

"Woah!" She balances herself. "How the heck did you lift me like that?" She looks between the two of us, and I'm fucking offended.

"Do I look like I can't *lift* you?" I glance down at her frame, and she does the same.

"Well, I'm pretty heavy and—"

"And I look like I can't lift you?" I shake my head at her before climbing the chair. "Just tell me how you want it."

She instructs me to move it every which way, and I'm damn near at the end of my rope when she finally decides it's perfect.

"This is exactly how it already was." I point out.

"No, it wasn't," she states matter-of-factly as she walks off before I can respond.

Chapter Four

SAGE

"**B**EFORE I SHOW YOU," I start warning my brothers before they have a heart attack. "It's a *little* revealing, but just imagine we were at the beach, and this was a regular bikini."

"Yeah, no," my twin starts. "I'm good."

I bite back a laugh.

"For once, I agree with August." Sire agrees.

"Bonus bro," I tilt my head to the side. "Please!"

A smile reaches his face at my name for him, and I admire how happy he looks to hear it. I call him that because we adopted him when we were younger, so he's a bonus addition to our family, but I really do believe he was always meant to belong with us.

"I need to know if you think this is better than what I have. I need to win this!"

I'm on my way back to New York after spending the weekend with Royal in Chicago, and like last year's contest, which she won, she's doing something similar, so it's pretty sexual.

"I like the idea you have now, Sage." August voices, and I let out a breath as I sank into my seat on the plane. The boys have a private jet and, thankfully, let me use it quite a lot.

"You guys always have such different ideas, and I think that's what makes the contest cool." Sire starts next. "Don't make yours like hers."

"Okay, well, *hers* won, so clearly, this is what the people want." It wouldn't take much to make my project a bit sexier. It'll actually be very easy since we already have a group of hot men and stunning girls.

The boys don't budge, but I send them the pictures of the other girls since they're so opposed to seeing me in anything less than a T-shirt.

"Damn." Hazel pops her head into the screen, and August smiles before kissing his girlfriend. "These girls are hot. I vote on making your project sexier."

August laughs as she disappears, and I chew my lip in thought.

"Let me call Lis." I kiss my brothers goodbye before calling my sister and she answers after a few rings.

"What do you want?"

I let out a laugh, and a smile paints her face.

"I don't *want* anything."

She keeps her gaze on me like she doesn't believe me, and I smile at how pretty her blue eyes are. They're not a deep blue but more like a clear sky. When we adopted Sire, we didn't get to officially adopt Lis, but that doesn't change anything. She's my sister just as much as the boys are my brothers.

"I call bullshit." She rolls her eyes before walking out of her apartment.

"Where are you heading?"

A smirk grows on her face, and I immediately shake my head at her. "I'm on my way to piss off our lovely brother. You know it's my favorite hobby."

I tilt my head back with a laugh as she walks to her car. She and Sire fight all day, and she starts most of it, but it's too funny to even be bothered by it.

I give her the rundown on my dilemma, and when she echos Hazel, I decide to listen to them.

The connection starts to get bad, so I kiss my sister goodbye through the phone and brainstorm some ideas.

We're *really* behind since I lost my original photographer. I think she lied about having past experience so she could work with me, which is honestly cute, but I could be disqualified since it's technically cheating. I had to get rid of all the pictures she took and start from scratch.

Liam isn't the worst photographer, and it's been fun bugging him and making him move things only to put them back in their original spot. I really do think he's the sweetest guy after you break the ice, and I've made it a goal to make him laugh at least once before this project is over in two weeks.

My brothers made a lot of comments about how I shouldn't work with the Yankees since they always bump heads with their players. They didn't name anyone, but I've been working with five Yankees players, six with Liam, for a few weeks, and all of them seem cool. I think it's just an ego thing with my brothers.

When I land, there's already a car waiting for me, and I step in when the driver opens the door for me.

After grabbing a coffee, I walk over to the studio. New York is freezing compared to LA right now, but it's better than my weekend in Chicago.

A smile touches my lips when I notice Liam's motorcycle outside, and I quickly walk up the steps to the studio.

I hear two sets of voices as I walk up the stairs, and it sounds like Liam and someone else.

"Just let me see!"

I round the corner and see a boy I don't recognize reaching for something in Liam's hands. He isn't that much shorter, but Liam pushes his arm away and keeps the camera back.

"Fuck. Off," Liam bites out.

I stifle a laugh as Liam shoves him away.

"She will drop dead if something happens to this camera." Liam shoves him again. "Get your grimy hands *off.*"

Liam storms away but stops short with a frown that softens as his eyes meet mine.

"Good morning!" I walk over to them, and Jordan looks up from the couch before looking between all of us. I glance over to the guy they're with, and his cheeks slightly blush. "I don't think we've met?"

He doesn't answer, and Jordan rises to his feet. "This is the friend I asked if I could bring along?" He shoves his friend, making him take a step towards me.

"Moon," is all he says, and I give him a small smile.

He shakes his head softly before taking a step back. "I meant my name is Moon." He laughs softly, and I tell him it's nice to meet him before walking over to the couch.

"I'm actually glad some of you got here early." I pull out my iPad, and the boys walk over to me. "I was working with one of the other contestants, and I think we should make a slight change in–"

"Again?" Liam mumbles, and when I look up at him, he's shaking his head at something. "I'm going to be stuck here all year." He sinks into the end of the couch with a groan, and I stifle a laugh before pulling up the pictures from Royal's photo shoot.

"What do you think about changing our third section to something like this?" I turn the iPad to them.

"Shit," Jordan mumbles under his breath, and I glance down at the iPad again.

"Is that a no?" I swipe for the pictures of me before turning the iPad back to them, and Moon suddenly looks everywhere but the iPad. "What?"

"Nothing." Jordan shrugs. "All of my teammates would appreciate the change." He chuckles before sitting back on the couch.

When *my* team trickles in, we get started on my hair and makeup. I voice my idea to them and they also agree. Since we're doing five sections and outfits, I think it won't be too similar to Royal's since only one section would be more sexual rather than all of them like hers.

"When do you think you'll be done shooting the video?" Annet, my hair stylist, continues to curl my hair, and I let out a breath at the reminder.

"With the way I schedule it, the last part should be filmed during the last week."

She reminds me how that doesn't leave a lot of room for editing and reshooting in case we have hiccups, but at this point, we'd have to wing it if there were any more mistakes.

"Did you see Mr. Moore's interview last night?"

I slightly sit up in my seat as Cara, my main makeup artist, walks over with her phone.

Annet lets out a breath at the sight of Vincent Moore. "God, that man is too fine for his own good."

He totally is, but I don't voice my agreement, and instead, I focus on the interview.

"In regards to your post about your excitement with The Core Eight's friendly annual contests, whose piece are you most excited to see?"

I watch intensely as he sits there with his usual glare.

"All eight of the ladies come up with very creative pieces each year, and I enjoy seeing their improvement every year, but my eyes are on Sage Loana and Quincy Lock."

My jaw drops before I let out a squeal. "Oh my god!" I quickly grab my phone before calling Quinn. She answers immediately, and before I say anything, my jaw drops. "You look beautiful!" I feel my eyes water as I take her in. Quinn has vitiligo but has been using makeup to cover it up, at least until now. She was in a horrible relationship with someone who made her feel ashamed of how she looked, but she stands here now, so sure of herself.

"Please don't make me cry." She lets out a soft laugh as she nervously plays with her curls.

"I'm so proud, babe."

She looks so confident as she smiles at the camera. "Yeah, well, I was tired of letting people control my life." She holds her head up high, and I love how free she looks.

"Look at your phone. *Now.*" I send her the link, and when she starts screaming, it's safe to say she got the message.

"Holy shit!" Quinn drops her phone, and I think she's jumping.

"Right!" I let out another squeal and my entire team laughs around me. We watch the rest of the video, and he mentions the rest of The Eight, so I text the group chat, and my phone blows up as all of their messages come in.

Being that we're all in his upcoming show, we've met him a few times, but hearing he has his *eyes on me*?!

I let out a squeal, and the girls laugh at me again.

I keep texting in the group chat after my hair and makeup are done, and as much as I'd love to sit and text my girls all day, I tell them we need to get on a group call later tonight and tuck my phone away.

My baby models get their hair and makeup done, and the rest of the boys come in later, but once everyone is in, I voice my new idea, and as Jordan said, no one is against it.

I have Trey, one of the guys on my outfit crew, run out and find some cute lingerie for the girls, and considering we're in New York City, it only takes him an hour, but in the meantime, we film.

The contest consists of three to five outfit changes and one video. Filming is my strong suit since I vlog almost every day, so when Stel and I won the vote to add a video to the contest, I was ecstatic.

When Trey makes it back, I have everyone change and as I look around the room, I smile to myself at how good everyone looks. I glance over at myself in the mirror, and I feel good... *pretty* even, but as I stare too long, every curve and stretch mark makes me feel like I need to crawl out of my skin. I blink the sudden tears out of my eyes, and when I glance around the room, a few people are smiling at me, but their gaze is suffocating, so I walk off to the bathroom.

Resting my hands on the sink, I force myself to swallow the sour taste in my throat, but all I can think about is how much I ate last night. I skipped breakfast to compensate for it, but as I watch my reflection, I feel bloated. I rush to the toilet and force two fingers down my throat, throwing up everything in my stomach.

I blink the stinging in my eyes and rush to wash my hands when someone knocks on the door. I take a deep breath and paint a smile on my face as I turn and open the door.

"Hey, you okay?" Annet asks gently before her brows furrow. "It sounded like you were throwing up. " She watches me carefully, and I give her a bigger smile.

"Yeah, I feel better." I walk off before she can question me and keep my smile intact as I grab a piece of gum. "Okay, let's take these pictures." I glance around the room for our photographer, but Liam isn't in sight. I debated giving him a minute, but we honestly don't have time to waste today, so I go in search of him.

The only trace of him on the second floor is his helmet, so I know he didn't leave. I decide to check downstairs, and as I make it to the last few steps, my eyes land on his back.

He's wearing his jacket as always since it's pretty chilly in here. He holds his phone to his ear, and my eyes trace the tattoos covering his hand. I glance down at his other hand, which is also covered in ink, and my mind wonders how far his tattoos go.

He's always covered since he isn't in any of my pictures, so he doesn't walk around shirtless like the other guys, but his neck is also drowning in a dark design.

"Is she okay, though?"

I pause at the last step, hearing the worry in his voice.

"Okay, so *what* do you need?"

My brows slightly raise at the sudden shift to annoyance in his tone.

"I already told you I can't go. Call me if there's an *actual* problem." He ends the call before whipping around, and my feet forget how to function when his heated gaze meets mine.

"Is everything okay?"

He lets out a tired breath before running a hand through his blonde hair. "Why do you keep doing that?"

"Doing what?"

"Asking me if I'm okay. Why do you care?" His words aren't harsh, but his genuine confusion surprises me.

I shrug, not entirely sure myself. "I just do? I care about everyone..."

He watches me for a second before brushing past me. I turn on my heels and follow him up the steps.

"I wasn't eavesdropping or anything," I clarify for, I'm not sure what. "I only just stepped downstairs and only because I was looking for you."

"Okay," is all I get before he grabs the camera.

"If you're not up for it today, you can—"

"I'm fine, Sage. Go sit over there and look pretty so I can finish."

I steal a glance at him, and he's already shaking his head.

"That sounded really bad," he mumbles as he rolls his eyes, and I bite back a laugh.

"Look who has a dirty mind now." I tease, trying to get a smile out of him, and I swear his lips twitch. His eyes cast down my frame, and I feel my entire body flush as his eyes cast down my frame in approval.

"This is the change you were talking about?" He slightly brushes my jacket, opening it a bit more to reveal my lingerie set.

I nod softly, losing my next words with the way his blue eyes stare into me so intensely. Every ounce of uncertainty I felt in this outfit slowly faded with how his eyes practically undressed me.

"Remind me of the *vibe* you were going for?"

I bite back a smile at the way he says *vibe,* and I know he's only teasing me. "The third section is supposed to be... sexier."

He nods slowly, his eyes scanning every inch of me. "Are you ready?"

I don't respond at first, then shake my head at the sudden cloudiness. "For?"

He lifts the camera. "The pictures."

I choose to nod, not trusting my voice.

"Unless you have something else in mind?" He trails off as he tilts his head to the side.

"Are you flirting with me?" I shake my head at how ridiculous that sounds, considering this man has two moods: neutral and leave me alone.

"I asked a simple question." He shrugs ever so innocently, but the *smirk* on his pretty face is far from innocent. "If your mind is elsewhere, that's on you, pretty girl."

He needs to stop calling me that if he expects me to think he isn't flirting.

"My mind is on my work."

"So is mine." He shrugs again. "So, are you ready, or did you want to take that off?" He gestures to my outfit, and my jaw falls open just a bit.

"*What?*"

"The jacket," he clarifies, and when his smirk grows, I feel my entire face burst into flames. "Looks like your mind isn't *just* on work, Sage Loana." He takes a step towards me, and I snatch the camera.

"Yes, it is." I walk off, my face still warming, and I hope it isn't noticeable to anyone that he made me so flustered. I *swear* I hear him chuckling behind me, but when I turn, he just watches me with his usual *look.*

He follows after me and plucks the camera out of my hand. "You never told me how you were going to help me get in my coach's good graces."

I busy myself with fixing the props on the bed we're taking pictures on even though they're perfect. The truth is, I have no clue how I'm going to help him. I don't even remember his coach's name.

He flops onto the bed beside me, ruining the pillows I just fixed. "I'm starting to think this is one-sided when it was supposed to be a symbiotic relationship, Sage."

Why is he suddenly so chatty?

I glance over at him as he lays on the bed lazily. He keeps his eyes trained on mine for a beat, but slowly, his eyes drag down to my chest, and my breath gets caught in my throat as the tip of my ears starts to warm. He keeps his eyes on my body, and I watch them trail lower. His eyes snap up to mine, and when I don't say anything, a smirk grows on his face.

"Are we ready?" Someone asks from behind the lights, tearing Liam's eyes away, and he rises from the bed.

"Yup." He glances down at me again. "Sage was just deciding if she wanted to take this off for me or not." He studies my frame, and his eyes *aren't* on my jacket anymore.

"It's staying on." I whip around, and when I walk off, he *definitely* lets out the softest laugh, and a smile grows on my face at how sweet he sounds.

Chapter Five

LIAM

FOR THE PAST THIRTY MINUTES that I've been here, with my eyes following her every movement, I haven't mustered up the courage to walk up to her.

I glance down at the flowers in my hands, and I almost change my mind and make someone give them to her for me. The last few times I've done that, though, I wished I had just spoken to her, so I just do it. I walk over, and the minute her eyes land on me, I see the confusion grow on her face.

"What are you doing here?" She sounds so bitter, but I keep my feet planted.

"Hi, Mom."

She looks back out the window with a huff of disapproval, and I almost walk away, but I swallow the sour taste in my mouth and crouch to her level. "I got you flowers."

"I'm not blind."

I feel a smile touch my lips because she has the nerve to wonder where I get my attitude from. I don't say anything, and when she turns to me, I see her confusion again.

"What are you doing here?"

I study her for a beat, then raise the flowers.

"Are these for me?"

I look between her lost eyes, and I suddenly feel so small. She looks back over at me, and I nod in return before kissing her hand.

"Yeah, Mom. They're for you."

She takes them, and after bringing them to her nose, she looks back out the window. I sit there with her for a few minutes, and when it starts pouring rain, I watch her close her eyes peacefully to the sound of the thunder.

"It's a beautiful day," I say, hoping it'll jog any memories of when she'd say that whenever it rained, but then she looks over at me with a wave of new anger.

"Why are *you* here?"

I might walk into oncoming traffic if she asks me that again.

I let out a soft sigh and force myself to speak as nicely as humanly possible. "I came to spend some time with you." I reach for her hand, and when she snatches it away, I decide we're done here.

"*Now* you want to spend time with your family?"

I immediately rise, but I don't think I can get out of here fast enough.

"Where were you when Shanti died?" She looks up at me with so much hate, I don't even recognize her.

"Goodbye, Mom."

I turn on my heels, but she barely lets me take a step.

"Of course, you're leaving. It's what you're good at."

I stand there for a full breath before I walk off. My eyes land on Capri, Mom's nurse, and she's already making her way to me.

"Liam—"

"Call me if she worsens."

"You should—"

"*Call me* if she worsens." I try to walk around her, but she steps in my way with her hands up.

"You really should stay, Liam."

I let out an annoyed breath, and I feel myself getting hot with anger.

"You have to remember that she doesn't mean what she says, I know—"

"You *don't* know, and she certainly sounds like she means everything that comes out of her mouth, now if you'll excuse me I—"

"You said you'll spend half an hour with her." She sends me a pointed look, and I hate that she cares so much, but it's good that she does.

"I've been here for—"

"You have not spent the entirety of your stay with her." She gives me a warning look when I roll my eyes, but I don't apologize. "Go back and try again; she doesn't look angry anymore."

"She's always angry."

"She isn't. She has *Alzheimer's*." She reminds me.

My eyes snap back to Capri, and she gives me a sympathetic look.

"So it's just me she's angry with; that's great to know." When I walk off this time, she grabs a hold of my hand.

"It'll be good for her if you stay a bit longer, Liam."

I don't turn around, but she goes on. "You haven't seen her in a while. She doesn't spend a lot of time with the other residents, and it's important that she socializes."

I turn now. "Well, if it's so important, and she's clearly not getting that here, then maybe I'll have her moved."

She lets my hand fall, and she shakes her head softly. She doesn't say anything else, but I let out a breath.

"I know you're just trying to help." My voice comes out a bit gentler, and Capri looks up at me like she's waiting for more, but I don't offer anything else.

"And I know you're trying to apologize, so I'll wait."

"You do that." I walk past her, and just as I do, I hear her let out a quiet laugh. Capri has been my mom's nurse since I first brought her here just over two years ago. I didn't want such a young nurse, but she really is the best. I know she knows I don't mean the shit I say, but I tell myself not to bite the hand that literally feeds my mom.

I almost get a chair to sit beside her, but I honestly don't think I'm going to stay those full thirty minutes, so I stand behind her instead as we face the window.

"What'd you do today?" I watch her reflection as she opens her eyes, and when she hums in thought, I let out a relieved breath.

"I think I went for a run." She nods to herself like she actually believes that. She isn't that old, and she can definitely run, but she *doesn't*. Even before she got sick, she hated running.

"I don't think you did." I watch her reflection morph into confusion, and I feel myself growing angry that this disease is killing her brain slowly. "I'm kidding, Mom. You did go for a run."

She doesn't look confused anymore, and that's all that matters right now.

"I need to start cooking dinner soon." She stands from her seat, and I almost stop her, but then she walks over to the table. "Come help me."

I watch her as she takes out a puzzle, and I have absolutely no clue if she thinks she's cooking or if she meant to say she wants to do a puzzle, but I sit across from her at the table and do the damn thing.

We work in silence, and whenever she starts putting two pieces that don't fit together, I swap them for ones that do. She only hums here and there.

"Okay, sweetie, I seriously need to get to work now."

"We didn't finish—"

"Really, Liam, you're going to make me late." She rises from her seat. "I love you, bye." She kisses my hair and rushes over to the couch for a bag I can only hope is hers because she pulls papers out and starts writing.

She didn't work before she came here. I don't remember her ever having a job, but I continue the rest of the puzzle as I steal a few glances at her and she looks focused on whatever she thinks she's doing so I don't join her when I finish the puzzle.

I'm still watching her when Capri comes next to me. "Will you be joining us for lunch?" She sounds hopeful, but I shake my head as I rise from my seat.

"I should go."

"You don't need to."

I look down at Capri, and she's watching my mom with a smile. "She's the CEO of a different business every day."

Miss CEO now has a phone to her ear. I look at Capri in confusion, and she reassures me that the phone only works with the people in the house, so the only people she can talk to are the nurses.

"Thank you for everything, Pri." I walk over to my mom before she can reply, and just as I do, she looks like she's about to lose her shit.

"Liam!"

"Mom!" I fake my surprise, but it's dripped in a dry tone, and it only confuses her more or maybe makes her angrier, I'm not sure.

"Sweetheart, please, okay? I'm very busy right now."

"I'm sure you are."

She sent me a pointed look, and I'm honestly surprised she picked up on my sarcasm.

"I was just leaving. I came to say bye."

"Oh." She stops shuffling her papers and just looks around at all of them like she's trying to make sense of something. "If you really would rather be out with your friends than help me with Shanti, then that's fine."

"What?" I feel my blood run cold and it's like I'm seventeen all over again and we're having that same fight.

"Now she's crying." She shakes her head and turns for something but stops to say something else. "I'm not going to stop you from going to this party, Liam. It's New Year's, and you want to be with your friends, I get it, okay? I–"

"You were seventeen once, too. I know, Mom."

She studies me, and I say what I wish I had said that day. "I'm not going to that stupid New Year's party. I'm going to stay here with you and Shanti."

Her smile is back, and when she pulls me in for a hug, I feel my mouth suddenly dry. I clear my throat and hug my mom. Letting my eyes fall shut, I take in a breath of her flowery scent, but then she pulls away too soon and walks off.

I don't know if she's really stuck reliving that day again, but I decided to stay for lunch in case she is because I need her to think I stayed with her that night.

Halfway through lunch, though, she asks who I am, and I respond with a tight smile before I get up to leave.

I'm just about to reach the door when I hear Capri from behind me. "Will you be at the next family night?"

I stall but don't turn to face her as I try to imagine how that would go. If she's angry with me the entire time, it won't be fun for either of us, and if she doesn't even remember me, then I would rather not come at all.

Before she got sick, we were really close, and before we lost Shanti, we were even closer, but now... It's just too hard to be around her, and I'm giving it my best shot, but it's not enough.

"I have a lot of back-to-back games at the start of the season."

I hear her sigh from behind me, but she doesn't push anymore.

"But I'll try to come." When I turn around, Capri is watching me with a hopeful smile, and when I glance behind her, my mom laughs at something one of the nurses says.

I watch her smile for a few seconds, but when my chest suddenly feels heavy, I walk out in a hurry.

It's not raining anymore as I slip my helmet on, and I soak the freeing feeling as I speed down the street.

Jordan starts calling me, and I don't answer, but he calls again, and it's ringing in my damn helmet, so I just pick up.

"Liam!"

"Sage?"

She lets out a breath, and I slow down a bit.

"Where are you?" She goes on before I can answer. "Jordan told me you won't be here today? What the heck!"

I shake my head at her, and I don't think this girl knows what a curse word is. "I'm sure you can find someone to take your pictures. The world will keep rotating without me."

She sighs again, and I bite my tongue not to laugh at how dramatic this woman is.

"Moon has been taking them for me, and I love him, but they are not the same. You need to get here. Right now, mister."

I roll my eyes at how she says she *loves* Moon. He's been tagging along to all of our shoots the last few days, and I don't think it's an exaggeration when Sage says they're *besties*.

"Not the same huh? I'm flattered." My tone is drier than the desert, but she laughs as if it weren't. I steady my bike so I don't have to hold it as I drive down the street and fix my helmet. I also turn my volume down because while she has a beautiful laugh, I can't hear anything else around me.

"Are you driving right now?" She must've heard the honking around me, but I grab onto the handle again and speed off before responding. "Wait, you're on your *bike*? Why are you on the phone?"

"Because you're having a heart attack over my absence."

She laughs again, and it should not do the things it does to me. I tell her she's in my helmet, and she says she *knows* that but voices how I shouldn't be distracted, and her sweet laugh sure is a damn distraction.

I speed up, trying to fill myself with adrenaline rather than lust, but all I can think of is her in that damn lingerie set.

When Capri called me, I didn't want to come to see my mom, but after having a hard-on for half of Sage's photo shoot, I quickly realized if I spent another day with her, I wouldn't be able to stay away.

I came to LA with the excuse of seeing my mom, and with Sage's project ending soon, I figured I could just get out of the end of it, but now she's calling me as if her world is ending.

"So you're on your way, right?"

"I'm in LA and–"

"I can send you a jet."

"Sage–"

"*Please* come."

Fuck. I'm fucking fucked.

"Fine," I tell her I have my own plane, which surprises her for some reason, but five hours later, I'm in New York for her.

In the time it took me to get here, I guess she told everyone to leave and come back once I arrived because they only just started setting up when I walked in.

"Liam!"

I turn around, and Sage beams as I walk over to her. She glances down at my helmet before a confused look covers her pretty face. "I thought you were in LA?"

"I was." I set my helmet aside before leaning against the couch to be at eye level with her.

"Do you have a bike here and in Cali?"

I nod in response, and she picks up my helmet before examining it. "How many bikes do you have?"

"Five."

She nods to herself before picking up my helmet a bit more but freezes. "Do you mind if I try it on?"

"Knock yourself out."

She smiles before slipping it on, and seeing her wear my things isn't helping the whole *stay away from her* thing. She pulls out her phone and snaps a few pictures before lifting the visor and looking at them.

"This is cute." She nods again before examining how she looks on her camera.

"Please don't use *cute* in the same sentence as my *helmet*. It's far from *cute*. *Babies* are cute. My helmet isn't *cute*, it's cool."

She *laughs* at me, and I snap the visor shut on her, which barely muffles the sound of her growing laughter. "That sounded very defensive."

"Can't hear you."

"I said–"

"Still can't hear you."

She opens the visor, but I shut it again, and she's *hysterical*. I watch her for a beat, and it's in that moment I decide fuck her brothers and fuck staying away.

Chapter Six

SAGE

I HAND SIRE A CHAMPAGNE glass, and he looks between me and the glass, raising a questioning brow.

"Apple juice," I whisper before showing him mine with the same liquid, and he laughs before taking the glass.

"Thanks, Sage." He smiles down at me, and I pull him in for a side hug.

"You sure you're fine with everyone drinking?" I keep my voice hushed as I look up at him. "Because I'll get rid of the bottles and–"

"It's okay." He kisses the top of my head, and I nod to myself before deciding to trust him.

Sire is a few months away from making a year sober from alcohol. He's been sober from narcotics for a while, but he's been having a hard time with this goal the last few years; it's really important to our family that he makes it.

Most of the girls have a glass of wine or champagne since I'm hosting a small watch party of Hollywood's It Girl. They're announcing the winner of our contest, so all of my friends came over today to watch.

The vote is open to everyone around the world. While we could have asked Florence who won, it's more fun to sit around the TV and have it announced to us. We could also use the break after the past few weeks of stress.

"You *need* to try this." August pushes his burger into my field of vision, blocking me from the screen. I quickly turn my face away, using a hand to get him to back up.

"No, thank you." I glance down at his plate, stacked with all the food we ordered. I looked at the menu before they ordered, and everything on his plate had an insane amount of calories. I have no clue how August is unbelievably fit. My stomach grumbles quietly as I look between his onion rings and cheese fries, but I had a big breakfast, and I'm certainly not going to eat any of this greasy food if it means gaining a single pound.

"No, trust me, it's so good." He holds his plate out to me, but I take a small step back.

"Eat some for me, I'm not hungry." I smile up at him and a crease grows in his brows.

"Are you okay?" He keeps his voice soft as his green eyes look between my identical ones in concern, and I hate this twin telepathy thing sometimes.

"Yeah." I force a smile, and Royal grabs me before he can question me, but I still feel his worried eyes on me.

"It's starting!" Royal yells to the room as she pulls me onto the couch with everyone, and we all quiet down as we zone in on the TV. They show all of our pictures and videos, and the girl's reactions to each other's projects are the best part of this.

"Well, I fucking lost." Macey sinks in her seat as they show Stel's pictures.

"We can't all be winners." She taps her leg. "Better luck next time." They tease each other on my couch, and I laugh before turning back to the TV.

"Holy shit, Sage!" Royal praises as my video plays, and I'm genuinely shocked everything came out as good as it did, considering the amount of hiccups and changes. I look over at my group of baby models, and they record themselves proudly on TV before quietly squealing with each other. I bite back a laugh and snag a picture of their excitement. I invited everyone who was a part of my photo shoot, and some of the boys were able to make it, but Jordan, Moon, and Liam were busy, which kind of sucks since they helped the most, but I don't let it disappoint me too much.

When they show Quinn's section, everyone gasps before clapping for her. All of her models were other girls who have vitiligo and they all look *gorgeous*. "Quinn, this is beautiful!" I turn to look at her, and she wipes her tears away as she smiles over at me.

"You have no idea how hard that was." Her voice slightly breaks, and I, along with the rest of The Core Eight, get up to hug her.

"Talk about the biggest fuck you to your ex," Coral exclaims before she hugs her best friend again, and we all let out a laugh.

"*Like always, let's start from least voted to most!*"

Everyone is holding their breath as they start eliminating each of us. I wish they'd just share who the top two were rather than showing who essentially got last place, but whatever.

Macey, Helena, Coral, Royal, and Quinn get knocked out in that order, and while most of them are bummed, Quinn is ecstatic that she placed top five.

"*In third, we have... Stellamae!*"

The room cheers for her, although she sinks in her seat.

"We can't all be winners." Macey taps her leg. "Better luck–"

"*Mace.*" She warns as she shoves her hand away, and Coral and Quinn laugh at them before sharing a look. We think they're hooking up, but we're waiting for them to come out to us.

"*In second, we have... Sage Loana!*"

I shoot up from my seat with a scream before pulling Nin to her feet. "OMG! YAY! YOU WON!" I shake her arm, and she pulls me in for a hug as they announce her as the winner.

Everyone congratulates her, and while she'd normally hate the attention, her empty wine glass is to thank for her boldness tonight. She struts to the TV and bows with a pretty smile. "Thank you, thank you." She flips her hair a few times before pretending to blush as we applaud her, and as she makes it back to the couch, I pull her in for another hug.

"Congrats, babe," I whisper before kissing her cheek. "I still can't get over how perfectly you were able to imitate the moonlight."

Everyone's piece was great, but I'm so happy Nin won. She added handmade traditional Thai outfits, and with her lake setting, she looked ethereal.

Everyone stays, and the night turns into more of a cel-ebration for Nin. After a while, Jordan and Moon text me with their congratulations. I'm not sure why, but a part of me waits for Liam's message. A few other friends text me with their congrats, and after every message I check my phone, and a ting of disappointment seeps in every time it's not him. As the night ticks away, I think he isn't going to text me, and a part of me is bummed I won't be seeing him anymore. It was fun bugging him with the lighting and trying to make him laugh the last few weeks.

When my phone rings again, I pick it up lazily, and a smile quickly grows on my face when I realize it's him.

Liam

> All that work and you only get second? That shit is rigged. You owe me a month of my life back.

I let out a laugh as I type out a quick response.

> It's not rigged! I'm happy with second.

> I can't give you back a month but I can give you a night?

As his bubbles appear, I shake my head at how bad that sounds, but he beats me to it.

> Are you flirting with me??!!!

I throw my head back with another laugh and I can only imagine all the extra punctuation was to emphasize my voice.

> I asked a simple question...

Seriously though, come to LA this weekend! It's Trey's birthday but we're also celebrating our hard work. Everyone from the shoot and a few of my friends will be there.

I don't even know Trey.

You know me! Plus, I kinda want to see you again

Just kinda?

I take a minute to respond, trying to decipher if he's actually flirting this time.

Less than kinda.

It's a sin to lie, pretty girl.

His nickname brings a wave of heat to my face, and I bite back my smile as I respond.

I would never lie.

You better come to the bar this weekend. You didn't come to my party today & you're actually nicer than I thought you'd be. We need a proper goodbye.

Why does the end of your contest have to be goodbye?

True...

"What are you smiling at?" Coral's voice drags me out of my thoughts, and when I look up at her, her eyes are on my phone.

"Nothing." I offer her a smile and swipe out of the messages. I, of course, don't care if Coral knows who I'm texting, but she's notoriously nosey and going to ask about Liam every chance she gets, and I don't even know what's going on *if* anything is even going on.

Liam is cute, and I've grown to like his company... along with his nickname. I don't want our friendship to end, but that's all it is right now, a friendship.

Quinn pulls Coral away, and I open our messages again.

> Didn't you tell Moon you don't like having friends?

> Yes.

I'm in the middle of typing when he sends another message.

> I'll see you this weekend.

LIAM

"I LIKE YOUR TATTOOS." SAGE looks down at my arms, nodding to herself.

I sidestep as someone walks past. Sage follows me as I take a seat at the bar, and she remains standing in front of me, keeping us at eye level.

I wasn't going to come here since it isn't my scene. Bars are, but it's more of a party scene here because of her friend's birthday, and I don't really know any of them. I wanted to see her, though, and Jordan and Moon also tagged along.

I almost tell her she's already seen my tattoos until I realize she hasn't since I never wore anything less than a jacket in the studio back in New York, considering it was usually colder in there.

"I posted a poll the other day asking if sleeves or sticker tats were hotter, and sticker tats somehow won by four percent, but I think my followers would change their minds if they saw you." She shakes her head as she realizes what she just said. "I meant your tattoos, not you."

"Right," I tease, and her smile doesn't falter.

"I don't mean that you're not hot because you are; I just mean if they saw your tattoos, they'd agree that sleeves are hotter," she says matter-of-factly, her usual nervousness gone.

I simply nod in response. "I have a few more tattoos."

"How can you possibly have more? Your arms and neck are completely covered." She looks back down at both of my sleeves, studying each design. "When did you get your first one?" She leans against the bar.

"When I was sixteen."

Her jaw drops. "Why so young–" She shakes her head and waves her hand as if she were waving away her words. "Wait, how'd you get it that young? You have to be eighteen to get tatted."

I lean past her for a chair and bring it closer so she can sit. "I knew someone who did tattoos, so my age didn't matter."

She nods in understanding as her attention shifts back to my arms. "Which one was it?" She goes to touch my arm but stops. When she looks up at me, I give her a nod, and she runs her hand along my sleeve.

"I covered it up. He did a horrible job, and my dumb ass picked a stupid design."

She asks me what it was, but I only shake my head.

"That bad, huh?" She throws her head back, laughing loudly, and I only watch her pretty dimples. From the corner of my eye, I can see a few heads turn our way, but I honestly can't blame them. *She's hot, and her laugh is perfect.* My eyes travel down her body, and I mentally scold myself before refocusing my attention on an equally appealing part of her, that damn smile.

"You couldn't torture me to show you that shit," I mumble. My eyes meet hers, and she laughs harder.

"Well, now I need to see it."

"No," I say dryly, and she only smiles at me. "Do you—"

The bartender cuts me off as he sets a drink in front of her. "I think you've gotten the most drinks yet are somehow the most sober one in here."

She laughs softly in return, but not like before. She seems uncomfortable now as she looks over her shoulder. I glance around the room with her, and my eyes land on a group of guys down the counter who are already smiling at her. I look between the drink and her, and her smile is clearly forced.

"Thank you," she says sweetly to the bartender then smiles at the group of guys, but it doesn't reach her eyes, she just looks more uncomfortable.

I look over at the bartender before he can walk away. "Don't bring her any more drinks."

"I'm just—"

"I don't care."

He looks offended, but I, again, don't care.

"If someone else buys her a drink, tell them she's not thirsty—better yet, I'll tell them myself. Which one of them sent this one?"

"Hey," Sage cuts in before he can answer.

I look back over at her, and the bartender quickly takes the opportunity to escape.

"*What* is your problem?"

I pull in a deep breath and force myself to get my short temper in order.

"I don't have one. Do you want them to continue to send you drinks?"

"Well, no, but—"

"And it's making you uncomfortable, right?"

"Well, yes, but—"

"Okay, now neither of us has a problem since they won't be sending you any more drinks or making you uncomfortable. Right?"

She lets out a scoff and shakes her head with a smile. "Don't take offense to this, but you're kind of an asshole."

I turn her chair so she's facing me with her legs between mine. I glance back at the group of guys, and they can't even see the side of her face anymore, which earns me a few eye rolls.

"No offense taken." I look back over at her. "Do you have any tattoos?"

She studies me for a second before answering. No one else sends her any more drinks, and she doesn't look uncomfortable anymore. She asks what each tattoo means, and only one has a special meaning to it, but I just tell her I thought they'd look good, and she agrees that they do.

"In case you think I forgot," I start, and immediately, a guilty look covers her face. "You still owe me one for taking all those hot pictures of you since you never helped me with my coach."

She shakes her head with a small smile before her eyes narrow on me. "Hot pictures?" She turns her head to the side before holding her heart. "You just admitted I'm hot. You're flirting again."

I shrug, taking a sip of my water. "You said it first," I remind her. "And maybe I am flirting."

She watches me, and I bite back a smile at how her words are suddenly lost.

"How about this?" I pull the bottom of her chair, closing the distance between us. "Forget about my coach. I honestly couldn't care less about him."

"But you said—"

"I know what I said, pretty girl." I study her face, and when my eyes cast down her frame, I think, *fuck it.* "How about you help me get you out of my damn head instead?"

She blinks twice. "You've been thinking about me?"

"More than I'd like to admit."

She tilts her head back with a laugh, and a few heads turn to watch her again. When she gets herself together, I rise to my feet and nod to the door. She glances over her shoulder before looking back at me, and a smirk pulls at my lips as she shamelessly checks me out. She nods once before giving in.

She takes a few short steps to her friend to whisper something in his ear, and they both look over at me.

Her friend gives me a once-over, then gives her a knowing grin. "He's hot." He winks at me before turning back around and taking a shot that, I'm pretty sure, just solidified his blackout.

She tells her other friends she's leaving with me and cautions them to watch the birthday boy before turning back around. On our way out, everyone who was watching her was now watching *us,* and I didn't miss the glares of jealousy I got.

I almost go over and very politely ask them if they have an issue or if there's just a stick up their ass, but then she looks over her shoulder at me, and as my eyes meet hers, my feet seem to have a mind of their own as they keep me close behind her.

As soon as the door to the bar closes, the lack of noise brings us out into a different world. It's cooler out here with the lack of people, but the LA heat is still present, even with the sun being set.

"My car is this way." I gesture to the right.

She hesitates as she looks where I pointed, down the dark street. "You're not going to, like, murder me or anything, right?" There's only a bit of light out here so I can just barely see the gentle smile on her face.

"I guess you have to just find out."

A smile grows on her face as she makes her way to me. "Well, just a heads up, I can definitely take you."

I give her a once over. She's in heels that wrap up her calves. Even if she can fight, I don't think she'd get far in those shoes. Then again, she won *Best Walk in Nine-inch Heels,* so maybe she can.

Plus, she isn't tiny. With these heels, I can kiss her forehead perfectly; she probably sits at 5'10 without them on.

"You think you can take me?" I turn my head as we round the corner, and she nods, her head up tall.

"One hundred percent, yes." She looks forward. When my car is in sight, I unlock it, and she makes her way over after seeing the lights flash.

I open the back seat and nod for her to get in. I slip in after her, and she watches the roof of my car, the starlight ceiling rivaling her eyes. "Don't you think the Wraith is better?" She glances around my car before looking over at me.

"There isn't this much space in the back seat of a Wraith." I take her hand, guiding her onto my lap, but she pauses and looks down at my lap, sort of laughing.

"I'm going to crush you."

I falter for a beat. I can't tell if she's insulting me *again* or herself. I glance down at her thick thighs, but instead of replying, I pull her onto my lap.

My hands find her hips as she straddles me, and I spread my legs more, leaning back. "Perfect," I tell her, and she feels tense, but I lean into her neck for a soft kiss, and she relaxes.

"Is that really what you took into consideration when buying a half-a-million-dollar car?"

"Absolutely; think about how unfortunate it would've been to spend all that money on a car, and we couldn't even do this." My lips crash with hers, and I don't come up for air, but I don't need air; I have her.

The *month* of torture finally pays off as my tongue explores her mouth. The minute she lets out a soft moan against my lips, all bets on playing nice are off. Her tongue slides against mine, and my hand finds her ass. The blood rushes to my cock as she slowly grinds against me. I bring a hand up her inner thigh slowly, fondling almost as I realize how soft her skin really is. She slows the kiss as I slip my hand into her underwear, and if I wasn't fully hard before feeling how wet she already is, I sure am now.

She lets out another soft moan as I slide my fingers in and out, but that doesn't last more than a minute.

"More," she whispers, and her hands find my belt, working it off. Her lips meet my neck in a rush. Her needy kisses beg for more as she memorizes my skin. I work my pants down for her, and she quickly rewards me as her mouth lands on mine.

I lean forward and grab a condom from the pocket behind the front seat before slipping it on. Bringing my hands back to her hips, I adjust her to slide onto me, but she pulls away and looks between us, although it's too dark in here for her to see what she's looking for.

"Do you—"

"Yeah." I kiss my way from her jaw to her lips as she slides her hand down my length to check.

"You did that fast."

"Practice makes perfect, pretty girl." With my hands on her waist, I bring her down on me, and the minute I'm in, I let out a sigh. Something deep in my core awakens being in her like *this*. "You feel really fucking good."

She lets out a quiet, pretty moan as her head falls on my shoulder, her long braids curtaining around her face. "Thank you." Her voice is breathless as she moves against me, and I shake my head at her politeness.

I wait for her to do more, to do *something*, but she keeps her slow, soft pace as she makes every sweet sound under the sun. I groan and try to go harder, but I really can't in this position.

"You fuck just how you look."

"How's that?" She asks quietly before I pull her away from me.

"Innocent." In a quick move, I flip us and lay her on her back. She lets out a surprised huff, but before she can say anything, I'm pounding into her. She fills the car with her moans, louder with each stroke. "There we go." I keep one hand on her waist and the other on the door above her to steady myself.

Leaning in, she puts her hand on my chest before our lips meet. "That hurts."

I slightly flinch at the pain in her voice and kiss her cheek twice before pulling out softly. She moans in my ear, and a chill runs down my spine. *How can she sound so good?* She runs a hand through my hair, burying her face in my neck.

"I thought you said you could take me?" I feel her smile against me, and I kiss the side of her face again. "Take it for me."

She makes more perfect sounds as I return to fucking her, and *fuck* does she feel good, but she takes it better. I let my eyes fall shut as I listen to the sounds she makes, and when she calls out my name, I lose it. She finishes close behind, and I bring my mouth to hers, swallowing the last of her moans.

As I collect myself in the space between her neck and shoulder, she runs her fingers through my hair. After maybe a minute, I pull out, and I don't miss the soft sigh that escapes past her lips. When I lean away, it's still too dark to see much, but I make out her frame as she adjusts her dress.

I slip the condom off before fixing my pants. Grabbing a napkin from the middle console, I hand it to her before kissing her cheek. "You took it so well."

A shy smile grows on her face as she avoids my eyes and cleans herself. I smirk down at her before stealing a longer kiss.

Taking the napkin from her when she's done, I turn to open the door, but she stops me. "Please do not tell me you're about to toss that condom on the side of the street."

"That's disgusting." I step out of the car, but she's still watching me.

"Is it broken?!" She sort of whisper-shouts, although I'm not sure why since no one is around.

"It's not, you're just really wet."

Her jaw opens a bit, and she turns away as if she's shy again. I shake my head at her, biting back a smile, and walk to the garbage at the corner to dispose of the napkin and condom, but double check and it's not broken.

When I walk back, she's stepping out of my car and fixing her dress. I lean in my car for a napkin, and when I turn to her, she's still standing there. She glances at me, then turns to something behind her.

"Yes?" I wait for her to say whatever she's clearly waiting for.

"You–" She shakes her head, and I think she rolls her damn eyes. "Nothing, get home safe." She turns on her heels and walks off.

"What–" I cut myself off since she's still walking away from me.

I walk around and slide into the driver's seat. I do a U-turn just as she rounds the corner. I look between the road and her as she continues walking. It looks like the guy in front of her is saying something, but she only gives him a small smile.

I slow down as she stops for something, and someone honks behind me, but when I don't move, they drive around me. It's only when I see her walk back into the bar that I speed off.

Chapter Seven

SAGE

"**O**H MY GOD!" I GRAB the door before I fall and quickly make my way to my room more carefully. I answer the call just before it ends, and Helena's pretty face pops up on my screen.

"Why are you in a robe?"

I look down at myself and rush into my closet. "Please don't tell me you're downstairs," I beg, frantically looking for the outfit I laid out last night. I'm never late when I have photo shoots, but my phone died last night, and I forgot to put it on the charger. My other alarm woke me up, but it was set for thirty minutes *after* I needed to be up.

"I'm not downstairs," she says matter-of-factly.

I let out a breath of relief as I slipped my pants on.

"I'm at your door." My doorbell rings.

"Ugh! Okay, one second." I only have a bra and my pants on as I rush for the door. The minute it's open, I'm already turning back around.

"Who's doing our makeup? My team said they won't be there," Helena voices as she lets herself in.

"Angie said someone from the brand deal was doing our makeup." Angelica is my agent, who I love, and she's never wrong about anything related to our work so I'm sure our makeup is taken care of.

I have two photo shoots today, which means two different makeup looks, and I usually have my team come with me to do all of this for me, but the brand we're shooting with today said they want their team to do our makeup.

"It feels *so* good to be back on our regular schedule." I let out a relieved breath as we walk into my room.

"Ugh, I know," Lena agrees. "The contest was consuming every second of my day the last month."

I don't voice that I know the feeling since I'm sure she knows. "It was fun, though. I'm just excited to be home and officially kick off our modeling season."

"Speaking of, we need to be there in an hour, and it's an hour's drive. What else do you need to do?" Helena glances down at my bra and jeans.

"I'm almost ready," I voice as I slip my shirt on. Since our clothes will be at the studio, I'm wearing something simple today.

"Sneakers or heels?" I hold both shoes, and she chooses the heels. I slip them on, then give myself a once over in the mirror. I adjust my jeans and turn to the side. "I know I don't need a belt, but do you think I should add one? It's behind you."

She turns to grab the belt, and I watch in the mirror as she runs her hand along the diamonds admiringly.

"Is this a Sloan Rue belt?"

I nod and turn with a smile, and Helena's eyes are on the *JS* logo. Josephine Sloan is the biggest model to ever walk a stage. When she made her clothing line, Sloan Rue, it, of course, blew up. After her passing, she left the company to her daughter, but Vlaire doesn't make clothes anymore, so every Sloan Rue item is a limited edition.

"How did you get this?" Helena puts the belt around her waist and looks at herself in the mirror.

"I reposted this video of some girl talking about how she'd rob whoever had this belt," I shrug and laugh at the reminder of it. "Vlaire ended up sending it to me."

Helena's jaw drops, but she quickly recovers and shakes her head in disbelief as she hands me the belt. "I still can't believe you are friends with Josephine Sloan's daughter." She shakes her head again. "Either you wear it, or I'm robbing you right now."

I take it from her with a laugh and put it on, and I'm glad for it because it completes the look. We rush out the door and to Helena's car, but I turn to her before she drives off. "Let me grab a coffee real quick."

"Sage, we–"

"We won't be late. There's no traffic, I checked. Come on, I know you want one."

She lets out a sigh at the smile I send her way. I bat my eyelashes for her, and she shakes her head disappointedly. "You're lucky I love you."

I lean over to kiss her cheek when she pulls in front of my favorite coffee shop in the entire country. I already know Helena's order since she hasn't switched her order in years.

We met at a casting when we were nineteen, and even though I ended up getting the part, we stayed in touch, and nine years later, we're best friends.

When I walk into the coffee shop, the cashier, Rob, smiles over at me. "What will it be today, Sage?"

"I'll have a Surprise Me Drink, but make it something with coffee, please." I add Helena's drink as well, and he puts in the order. As I reach into my bag to grab my wallet, Rob waves a hand dismissively.

"It's on the house."

"Again? No, you guys can't keep letting me have free drinks. I can't remember the last time I paid in here, and I'm starting to feel bad."

"Of course, we can, and don't feel bad," Cee Cee, my favorite barista in here, chimes in as she walks over to the expresso machine. "Where are you going? You look so cute."

"She always looks cute," Rob mumbles, and when I look over at him, I notice his cheeks blush. I smile at both of them before telling them I have a photo shoot.

"What brand is it for today?"

I slide over to the pickup side as someone comes to order. "This first one is just something small and later today is with Cartier."

"Cartier?!" Cee Cee glances over her shoulder at me. "Bring me back a pair of earrings."

I let out a laugh because she says this every time I tell her which brand I'm shooting with. Jewelry line, clothing line, shoes. It's always the same joke with her, but it never gets old.

She finishes my drink and has me try it right then and there to see my reaction.

"Hmm." I take another sip and look back down at my cup. "What is this?"

She tells me something that isn't even on the menu. "Should we add it?"

"Definitely!" I glance at my watch when it dings, and it's Helena. "Okay, I need to go." I quickly add a hundred-dollar bill to the tip jar. They both send me a pointed look, and I send them both a quick air kiss. "Love ya."

I don't miss the way Rob's cheeks heat as I turn, and I give him a small smile. He's so cute but also so young.

As I walk out, I notice Helena leaning against her car. My eyes catch someone behind her, and as if he can sense me watching him, he glances up, and a smile touches my lips.

I watch as Liam's eyes roam along my frame, and when his eyes meet mine, my smile widens as I wave at him. He nods my way but barely even looks at me as he turns around.

"Do you know him?" Helena takes her drink, and I keep my eyes on Liam's back. I haven't seen him since last week when we... anyway, I've never seen him around here, so I'm a bit thrown off, but it bugs me more that he just acted like that. We only texted maybe once or twice in the last few days, but a part of me is shocked he totally acted like he didn't know me just now. When he said he wanted me to help him get me out of his head, I didn't think he meant literally...

"I guess not." I debate, walking over, but Helena climbs into the car, reminding me we are in a rush, so I follow suit.

The entire ride, the car fills with our excited voices about our upcoming show with Vincent Moore. Being that it's only a week away, we're all losing our minds from the excitement but also the amount of energy it's taking. Big shows like this always take so much preparation, but considering it's Mr. Moore himself, no one has voiced a single complaint.

We made it to the studio with time to spare since, as I said, there was no traffic. As soon as we walk through the door, we are ambushed by excited staff and swept along with directions and instructions.

Since Helena and I are signed with Magic Model, most of our photo shoots are set up through them. I get other brand deals, of course, but the company sets up maybe half of them.

"Okay!" The woman who introduced herself as *The Boss* starts yelling out orders. "Our girls are here. We need hair and makeup for Ms. Rogers." She leads us to the back, and we take our seats in front of two vanities. It is a whirlwind as hair, makeup, and clothing designers work to get us ready for the first look.

"Oh *God*, did you see Mel's post?"

I turn to Helena just as she looks up from her phone. She passes it to me, and I smile at the post Mel made. She models with us and was one of Quinn's baby models in the contest. Helena doesn't like her, but I can't remember why.

"She looks so pretty! Blonde suits her so well."

Helena lets out a scoff and turns the phone back to herself.

"What?"

"She totally went blonde because I'm blonde." She rolls her eyes, and I feel my brows furrow.

"You're naturally blonde, Lena." I look at her, confused. "It's not like you just changed your hair and she–"

"Yeah, well, the other day we were at the studio, and someone complimented my hair, and she interrupted and immediately started going off about how she was dying her hair blonde."

I still don't see what this has to do with her...

"Mel has been talking about going blonde since I met her." I shrug. "She just couldn't because of her previous contract."

She just got signed with Magic Model and was finally released from the horrible company she was with. That girl has horror stories for days. The CEO of that agency needs to step on a few legos for the rest of his life. The things I hear about him and how controlling he is with his girls make me forever grateful that I decided to sign with Magic instead of them.

Helena doesn't say anything else.

"Stop being mean, Lena. She's so sweet, and you barely know her," I scold her with a smile.

While I love taking in baby models, Helena hates making new friends. She doesn't reply as staff make their way over to us, and we get started. They start Helena's hair as they do my makeup. I scroll through my emails and forward potential brands I'm interested in working with to Angie.

When I put my phone down and glance at the mirror, something seems off. I only have concealer under my eyes, but it looks too light. I look over at the rest of the makeup and grab the foundation, which is also not my shade.

"Is everything okay, Ms. Loana?"

I turn to the makeup artist with a smile. "You can call me Sage."

She nods shyly.

"I think this is too light. Can we get a darker shade?"

Her entire face flushes as she searches her bag, and I try to tell her it's okay, but my reassurance doesn't help. She pulls out another shade, but they look the same, and it's three, maybe four shades lighter than me.

"This is all I have..."

I give her a tight smile. I steal a glance at the rest of the makeup and even the contour is too light. *Why don't they have anything in my shade?*

"You're joking."

I look over at Helena at her rough tone. "It's fine." I give her a smile and shake my head, but she doesn't take the hint.

"No, it isn't, Sage. This is so unprofessional." She turns to the makeup artist. "You guys should know her shade and have it." She waves off the stylist who's trying to do her hair. "Get your boss in here."

"Helena, it's fine. It's not her fault that—"

"Sage, stop being so damn nice. I bet you all my shoes that my shade is in that bag." I glance at the makeup bag, and Helena's lighter shade is certainly there.

I let out a sigh and rise from my seat. Everyone is apologizing to me as I wipe the bit of makeup from my face. I turn to the makeup artist I was working with, and she looks like she's about to cry.

"It's okay." I ignore the huff Helena lets out, but she's right. This is unprofessional and it also isn't the first time different teams we work with haven't had a makeup shade that matched my dark complexion.

I put on a smile and grab her hand. "It's not your fault. I actually might have my makeup in the car, let me check."

She's already nodding as I barely finish my sentence, and I drag in another breath as I grab Helena's keys from her bag. The minute I'm in the car, I'm calling Angie.

"How's my girl doing?"

I smile at the clear affection in her tone, relaxing in my seat. "Good..." I trail off hesitantly.

She lets out a sigh. "You haven't even been there for twenty minutes. Tell me what's wrong so I can fix it." How does she know something is wrong? No clue, but I love her for it.

"They don't have the right shade for my–"

"No, the hell they do not."

I let my eyes fall shut. I know this is an issue, but I feel so bad that Magic is going to blacklist this brand over something like this. The biggest problem with modeling is the lack of representation, and because of that, Magic Model is so popular considering our diversity. When they hear that the brands who collaborate with us don't have our makeup shade or stylists who don't know how to do our curly hair... it's an issue.

"Walk, Sage."

"Angie, no. I can't—"

"You can and you will. Stop being so damn nice. This is the exact reason you have your own team who does your makeup and laces your damn shoes. You're Sage Loana *Hale.*"

I cover my face with my hands. I don't care if I was the CEO of our company. I can't walk out on this photo shoot. That's so mean.

"The other reason you have your own team was to avoid shit like this from happening, but what did they say?" She doesn't let me reply. "*They have an amazing team and would love the privilege to do your makeup.* Never again!"

I don't know why I even called her. I let out a sigh and grabbed Helena's lipgloss as I put her on speaker.

"They're not only wasting your time but the fact that they don't have your shade at all?! Are they using makeup from shitty brands that don't have shades darker than Caramel and *Chestnut*?"

"Yeah..." The minute I saw the makeup brand, I knew she was wasting her time checking her bag.

Angie is quiet for a while as I play with the lip gloss.

"Get the hell out of there!"

I jump at her sudden outburst, then break into a laugh at how loud she's being. "Angie, please just let me stay. I can do my own makeup and–"

"Absolutely not. You probably don't even have it with you. What? You plan on driving home to get– no, you don't *do* your own makeup, Sage. You're a Magic Model."

"I don't think I'm too good to do my own makeup..." I pull the mirror down as I apply some gloss.

"You are, you're just too damn humble." She lets out a sigh.

I think being humble is a great thing, but I don't respond.

"I already had someone call them. The shoot is over. Since you're too damn nice, have Helena grab whatever you left in there and come to the studio, we can move up the photo shoot with Cartier. I just texted your team; they'll be waiting for you." She ended the call by telling me not to stress over this, although her words didn't make me feel better.

I let out a sigh and text Helena, but she's already making her way out with my purse. I stifle a laugh at the clips still in her hair and the concealer under her eyes. The minute she's in the car, I turn to her.

"Please don't tell me you yelled at them."

"I didn't." She shrugs as she grabs the makeup wipes in her bag. "I yelled at their boss."

Oh, God. I cover my face with my hands.

"Don't feel bad, Sage. I don't understand why you don't see the issue with this."

"I do, but–"

"But nothing. Our team would've never been that unprepared. Don't feel bad we left, we couldn't do the pictures either way because *they* didn't have *your* makeup. That's not your problem, and it's not your job to bring your own makeup."

I only nod in response because everything she's saying is true.

"They would've had you looking like a clown in that shade." She tosses the used makeup wipe out her window as she drives off, and I shake my head at how often she litters, but I don't waste my breath.

I see her glance at me from the corner of my eye, but I keep my gaze ahead of me.

"Okay, what if it was your hair? What if you didn't have your braids in, and they needed to do your hair, and we had another DC incident."

I literally cringe at the reminder. We flew to DC last year, and once again, the brand we were filming with wanted to show off their *great team*, but they *ruined* my hair. I think I cried the entire trip.

"Okay, you proved your point," I finally relinquish, trying to squish the guilty feeling in my gut.

She thankfully changes the topic and goes on about how excited she is to work with Cartier again because the guy they usually send is hot. He is, and they're constantly flirting.

Both of our phones light up, and I know it's probably from the agency. I immediately grab it when I notice it's our updated meal plans. As models, we, of course, need to keep in shape, but as I read mine, I notice it's a lot different than my last one. I pick up Helena's phone, and she also got the same email.

"Can I see what meal plan they sent you?"

She gives me the green light, and I unlock her phone.

"Hmm." I look at her last one, and they're pretty similar.

"What?"

"They changed my meal plan, but yours is so similar to your last one."

I look over at Helena when she doesn't answer, but she keeps her eyes ahead.

"What?"

She shrugs in response before stealing a quick glance at me. "Maybe because you put on a bit of weight." Her words are soft, but they somehow still cut. "And that's fine; you're a plus-size model, Sage."

I only nod in response and put her phone back. We're quiet for a few minutes, and I feel her stealing a few glances at me, but I keep my eyes fixed on the road.

"Stop overthinking this, Sage." She places her hand on my thigh, and I turn to her with a forced smile. "You're our best model—after me, of course."

She flips her hair playfully, pulling a laugh out of me. She and I are always toe to toe for everything, so I don't think her words are true, but either way, I don't see her as competition since we're best friends.

She looks back over at me, the playfulness gone. "Your weight doesn't change that, Sage. You're beautiful."

I only nod in response with a soft smile and she lets out a sigh. "Just follow my meal plan." She shrugs.

My brows furrow as I look back down at her meal plan and study how different ours are. "Are you sure it's okay for me to do that... again?"

"You did it last summer, and you were fine." She shrugs as I sit in thought. I *did* lose weight when I followed her meal plan last summer, but Angie also yelled at me so badly, I freaking cried. She made it such a big deal and was talking about all of these health problems I didn't even understand or have. I was fine. I was hungry and a bit lightheaded, but I lost weight.

"Yeah, maybe I will." I nod, more to myself.

"Good."

I turn to Helena, and she has a bright smile on her face. "You look amazing now, but your summer body last year was literal goals."

I laugh softly but clear my throat when it comes out weird... maybe she's right.

We sit in a comfortable silence for the rest of the drive, but as Helena pulls into her parking spot in front of Magic Model Headquarters, a sense of serenity washes over me as my eyes land on the huge glass doors. The gold M handles catch my eyes as we head for the doors, and I let out a content sigh.

"I love it here," I say, mostly to myself, and Helena agrees as we walk in. MM Headquarters is five times bigger than the studio we were just in, and considering how much time I spend here, it feels like home.

"Good morning, ladies!" The front desk man waves cheerfully before he takes the ID from the girl in front of him.

"Good morning, Cal!" Helena and I voice in sync as we slip into the elevator. The ride up to the third floor is fast, and I feel a smile tugging at my lips when I step off the elevator and hear laughter coming from one of the common rooms.

Turning the corner, I peek into the makeup room where all of the models get ready, and a few heads turn my way. "Sage, hey!" Mel's pretty smile paints her face.

"Hello, pretty. I love your hair!" Seeing it up close, blonde really does suit her. In the corner of my eye, I can see Helena walk away, but I don't comment on it as Mel thanks me. My team quickly stands from their seats and tells me they'll meet me in my room before I tell the other girls I'll see them later.

Helena slips into her dressing room as I make it down the hall, but since we both need to get ready, I head for the end of the hall. Passing by Quinn's room, I pluck the green dry-erase marker from the velcro and write a small message on her board. Next to her door is Nin's room, and I pick out a daily affirmation from the small cup she has outside her door.

You alone, the way you are now, are enough.

I feel myself go still as my brain shuffles through my conversation with Helena in her car. Before I can decide whether or not the universe is trying to tell me something, a door opens.

"Loana!"

My eyes land on Coral, and her smile pulls one out of me. I love that she just calls me my middle name. She and a few of the other girls do that, and I smile like this every time I hear it.

"I heard about the makeup shit show, but I'm running late, so tell me later." She points at me eagerly as she walks away backward.

A laugh bubbles in my throat at how nosy she is, but I promise to give her the scoop before I walk a few steps to my dressing room. As a Core Eight girl, we all have our own rooms, and as my eyes land on my name on my door, I feel a sense of pride. While this has always been the goal since I first signed with Magic Model a few years ago, I had no clue I'd make it this far, but seeing my full name on this gold plaque reminds me that this is real.

I snap a picture of the plaque and post it to my story with the caption *Back to work*. Just as the door shuts, someone is knocking. I turn on my heels and let my team in.

Sitting at my vanity, my team sets up around me before we fall into our routine. I let my eyes fall shut as they start my makeup. "What do we think about my hair? Can we style it in these braids?"

"Of course, we can." Annet shows me a few different hairstyles on her phone, then gets started on my hair when I pick one.

"You have three different outfits you need to change into by the way." One of the girls who is off to the side voices.

"Three? We're modeling jewelry. Why so many outfit changes?"

She shrugs and apologizes for not knowing, and I laugh softly.

"Please don't apologize."

She apologizes for apologizing, and I steal a glance at her but don't recognize her.

"What's your name?"

She glances over at Cara before her eyes settle on me. "Lynn," she mumbles.

I smile at her, and Cara tells me she's new and is shadowing under her.

"Well, she can't learn much by shadowing, can she?" I peek over at Lynn. "Come, you can finish my makeup." The room falls quiet, and I look around at them in confusion. "She *is* shadowing as a makeup artist, no?"

"Yes." Cara clearly forces a smile. "But today is an important photo shoot and—"

"Every day is an important photo shoot." I laugh softly. "You'll be right here to help her if it doesn't look good, let's give her a chance." I shrug and Lynn looks at Cara for approval.

Cara only nods towards me since it is my call, and Lynn trains her hopeful eyes on me. "I'm sure," I reassure her.

A smile lights up her face as she makes her way closer and continues to blend out my makeup. My base is already done, which I personally think is the most important part, so she starts my eyes.

Cara barely gives any pointers, and before I know it, Lynn is applying the setting spray. She steps aside so I can survey myself. I glance at her in the mirror, and she fiddles with the setting spray nervously as Cara stands beside us, waiting for my reaction.

"Well, you don't need to shadow Cara anymore."

Lynn's shoulders drop, and Cara shakes her head, her glare settling on Lynn.

"Because it's amazing," I quickly clarify.

They both look over at me, and Lynn's eyes widen as her disappointment turns into disbelief. Beside her, Cara holds her head up proudly.

"Keep up the good work," I tell Lynn before turning to Cara. "You're a good teacher."

She nods gently as she thanks me before exiting the room with Lynn. My outfit crew brings in my clothes over, and I get changed before heading out to the photographer.

The photo shoot goes smoothly, as always, and ends fast, and I'm thankful for it after this morning's drama. I head back to my room to change but stop short when someone calls my name.

"Here you go." The photographer hands me a small red leather box. "Please accept this gift on behalf of the company; it's been an honor working with you."

"Awe, thank you so much. Likewise." When I open the box, a small gasp escapes me. Beautiful stud diamond earrings shine back at me. I love them, but I already have a pair of them. I don't tell him that, though, and thank him again before heading for my room. After I change back into my clothes, I grab the earrings and meet Helena in her car. On the route to my house, I debate on what to do with the earrings, but when Cee Cee texts me to tell me someone else loved her Surpise Me drink, I have her drop me off at the coffee shop.

"Back so soon? Just admit you're in love with me." Cee Cee flirts, and I smile at her as I bat my lashes.

"I confess," I play along as I make my way to the counter and pull the box from behind my back. "A token of my affection."

"You're joking." She takes the box, and when she opens it, her jaw drops. "You are *joking.*"

I laugh at her shock, and she only stares at me dumbfounded.

"I didn't mean it when I said to bring me a pair of earrings! No, I can't—"

"Please take them. They gave them to me, and I already have a pair of those."

She looks back at the jewelry in her hands. "I think this can cover *all* of my student loans."

I can't stop smiling as a warm feeling settles in my chest at how grateful she looks. "Sell them." I shrug. "I can always get you another pair as a graduation gift, but only if you apply to that grad school you were talking about."

She walks around the counter to pull me in for a hug. "Thank you so much!"

I hug her back, and she squeezes me tightly before letting go. "This guy was flirting with me today." She smiles and flips her pink hair over her shoulder, and I can't help but laugh.

"Every guy flirts with you."

She smiles and raises her brows twice, which makes me laugh harder.

"Did you entertain him?"

"Of course I did. Straight men think they're so funny." She rolls her eyes and calls him dumb while pointing at the pride flag pin on her apron.

"Are you talking about that blonde guy?" Rob asks as he walks around the counter. "Because he wasn't funny, he was actually really rude."

My brows furrow at his tone.

"No, but that one was actually hot and coming from a very gay girl that says something."

Now she has my attention. "Spill, what'd he look like?"

Cee Cee shrugs and looks back down at her new earrings. "Really tall white boy, blonde fluffy hair, tons of tattoos."

I go still, and pictures of Liam blatantly ignoring me this morning fill my mind.

"He wore all black. I don't think he's seen color a day in his life."

"Yeah," Rob laughs now. "I think he had a stroke when he walked in here."

I look around the room and can't help but smile. It looks like a unicorn was thrown up here, and I love it.

"What name did he give for his order?" I ask lightly, letting my curiosity get the better of me.

"Luke or something." Cee Cee goes back around the counter, and Rob rolls his eyes at her.

"It was Liam." *I knew it.* I think of shooting him a text but convince myself not to be that girl, especially not after how he acted earlier.

Chapter Eight

LIAM

"**A**RE WE GOING TO THE club or not?"

I let out a sigh, ignoring him as I scroll through my phone. When I don't reply, Jordan asks again.

"I heard you the first time."

"So, can you maybe not ignore me?"

I keep my eyes on my phone.

"Cool." He sits on the couch beside me, and the irritation seeps into my blood as our shoulders touch. I look up at him, but before I can tell him to back up, he's back on his feet. "Got it." He nods once before sitting a few feet away from me.

When he doesn't leave my house, I turn my phone off and look over at him. "What do you possibly want from my life?"

He turns his head to the side. "What's your problem?"

"You're about to find out if you don't leave."

He doesn't leave. "You're being bitchier than usual." Before I can respond, Moon walks in, his mouth full of *my* food.

"These chips are really good." His voice comes out muffled as he stuffs more into his mouth, cheese covering his fingers, and I briefly close my eyes as some chips fall onto the ground.

"Jordan, get your friend." I pinch the bridge of my nose as Jordan laughs from beside me.

"I recognize this attitude," Jordan voices. "You need to get laid."

I ignore him and look back over at Moon to tell him to clean the mess on the ground, but he nods in agreement and starts talking before I can.

"Speaking of, you and Sunshine?"

"Who the hell is Sunshine?" My eyes narrow in annoyance.

"Sage," Jordan voices as if I should've known that. "Her whole aura is rainbows and sunshine. We've been calling her that for weeks."

"*That's* who you two have been talking about?"

Moon waves me off before turning serious for once in his life. "You slept with her then *ignored her?*" He shakes his head. "Dick move."

I almost ask when the fuck she told him that, but Jordan whips to me so damn fast; I'm surprised he doesn't give himself whiplash.

"You *slept* with her?!"

I let out an annoyed breath as his heart attack passes.

"Did the argument with Griffin the other day not speak for itself?"

"I slept with her before I saw him." I roll my eyes at him as I look back down at my phone. Seeing him was actually the reason I ignored her back in LA, and I'm sure it was a dick move, but I was still sore from my fight with Sire over something not worth remembering, a physical reminder that Sage isn't worth the headache. Her brothers have never fought fair, and I'm not scared of them; I just don't feel like getting jumped by them again. While I love pissing them off, this rivalry can get exhausting at times.

"Why is it a pissing match every time you see each other? Just because of college and baseball rivalry?" Moon looks as confused as he sounds, and I mumble that there's more to it, but I'm too tired to even get into it.

"You ignored her, so I'm assuming you're going to..." Jordan waits for me to finish, and when I don't, he throws his hands in the air. "You know what? I tried being a good friend and keep you two apart since *you* told me not to let you get close to her, but since you want the Hale brothers to cut your dick off, knock yourself out. I hope the sex is worth it."

It is, and so is her damn smile and pretty dimples.

I only told him not to let me get close to her because she's drop-dead gorgeous, and I knew I'd end up sleeping with her. Considering how close she seems with her brothers, I figured it would've slipped and cost me a pretty black eye, but it hasn't, so maybe I was being careful for no reason...

"You look like you're scheming." Jordan sits up as he watches me.

I kick them both out, and without them, I finally have peace. I go back to scrolling through my phone, but as if saying her name three times makes her appear, she pops up. I don't follow Sage on anything, yet she still pops up on my feed from time to time. It's like I can't get away from her.

This one is an ad for Cartier. She's in all white, looking as innocent as ever. She isn't smiling in this picture as she models a necklace and a few rings. The picture is zoomed in, and every inch of her shown is flawless. She's looking off to the side, the emeralds in her necklace matching her eyes. Her hands are resting on her chest as she shows off the gold rings that look like they cost a million dollars against her dark skin.

All the images of her in my car come to mind, and I'd be lying if I said this was the first time I had thought about her. After I saw her smiling at me and fucking waving all friendly, I couldn't get her out of my head, and I don't know why. I shake my head of my thoughts as I scroll past the picture, but not even two minutes pass before another picture of her appears.

"You're joking." It's the same ad, but she's in a red outfit now, smiling; she shines brighter than the jewelry around her. It looks like the picture was taken in the middle of her laughing, and she looks over her shoulder at whoever is pretending to put her necklace on her.

I tap on the page, and I'm not sure why because, as I expected, the last six posts are all of her. She has some pictures with some blonde chick, but Sage is clearly the center of this photo shoot. She looks perfect in every single shot, effortlessly perfect.

I decide to shoot her a text.

Hey.

Her text bubbles pop up after a minute but then disappear. I give her another minute, but she doesn't reply, and
under my message *read* appears.
Did she just turn her read recipes on?

So you just use me for my photography skills then
toss me aside? Cold.

Oh, you should not be talking about using people
then tossing them aside and being cold.

Okay... clearly, she's offended I ignored her, although I
could've guessed that since she felt the need to tell Moon.

I decide not to go back and forth with her over text, but
as I reread her message, guilt eats at me, and I call James,
my pilot.

"Mr. Walker?"

"Can we have the jet ready to leave in forty-five minutes?
I need to go back to LA."

There's a hesitation on his end. "So soon? You only just
landed in New York last night?"

"Can we leave in forty-five minutes or not?"

"Yes. Yes, of course."

I end the call and get up for a quick shower.

I LOOK OUT OF MY car and watch as people walk in and out of
this weird coffee shop. Whoever designed this place needs
to be fired because it was obvious they couldn't pick one

design. There's so much going on, and the entire place looks like sunshine and rainbows. I shake my head at the reminder of Jordan's nickname for Sage, and of course, she likes it here. This place is the location version of her.

I keep my eyes on the door, but after just a few minutes, a few people start to notice me. If I could simply play baseball and cash in my checks without the fame, I would. After I give one person my autograph, I put my car window up so no one else can ask or take pictures of me.

I start to think she just came here that one time, but just as I'm about to drive off, I glance in the mirror and see that smile of hers. She's talking to a girl beside her, and I put my window down a bit.

"I promise–" She laughs loudly as she takes the hand of the girl she's with. "No, I promise when they first opened all of the drinks were horrible, but their current barista is amazing." She walks right past me, and they go into the shop together.

I wait outside for her, and the girl she was with comes out first. When I glance into the coffee shop, she's lost in a conversation with both baristas. I have no clue what she's saying, but the guy who should be taking orders is just *watching* her. His face is red as fuck; as if he's in love and is about to get on one damn knee. I decide to go in after all and grab the small bag in the seat beside me. The minute I walk in, my ears are assaulted by the torture music they're playing, and I curse myself for putting my ears through this, but I walk further in.

"Oh, I love this song!" *Of course, she does.* The cashier, unfortunately, puts it louder for her. She starts dancing, swaying to the ear-bleeding music with a beat that doesn't sound so terrible now that she is moving to it.

I walk over to the fridge since I've been watching her for way too long. I grab a water, and when I turn, her eyes land on me. She stalls in her movement, looking like a deer in headlights with her doe eyes as embarrassment covers her expression.

"Sage," I say cooly with a small nod.

"Hey..." She trails off, looking a little confused by my appearance.

I walk to the counter, and she moves aside so I can pay. I feel her curious gaze boring into me, but she doesn't speak up again. When I glance over at her, my eyes scan at the rest of her frame, and I really take her in. She's in a skin-tight pink dress that fades into purple at the end, and it hugs every last one of her curves perfectly. The bright color makes her skin look as good as ever.

She keeps her eyes on the barista in front of us as she plays with the end of her hair. She doesn't have braids like the last time I saw her; instead, it's curly and a really light brown, reaching her waist.

Sage finally looks at me again, filling the awkward silence, "I don't normally see you around here. Did you recently move?" It's clear she's just asking out of politeness, and I don't miss how standoffish she's being.

I shake my head. "I have a penthouse downtown, but I don't live here."

She looks confused, but I don't elaborate on how I'm only ever in LA for my mom. Before she can ask another question, because I'm sure she's going to, I hand her the small bag in my hand.

"What is this?" She's already peeking into the bag as she asks.

"Open it." I grab her drink, allowing her hands to be free.

She opens her gift, and her smile lights up the entire room as she pulls out the camera. "Is this for *me*?!"

I nod in return, and her smile somehow grows as she studies me. When we were working on her pictures for the contest, she mentioned something about wanting a new vlogging camera and considering she looks ecstatic, I'm assuming I remembered correctly, and this was the one she wanted.

"Is this you saying sorry for ignoring me?" She takes her drink back and gives me a pointed look, but I don't miss the way her lips curve upwards.

"Does that pretty smile mean I'm forgiven?" I voice, my eyes on those dimples.

She averts my eyes, hiding her smile. I put my hand on the small of her back as I guide her out of the coffee shop because beside her, are two nosy baristas who were in our entire conversation.

"It's going to take more than an expensive camera for me to forget you blatantly acting like you didn't know me after *sleeping* with me." She keeps her voice light, but I sense the hurt under her tone, and it makes me feel like a bigger dick.

As we approach my car, I open the driver seat door and nod for the other side. "Let me make it up to you."

She crosses her arms as she watches me. "How?" She looks skeptical.

"Get in, and I'll show you." I'm sure she wants to use her new camera, and while it's for vlogging, she can get nice pictures. There's a park downtown that I'm sure she'll like.

Her eyes slightly narrow as she studies me but after a beat, she walks around the car and slides in. I get in after her and then turn to her when she starts talking.

"Are you going to tell me why you completely brushed me off the other day?" She puts her drink in the cup holder before folding her arms across her chest and crossing her legs. "First, you're nice in the bar—well, at least you were nice to me. Then we hooked up, and you can't even walk me back to the bar. It was very dark, and drunk men were everywhere."

"You were fine-" Cutting myself off, I shake my head at the reminder. "*That's* why you stormed off with a little attitude? Because I didn't offer to walk you twenty feet?"

"Yes, it's *rude*. How do you know I was *fine*? You just drove off."

"You were fine." I nod once as I remind her.

She keeps her eyes fixed on mine, a small furrow growing between her brows. "I'm confused, Liam. You said you don't live around here... did you come all the way over here to give me a sorry gift? You don't seem like the type of man that apologizes for being... well, an ass." She keeps her voice light, her eyes still watching me like she can pull my thoughts from her head to hers.

"I'm not the type." I open my mouth again to tell her I also don't like being ignored but quickly close it because I realize how ridiculous it is that I came here and got her an expensive camera because she sent me a smart text after *I* ignored *her.*

What am I doing with this woman?

"Well," She starts again, pulling me out of my thoughts. "You're going to have to say it." She holds her head up high, but I don't try to form the words I desperately hate saying.

When I say nothing, she shakes her head and grabs her drink before turning for the door. The flash of hurt in her pretty eyes makes me lean over her to close the door as she opens it. I keep my hand on her door as I turn to her, and she goes still, keeping our faces inches apart. "It won't happen again," I say, meaning it.

My eyes land on her lips, and I close the distance between us, kissing her gently. She pulls away first, leaning her head on the seat. "Is that how you say sorry? Gifts and kisses?"

I watch her carefully, and the hint of hurt is still in her damn eyes, and the sight makes it feel too small in here. I didn't think not saying hi to her would affect her this much. "It could be." My hand lands on her thigh, but when I lean in again, she puts a finger on my lips.

"Use your words first." She drags her finger down to the bottom of my chin slowly, tilting my head up so my eyes will meet hers again. *How does she look prettier now than she did five seconds ago?*

"I'm sorry for ignoring you, Sage," I force out, and the crease in her brows eases as the corner of her lips rises. Past her shoulder, I notice the guy barista still watching us, and while my car is tinted, I still pull away and have the car drive us to the park.

Glancing back at her, she has her eyes on the wheel. "Oh my God, this is so cool."

I feel a smirk tug at my lips at how easily distracted she is. "Have you never been in a Telsa?"

She shakes her head, her bangs falling in front of her eyes. "No, I have. My brother has one. I just never been in one while it drives itself." She reaches into her bag for something. "I need to call him, he literally said-"

I swiftly cut her off. "Call him another time." I'm sure he's going to ask whose car she's in, and I don't want him to know that. "Let me see the camera."

She tucks her phone back into her bag mindlessly before handing me the camera, and I plug it in to charge before telling her about the features it has.

"You learned about the camera?" She has a teasing smile on her face as I start setting it up for her, but I don't respond.

We get to the park and when we step out, she's already taking pictures on her phone of the cherry blossoms. "This is so pretty." She looks up at the trees in awe as a few petals fall around her, and she looks gorgeous.

I snap a few pictures on her new camera, and she doesn't even notice at first with how distracted she is with the trees. When she finally turns to me, she tilts her head to the side. "I *knew* you were a nice guy under all that attitude."

I roll my eyes at her, but she only bites back a laugh.

"Are we besties now?" She teases.

"Moon might have a heart attack if I take his title as your best friend."

She lets out a laugh, and I snap a few more pictures of her.

"What changed?" She looks skeptical, and it offends me that she thinks I'm incapable of an act of kindness for no reason.

I close the distance between us and fix a curl that's out of place. "Nothing changed, pretty girl. I just felt bad for ignoring you." Even I can admit it was messed up, and her feelings being hurt affected me more than I'd like to admit.

She nods gently as she focuses on me. "You don't have a girlfriend, right?"

I feel my brows furrow as I watch her watch me. "No?"

She looks relieved, and I quickly clarify.

"That's because I don't do girlfriends."

She looks offended now as she leans away. "Oh, I wasn't asking for me. I just had this guy flirt with me yesterday, and he had a very pregnant wife. I'm traumatized."

I shake my head at how dramatic she is. "I'm not even flirting with you."

"Maybe not, but your girlfriend wouldn't appreciate the kiss we shared earlier." She points out.

"The girlfriend I don't have?"

She must sense that I don't believe her because she looks offended again. "Don't get me wrong, you're cute and all, but you don't really meet my standards." She says it so casually, it actually offends me.

"I don't *meet your standards*?" I ask, giving her a once-over as I try to understand what that even means.

"Why are you looking at me like I don't have standards?" She crosses her arms.

"Because I'm good enough to fuck you but not good enough to date you? What kind of shit is that?"

"Okay," She puts a finger up as she starts, "Don't say *fuck you* like that. It sounds gross. You're just... well, rude to everyone who breathes your air." She puts her hands up in defense. "Moon's words, not mine; plus, you don't open doors for me or walk me back to bars at night, and I know I can do that on my own. You should *want* to, but you don't. Nothing's wrong with that. I just know my worth."

"And sleeping with me is fine?"

"You meet casual sex standards. You also seem like a great friend, but I don't see it becoming more."

This feels a lot like I just got rejected, and I'm glad Jordan isn't here to witness this because it's very humbling.

"Okay..."

She looks up as more petals fall around us, barely sparing a glance at me as she gazes at the scenery.

"Well," I close the distance between us and hold her chin so she's looking at me. "I want another night with you." My finger brushes her bottom lip, and she looks breathless now as she watches me. "Can we do that? Casual sex?" I keep my voice low as I look between her pretty green eyes.

She leans forward, but before our lips can meet, she pulls away again. "If you ignore me again—"

I bring my lips to hers before she can finish her sentence. "I won't."

She watches me carefully before she nods.

Even if I did want this to become more, I wouldn't make her succumb to that. She deserves better, and I'm glad she knows it.

We stay to take more pictures and videos of her, but she gets a call and realizes she's late for work, so I give her a ride.

She talks the entire way there about maybe seven different topics, and I don't say much the entire time, but she doesn't seem to mind or notice as she rambles.

"Thanks for the ride."

"I'll text you later. Don't ignore me."

She glances over her shoulder at me, and the guilty look on her face alone tells me she knows I know she put her read recipients on, so I knew she was ignoring me. She only nods before opening the door, and the minute she's out, a group of people notice her, and a ton of cameras are in her face. I hear her laughing at something one of them says, and after taking a few pictures with them, she waves them goodbye and walks into the building.

A few of them turn to my car, but I leave before they try to figure out who's in here.

Chapter Nine

SAGE

"**C**AN SOMEONE GIVE ME A rundown of the changes?" I look around the room as Annet touches up my hair.

"What changes?" Angie looks around the room, and I can see her annoyance growing when no one answers her. She hates last-minute changes, and while I'm fine with adapting to them, she's ready to fire people.

Today's our runway show for Vincent and *nothing* can go wrong, so I understand her worry, but everything's going to be fine... I hope.

"It's–"

"So help me God, Sage, if you say it's fine."

I laugh softly, and she sends me a glare, but a second later, she's smiling when I stick my tongue out at her.

"What changes?" Her tone is a lot softer now, and I smile in the mirror.

"Nothing big. Royal is stuck in Chicago, so they want me to take her place."

"They want you to model her outfits along with your three outfits?" She looks like she's having a stroke, and I let out a sigh, but before I can say anything, she goes on. "Absolutely not. Why didn't they run this by me?"

"Because they knew you'd say no." When I roll my eyes, she points at me and tells me to watch it. I laugh at how motherly she is. "Angie, I already agreed and–"

"Of course you did." She looks up at the ceiling. "Of course she did!"

"Ang, she was supposed to model twice in the middle, and I'm opening the show, so–"

"Sage, three outfits are already pushing it. Everyone else modeling one to two pieces and–"

"And Mr. Moore directly asked me to model all five pieces. How the heck was I supposed to say no to *the* designer himself?"

Angie goes still, and she watches me as my words sink in. I know it's because she didn't know that last part, but I was pretty shocked myself. Vincent freaking Moore was just here ten minutes ago, and he was going bananas over Royal not being able to come. We have backup models for this, but he was adamant that I wear the two outfits Royal was supposed to wear and said he could have them tailored before the show tonight.

"What?"

I laugh softly at Angie's face.

"Mr. Moore is *here*? I thought we wouldn't see him until his event tonight?"

"Me too, but he drove down here when he heard about the flights being delayed." I shrug, and Angie still looks dumbfounded, but I don't blame her. I was trying to contain myself when he walked in here.

"Okay, fine." Angie lets out a breath, and it looks like she was holding it the minute I brought up Vincent's name. "So we need all hands on deck. This is the most outfits you're modeling in the shortest time frame, but–"

"We can make it work." I glance in the mirror at my outfit team. "Right?"

"Of course." They agree with various noises of agreement, too focused on making sure I have all of my jewelry pieces for each outfit, and I'm only a tad bit nervous, but I have faith in them. Switching outfits with such little time is an outfit malfunction waiting to happen, but after all of the years we've been working together, I really do have faith in them.

By the time my hair is ready, it's time for the meeting, but just as I stand, my door flies open.

"Mr. Moore came to see you?!" Florence, the CEO of Magic Model, storms in, and her tone causes a shift in the air. Rather than being nervous about the show, I'm now nervous about her potential rage. "What did he want? What did he say? What did you *do*?" Her eyes narrow on me.

My brows furrow at Florence's last question, and when I glance at the door, the rest of The Core Eight, along with a few other models who are supposed to be at our meeting, are standing at the door.

I tell them they can come in, and they do.

"Hello?!"

I turn back to Florence, and when I tell her everything, her jaw is on the floor, along with everyone else.

"This," she points at me. "This is why you're my favorite."

I burst into a laugh when she pulls me in for a hug. She starts giving *my* team orders, and the whole meeting turns into her making sure tonight runs smoothly for Mr. Moore.

By the time we're getting ready for the event, my team seems nervous, so I turn to them before we leave.

"Hey,"

They all pause what they're doing and turn to me.

"You guys seem stressed, and it's going to stress me out, so let's please shake the nerves off."

They all say they will and apologize, and I laugh at how scared they still seem.

"Okay, listen, let's just forget everything, okay? First, forget everything Florence was saying about you guys not having room to mess up." While that was true, and they really can't mess up tonight, I don't want that pressure on them. "She was just nervous, but I know you guys know what you're doing. You guys are also *my* team, not hers. We'll do things the way we always do them, so please toss the ridiculous checklist she made; it's confusing me, and Angie already made one."

My team nods, and my outfit crew laughs as they throw away the paper Florence gave them.

"Second, let's act like Mr. Moore wasn't just in here. It's a regular Magic Model show. We own the stage and building; it's about us." Our shows always run perfectly because everyone is most comfortable, so we just need to act like it's our show. They glance at each other before turning back to me, and after a few seconds, I get nods in return.

"Another thing, and I mean this very humbly, but while he's Vincent Moore, *he* asked for *us*. If he wanted his team to do my hair and makeup and dress me, he would've told them to do so. You're all worthy of the job you have, so please act like it." I give them all a pointed look, and I can see the last few nerves leave as they stand straighter.

"Okay, good. Let's do one more check and go."

I take a seat as Angie runs through the routine checklist, and my team makes sure everything is in order.

When I get the green light that we're good to go, I rush to stand up, but my blood suddenly runs cold, and dark stars flood my vision. I fall back into my seat and take a drink of water, just waiting for the cold feeling to pass as it usually does.

Figures I'm a bit light-headed since I didn't eat all day today... or last night. I'm getting hungry, but I'll have my one meal tonight and stick to Helena's meal plan.

When the feeling passes, I stand a bit slower and ask one of my girls to grab me a juice. Annet gets it for me before walking me out to the limo, where I meet Helena and Mel.

"Are you nervous?" Mel teases, pushing my knee playfully.

"Honestly, not as nervous as I think I should be. I am hungry, though," I admit with a sheepish grin when my stomach growls.

"Do you stress eat? Because same–"

"You shouldn't."

We both turn to Helena, but she doesn't glance up from her phone. "Don't eat before the show, Sage," she cautions.

"Why?" Mel asks for me, and Helena sends her the rudest side-eye. I send her a look to be nice, but she ignores me, looking back down at her phone.

"They're tailoring two new outfits for you as we speak. That's way too last minute and the last thing you want is to not fit in it. Eat after the show."

I don't say anything and lean back in my seat. I look back over at Helena and study her frame. She's in a gold dress that makes her look stunning, especially with her blonde curls. My eyes stay on her flat stomach and the rest of her thin figure.

I know I'm bigger than she is, and I don't think that makes her any better or prettier than me, but... *she* doesn't need designers tailoring outfits for her.

When I look over at Mel, she's already watching me with a sympathetic look. I give her a bright smile and shake my head, silently telling her not to say anything about Helena's attitude. I'm nervous enough as it is with the show, and I know Helena doesn't really like Mel for whatever reason; I don't need the stress of them arguing.

I look down at Mel's frame, and she looks really good even though she mentioned her stress eating. Maybe it's okay if I have a small snack before the show? I let out a sigh at my conflicted thoughts and push them away entirely because I need to be in a good mood for tonight.

I see the paparazzi lights flashing from a distance as we pull into the main entrance. Mel's eyes are glued to the window, and I reach for her hand. She's only ever modeled with us at Magic Model shows, so this is her first big event, which means it's probably the first time she's had to face *this* much paparazzi.

"I remember how nervous I was when I first had to encounter this much paparazzi." I feel the nerves bubbling in my stomach at the reminder, and Mel asks me when that was as she keeps her eyes out the window. "It was the night they announced us as The Core Eight. I didn't get out of the car until my twin came to walk me out." I laugh at the memory, and Mel turns to me, her brows pulled together.

"I remembered that night!" Mel's face lights up. "I watched the whole show at home; you didn't look nervous at all. That was actually the day I added working with you to my vision board." She adds that last part sheepishly, a blush coming to her cheeks.

"I was terrified." I laugh as I admit it. "Your vision board is your reality now; stand proud because you should be." I squeeze her hand and give her a small tip. "If they know your name, they're all going to call you. Don't look for who's trying to get your attention. Either look forward and walk or glance between all of them."

She nods as I go on.

"If they *don't* know your name, they will after tonight. Don't cover your face from the flash, you're new so don't hide."

"Right." She nods again.

I give Mel a smile, and she returns it.

"You're fine."

She repeats after me before the driver opens the door for us, and Helena steps out. I follow after her, and there's somehow more flash.

Helena walks ahead, but I hold a hand out, and the minute Mel takes it, I can tell everyone is shocked because it's normally just Helena and me.

"Who is that with Sage Loana?"

"Sage, over here!"

"Who's the girl in red?"

"You look beautiful, Sage Loana!"

"I love the dress, Sage!"

I smile and wave at all of the cameras but don't stop like I usually would. I love talking to paparazzi, but more cars are going to start pulling up, and I'd hate to have a traffic build-up at the door.

As we step into the hall, Mel lets out a breath. "Wow, I think I'm blind."

I burst into a laugh and assure her she'll get used to it. I keep my hand in hers as we walk in, and as people walk up to greet me, I introduce them to Mel.

I glance around the room and notice a few Magic Models mingling with the designers who were invited. Most times the models would be in the back, but Mr. Moore wanted us to *show face* so his guests could see us since there were rumors that he wouldn't be able to get all of us here, and technically, he didn't, but that's because of an issue with the airline, not because Florence denied him.

"There's a lot of designers here," Mel mumbles to me, and when I follow her eyes, they're on Colette Dubios, the face of Paris in the designer industry.

"Yeah," I take in her stunning pearl dress before reminding myself not to stare for too long.

"I know being a Moore Girl is every model's dream, but when I work with *her*, I think I can say I finally made it," Mel mumbles, and I squeeze her hand to pull her away from staring. "How come people are making a big deal about us being here when it's Vincent's show?"

I almost think she's joking until I remember she's still new to Magic. "It's pretty hard to get every Magic Model to walk in your show. Florence likes to say we're untouchable and exclusively *her* girls, which is true. We don't model in shows she doesn't sign off on to keep up that image, and maybe it's just because he's Vincent Moore, but he got all of us."

"Why was that again? I mean, I'm not complaining. I'll model for him every hour of the day in my most uncomfortable heels, but he has the best models in the world."

"He said with this new line, he wants new girls to model them, but," I lean into her and smile when I notice people are watching. "Don't say anything, but Angie said this was his way of scoping out which models he wants to sign as Moore Girls." She only told me, and I don't know if it's true, but I told The Eight.

Mel's eyes widen, and when I squeeze her hand and force a smile, she changes her face. I walk over to Nin when I see she isn't talking to anyone, and the look of relief on her face tells me she's grateful for having someone to talk to.

Everyone is loving Mel and I feel my excitement buzzing off of my cells. She didn't get a lot of attention with her last company, so I'm happy for her. She's going to kill it tonight, and if I could let her model one of my pieces just to get her out in the spotlight one extra time, I would.

After more mingling, Mel walks over with two plates full of small appetizers that she snagged from a passing waiter. I almost refuse her offer, but my stomach grumbles, so I decide to take it, and I feel the energy return to me after eating with her.

"They were all screaming for Sage." Mel shoves me playfully.

"Yeah, paparazzi always do that; they freaking love her."

I laugh at Nin but then bring a hand to my stomach because my dress feels tight. I take in a deep breath but immediately stop because my dress definitely feels tighter.

"You okay?" Nin studies me, concern clear on her face.

"Yeah." I smile at the girls, then turn when someone grabs my arm.

"The new outfits are ready," Angie says quietly. "Let's do a quick try-on to make sure we're good."

I nod, but when I glance down at myself, I tell her, "Let me use the bathroom–"

"Sage, it'll be quick, just–"

"I'll be quicker." I rush off to the bathroom before she can stop me.

Locking the door behind me, I bend down to check for feet under the stalls and let out a sigh of relief when they are empty. I turn a faucet on before walking into the last stall. I take a deep breath, and when I feel my dress tighten around my waist, I don't think twice and lean over the toilet before forcing two fingers down my throat.

Everything I ate came up after three tries. My dress doesn't feel like it's about to pop anymore, but I make myself throw up one more time for good measure.

I blink my watery eyes before I ruin my makeup. When I'm done, I flush and wash my hands. I glance at myself in the mirror and turn to the side. Running a hand down my stomach, I turn my head to the side and chew on my lip.

My brain seems to pick apart every other part of myself. The way my big thighs rub together instead of having a thigh gap like a few of the other girls. I turn my head to the other side as I take in my arms next.

I felt gorgeous in this dress before, but now–

Someone knocks on the door and I jump out of my head. I eat a gum before unlocking the door and my jaw drops.

"Sage mother fucking Loana *Hale*!"

I let out a squeal before pulling in Vlaire for a tight hug. "I didn't know you were going to be here! You usually let me know. We could've hung out before this!" I know she's acquainted with Vincent, considering her mom, the icon herself, modeled for Vincent's mom before the Moore company was passed to Vincent, but she *always* calls me when she's in the States.

"I wasn't going to come." She shakes her head softly, and I pick up on her somber tone, although she voices her words with a smile. "Vincent just reminds me too much of my mom." When she smiles this time, I pick up on how forced it is.

I pull her in for another hug, and her arms come around me. "I'm so sorry again for your loss, Vlaire. If it all becomes too much for you, you know you can come backstage with me. No one will dare say anything to you." I pull away and kiss her cheek gently. While it's been a little over a year since her mom passed, I can't imagine ever getting over a loss like that, especially with the constant reminders.

"Thank you, Sage. Mamãe would've loved you. I hate that you never got to meet her. " She takes both of my hands and holds them out as she studies me from head to toe. I feel uncomfortable under her unwavering gaze after a beat, but she watches me like–

"Beautiful." She shakes her head. "Ugh, I love you. I literally only flew here for you." She beams, her heavy Brazilian accent weighing on her words.

I feel my face flush and laugh as I thank her.

"Is it true you're modeling *five* pieces?" She sort of whispers as she leans in.

"My agent is going to murder me if I confirm or deny, so I'm going to slowly walk away." I nod yes, and she squeals as I rush off with a laugh.

I hold my breath the entire time I try on the two new outfits, and they thankfully fit. I'm sure it wasn't too hard to adjust them since Royal and I are closest in size among The Eight.

The new pieces are practically shining on their hangers. One is a diamond corset dress with a fluffy short-cut shirt. The other is a dress, and the way it flows gives the illusion of fire—did I mention they are *gorgeous?!*

As I'm slipping out of the dress, all of the girls start trickling in, and just like that, the show is starting. We touch up my hair and makeup once I'm in my first outfit. I'm opening the show, so the second the cue song plays, I'm walking out on stage.

I see a few scattered flashes, but I shut out the room and its distractions, keeping my focus on my picked-out point at the back of the room and walking the way we rehearsed.

I notice Mr. Moore at the end of the stage. His face is stone cold as he watches me and the rest of the girls. I look back up and stop to pose. A few people take pictures, and I hear comments on my dress before I turn and walk back down.

I pass Helena on my way back up the stage. We both stop at the same spot, like rehearsed, and walk around each other before posing. I'm sure the ends of our dresses look amazing as they chase each other. More cameras are out now, and we give them a few seconds before continuing.

I step behind the curtain and am swept away to change. Everyone works quickly on me. Two people work on my jewelry. One works my dress off, and another helps me out of my shoes.

It took me a very long time to get comfortable with being naked in front of my team, but after a lot of trust-building activities and long speeches, I barely notice. Mainly because they're so focused on the task at hand, and I know they're barely looking at me more than they need to.

I'm trying to put on the headpiece that goes with my outfit, but Trey takes it from me and says he'll do it as someone is tying the back of my corset.

The headpiece looks like a necklace, and a few diamonds fall on my forehead; it completes the look perfectly.

I'm back on stage a few minutes after I'm ready, and we honestly did that a lot faster than I thought we could.

I notice a few confused looks when people see me back on stage so soon. A few people look down at the program and whispers are being shared. I glance at Mr. Moore and he looks proud that he shocked everyone.

The rest of the show flows heavenly, to quote Angie's dramatic words, but she's not wrong.

"You are killing it!" Mel comes around to me with the brightest smile.

"Thank you, thank you."

I blow her a kiss before walking back out. I'm on autopilot by the time I'm changing out of my second-to-last outfit.

Everyone wishes me good luck as I walk out in the closing dress. My eyes land on Vincent as I walk down the runway, and I almost falter when he cracks a small smile.

I pose at the end of the stage, and on my way back, every single person stands to applaud. I've never heard an audience so loud, and the second I'm backstage, I'm literally squealing.

"Oh, em gee!!" I collect my team in a group hug and congratulate them on our success before thanking them for making sure everything ran so smoothly. I was so damn nervous something would go wrong with the amount of pieces in such a short period of time, but it was *perfect*.

"Where's Sage Loana?"

I go still at the sound of Vincent's deep voice resounding through the dressing room. He only just finished his speech, but I thought he was still on stage, so when I turn to see him watching me, I don't move an inch for a beat.

"Mr. Moore." I smile up at him, and the entire room feels thick as he watches me with his usual glare.

"You did amazing. Thank you again for modeling all of those extra pieces." His thick accent drips from his words as his dark eyes bore into mine.

"Thank *you* for the opportunity." I feel my smile widen, and he gives me a single nod before walking out. I turn to everyone else in the room, and they're just as shocked as I am.

"I don't think Vincent Moore has *ever* thanked or even complimented a model before." Florence studies me like I just appeared from thin air.

I feel someone grab my arm, and I turn to find Angie smirking at me. "He loved you out there."

I laugh softly at her. "That's not what he said, he–"

"He may well have."

I feel a flutter of butterflies in my stomach at her words.

"I told you this may as well have been an audition. He's going to be watching you now."

"You think so?!"

Angie nods, and I feel my nerves heighten. It would be a dream come true if I were a Moore Girl. Of course, I love modeling for Magic Model, but I want to be at the top of my career. I'm already there in the States with Florence, but Vincent Moore would take me to an international level.

Before I can make sense of what doors may have opened for me tonight, someone is barging in.

"YOU KILLED IT!" A loud voice fills the entire backstage.

I break into a laugh at how loud August is. He makes his way over to me and pulls me in for a tight hug. I pull away from him, and the second I do, my other brother is lifting me with a spin. He's done this since we were kids, and I have no idea how he's still able to pick me up *and* spin us.

"You really did kill it, Sage. Everyone is talking about you out there," Sire says once he puts me down.

"Thank you, guys!" I squeal in excitement, simply because they're here, and hug them both again. I knew they'd come for the runway show, but I didn't see them in the crowd.

"Sorry, do you guys have passes?"

I pull away and turn to a woman wearing a headset and holding a clipboard.

"They're my brothers, it's–"

"Oh, I'm so sorry, Ms. Loana. I didn't know–" She looks between August and me, and before she can ask, August speaks up.

"Yes, we're twins," he says with a soft laugh and she looks between the two of us, taking in our nearly identical features.

"Right." She looks between all three of us now. "I'm sorry again and–"

"It's okay, really."

She apologizes again before rushing off.

I let out a laugh and the boys turn to me. "Are you mean to these people or something? Why was she so sorry?" Sire teases, and I playfully shove him.

"I am not mean to anyone!" I don't know why people get so flustered when they make mistakes around me; I'm nice to all of my staff.

August starts talking about everything he loved about the show, and when Sire tells me he was on the edge of his seat out there, I know he isn't exaggerating.

When I look back over at Sire he's watching me with a smile. "I think this was your best show yet."

I feel my excitement growing as I grab his hand to contain myself. "Thank you, bonus bro. I thought so, too!"

I get lost in another conversation with my brothers, and all of my nerves from earlier never return. I think the world could be ending, and my brothers could somehow make me feel better.

Chapter Ten

SAGE

"**A**RE YOU SURE YOU'RE OKAY?" I glance at Sire's busted lip.

I called August to ask for his opinion on my outfit, but he brought up some fight they got into, so I called Sire to make sure he was okay. Not only does he look unharmed besides the lip, which he claims was a cheap shot, but he is relatively unfazed, so I know it's not serious. I'd normally scold them for fighting, especially in public, as such big public figures, and I don't condone violence, but they said this guy started it for no reason, which isn't cool.

"Yes, Sage. Finish your makeup."

I glance at Cara, and she tells me it's okay to keep talking, but I really should let her get back to work, so I tell Sire I love him before hanging up.

"Sorry about that." I put my phone down and turn back to Cara.

"It's okay." She gets her makeup pallet, and I close my eyes as she starts applying my eyeshadow. "I hope this isn't inappropriate, but your brothers are hot." She sort of whispers, and when I laugh, I sense her relaxing.

"It is inappropriate, but I want you guys to feel comfortable enough around me to make inappropriate jokes."

My team has been working with me for almost a year now, and I feel like they are comfortable around me, but they're too professional.

"We are," Annet voices. "Angie sort of traumatized all of us, and we would prefer not to end up like your last two teams, so we try to be on our best behavior."

I cringe at the reminder of my past teams. Annet has been here the longest as my personal hairstylist, so she knows how both catastrophes went. I was too nice, as Angie put it, and they got way too comfortable. A lot of them didn't even listen to me, and I'm not a demanding or bossy person, but I am sort of in charge, in this room at least, and it was just a nightmare.

Angie fired them because I felt too bad to do it, and when my new team came, she was strict with them. She eased off after a while, but it clearly took a while for them to warm up.

"That's fair, but Angie is *my* agent. I love you all and won't fire you because you called my brother hot, so please don't be afraid to talk to me like I'm your friend because I like to think we are... friends, I mean."

I still have my eyes closed, but when I feel Cara steps away, I open them and glance around the room.

"That's good to hear."

"Yeah."

"No, literally."

I laugh at how they all seem to suddenly breathe normally.

"On a serious note, your brothers are really hot," Lynn voices, and Annet agrees. I try not to cringe when they start fawning over them. "August has a girlfriend, right?"

I nod with a smile. "Yup, he's been with Hazel for a while now." August is so obsessed with that girl. They started dating in college and he told me about her the same day he met her. She is practically my sister-in-law at this point. I love her.

"But Sire..."

I glance at Lynn as she passes Cara a different brush.

"He's single, right?"

I shake my head no but don't elaborate. Sire *is* technically single, but the whole family is holding their breath on the chance that he'll get back with Vidia because they're meant to be, and no one can tell me otherwise.

Ever since he and Vidia broke up, the mention of her name alone would set him off, but she recently moved back to LA, and now I think their relationship isn't too bad. I'm honestly not sure where they stand, but if they don't get back together, then I refuse to believe in love.

A few of the girls look discouraged at the fact that they're both unavailable and I bite back a laugh.

Angie walks in a few minutes later with Mel.

"Hello, pretties."

They both smile at me, and Angie nods her head off to the side, indicating she wants to speak with me alone.

"You can speak freely in front of everyone here, Ang."

She glances around the room, and I remain seated, waiting for her to speak. I trust my team, plus they all signed an NDA, so I wish she trusted them like I do.

"Mr. Moore invited you to his event tomorrow tonight."

I turn in disbelief, and Ang smiles proudly at me.

"I didn't know he was having another runaway show?!" I eagerly grab my phone to look for a message I might have missed, and as soon as I open my email, I see a message from Vincent sent a few minutes ago.

I'm already reading it as Ang starts explaining. "It's not a runway show. It's going to be like the after party he had the night of the show, classy and calm."

I nod mindlessly as I read the rest of his email. "He wants me to wear one of his new pieces?" I look up at my agent, and she looks so excited, you'd think she was the one who got invited to *another* Moore event.

She picks up the bag in her hand, and I stand up, remembering to rise slowly since I only had a small breakfast today.

"When did he send this?!" I eagerly peak into the bag, and my breath catches my throat when I see the material of the dress.

"Someone *just* dropped it off."

I pull out the dress, and every person audibly gasps. "Holy cow, this is—"

"Beautiful."

"Stunning."

"Wow."

I place the dress against me and turn in the mirror, and... *wow*. It's a perfect emerald green, practically matching my eyes. One side is strapless, while the other is covered in diamonds that crawl down to the chest. They shine so bright;

I wouldn't be surprised if they're real. I lift the dress a bit higher and notice a slit, sure to reveal one of my legs.

My team crowds around me to admire the dress in the mirror and my face is starting to hurt with how much I'm smiling.

"Okay, let me put it back before it gets dirty." That would be a freaking nightmare. As soon as it's in the safety of the bag, I steal another glance at it and let out a small squeal. "Oh em gee!"

The room is filled with everyone's laughter, and I glance at Ang in the mirror as I sit back at my vanity. "What does Helena's dress look like?" My makeup team gets back to work, but in the mirror, I notice Angie's brows furrow.

"She didn't get invited."

Cara freezes in the middle of blending my foundation, and the rest of the room goes quiet.

"Are you sure?" I assumed Helena also got invited since we usually both get invited to things like this. Brand deals and designers, of course, want the biggest models in the industry, and Helena and I are head-to-head for a lot, which is why we do a lot of our photo shoots together.

Angie isn't her agent, but she knows everything about everything, so when she confirms with a head shake, I have no words.

Cara and Lynn swap as they do my makeup, and I'm quiet for a few minutes. I steal a glance at Mel, and she's already watching me. She shakes her head at my silent question, but it's understandable why she wasn't invited since she's still new here.

"Was Quinn invited?" She was getting a lot of publicity after Vincent's show but Angie shakes her head no. "Nin?"

No again.

I open my mouth to say another one of The Core Eight, but Angie beats me to it.

"Mr. Moore only invited you."

I open my mouth, but nothing comes out, and I close it again.

What?

I'm shocked at first, but then I immediately feel horrible. All of the other girls were amazing at Vincent's show, yet I was the only one invited to his next event.

"Maybe it's just his way of saying thank you for modeling so many extra pieces."

"Or maybe he wants you to model for him."

"No way." I let out a nervous laugh, but I feel my excitement building up at the thought alone. Angie only shrugs with a smirk playing on her face, and when I glance at Mel, she raises her brows.

"You better not turn him down if he offers you to be a Moore Girl." Angie sends me a pointed look, but I didn't need the warning. I'd have to be insane to turn down *anything* he asked of me.

Cara and Lynn finish my makeup, and before I know it, I'm smiling at the camera for my new headshot pictures.

Since we took twice as long, I'm not done until an hour after what we were supposed to be, and that doesn't seem bad, but I was up until the sun rose because I was editing a video. I was able to post it on time, so I guess it was worth it.

I post a video twice a week on Famoura, and when I miss a video, my followers literally blow up my DM's. It's honestly sweet to see how much they love my content, but it can be a bit overwhelming at times. Like last night.

Helena came out to see my headshot pictures, and as we walk to my room, I can't stop myself from asking what I'm dying to know. "Did you get invited to the Moore event tomorrow night?" I know Angie said I was the only one with an invite, but maybe Helena also got an email and didn't tell—

"Nope."

My head snaps to her, but she keeps her eyes forward as we walk.

"I have a photo shoot anyway, so it's fine; I didn't want to have to cancel."

"Oh." I nod to myself. "Who's the photo shoot with?"

She only shrugs but doesn't say anything else. I know the rest of The Core Eight have two huge photo shoots tomorrow, but I thought Helena wasn't in it, either way, I don't question her.

"Vincent sent me the prettiest dress ever. Wanna see—"

"I'm running late for something."

I stop short when she suddenly pivots.

"Send me a pic, though."

"Oh, yeah, okay."

She walks off but turns to me. "Congrats, by the way." She sends me an air kiss, and I feel my smile growing.

I walk into my room, and as I grab my things, I get a Famoura notification.

L. Walker started following you.

I open the app, and when I click on Liam's account, a smile touches my lips when I notice he's only following one person. I follow him back, although he has no post, and a second later, I get a text from him.

I like his message before tucking my phone away.

This whole friends-with-benefits thing worked out perfectly for both of us, and I'm glad I was honest with him about not seeing this becoming more than what it is.

The drive to my house isn't too long, and as I park, I notice Liam driving up behind me.

By the time I'm out of my car, he has removed his helmet and climbed off his bike, closing the distance between us.

"Hey." I smile up at him, and to no one's surprise, he doesn't smile in return.

"What's up," he glances at my hair before his eyes meet mine again. "Your hair looks pretty. Did you just get it done?"

"Thank you! Yes, I just did it yesterday." I run a hand through my faux locs as we step into the building, and when he walks in front of me, I get a closer look at his helmet.

"How'd you get a KD helmet? That one just released and there were only two of them."

He looks down at his helmet, and when he looks over at me, he looks like I'm speaking a different language. "How do you know that?"

I laugh at his obvious shock as we step onto the elevator. "Because my brother has the other one and was just about ready to give his firstborn for it." That's not an exaggeration, August literally said he'd give up his firstborn child for that helmet and Hazel did *not* find that funny. They don't even have kids, and I don't think she wants any, but she hates that he even has a bike.

The boys used to street race, and August never really let that life go, but Hazel hates it, so he doesn't do it. He'd never give up his bike though, even if he barely rides it anymore.

Liam rolls his eyes at something before looking forward. "I'm acquainted with the designer."

My jaw drops. "You're *friends* with *Kai Drew*?!"

"Acquaintances." He corrects me, but he says it like it's *nothing.*

"I think my brother would kill to be friends with you."

He lets out a scoff and turns to me. "I can bet this helmet he wouldn't." He's stepping out of the elevator before I can question him. Since my penthouse is the only one on this floor, he walks straight to my door.

"How come you don't follow anyone on Famoura?"

He shrugs as I unlock my door. "I don't like anyone enough to care about what they post."

"But you followed me?" I say with a laugh, and when I look over at him, his eyes are already on me, but he doesn't say anything and a smile creeps onto my face. "Is that you saying you *like* me?" I tease, and he rolls his eyes at me, but I swear I see him biting back a smile as he steps into my apartment.

"It's just social media."

"Hey, they're your words, not mine." I put a hand up in defense as I smile over at him. "Just admit it." I tilt my head to the side, and he shakes his head at me as he closes the distance between us.

"I followed you to see these pretty dimples." He kisses my cheek, and with him being so close, I steal a kiss on his lips.

"And because you like me," I add, and a smirk tugs at his lips.

"Whatever helps you sleep at night, pretty girl."

I feel my brows furrow when I notice a bruise forming under his eyes, but he walks over to my couch, and I decide not to probe him about it.

"Do you want to watch a movie? I saw this video of a girl reciting Bling's and Cyrus's entire rap battle, so now I want to rewatch *Let It Shine*. Have you seen it before?"

He nods and takes a seat on my couch. I tell him I'm going to change out of this dress and rush off to my room. I think of putting on regular clothes, but I don't plan on going anywhere, so I throw on the pajamas I wore last night, and it's a little revealing, but it's nothing he hasn't seen. I walk into my kitchen and put some popcorn in the microwave before pulling out my phone to order some food.

I've been following Helena's meal plan, so I make sure I get something on her plan. I've still been hungry after every meal since her suggested portions are smaller than mine, but I don't mind. It's sort of like a diet.

When I walk to the couch, I notice Liam on the phone. "I told you *I can't*, and after last time, I don't want to."

My brows furrow as his voice morphs between concern and annoyance, it sounds as if he's having the same conversation from the studio.

I pick up the control and turn to the TV.

"I'll send her some flowers or something. Tell her it's from me." He definitely sounds annoyed now. I steal a glance at him, and he looks a bit worried again. "Fine, I'll go see her." It sounds like the other person is saying something, but Liam hangs up.

"Everything okay?" When he doesn't respond, I turn to him, and he's nodding as he types something into his phone. I have no idea who the *she* is that he was talking about, but she clearly made him upset, and I really, really hope he doesn't have a girlfriend, and if he does, I hope they only recently got together because I would feel so bad if he cheated on her with–

"Why are you making that face?"

I change my face as I turn to him. "Are you *sure* you don't have a girlfriend?" I blurt out, and he studies me for two whole seconds before looking back at his phone.

"I don't have a girlfriend. It's family."

I nod in return as he looks back at his phone, but it's clear something is upsetting him.

"Is there anything I can do?" I ask gently, and he shakes his head before turning his phone off and turning to me. "You look like you need a hug." I open my arms out to him, and he watches me with a confused look.

"You really are too good for this world, beloved." He almost sounds disappointed, but I don't respond and hug him instead. He feels tense at first, like he's never been hugged, and doesn't know what to do, but I squeeze him tighter, and his arms immediately come around me.

Chapter Eleven

SAGE

"THANK YOU SO MUCH!" I hug Annet again, and she laughs at me.

"Stop thanking me, Sage. This is literally my job."

I look in the mirror and touch my hair again. With the Moore event tonight, I really wanted a new hairstyle. I know this is Annet's job as my personal hairstylist, but I'm grateful she pulled off this new hairstyle.

We always have my hairstyles planned out a few days in advance, but I told her I wanted a blonde wig last night and she made it happen.

"I know it's your job, but seriously, you're the best for pulling this off so fast."

She smiles proudly in the mirror, and after she takes a few pictures of her work, she leaves.

I grab the physical copy of Vincent's invitation and let my fingers run along the pretty ink. He has someone handwrite all of his invitations, and whoever they are have amazing freaking handwriting.

I read over the part where it says I can bring a plus one, and I definitely want to bring one of my friends since none of our other girls were invited, but I feel like it's too last minute to call anyone.

Considering this is a Moore event, I decided to just call Helena, and maybe she'll consider canceling her photo shoot to come with me.

The FaceTime call rings a few times but then it ends and I get an auto message from her saying, *working*.

I stare at our messages, and she only loved the picture of the dress, so she must be really busy because she usually gets excited and calls me to see how I look in my outfits, but she seems off, and I can't tell why. When I texted The Eight group chat yesterday, she also didn't reply.

I decide not to think much of it and call Mel instead. Going to this event would be great for Mel to get her name out there, and I love giving baby models a boost. She answers after a few rings, and she's in the middle of blending her eyeshadow.

"Hey, Sage."

"Hello, Mel Mel. Are you busy?" I notice her smile growing before she sets her phone up against something.

"Not really, what's up?" Before I can answer, she glances back at the screen, and her eyes light up. "Oh my God, your hair looks so freaking good."

"Right!" I look up at my mirror again, and I'm officially obsessed. I know I say this every time, but this might be my favorite style yet.

"Annet knows what the hell she's doing. That wig is going to look great with your dress tonight."

At the reminder of why I called, I go on. "Speaking of, would you like to be my plus one tonight?"

She goes still before turning to the camera.

"I know it's so last minute, and you only have a few hours to get ready, but I don't want to go alone, and I think it would be great if you went and met some other–"

"Are you serious?!" When she shoots up from her seat, I think I have my answer. "Oh my god, of *course* I'll come! Thank you!"

I laugh at her excitement, but then she looks around frantically.

"I can't do my own makeup for a Moore event!" She starts wiping off the bit of makeup she has on, and I tell her to come over since Cara and Lynn are on their way for my makeup. I'm sure they can also do hers.

"Shit, what the hell am I going to *wear*?!"

"I'm friends with the owner of one of the dress stores down at Rodeo Drive. I'm sure we can find something."

She thanks me profusely, and I break into a laugh as she starts packing her things. I shoot Annet a quick text, asking if she can come back to do Mel's hair, and like the saint she is, she says she's turning back.

"ARE YOU SURE I LOOK good?" Mel glances down at her dress *again,* and I grab hold of her hands, causing her to look up at me.

"Yes, Mel." I give her a warm smile, and she takes a deep breath, nodding. "I wouldn't let you walk out the house if you didn't look good, and I certainly wouldn't have let you come to this event if you didn't look amazing."

"Right, I just feel so underdressed. Everyone is going to be in custom outfits by huge designers, and I'm–"

"You look great, babe. It doesn't matter if you didn't get a custom dress. You could wear a trash bag and make it work."

She smiles at me as she sits taller, and she looks much more confident. I ask her if she's ready, and when she says she is, we climb out of the car.

I thank the driver before walking into the hall, and there are already a lot of people here. A few familiar faces come up to me, and I'm surprised I know more people than I thought I would.

"Ms. Hale."

I turn at the sound of that familiar Italian accent, and Vincent is walking to us with a beautiful woman on his arm.

"Thank you for coming." He leans in and kisses my cheek gently.

I greet him the same way in return as I thank him for the invite, and his eyes land on Mel beside me.

"Is this your plus one?" He holds a hand out to her, and as she takes it, he kisses the back of her hand. I love the way they greet people in his culture.

"Yes, this is Mel Jimenez. She models with me at Magic."

He takes in her outfit. "I remember from my runway show the other night." He nods at Mel in approval, and her cheeks redden at the attention.

Vincent introduced the woman he's with as his wife, Nora, and she leans in to kiss both of my cheeks before greeting Mel the same. "Vinnie was wondering who you'd bring tonight." Nora nudges her husband like she's teasing him, but his glare doesn't falter.

"May I ask why?" I voice shyly and he looks between Mel and me then shrugs.

"You stood out to me at my show, Ms. Hale. I didn't invite any of your other colleagues, but you've been in the industry long enough to know there'd be opportunities here for your plus one. I wanted to know who you want those opportunities for." He gestures towards Mel. He doesn't say anything else, but he looks at Mel like her being my plus one made him notice her in a new light, and now I'm even happier I brought her.

"Ms. *Hale*?"

I feel my entire face light up at the sound of that voice. I turn on my heels and force myself not to run to her only because everyone in here would think we're insane.

"Ms. *Sloan*?" I keep my voice hushed but say her name as if I were her biggest fan and meeting her for the first time. She laughs and pulls me in for a tight hug. I told Vlaire I was going to be here tonight since it was a no-brainer Vincent invited her and I'm glad she was so willingly to come. I guess the fashion show wasn't too hard on her the other night.

She pulls away but quickly pulls me back in for another hug, and I squeeze her back with a laugh. When she pulls away again, she holds my hand and glances at my hair. "The blonde? *So* your color." She glances down at my dress, now nodding in approval. "Wow."

"Right?!" I go still and immediately turn to Vincent. "Oh my goodness, thank you so much for the dress, by the way. It's beautiful."

He nods in response, and I swear I see him crack a smile.

"Thank *you* for wearing it tonight."

I didn't think I had an option, but either way, I didn't want one.

"Do take pictures in it tonight."

I assure him that I will, and after his wife says it was nice meeting us, they walk off.

Mel stands off to the side shyly, but I pull her closer.

"Vlaire this is Mel, Mel this is Vlaire." They give a quick hug to each other, but Mel is as stiff as a board and barely remembers to bring her arms up for the hug. I stifle a giggle behind my hand at how starstruck she is.

"I'm sorry." Mel shakes her head but still looks shocked to be standing in the same room as Vlaire. I don't blame her. Vlaire is royalty by blood to us models, even if she doesn't model.

"How did you two meet?" Mel glances between the two of us, keeping her focus on Vlaire as I explain.

"We had exchanged interactions on Famoura, and when I was in Brazil, her hometown, for a shoot, she offered to show me around."

Vlaire smiles over at Mel as she elaborates. "I wasn't on social media very much at the time." She glances at me, and I offer her a reassuring smile, remembering that was around the time her mom passed. "But on the rare day that I logged in, I saw a compilation of her best shows that a fan edited, and she reminded me so much of my mom. I reposted it on my story, and we were practically internet besties until we finally met in Brazil, as she mentioned."

I feel my heart warm at her words. "I am nowhere near Sloan status," I voice with a nervous laugh.

"At this rate, I'm sure you'll reach it." She nods behind me, and just as I turn, a man Vincent is talking to swiftly shifts his gaze aside from me. "I know him very well. It won't be long before he offers you a pretty, multi-billion-dollar contract and sweeps you away from Magic."

I turn to her, unable to find any words.

"Wait, really?" Mel voices for me, and when Vlaire nods, I will myself to remain calm and badger her for details on what he may have told her later since people are watching.

I notice a few cameramen have gathered around awkwardly, waiting to take a picture. I signal them over with a welcoming smile, and the flash is immediately in my face. When I look over to the side, Vincent is watching with a prideful smile.

Chapter Twelve

SAGE

"WOULD YOU GUYS LIKE TO say hi to my vlog?"

All of the girls look up at me with a smile as I turn the camera.

"Hey, vlog!" They sing in sync as a few of them wave.

"Is that a new camera?" Stel voices as she sits up like she's going to run over.

"It is!" I tell her, and the vlog, what camera it is and mention that the link will be in the description.

"You lucky bitch," Stel voices playfully as she sinks into her seat. "Did they send it to you? Because I've secretly been dying for a partnership with them."

I tell her it was a gift and smile at the camera before reminding myself to thank Liam again.

I tell the camera I'll see them in a bit, and I turn it off before turning to the group. "Anyways," I flop onto the couch beside them. It became routine for us to hang out in Quinn's room between shoots. I'm not sure why we collectively chose her room, but she says she loves having us in here, so it's become our spot, and we even prefer it over the lounge.

"How's everyone's day going?"

We chat for a bit about our various days and what we did at work before Nin invites me to lunch with them at her family's restaurant. I almost decline since I don't have the appetite to eat. I'm not sure what it is, but my appetite has been shot recently, which I guess isn't the worst thing. I haven't eaten in two days, and the pumpkin spice latte I had is starting to feel like it's not enough. I end up agreeing to go to eat with them since I miss hanging out with them outside of work.

After a beat, the room falls quiet. I look between the girls, but they just stare at me.

"What?"

"What do you mean *what*?" Coral repeats my question as if it were absurd to ask. "How did the Moore event go? It's been days, and my nosy ass is tired of being polite. *Who* was there?"

I burst into a laugh when she leans forward like she might pounce at me. I tell her how the night went, and everyone else in the room has their eyes on me as I explain. They ask for pictures, and I let them scroll through my camera roll.

I look up at the sound of the door opening, and a smile touches my lips when I notice Royal. I feel my brows crease at the annoyed look on her face, but she rants before I can question it.

"Your friend is right behind me, and she has an attitude." She rolls her eyes before flopping next to Quinn. I'm sure she's talking about Lena, and I bite back a laugh at how she always calls her *my* friend when she does something to annoy her.

"What happened?"

"Shit," Quinn starts before looking around the room. "I forgot to fill you in, she—"

Helena walks in, and Quinn falls quiet.

"Hello, pretty babe." I smile over at her.

She barely glances up from her phone as she mumbles a hello in return. I look back over at the girls, but when I notice them watching us, I feel my brows scrunch. "What?" I whisper, but it's clear they aren't going to say it in front of Lena.

Coral looks over at Quinn, but when neither of them says anything, I look down the couch at the rest of the girls, but no one speaks up.

"Are we still getting lunch after these pictures?"

I look back over at Helena, and she's looking at Nin now.

"Yeah, that's the plan..." Nin looks over at Stel and they both share a weird look before they glance over at Macey and Royal, and I have no idea what I missed.

"We're going after our group pictures, right? Not your solo ones." I turn to Nin, and she nods quietly.

Today's probably my favorite day to vlog since we're doing billboard pictures. Group photos are always fun.

"What time is the photographer getting here?" We look over at Helena and she's fixing her gloss in Quinn's mirror.

"He should be here soon." I smile at her usual impatience. When I notice the glitter in her lipgloss I let out a soft gasp. "Omg, can I see your gloss?" I'm already making my way to her, but just as I reach her, she puts it back in her bag.

"We can't have the same gloss in these pictures, Sage."

"What—"

"We're going to be late." She rises from her seat and walks off without another word, and I look over at the girls.

"Okay, what is going on?"

Royal speaks up. "She's upset about the Moore event. She wanted to go." She rolls her eyes, and instead of responding, I follow after Helena.

"Hey."

She doesn't stop, but I keep up with her fast pace.

"Lena, what's wrong?"

She still has her back to me as she shakes her head. "You're seriously asking me that?" Her tone alone tells me she's more upset than I thought, but I'm so confused.

"Did I do something?"

She turns on her heels so fast I almost bump into her.

"Why did you invite *Mel* to go with you to the Moore event?"

I open my mouth, but she doesn't let me get a word in.

"Of all people, you take the girl you *just* met to one of the biggest opportunities of our lives?"

"Helena, I would have invited you, but you had a photo shoot? You said-"

"I would've canceled for Vincent Moore, Sage."

"You said you didn't want to cancel?!" *I am beyond lost right now.* "And I called you that day to invite you as my plus one, but you declined my call and said you were busy?"

"And you invite *Mel*?"

"You said it yourself, that event was a huge opportunity, and if I could let all of the girls tag along, I would've, but the rest of The Eight were busy with the Angels and Elaine's photo shoot. It was great for Mel, so what's wrong?"

Helena shakes her head as if I'm the crazy one who's not understanding, but I genuinely don't see the problem and none of the other girls seemed upset, if anything, they were the opposite. They were only being weird once *she* entered.

"We started this together, Sage."

"I–"

"We've always talked about being Moore Girls, and now that you have Vincent's attention, it's like you completely tossed me aside." She sounds so... betrayed, and it hurts that she even thinks that.

"Helena, that's not what I'm doing. You know I want to see us *both* at the top, no matter who gets there first. I swear you were the first person I called when I saw I could bring a plus one."

She lets out a sigh, and I grab a hold of her hand. "You're my best friend, Lena. I wouldn't intentionally *not* invite you to anything, and for you to think that of me hurts."

She shakes her head and pulls her hand away. "I just need some space."

I keep my gaze on her as she walks off without another word. I decide to just leave her alone, and the rest of the girls descend from Quinn's room. I, of course, fill them in, but they only roll their eyes and tell me not to overthink it. I guess they're used to Helena's random attitude and fits.

"I can't believe she really thinks that low of me."

"Oh, girl, please. We all know you're an amazing friend," Royal starts, "I *been* told you I noticed sneaky hater vibes from her," she voices as she ties her braids in a high bun.

"Yeah..." Stel goes on. "I didn't want to say it since you two are besties and have been here longer than me, but she's also really mean to—well, every new girl. It's weird," Stel adds, and she's right, but I never sensed Helena being jealous of me.

Someone is sent over to get us and we get started with our group pictures. Royal unfortunately needs to sit out on these since she's on probation for missing the Moore runway show. Thankfully, she gets to stay and watch, vlogging for me off to the side, and it isn't too awkward as we take our group pictures with Helena.

Stel and Macey get closer as we pose *and* get touchy. Not inappropriately, and if you didn't know they had something going on, it'll look like they're just working, but I can feel all of the girls stealing glances at them.

When Royal moves to the side to get shots of the secret couple, I remind myself to cut whatever they don't want to be shown in my vlog. I'm not sure why they're hiding their relationship; it makes me doubt if they're actually together and their flirty comments to each other are jokes, but I sense it's more.

As planned, we end up having lunch at the Thai restaurant Nin's family owns, but Helena bails.

Nin's dad comes out to say hi to us before whispering something to Nin in Thai. She shakes her head at him softly before inviting us to come over to his house later today so he can cook for us.

We all thank him for the offer, and I'll be busy, but a few of the other girls say they'll be there. I glance at Helena's meal plan since I'm still following it and order something similar. I force myself to pick at some of it because I don't want to offend Nin, but it has nothing to do with her dad's food. The bit that I do try is amazing, but I just don't have an appetite.

After we ate, we did a bit of shopping because we were so close to Rodeo Drive and just couldn't resist.

Helena ends up texting me an apology and says how she's *just stressed*. When I show the girls, half of them say to respond while the other half tell me to ignore her. Considering she's still my friend and we have to work together, I just like the message and tell her to forget it.

After a while, we each go our separate ways, and I'm heading to my car when Moon texts me.

Moon Pie

> Heyy! Liam just said he wanted to see you and when I asked if I could come, he said no :(

> You're cool with me tagging along right?!

Before I can type out a response, Liam texts me.

Liam

> Do not tell Moon he can come over.

I stifle a laugh as I like his message.

> I'm being serious. Stop laughing, and please do not invite him over.

I break into a laugh as I go back to reply to Moon.

> Of course you can come!! Meet me at my place, I'm on my way now!

I give him my address and slip into my car.

Chapter Thirteen

SAGE

"WHEN YOU LIKE A MESSAGE, that means you're agreeing with the person," Liam grumbles from my couch as I let Moon in.

"Hi, friend!" Moon beams at Liam, who ignores him. I bite back a laugh as Moon pulls me in for a hug. When he pulls away, I study his features and I want to guess where he's from but decide to just ask.

"I'm Malaysian and Japanese." He smiles at me when my jaw drops.

"I *swear* I was going to guess Malaysian!"

His smile widens as he looks into my eyes. "Okay, I'm trying to guess where you're from, but the green eyes are really throwing me off right now." When he turns his head to the other side, I let out a laugh.

"Mom is Haitian, and Dad is Jamaican." I have Dad's green eyes, and besides my twin, we're the only ones in the family with them, so I'm not sure where the gene came from.

Moon nods in thought. "Yeah, I was *so* off."

We settle on the couch with Liam, and when Moon sits too close to him, he shoves him away.

"Hey! Don't be so rough."

He rolls his eyes at me, so I pinch him for being *rude*. He looks down at his arm before looking up at me. "Did you just pinch me?"

"Yes, don't be rude."

He lifts his hand, but I see it from a mile away and shoot up from my seat before he can pinch me.

He gets up after me, but I run around the couch, and he stops in front of it. "Don't make me chase you, Sage."

I let out a laugh as I ran around the couch again.

"Come here."

I don't, and he walks after me, but I run to the other side again.

He lets out a breath, and another laugh escapes past my lips.

In one swift move, he hops over my huge freaking couch and grabs me. I let out a squeal as he scoops me into his arm and over his shoulder.

"Oh my God!"

He pinches my *butt,* and I squirm in his arms with another scream.

"How the heck are you lift-"

"Stop-" He pinches my thigh again, and I try to swat him away. "-asking me how I can *pick you up*." He pinches me again, much harder.

"Ouch!"

"Do I look like I can't lift a woman?"

"I never said-"

"You implied it. *Stop* doing it."

"I only meant that I'm-"

"What? *Too heavy?* Don't even say it, Sage Loana."

My voice is nowhere to be found at his sharp tone, and I certainly don't say that those were my exact same thoughts.

He tosses me onto the couch, and I shake my head from the dizziness as he flops next to me. He pulls my Dodgers blanket out from under him when he sits on it, and my jaw drops as he *tosses* it aside.

"You are so rude!" I let out a soft laugh as I pick up the blanket from the coffee table in front of us.

"Don't take offense, Sunshine," Moon voices from my kitchen as he raids my cabinets. "He's a Dodgers hater."

I look back at Liam, and he's watching Moon with his usual glare.

"You hate the Dodgers?"

He nods once.

"Why?"

He turns to me and leans back in his seat. "I'm with the Yankees," he shrugs. "They're one of two teams that usually beat us in the playoffs."

"My brothers also mentioned not liking the Yankees," I hum in thought as Liam watches me blankly. "Have both teams always hated each other?"

He shrugs. "I don't know the entire MLB history."

"Well, maybe not, smarty pants, but do the players genuinely not like each other, or is it a historical rivalry that you guys feed into? Like, if you were traded to the Dodgers, would you feel the same way about the Yankees?"

Moon chimes in. "I think he just doesn't like-"

"Moon." Liam cuts him off before he can finish his sentence. He's glaring at him, and when I glance over at Moon, I see that he looks confused.

"What?" Moon looks between Liam and me. "I was just going to say-"

"Stop talking and stop ransacking her cabinets." Liam rolls his eyes before turning back to me and pulls me onto his lap. "The hatred between the teams doesn't matter." He kisses my cheek.

I kiss his lips before glancing over at Moon. "What were you going to say?"

Moon glances at Liam before shrugging. "I forgot." He looks back at my cabinets. "Can I have some of these marshmallows?"

"Yeah, sure."

He grabs them before walking over to us. "Random, but I thought your full name was Sage Loana this entire time. Am I the only one who gets that?"

"A lot of people assume that, but they catch on to the fact that I'm a Hale." I smile proudly.

"Yeah... that's still shocking." Moon glances over at Liam again.

"Why?" I look down at Liam, but he's just glaring at Moon. "What's wrong with you two?"

"He's just a weirdo," Liam mumbles.

I shake my head at him as I turn back to Moon. "How come it's so shocking? Are you, like, a stalker fan of my brothers?" I tease.

Moon laughs in response. "I just mean it's shocking that I'm friends with you. Your family is so dope." He shrugs sheepishly.

"Aw, that's so sweet. I think you're way cooler than my brothers, though."

"My ass," Moon mumbles, and I break into a laugh before turning to Liam.

"Have you ever met my brothers? Like at games and stuff."

He only nods in response before stealing a kiss.

I pull away, but he steals another one. I let out a soft laugh and put a hand on his chest to push him away. "Stop that," I whisper, but he tries to kiss me again, and when I pull away, he tickles my side. "Alright!" I'm hysterical as I give in and let him have another kiss.

I pull away quickly since Moon is still sitting a few feet away from us. "Okay, that's it." At the reminder of full names, I ask Liam, "What's your middle name?"

"I don't have one."

Hmm. I know a few people who don't have middle names, but that's kind of boring. Maybe his parents thought nothing went well. Or maybe they were just lazy...

"Why are you lying to her?" Moon chimes in.

I let out a soft gasp and look down at Liam, but he only returns it with a bored look.

"Well, are you?"

He rolls his eyes at me and pulls my shirt up just a bit so he can rub my stomach. "You know I'm not."

"I don't know *anything*." I put my hands up in defense like I'm being questioned for murder or something, and he shakes his head at me.

"Oh, come on, you know my middle name."

He doesn't respond.

"Just tell me in my ear, and I won't tell anyone."

I lean down to him, but he softly pushes my head away. "You'll scream it from the damn rooftops."

"Ah ha!" I jump off of his lap. "So you do have a middle name!" I point at him accusingly, but he only looks up at me, confused.

"What?"

"You just said I'll scream it from the rooftops, which is an exaggeration if you ask me, but if you didn't have one,

I wouldn't be able to scream it anywhere." I cross my arms because I caught him. "Liar."

His bored expression doesn't falter as he pulls me back to his lap. "Don't call me that." He takes my arm and drapes it around his neck, and I smile at how touchy he suddenly is. "I meant if I did have one and told you."

"I'm sorry, but I sense you're lying." I give him a weak shrug. He opens his mouth, but he's interrupted.

"He is," Moon voices.

"Do you know it?"

"Yup." He casually leans back in his seat and I look back at Liam, once again shocked that he really lied.

"He's full of shit." Liam waves Moon off and starts rubbing my arm that's around him. I stare into his soul, but he doesn't pay me any mind. Instead, he leans forward to kiss my cheek a few times.

"Just tell her, man."

Liam lets out a sigh but keeps kissing me, making his way across my jawline.

"I know it's embarrassing, but it's okay."

Liam lets out a bigger sigh, this time as he pulls away. "*Leave.*"

I turn to Moon and raise my brows, but he only giggles.

"Tell me." I keep my eyes on Moon since the man under me wants to keep his middle name locked up like Fort Knox.

"It's Leslie." Moon laughs before he barely finishes his sentence.

I look between them, and Liam only shakes his head.

"Leslie?! Your middle name is *Leslie*?"

"No, it isn't."

I immediately break into a laugh, and Liam does not look an ounce amused.

"Liam Leslie Walker." I laugh again. "It actually has a nice ring to it."

"That's not my name." Liam sounds so defensive, but I can tell it's true.

"Don't lie to me, Liam Leslie." I snort, and he looks bored.

"I won't be answering you if you call me that." He picks up his phone, but this is too good.

"Oh, don't be ashamed of your name, Liam Leslie."

He rolls his eyes and looks over at Moon. "I'm kicking your ass."

Moon and I are a laughing mess, and Liam doesn't pay us an ounce of attention. He starts drawing a few shapes on my thigh before looking up.

"Moon."

"Yeah?" He turns to Liam.

"Leave." When Liam's hand slips into the side of my shirt, I realize why he wants Moon gone, but I give him a knowing look.

"I want him to stay, and either way, you can at least ask him nicely."

"I don't think he knows what that means."

I look over at Moon.

"He's actually never said please or thank you, like ever."

Liam doesn't deny it, and I remember Rob mentioning something similar when he ordered a drink at the coffee shop.

"That's rude."

"Yeah." Moon sends him a stern look but Liam isn't looking at him. "The other day he said he would never beg for anything, not even his life." That sounds like something he'd say but I still glance down at Liam.

"What if someone had a gun to your head?"

"I wouldn't beg."

"*Really*?"

He nods once and keeps his eyes down as he rubs his hand up and down my thigh. I let my arm drape around his neck like before and lean in a bit.

"You okay?" I whisper into his ear before I kiss his temple.

He seems... off, but he only nods and keeps his eyes on the ground.

"Are you sure?" I run a hand through his hair.

"I'm fine." His words aren't harsh but numb instead. After a beat, Liam glances up at me. "Want to help me with something?"

I nod eagerly, and he kisses my lips. "I need to pick out a gift for someone."

"Oh, I'm so good with gifts! Who is it for?"

He hesitates before saying, "Someone."

I watch him carefully before nodding with a smirk. "A surprise, I like it."

He shakes his head at me, and I kiss the smirk on his lips.

"If this is your way of trying to figure out what I want for my birthday, I want to make it very clear that I don't accept early gifts because they're bad luck."

"Who told you that?" He watches me suspiciously, but I wave him off.

"They just are." I ruffle his hair as I lean my back against him. "Is the gift for a boy or girl?"

"Girl." He returns to drawing shapes on my thighs, as I think.

"Get her a purse. You can never go wrong with a purse." Am I biased because I love handbags? Yes, but it's true, and they make the best gifts.

"She wouldn't use it," Liam mumbles in response and I hum in thought.

"Well, what does she like to do? Those make the best gifts."

Liam takes a minute to think, rubbing his palm down my leg. "Puzzles."

"Puzzles are great! I saw one that was all white and missing one piece. That'd be a cool gift."

I feel him shaking his head from behind me. "You lied about being good with gifts."

I stifle a laugh as I elbow him. He tickles me in return, but as I squirm in his lap, he stops. "Okay," he grumbles as he holds my hips firmly. "I need you to stop moving so much if you want your friend to stay so damn bad." He keeps his voice low, and I feel my brows furrow but go still when I feel him getting hard through his pants.

I feel a heat come to my face, but when I glance at Moon, he's zoned into whatever show he's watching on my iPad.

"Tell him to leave," Liam mumbles so quietly that I barely hear him over my racing heart.

"Get a custom-made puzzle." I ignore him and swiftly go back to what we were discussing. "You can order it online and submit the picture you want the puzzle to be."

He doesn't respond, and when I turn to look at him, he squeezes my hips. "*Sage*," He warns, and I bite back a laugh as I turn back around.

Deciding to put him out of his misery, I get up to sit beside him instead, but as I rise, I instantly need to sit back down when my vision goes completely dark.

"What's wrong?" Liam grabs my hand before turning my face to look at him.

"Nothing." I shake him off, but my vision is still blurring, and my blood is running warm.

"It doesn't look like *nothing*. Are you dizzy?"

"Just a bit." I try to convince him that I'm okay, but he isn't hearing it.

"You probably just need to eat." He walks to my kitchen, and I, again, try to tell him I'm okay and I'm not hungry, but he completely ignores me as he raids my cabinets.

"Maybe your blood sugar is just low. You need sweets." Moon nonchalantly hands me a marshmallow, but I decline and turn back to Liam.

"Liam, really-"

"Why are you being so weird about this? You looked like you were about to pass out; just eat."

He has his back turned to me, but my eyes still fall to the ground, and I don't say anything else as he makes me a sandwich.

Just eat. He says it as if it were as easy as breathing, and I feel a knot form in the back of my throat because it *isn't* that easy.

When he hands me the sandwich, I mumble thanks, and since he has his eyes on me, I just take a bite of the damn thing and force it down. After a few minutes and very small bites, Liam gets a phone call and says he has to go. Moon tries to stay, but Liam pulls him up from my couch and drags him out.

I sit back down in front of the huge sandwich and eating with the girls earlier opened my appetite, but considering I barely ate in two days, I'm *so* hungry it's nauseating. I force myself to take another bite, and it's as if there's something physically blocking me from swallowing because I *can't swallow it*. I try to force it down with water, and when it finally flows down my throat, it feels like I'm swallowing thick, wet cement, and tears sting the back of my eyes.

I take a deep breath and force myself to take another bite. I know I need to eat this, but every bite feels harder than the last.

"You're being ridiculous, Sage. Just eat it," I whisper before compelling myself to take another bite. I clear my mind of everything, and the mental barrier fades as I swallow. I nod to myself as I take a small sip of water, and I get on my phone to distract myself. I take another bite as I scroll through my feed. Tapping on the 99+ likes and comments, my eyes land on one.

Lucky8797: That color is not flattering on you. Or maybe it's just the dress. No hate, but have you thought of going on a diet?

Everything in my stomach bubbles, and it feels like acid is seeping down my throat as I force another bite. The replies are defending me, but when I see another person agree, the sandwich in my hand sends a wave of disgust through me, and I'm suddenly standing over the garbage as it all comes back up.

Chapter Fourteen

LIAM

"I DON'T SEE WHY I couldn't stay."

I ignore Moon as I type out a message to Capri but pause to steal a glance at him. "Did Sage seem weird?"

"What do you mean?"

"When I asked her to eat after she got dizzy. Did she seem weird?"

He shrugs.

"She hasn't told you anything? You think she's fine?" I study him for a beat.

"She said she was fine." He shrugs again. "I think she just needed some sugar. I get like that sometimes, plus she works a lot. I'm sure she's fine."

I let out a breath before looking at my phone again. I can't shake off the worry from seeing her lose her balance earlier, but at the same time, she *did* keep saying she was fine...

"Are you *worried* about her?"

My silence is the only answer he gets.

"I think you like her."

I can *hear* the smile in his voice. I tell him to stop talking and it only makes him laugh.

"I can't wait to tell Jordan you're in love with Sunshine."

"Shut the hell up, kid." I roll my eyes at him and when Capri replies to my message and tells me my mom isn't *too* bad, I decide to stop by my house before going to see her.

I slip into my car, and Moon climbs in after me. "Tell Jordan to meet us at my place to pick you up. I don't have time to drop you off at your place." I speed off, and I can see him smiling in the corner of my eye.

"You're willingly taking me to your fancy penthouse?"

I ignore him.

"I could've stayed with Sage."

"I didn't want you to," is all I say, and he's quiet for a few seconds, but I feel him watching me.

"Worried about her *and* jealous? Yeah, you like her." He laughs to himself, and I shake my head at him.

We're stepping out of my elevator, which leads into my living room, when my eyes land on Jordan, and he's tapping his helmet nervously. The minute he sees me, he pushes off from my couch and crowds us at the entrance frantically.

"You said SOS?" He scans the two of us, and I shake my head at the way Moon abuses that damn code.

"Your guy is in love."

Jordan looks over at him, but before he can respond, my phone starts ringing. My eyes land on Sage's name, and I don't need to look at Moon to know he's smiling when I answer.

"Hello, Liam Leslie." She giggles before her entire sentence is out, and I shake my head at her. I don't answer her because that's not my damn name, but she's still laughing. "Are you there?"

"Yes."

"I—oh. You sound upset. Are you sure everything's okay?"

No, my mom is slowly losing her memory and dying.

I let out a sigh and rub my forehead. This woman cares so much, and it's weird to me, but it unbalances me more that I like it. When she asked me if I was okay earlier, it did something to me. I haven't had someone care about how I felt in a while, and she *always* cares. From the very first day she met me, she has cared, and I don't know what to do with this feeling that seeps into me every time she asks that question.

"Are *you* okay?" She was laughing when she answered and now she sounds concerned for me but there's something else in her tone I can't decipher.

She takes a beat to reply before telling me she's fine.

"You sure? Are you still dizzy? Did you finish eating?"

"I'm *okay*, Liam. Moon left his phone here. I can drop it off since I want to hang out with him. Can you send me his address?"

"I'll pick it up another day."

She's quiet for a few beats, but I wait for her to respond.

"Are you sure he doesn't want his phone today? I know I would, and I don't mind taking it to him. Where is he now?"

I look over at him, and he turns his head in question. This is the least of my worries right now, but to satisfy her, I tell her I'll go back for it.

"Okay, perfect. Are you going to be too busy to stay for a while when you come to get it?"

I'm quiet for a beat as I try to decipher what she wants. "Too busy for what?"

She doesn't answer right away, then: "You know..."

I feel a smirk tugging at my lips, and I slightly cock my head to the side, although she can't see me. "I don't know *anything*."

Her laugh fills my ears, and I briefly close my eyes, feeling my stress from Capri's call somehow start to fade. She sounds like she's waiting for me to say something, but when I don't, she says, "Are you really going to make me say it?"

"Yes."

She's quiet, and I don't think she's going to say a thing.

"You can either say it, or I just won't go."

I hear her let out a breath, and she's quiet for another second before she says, "Are you going to be too busy for us to have sex?"

"Not at all, pretty girl." I tell her I'll see her in a bit before I hang up. I hear someone clear their throat, and I almost forgot I wasn't alone. When I look back at the guys, they look like they're waiting for me to tell them something.

"I'm going to pick up your phone from Sage, so–"

"Wait–" Jordan looks between the two of us before settling on Moon. "Sunshine Sage?"

I look over at Moon, and he's watching Jordan with a smile.

"Why would she have your phone?"

Moon doesn't hesitate to tell him how he was at her house, and he sounds a bit too happy to have been in her presence.

Then he gets to the part of me *liking* her.

"You *like* her?!" Jordan stares at me as if I have grown another head.

"You two need to-"

"Does she at least have a single clue that her brothers *despise* you?"

"Wait, she doesn't *know?*" Moon looks between the two of us. "*That's* why you were acting so weird?"

"I wasn't acting weird." I keep my glare on him, but he rolls his eyes like he doesn't believe me.

"You straight up lied to her and tried distracting her by sticking your tongue down her throat." He turns his head to the side and sounds like he feels bad for whatever reason.

"I didn't *lie.*"

"Not telling her is lying, bro. This whole thing is fucked up." He gives me a once-over like he's actually mad at me, and I don't think I've ever seen him upset.

"What's fucked up? I'm not sleeping with her because of who her brothers are. Why do you even care?"

"Because it's *fucked up,* and I'm not lying to her for your ass." He crosses his arms like the child he is.

"I don't give a shit," I bite out.

"So you don't care if I tell her you and her brothers—"

"Shut up, Moon. I didn't tell her since it's not relevant."

"If it's not relevant, you'll tell her." When I don't respond, he nods once. "Case in point. You're an asshole, and she doesn't deserve that shit." He rolls his eyes and looks off to the side like he can't stand to look at me anymore.

"Shut the fuck up. You're acting like I'm torturing her." I shake my head at him.

Jordan lets out a scoff and I send him a glare. "Do you also have something to say?"

He shrugs. "You don't sleep with women more than once. I agree that this is fucked. I mean, come on, you're really telling me if she wasn't their sister, you would've stuck around for this long? Leave her alone, man."

I would have stuck around this long, but I don't voice another word since I don't have to explain shit to them. Sage is clearly close with her brothers, and if I tell her, I doubt she's going to want to continue this arrangement with me, and sue me, but I don't want it to end yet.

Jordan keeps his eyes on me, then his brows raise. "You really do like her."

"Get out."

"Holy shit! You're *falling* for her." Jordan looks *way* too excited.

"I've known her for maybe two months-"

"And you like her." Moon joins in now as he shakes his head at me. "If your feelings are genuine, I won't say anything, but you better tell her."

"Or what, Moon? Don't threaten me. Leave."

They ignore me, and Jordan looks over at Moon now. "What's he like around his girlfriend?"

"She's not-"

"Happy." He sounds confused before he turns to me. "I swear I saw you smile when you chased her around the couch. I have no clue how you're happy around her, considering you're a rainy cloud compared to her."

"I'm not-"

"You *smiled*?!" Jordan loses his shit again. "I need to see this! When do I get to hang out with you while you're being all mushy with Sunshine?"

"You don't. I'm not mushy with her. Leave. *Now*." At whatever look is on my face, Jordan puts his hand up in mock surrender, and they step into the elevator.

The doors are shutting as Moon says, "You better tell her."

Before I can respond, the doors close on him.

I'm going to tell her... just not today.

I head upstairs to grab something for my mom before heading out.

My helmet yells at me that Capri is calling. I drum my bike to the sound of the ringtone as I drive down the street and let it ring.

When I hear yelling, I glance at the side, and some old hag tells me to hold onto my bike with both hands. I almost flip her off, but my mom's voice rings in my head, so I simply nod and hold my bike before gaining speed and doing a wheelie. I'm ninety percent sure she honks from behind me and I possibly gave her a heart attack, but I couldn't help it.

Capri calls *again,* so I answer, and her voice fills my ears. "If you aren't going to answer emergency calls, I'll remove you from her emergency contact."

"If you called when there were *only* emergencies, I'd answer more often." I pull up in front of the house and see Capri's red hair from the window as she paces the hall. "What's wrong?"

"Can you-"

"Yes, I can come in today. I told you I would. I'm standing outside, but tell me what it is before I walk in there."

She turns around, and when I see the concern in her freckled face, I want to turn back around. I almost do, but Capri ends the call and walks outside. I slip my helmet off and stay seated on my bike as she closes the distance between us.

"She got worse..."

I shake my head at the thoughts of the last time I was here as I look over at the house. "Do you not notice how her bad days are becoming frequent when I visit? I don't understand why you want me here. She-"

Capri cuts me off. "It is in no way related to your presence, Liam. Trust me. You usually calm her, but if you just had a bit more patience-"

"Now I need more patience." I let out a scoff as I lift my helmet, but she stops me, and her eyes scream *this is exactly what I'm talking about.*

I let out a breath before resting my helmet on my lap. When I catch a glance at a figure in the window, I notice it's my mom fighting with someone.

I hate this.

"Tell her to come out here." I keep my gaze on my mom through the window as she backs away from one of the other nurses.

Capri doesn't question me as she goes back in the house, and a few minutes later, my mom walks out in a winter coat, and I don't even question where she got that shit from.

"Excuse me?!" She looks at my bike as if it just spoke and threatened to kill her. I stay seated and fight back a smile. This was her exact reaction the first time I got on a bike in front of her. I was sixteen, and it was my friend's dad's bike since my parents didn't want to buy me one. I learned to ride on his and was riding circles around his ass by the time our lessons were over.

"I got you something." I pull the bag out of my backpack and hold it to her, but she doesn't even glance at it.

"Get your behind *off* of that thing, little boy!" She storms off the porch, and I bite back my laugh at how she looks. I glance up at Capri, silently asking why the hell she's in this coat, but she only puts her hands up and shakes her head.

When my mom reaches me, she tries to grab my helmet, but I immediately pull it away from her. While I was messing with her two seconds ago, I'm not letting her fuck up my shit. I quickly get off the bike and shove the bag into her hands before she can touch my bike.

"Open it."

She looks between the bike and me, her motherly glare showing. "Whose bike is that?"

I shrug, and she folds her arms. She watches me, but I shrug again and bite back a laugh when she rolls her eyes so damn hard.

"Get your behind in this house, Pri and her friends are pissing me off."

I stifle a laugh as I glance over at Capri, who looks highly offended.

My mom storms off, but before she reaches the door, she turns back to me. "And get rid of the bike! You're *not* keeping it!"

"Yes, ma'am."

She nods, and when I hear Capri laughing, I step into the house and lock her out. She laughs harder, and with the glass door, she can see me flip her off as clearly as day.

I keep my eyes on my mom as I follow her into the house, and the nurses watch us carefully. When my mom doesn't acknowledge them, they back off.

We settle in the living room, and when she finally opens the bag, all of her anger seems to fade as she hugs Shanti's baby blanket. She doesn't say anything as she stares out the window and rocks herself while she smells the blanket.

Someone lets Capri in, but she doesn't interrupt us, and I stay with my mom for a peaceful two hours, which is our new record.

Chapter Fifteen

SAGE

I DON'T KNOW WHY, BUT I always get a bit nervous before castings. They always end up going really well, but it's still nerve-wracking, especially when it's with the agents who don't say anything and just sit in the corner judging.

I'm fifteen minutes early when I arrive, but I call August like I normally do before my castings or anything else that makes me nervous. He's good at making me feel better.

"Hey, Sage."

"Hi—what in the world are you doing?" I turn my head to the side but then flip my phone over because he's upside down.

"I saw something about blood flow to your head helping headaches."

I feel my brows furrow as I try to think of how that even makes sense, but it doesn't.

"Hazel did my braids too tight, so I'm trying to see if this helps." He explains, but the reason for his headache isn't the reason I'm confused.

"Your twin's an idiot."

I feel my smile return at the sound of Sire's voice. "Sire! Let me see him."

August tosses the phone, and Sire catches it. "You look so pretty." Sire smiles at me through the camera.

"You don't call *me* pretty."

My jaw slightly drops at Lis's voice.

"Because you're not."

I break into a laugh at how serious he sounds. Most siblings bully each other and say we're ugly, but Sire has never been like that with me. August sometimes is when Sire isn't around to scold him, but for the most part, they never joke about my looks, and I appreciate that our sibling bond isn't like that. Sire is clearly like that with Lis, though; you'd think he hates her.

"It's a freaking family event in there. I feel so left out. What are you guys doing?" I see Lisette walk over, but Sire pushes her away when she tries to take the phone.

"Get away."

"Let me talk to her!" They fight for the phone, and August yells about not dropping his phone just as it falls. "Was your screen already broken?" Lisette sounds guilty, and I'm positive this was her fault, although she's going to blame it on Sire.

"Are you kidding me?" August doesn't sound too mad, and I'm sure he doesn't care at all, but Lis quickly defends herself.

"It's Sire's fault!"

I burst into a laugh. I freaking called it.

"I just wanted to say hi to Sage, and he just needs to be a fucking asshole. Give me the–"

"Just take it."

I watch as he aggressively shoves the phone to my sister.

"Don't–" She swings at him. "–shove me."

"Hey! Stop hitting each other!"

"Oh please don't start, Sage." Before I can tell her not to be rude, she finally looks down at the phone with a smile. "You *do* look pretty."

I smile back at her as I thank her. "How are you doing?" I watch her closely and she looks pretty good. Better. She's been struggling with her addiction, hence the reason for her new emotional support animal, a turtle. I know she and Sire have been talking, and she seems... lighter.

While August and I always tell them they can talk to us, I think they find more comfort in talking to each other.

"I'm fine." She shakes her head at something. "I really am fine, Sage. Stop looking at me like that."

I change whatever look is on my face and give her a smile. "That's good." I nod in return. "I just wanted to check in, I feel like we don't hang out as much."

"Yeah," she rolls her eyes playfully. "Because you prefer hanging out with our loser brothers."

I let out a soft laugh as the boys shout that they're not losers, and she smiles over at me.

"Oh, don't give me that. You're literally with them right now, *without me*, and were invited to get coffee with us the other day and bailed."

She uses the excuse that she didn't feel like being around to hear Sire and his lovely ex-girlfriend argue all morning and I get what she means, I was the one who told her they sorta argue like a divorced couple. I thought those two were on good terms. Sire got injured a while ago and Vidia has been his physical therapist, but it's clear they don't like each other very much or at least they act like they don't.

We all bet on how long it was going to take for them to get back together. I said before their first game came up. Hazel bet after Vidia's birthday, and August said before the summer ends. Lisette is giving it til Thanksgiving, but I definitely don't think it'll take that long.

"How's it going with your modeling stuff?" Lis pulls me out of my thoughts. "You still loving it?"

"Of course I am."

She smiles through the screen as I continue. "I don't think modeling is something you can do if you don't love it. It gets stressful, especially since we're influencers to such a huge audience."

I've never gotten backlash or *canceled* for anything, but people can be so mean. I've had to put filters on my comments, but somehow, I still get hate on everything I do. For the most part, I get positive reactions, but the negative ones have left me in tears from time to time. I don't understand how someone can be angry enough to make a mean comment about how I look and act when they've never met me, but they definitely find ways to get under my skin.

I'm grateful my supporters are quick to defend me. I looked back at the comment I got the other day about my weight, and the replies turned into hundreds of *thousands* of comments from my supporters, tearing them to shreds. I might end up deleting the entire post because it's getting to the point where death threats are being made, and nothing should ever be that serious. After years of being a social media influencer though, I'm still learning to not read the comments and to definitely not reply. Most of the time, they comment mean things for a reaction.

"Good." Lisette nods once. "You better let me know if anyone is being an online bully so I can fight in your comments."

I tell her I will, even though I definitely won't. She can get a bit... aggressive.

"I have a casting soon. That's actually why I called. I'm nervous."

Sire leans into the frame and tells me not to be and that, *I got this.* It's cute, but this is why I call August when I'm nervous.

"That's so motivational, Sire. I'm sure she appreciates that." Lis rolls her eyes at our brother. "Get the hell out of here."

I bite back a laugh when Sire's jaw drops.

"Listen, you asshole, how about you look for your damn turtle before I step on it."

Lisette literally threatens to kill him, and August thankfully takes the phone back.

"Come save me from them, Sage. They've been fighting all morning."

"Why?"

"Because he lost Piglet!" Lisette shouts.

Sire says he cooked her turtle, and I think they start fighting again, but my twin and I ignore them per usual.

"I have to go in there soon, August."

"What's the worst thing that can happen?"

I smile at his usual question, and I sit there thinking about the worst-case scenario. "I could trip as I do my walk and break my leg." That's my biggest fear because then I can't even get up and walk it off because my *leg* would be broken!

"It could be worse than that, you could bump into the agent, spill their hot coffee on their limited edition designer shirt, and then when they tell you to forget about it and just do your walk, you trip, but as they try to catch you, you drag them down and break *their* leg."

I laugh at his scenario and definitely feel better. He always comes up with the worst-case scenario when I'm nervous, and I don't know how he always makes a different horrible situation.

"If that doesn't happen, it went well, right?"

"Yeah, thanks, August. I have to go now. I love you guys!"

"Love ya!" Sire yells out first.

"Don't break a leg!" Lis calls out next, and I laugh at her.

"Bye, Sage. I love you most."

I smile to myself at August's usual words before I hang up. I don't think he actually loves me the most because I don't think he could pick a favorite since he's so indecisive, but it's cute that he says that instead of *Love you more* or *Love you too*.

I climb out of my car and make my way into the building. After letting them know I arrived, I sat in the waiting area with a few of the other girls. I talk to them for a bit, then go back to my seat and listen to some music.

I'm not too nervous anymore, but I like a few minutes alone before I go in, so I blast my ears with some Adele. I make sure to keep my attention on the door in case they come out and call me since I can't hear much.

After the first two songs play, I glance around the room, and I notice a few girls talking to each other, but they keep glancing at me. I think someone may have said something to me that I didn't hear, so I pause my music.

"You're so mean." One of them laughs softly, and they look away from me, so I assume they aren't talking to me, but before I can hit play, the other girl responds.

"Is it mean if she doesn't know?"

I keep my eyes on my phone, but I feel my brows furrow at whatever they're talking about.

"I'm just saying," she laughs again. "I didn't know this was a casting for plus-size."

I go still, but I don't look over again.

"At least she's pretty."

The other girl lets out a scoff. "That's all makeup."

I almost glance around the room now because I'm not wearing any makeup, but I know I'm the topic of their conversation since I'm the only plus-size girl in the room.

"I guess it's good she wore makeup, but we're modeling with our body, not face, and *her* body is–"

"Sage Loana?"

I look over at a much younger girl, maybe sixteen, with a smile plastered on my face.

"I'm Ebony, the designer's daughter." She points behind her shoulder with her thumb at the room behind her where her mom, Elaine Wilson, is. "She told me you were out here, and I almost passed out."

I get up to hug her, and she laughs nervously.

"Did she say *Sage* Loana? As in Sage *Hale*."

I hear the girls start whispering again, but I only hug Ebony in return.

"Aw, it's so nice to meet you." When I pull away, she stares up at me in awe, and I can't get over how cute she is. I glance in the mirror behind her, and I can see the shock on the two girls' faces as they realize who they were just bullying, but I look back over at Ebony and keep my smile in place.

"Don't tell my mom I told you but you already got the job."

I laugh at how fast she rushes her words out.

"She's wanted you to model in her shows for months. I think she didn't reach out first to play hard to get and because her ego is bigger than her fake butt."

"Okay," I can't stop laughing now, and she pulls me in for another hug. "Maybe we should not spill all of your mom's secrets, yeah?" I tap the top of her head softly, and she nods before asking for a picture. We take a few, and she rushes back into the room.

I stand a bit taller as I turn to the girls who were just talking about me but are suddenly watching me like they might drop to their knees.

"Wow," one of them starts. "You are so much prettier in person, I-"

"Am I?" I turn my head to the side as I give her a sweet smile. "Or is it all the makeup I'm wearing?"

Her face drops, but I don't say anything else and return to my seat. They're both stuck in a place for a few seconds but then the one who was doing most of the talking walks over to me.

"I am so sorry I said that. I didn't know-"

"That I could hear you? No, that's okay because it's not mean if I can't hear you, right?"

She opens her mouth, quickly closes it, and tries again, but nothing comes out.

The door behind her opens, and they call her name, but before she walks in, I call out to her. "Modeling isn't just about your body, by the way. It's all in the face and walk."

She blinks twice.

"Good luck in there." I look back down at my phone and force myself to stay seated because the other girl is still out here watching me, and I refuse to rush off and let either of them know their words got to me.

When the door opens again, she walks out with tears in her eyes, and I know Elaine just tore her a new one because she's one of *those* designers. I would normally feel bad since this girl is clearly a baby model, and I'm not saying she deserved it, but maybe it's her karma.

I go in after her and walk over to the table to introduce myself.

"Let's see your walk first, and then we'll take pictures." Elaine keeps her tone neutral, but when I glance behind her at her daughter, she gives me a thumbs up with a huge smile on her face. I give her a small smile before walking to the back of the room.

I showcase my walk twice, and Elaine nods to herself as she writes something down. We take some pictures next, and I expect her to stay seated, but she gets up and stands behind the photographer as I pose.

"She's beautiful." Her voice comes out just above a whisper, and I almost thank her but realize I wasn't meant to hear that. I smile to myself as I look back over at the camera and give them a few more poses.

When we're done, she says she'll be in touch, and that's all I get before walking out. A lot of designers and agents are different at these things. Some are super friendly, others don't say a word to you, and the best tell you what you did wrong, nicely or not. You really never know what you're going to get, which is why I'm so nervous about these things, but her daughter definitely made me feel better. Even if she had no clue what she was talking about and I didn't get the job, it was nice meeting both of them.

I feel my stomach grumbling when I walk out because I made sure not to eat before coming here, but either way... I don't have the appetite. I feel the back of my eyes stinging as I think of how those girls were just laughing at me, and I know I shouldn't care what they think, but I *do*, and I hate that I do. I have Killian's photo shoot next, so I head to his studio. He's a friend I met in the modeling world, but I recently learned he's friends with Vincent Moore, which was a surprise to me.

I ate all day yesterday since my appetite was back, so I don't feel lightheaded as I go through the day on an empty stomach, but I grab a coffee anyway.

When I walk into his studio, I'm shocked it's so nice here. Someone brings me to Killian, and his face lights up when he sees me.

"Sage, thank you again for coming, love."

I tell him it's not a problem, and I lean in to hug him. "How did your photo shoot go?"

"It was a casting, but it was good."

He ends up taking me to the changing room, and I get dressed before they do my makeup to match the look he's going for. I have my hair in Fulani braids this week, so we don't have to style my hair.

I take a few solo pictures, then to my surprise, I take some with Killian, but we're done a lot faster than I was expecting, and I'm not complaining.

"Thank you for having me today. It was fun." I hug Killian goodbye, and when he pulls away, he kisses my cheek.

"Thank you for coming. All of your pictures came out stunning." He takes my hand. "*You* are stunning."

I keep my eyes on him as he brings my hand to his mouth and kisses the back of it softly. I try not to read too much into it, but a few of my friends said they think he has a crush on me, but I'm not too sure.

I give him a smile before waving goodbye.

Chapter Sixteen

LIAM

"**I**'M GLAD YOU WERE ABLE to make it." Capri smiles at me and I give her a nod before walking in. I glance around the room, and there are a few people here for family night, but I'm glad it isn't crowded because I don't want to socialize. My body is killing me from my game, and I'm surprised I even made it here on time, so no, I don't want to socialize with these families; I'm only here for mine.

I'm also running on almost no sleep because of my early game, and I could never sleep on plane rides. All the back-and-forth traveling between LA and New York is also catching up to me.

Since we lived in Cali before my mom got sick, I decided to keep her here; this is a really good place for her. Instead of being a typical nursing home, it's just a big house with three other residents and their personal nurses, chefs, and everything else they need.

It feels homier and it's the closest thing to a home I could give my mom since I travel a lot for games, and while I could buy a house for just my mom and Capri, since she's her nurse, my mom needs to socialize and at least here, with all the nurses, and volunteers who come to spend time with them, it's good for her here.

"Just a heads up," Capri catches up to me. "She's having a *really* bad day."

I glance over at my mom, and she's looking out that same window. When I make my way over to her, I don't say anything at first, but she looks over at me, and it's like she's seen a ghost.

"Mom?"

"*Leave.*" Before I can even say anything, she stands from her seat and takes a sharp step towards me. "Do you seriously think I want to see you after what you did, Eli?"

I swear my heart stops at the sound of my father's name. I don't know how long I stand there, but her eyes cut into me so fucking deep it hurts to breathe.

"Aria, this is Liam, your *son.*" Carpi takes hold of her hand, and I wait for her to realize her mistake, but she doesn't, and I don't think I've ever felt this... hopeless before.

"Leave before I kill you."

"Okay!"

I'm still stuck there as Capri tries to de-escalate.

"We don't say those things. Let's go to your room for a little while to cool down, and when we come back, you can apologize to Liam."

My mom opens her mouth, but Capri cuts her off before her words cut me again. "We're *leaving* now." She pulls her away, and I keep my eyes on them as they walk off.

Capri looks over her shoulder with an apologetic look, but I walk off before they can come back out.

I'm nearing my bike when I hear my name, but I don't stop.

"Liam, please wait!"

I swing a leg over my bike before starting it. Capri steps in my way and rests her hand on my helmet before I slip it on.

My eyes meet hers, and she looks at me so damn sympathetically. "Liam–"

"Capri." I shut my eyes and try not to yell because I know she's trying to help, but she needs to leave me alone. "I *just* got off a six-hour plane ride after a long ass game, and we fucking lost anyway. I'm tired. I'm in pain and–"

When my voice cracks, my head snaps over at her. "*Move.*" I struggle to keep my voice low, but I do. She takes a step back without another word. I slip on my helmet and keep my eyes away from her before speeding off.

I grip the handles so hard, my hands hurt, but I won't stop shaking, and these stupid fucking breathing exercises aren't working. My anger only heightens with every breath I take, making me speed between every car in my way.

When I get to my penthouse, I head straight for the gym and take out my anger on the punching bag. I'm not sure how long I'm in there, but I didn't put on my gloves or wrap my hands, so they're bleeding by the time I notice, but I also feel better, so I stay for another hour.

By the time I shower and climb into bed, I'm so beat I could sleep for days. Just as I close my eyes, my phone lights up with a message. I don't pick it up, but then it dings again, and I let out an annoyed breath before grabbing it.

Sage

Heyy

Are you in the city?

Yes.

Wanna hang out?

Hang out or fuck?

What did I tell you about saying that, Liam Leslie?

Have sex*

Thank you.

And both...

Tmrw.

I turn my phone off and turn in my bed, but then my eyes land on the gift I got for my mom. I stare at it for a few seconds, but the picture of us and my little sister facing me suddenly makes it hard to breathe, so I roll out of bed.

Omw*

"You look tired." Sage tilts her head to the side as she studies me.

"I am."

She opens the door wider for me and I notice her eyes drop down to my hands. "What happened?"

She reaches for my bandages, but I pull my hand away and mumble, "Punching bag."

I walk further in, and she doesn't question me as I fall onto her couch. I keep my eyes on her as she makes her way over to me, but before she can sit next to me, I pull her onto my lap.

A smile spreads across her face as she wraps her arms around my neck. "Why do you always make me sit on your lap?"

I shrug softly before pulling her shirt off. "I like the way your ass feels on my dick." I toss her shirt aside, and my lips land on her chest as I work her bra off.

"God, you are so vulgar!" She laughs softly, and I throw her bra aside next. I look up at her before taking one of her nipples between my teeth. She's suddenly quiet, and it fascinates me how shy she gets when I have her like this.

"How was your day?" I suck on one of her nipples as I rub her other boob, and she lets out a soft sigh.

"Good."

"What'd you do?" I slip a hand into her pants, and she sucks in a deep breath.

"Um..."

I watch her bite her lip as I work my fingers in her.

"Hmm."

"What'd you do today?" I kiss my way along her neck as she moves her hips against me.

"Work."

"What kind of work?" I add another finger, and she tilts her head back with a pretty moan. I let my eyes fall shut as she moans my name in my ear. My lips land on hers, and I kiss her softly as I make her come over my hand.

She's working my pants off before she can catch her breath, but I don't hesitate to help her take her pants off, too.

"You're staying on top." Not only because I lack the energy but also because I like her like this.

"Mhm." Her lips are on mine again as she rubs her hand along my length. My lips part for her tongue, and I slip a condom on before she slides down on me, and I swallow every sound she makes.

Her hands are in my hair, and my hand comes around her throat as I kiss her harder. I bring my other hand to her waist as I guide her to move the way I want her to. My head falls onto the couch, and when a soft moan escapes past my lips, I feel her pull away.

"That was hot."

I look up at her to find her already watching me. "Harder, Sage."

She does, and our eyes lock as she clearly struggles to hold it together.

"Are you going to finish again so soon?"

"No!" She's a horrible liar, and I bite back a smile when she slows down.

"Faster, Sage."

A whimper passes her lips, and she picks her pace but barely. "You okay?" I tease.

"Mhm."

"Use your words."

She moans in response, and when her leg shakes, I flip us over. "You're a two-pump chump." I pound into her harder and faster, and when she finishes, I don't stop.

"I am *not*!" She pushes my chest, but I barely move and smile into the crease of her neck at how defensive she sounds.

"You didn't even last ten minutes, beloved." I bring my hand to her clit, and she moans so loud, I feel myself smirking against her lips. "And you're going to come a third time."

"Shut. Up."

"You must've *really* missed me."

She shoves me harder this time, and when I look at her, she looks so embarrassed.

"It's only been a week."

She sends me a warning look I could never take as a true warning. "Liam—"

"Did you miss me, Sage?" I rub her clit softly as I leave a trail of kisses from her cheek to her ear. "Don't make me repeat myself."

"I did."

"You did what?"

"I missed you." Her voice is just above a whisper, and my lips land on hers as I finish. We both catch our breaths for a few minutes before I feel her kissing my neck ever so softly.

"Are you still tired?"

"Exhausted." I take in another few breaths, but when I pull out of her and feel how wet she still is, I force myself not to collapse. "But you want to go again." I pull away to look at her, and she nods shyly.

"Say it."

She avoids my eyes, and I officially get off on seeing her struggle under me.

"Can we—"

"Speak up."

Her eyes snap to mine, and she takes a deep breath. "Can we do it again?"

"Do what again?"

Her brows furrow, and her nose scrunches with the rest of her face. I kiss her nose and then her lips. "Say it."

"You know what I mean."

I pull away and put my hands up in mock surrender. "I don't know *anything*."

She pauses for a second but then tilts her head back. She laughs when she realizes I'm mimicking her again. I pull her back on top of me and watch her for a few seconds.

"What?" She looks between my eyes, and I shake my head before kissing her dimple.

"You're just so pretty."

Her smile widens, and I kiss her cheek again before standing with her.

"We can fuck again since you want to so bad."

She looks like she's about to tell me not to say *fuck* like that, so I shut her up with a kiss and lead us into her room. I've never been this far into her apartment, but I don't bother looking around. I lay her on her bed and slip off the used condom, dumping it into the trash by her bed. Rather than climbing on top of her, I pull her leg to bring her closer and kiss my way between her legs.

She's dripping, and I've barely been at it a minute, but I keep both hands on her legs as I fuck her with my tongue. She rocks her hips back and forth a few times, but I take my time, and when she starts whimpering my name, I glance up at her. I know what she wants, but I make her work for it.

I climb on top of her, and when she lets out an unsatisfied sigh, I pull away to look at her. "I know you didn't finish."

She looks confused at first, but I turn us over so she's on top again.

"Prove you can last long."

She realizes what I'm doing and looks offended. "That's not fair, I'm—"

"Trust me, I'm just as close as you are."

She looks down at my cock, and I watch her chest rise and fall faster. She doesn't say anything, but when she reaches over to her nightstand for a condom, she looks determined to prove she isn't a two-pump chump. I know she isn't going to last long, but I'm interested in seeing how long she can last.

She slides onto me hard, and her lips find mine as she fucks me perfectly. When she takes my bottom lip between her teeth, I let out a loud moan. I have no clue where this side of her has been, but I don't complain or stop her.

Her rhythm doesn't falter, and when I feel a tightness form in my stomach, I quickly remember this is a competition and I'm fucking losing. I bring my hand between us, and when I give her clit a soft stroke, she lets out a moan for me.

"That– that's cheating."

"We didn't set any rules, beloved." I flip us over, but she immediately turns us again and gets on top. I pull away to look at her, and I'm genuinely shocked she just did that shit.

"*Stop* cheating."

"Let me *win*." I flip us over again, and she lets out a frustrated huff.

Without warning, she pulls away from me so I'm no longer inside of her.

"What–"

Her lips crash into mine, and I feel her slip the condom off as she starts pumping me. Once. Twice—and I fall apart. I pull away from her in a rush, and she has an innocent smile on her face when she looks down at where I finish over her hands.

"You're a two-pump–"

"That doesn't count."

"Don't be ashamed, Liam."

I send her a glare, but her smile only widens.

"I'm going to fuck you up."

She breaks into a laugh, but I drag her back to me and slide the condom back on. "That does *not* count."

She opens her mouth to retort, but I slam into her, and all that comes out of that pretty mouth of hers is my name.

"It doesn't count." I pound into her harder when she smiles. "Say it."

She doesn't, and I fuck her harder. Her moans morph between light screams, but I don't stop. "Say. It."

"Okay, okay!"

"Okay, what, Sage?"

She shakes her head, and when my hand wraps around her throat, I swear I feel her pulse quicken.

"Don't make me repeat myself."

"I'm sorry– I'm sorry you lost." Her smile doesn't falter, and I let out a low chuckle. She's stubborn; I'll give her that.

"*I'm* sorry you won't be able to walk in any runway shows for a while." I try to get her to submit, but she doesn't. I don't know if I hate it or love it, but by the time she comes, so do

I, and when I collapse next to her, I don't have it in me to even try again.

"You are *so* fucking lucky I'm tired." I blink slowly as I fight to stay awake.

"Tired? Or a two pump–"

I cover her face with a pillow, and her laugh is the last thing I hear before passing out.

Chapter Seventeen

SAGE

I SWING MY CURTAINS OPEN and smile with my eyes closed as I soak up the sun. When I open my eyes, they land on the Peach sticker on my window, and my smile widens.

"It's morning, everyone! Today's the day, the sun is shining, the tank is clean, and we are getting out of–" I let out a fake gasp, and I notice Liam jump up from his sleep. He looks around frantically before his eyes land on me.

"The tank is clean!" I fake my shock again.

"What the *fuck* are you talking about right now?" He flops back onto my pillow and covers his face with the blanket.

"You don't know that line from *Finding Nemo*?" I point at Peach, the starfish, although Liam isn't looking at me anymore. "It's one of my favorite movies."

"The dumb blue fish?"

I let out a laugh and climb back into bed. "That's Dory, not Nemo." I think for a second and turn to the Dory sticker I also have on my window. "And she's not dumb; she has short-term memory loss."

"Okay, Dory."

I turn to Liam and he's shaking his head. "Sage," he corrects himself, and I bite back a smile. "Fuck, what time is it?"

I pick up my phone. "It's almost seven-thirty."

He lets out a very big sigh and covers his head with another pillow. "I'm *never* staying over again if you wake up this early."

"Well, that's rude. I thought we had fun." I feel a smile creep onto my face as I lean down to him. "My two pump–"

In a quick move, he slams the pillow over my face and keeps it there as he *suffocates* me!

"Dory—fuck, *Sage.*"

I let out a muffled laugh, and he pushes the pillow onto my face harder, which only makes me laugh harder.

"My brain is barely awake, so I'm going back to sleep, but tonight, you're in trouble."

I feel the bed shift as he flops back down, and when I move the pillow, I see him already falling back to sleep.

"Whatever you say, Liam Leslie."

"*Stop* calling me that!" He pulls the blanket over his head, and I break into a laugh as I hop out of bed.

As I'm crossing out the days on my calendar, my heart drops.

"Oh no!" I race for my phone and pull up the shelter's page, and when I see there are still a few animals that weren't adopted in time, I grab all of my things to leave. I posted about it when I walked past the shelter and noticed a few animals were going to be put down but, so many people are opposed to cats.

I'm looking for my car keys when I remember it's in the shop. "Dammit!" I try to order a car, but none are available, so I run back to my room. "Liam!" I pull the blanket off of him, but he immediately pulls it back over his face.

"Shut the curtains. You—"

"Liam, *please* let me borrow your car!"

"Are you insane?"

"Excuse me—"

He pulls the blanket off and looks me dead in the eyes. "I'm not letting you near my car with the way you drive."

I'm offended, but there's no time to argue. "Fine, then please drive me to the animal shelter."

He stares at me for two whole seconds before turning back around.

"Liam! Get up." I pull his arm, but he pulls away from my touch like I just burned him.

"You're going to yank my arm out of its damn socket. Don't fucking *pull* me."

My hands go up at the way he glares at me. "*Sorry.*"

He rolls his eyes before sitting up straight.

"Please drive me, Liam. I'd call my brothers, but they—"

"Alright." He stands from the bed, and I somehow just remember he's naked. My eyes slowly scan his body, and every inch of his body is covered in ink. I shake my head, turn on my heels, and rush into the living room to get his clothes. When I make it back to my room, he isn't there, so I hurry into the bathroom.

He's still naked, and I have no clue how he stands there, brushing his teeth with my spare toothbrush in *zero* shame.

"You're staring."

I blink, and when he wipes his mouth, he has a smile on his face. I study him for a breath, and I feel my shock pass as I try to memorize the way his lips curve.

"You're still staring."

"You have such a pretty smile."

His face is stone cold again just as the words leave my mouth.

"You should smile more."

"I'll think about it."

I shake my head at his bored tone but smile anyway before placing his clothes on the counter. "Please hurry."

"Mhm."

I leave him to get dressed as I pace the living room impatiently. When he walks out, he heads for the kitchen, and I stare at him dumbfounded as he opens my cabinets.

"Why don't you have any real food in here?" He opens another cabinet, and I think I lose my mind.

"LIAM!"

He turns so fast, he's a blur. His eyes widen as he searches me. "Why are you yelling?"

"We have to *go!*"

"Okay!" He walks out of the kitchen, and I hurry to the door. "Jesus Christ, you're *dramatic.*"

I tap my foot impatiently as I wave for the door.

"I am not about to run, Sage. Calm–"

"Do not tell me to calm down. They are about to kill three innocent kittens, and you're taking your sweet time like you don't care!" I pull his hand when he's within reach, but he immediately snatches it away.

"What did I tell you about pulling me like that?"

I ignore him as I head for the stairs, and when I turn, he's at the freaking *elevator*. I open my mouth, but he's already making his way towards me.

"Alright, alright. Don't have a damn stroke."

We race down the steps, and by we, I mean me because Liam complains his legs hurt like a baby. He tells me not to call him that and goes on about his baseball game or practice or something else I don't listen to because all I can think of are those baby cats.

I posted the flyer I saw earlier this week, and most of the animals got adopted, but these three kittens are somehow left. I've been calling everyone I know, but no one can take them.

I jump out of the car the minute Liam slows down, and he yells for me to watch where I'm going when I cross the street without looking. The light isn't for me, but I think the cars slow down as they see me.

I make it to the front desk of the shelter and ring the bell a few times.

"Are you a fucking *maniac*?"

I turn at the anger in Liam's voice, and when I realize it's pointed at me, I feel my brows furrow. He makes it to me in a few long strides, and when I take a step back, I hit the desk behind me.

"Do not run across the street like that ever again. That road is–"

"Okay."

"Do not cut me off."

"*Okay.*"

He lets out a breath, and I turn back around. "Jeez, don't have a stroke."

"Sage, I swear–"

"Excuse me!" I wave down one of the workers just as I see them passing behind the doors. I ring the bell a few more times, and he comes out almost immediately.

"Hi! I saw you guys still have three kittens that need to be adopted. Are they still..." I can't find the right words, but thankfully, he knows what I mean.

"Yes, we still have them. Were you thinking of adopting one of them?"

"Oh, well, *I* can't, but-" I turn to Liam with a smile, and he's staring at me like he wasn't listening to a word I just said. "-would you-"

"No."

"Oh, okay. How about you let me-"

"No."

"Okay, thank you so much for that!" I give him a tight smile, and if he picks up on my sarcasm, he doesn't let on. "I think you should recons-"

"No."

"Alrighty then!" I turn back to the worker with a smile. "Can you bring them out for us?"

He glances at Liam for no more than a second before he rushes off. When the door closes, I turn on my heels towards Liam, and he's already watching me.

I cross my arms across my chest as I wipe my smile clean. "Why are you being so rude?"

"It stinks in here, and you just ran across that street as if a truck wasn't making its way down the fucking road."

"I—"

"It's still my turn."

My mouth falls shut.

"If you want to run across main roads and play with your life for nasty cats, do so when you're not with me. Police reports take long."

My jaw is ajar, and he just stands there like he'd honestly rather be elsewhere. "Okay, I get you're not a morning person, but you don't have to be so mean." I turn back around. "I can find a ride home since you clearly don't want to help."

He doesn't answer me, but I don't hear him walking away. Either way, I don't care anymore.

I stand there for a few seconds, but I can't help myself, so I turn back to him.

"You know, I can *really* see those anger issues that got you into trouble with your coach. You should work on it."

He blinks twice before taking a step back. "Find a ride home, Sage," he practically spits out.

"I was already planning on it!" I turn around, but he grabs my arm and turns me back to him just as fast.

"Yell at me again." His eyes bore into my soul, and if he was angry before, he's *furious* now. I know he just told me to yell but I can no longer find my voice with the way he watches me. "Go ahead."

I swallow slowly, and he doesn't even blink as he watches me.

"You should go to anger management or something."

He pulls in a deep breath, but it looks like he can no longer breathe.

"You're turning red." My voice falls into a whisper, and he takes a few steps away from me.

Before either of us can say anything else, the back door opens again. I turn to find the worker with three baby kittens. I feel my previous annoyance fade as my eyes land on them. He places them on the counter, and I take a step closer but make sure not to touch them.

"They are so perfect." I feel a knot form in my throat but force it down.

The smallest one just lays there like she's falling asleep, and her brothers climb over her. I smile when she yawns and catches the other's tail in her mouth. Her brother turns like he's about to hit her, so I grab him, and he barely misses her small face.

I stroke his white fur, and the bigger one of the three walks over to me, greedy for attention. I pick him up next, and when they purr against my chest, I almost lose it, but I keep my tears at bay.

"Can I pay you to keep them a bit longer?"

The worker watches me carefully but shakes his head no.

"Name any price. Please?"

He looks intrigued now, but before he can tell me how much it's going to cost to let them live, Liam speaks up from behind us.

"How do you know he won't take your money and kill them anyway?"

My eyes widen when I notice the guilty look on his face, but he only lets out a sigh as he shoves his hands in his pocket. "I'm just doing my job."

I want to tell him he has a cruel job, but I keep my thoughts to myself and turn to Liam. He has his eyes on his phone when he speaks before I do. "Do not ask me again, Sage."

I look back down at the cats in my hands and hug them a bit closer.

"You want them so bad, you take them."

"Don't you think I would if I could?"

Liam doesn't even look up from whatever is so important on his phone.

"My complex doesn't allow pets and either way, I'm allergic to cats."

Liam's head snaps up to me now and a weird look crosses his face. "Put them down."

"No." I hold them closer, and Liam takes a step forward, his eyes slightly widened.

"Your face is breaking out, Sage. Put. Them. *Down*."

"I'm—" I sneeze, and when I rub my eyes, Liam pulls my hand away.

"Stop touching your face."

I itch my cheek on my shoulder but hold the kittens a bit longer.

"Sage, your eyes are starting to swell. Put those nasty shits down, *now*!"

When one of the kittens jumps, I take a step away from Liam. "You're scaring them."

"I don't—" He lets out a breath when I turn away from him. The smaller one is still on the counter, and I realize she's not sleeping, but she looks really weak.

"Is this one sick?" I sneeze again as I rub her head.

"*You're* sick."

I ignore Liam.

"We believe she is, yes."

"Can you just wait one more day before you put them down? I can—"

"I can't."

I can't hold back my tears anymore and I pull all three of them closer as I cry.

"Jesus fucking Christ. You—" Liam cuts himself off and snatches all of them away.

"What—"

"Go wash your hands."

"But—"

"Do you have your medication with you?"

"Yes, but—"

"Take it and go wash your hands." He shoves the kittens back into the arms of the man who's going to kill them. I try to reach for them, but Liam steps in my way. He opens his mouth to say something, but he goes still as he watches me. A few more tears trickle down my cheek, and it's mainly because I'm crying, but my eyes are also watering from my allergies.

"Fuck." Liam turns around and grabs all of the cats.

"What are you doing?"

"I'll take them if you walk out right now and take your damn medicine."

I look up at him from the kittens, and I feel my smile widen. "Really?"

"If you don't wash your hands and face and take your medicine in the next five seconds, they're staying."

I hurry off into the bathroom and get myself together. The cold water feels good on my face, and I drink some when my throat feels scratchy.

When I look into my bag, I realize I actually *don't* have my eye drops or Benadryl. Oops... There's not much I can do now so I blow my nose a few times and walk back out.

When the door closes behind me, Liam turns with all three kittens in his arms."Did you take your medicine?"

"Mhm." I reach to pet the sick one, but Liam takes a step out of my reach.

"Sage."

I keep my eyes on the kittens.

"Sage, I promise you I will snap their necks in an instant if you're lying to me. *Did you* take your medicine?"

"You don't have to be so violent."

He turns to the man, and I blurt out the truth. "I'm sorry! I forgot that I switched purses and didn't transfer all of my things."

He lets out an annoyed breath as he watches me, and if looks could kill, I think I'd die faster than these allergies are killing me.

"Jesus Christ, Dory."

I smile up at him, but he doesn't look pleased.

"Let's go." He walks ahead before I can respond, and I follow after him with a smile plastered on my face.

I sneeze three times before we even walk out, and my eyes begin to blur from how watery they get, but it doesn't bother me. Liam opens the back seat and places the cats down as he shakes his head at something.

When he turns to face me, I'm already watching him with a smile. His eyes roam my face, and he shakes his head again. "You look like you can barely see."

"I can see how happy you are to have three new kittens." I turn my head to the side as I look up at him.

"So you can't see." He nods once and opens the passenger door for me. "Get in and don't touch them."

I walk over to him and look up with an even bigger smile. "Thank you for taking them."

"You're a damn headache and a *half.*" He shakes his head, and he looks very upset, but my smile doesn't falter.

"*Thank* you," I voice again for the kittens. He doesn't answer me, and his cold expression doesn't falter, but I get on my tippy toes to plant a kiss on his lips. He kisses me back firmly before literally pushing me into his car and slamming the door.

I think he's mad, but I *know* these kittens won't be put down, so it's worth his anger. I look at myself in the mirror, and my eyes widen at my reflection. I don't feel as bad as I look, but my eyes are almost swollen shut, and I have hives on my cheeks and neck. I turn around to look at the babies, and when one of them yawns, I decide it was definitely worth it.

Liam climbs in, and I hum to the music as he speeds down the street.

"Can you breathe alright?"

"Yeah." I look over at him to find him already watching me, and he looks so disappointed about something.

"You're a headache, you know that?"

"You've mentioned it." When I smile, he rolls his eyes at me and looks back at the road. He ends up putting all the windows down when I don't stop sneezing.

I'm scratching my neck when he turns my face towards him. "Are you *sure* you can breathe?"

"*Yes*, Liam."

He looks between my eyes, and I feel myself smiling.

"Aw, are you worried about me?"

His hand drops from my face, and he turns back to the road.

"I'd have to care to worry, and I don't." He sounds bored of the topic at hand, but I don't let his lies get to me. "Police reports are long, remember?"

"Don't lie to me, Liam Les-"

"*Stop* calling me that, Dory."

I break into a laugh, but I start sneezing again. Liam leans forward for the glove compartment and hands me some tissue.

I thank him before blowing my nose. "Am I Dory now?" I look over at him, and he looks angry about something else.

"You *forgot* your medication for an allergy that's clearly serious?"

I don't answer him.

"And you *forgot* you didn't have it with you when you decided to rub those nasty shits all on your face?"

I don't answer him once again, and his anger seems to grow.

"Sounds like something a dumb blue fish would do."

"She's not dumb. She has-"

"Short-term memory loss, yeah. You clearly do, too."

I stifle my laugh and turn away from him so he can't see me smiling at him. We're quiet for the remainder of the drive, and I thought he was taking me home, but then he stops in front of the emergency room.

"Liam, I'm fine-"

He climbs out of the car and is already opening my side. "Let's go."

I let out a sigh and climb out, but when he walks off, I plant my feet.

"You're forgetting something."

He turns to me and looks around for something. I wave to the back seat, and he doesn't move.

"We can't leave them in there."

"Well, we can't take them in there."

Is he serious right now? I stay put but so does he. When I cross my arms he sighs so loud, I have to bite my tongue not to laugh.

"Fine. Are you capable of going into the hospital alone, or will your short-term memory get you lost?"

I laugh at him, and he doesn't look amused as he walks over to me.

"I have to go do something anyway. I'll see you tonight." He walks over to his side of the car, but I turn back around before going into the emergency room.

"Can I get a picture with them?"

"You can take a picture *of* them, but you're not going to hold them again."

"Can *you* hold them?"

He sends me a bored look, and I tilt my head to the side as I smile up at him. "Please?"

"Fine." He caves, and I steal a quick kiss before he grabs them. He holds all of them in his arms and they look even smaller than they are with how big his arms are. I try to get him to smile, but he tells me not to push my luck, so I don't.

"What will you name them?"

"I won't be naming them since I'm not keeping them."

"What?" My head snaps up to him, and he looks serious.

"Go inside, Sage. Your breakout is getting worse."

I'm also starting to feel worse, so I decide to argue with him about this later and get a few more pictures.

"*Enough*. Go inside before I–"

"Okay, stop threatening them."

He puts them in the back seat again before shutting the door.

"Thank you again." I smile up at him before planting a kiss on his lips.

"Go." He pushes me away, and I walk off before he actually drags me inside. "Call me when you get out."

I tell him I will, and when the sliding doors close behind me, I turn and expect him to be gone, but he's still standing there, watching me.

He nods for me to keep walking, so I turn back around. When the front desk lady sees me, she immediately gets up from her seat and opens the back door for me. I'm unsure why, but I steal a glance behind me, and Liam still watches me.

I give him a small wave, and he shakes his head, but I swear I see him smile before he turns for his car.

Chapter Eighteen

LIAM

I GLANCE DOWN AT MY arms, and when one of them hiss at me, I almost drop all three of them. "She's not here to protect your ass anymore. I'm not above taking you back there."

All three of them seem to cower at my words, and I look back up as I walk into the house. One of the nurses smiles when he sees me, but then he sees the three ugly cats in my hands, and his smile drops.

"I'm sorry—"

I cut him off before he tells me what I already know. "I know, okay. I just—"

"Liam!"

I turn at the sound of Capri's voice, and her face lights up when my eyes meet hers. She glances down at the cats and then at the balloons in my hands, and her smile doesn't falter.

"I think we can make an exception since it's a holiday." She rests her hand on my arm and guides me in as she tells the other nurse not to worry. He doesn't question her and we walk into the house.

"How is she today?"

"She's been really good."

I let out a breath, and when I look over at Capri, her smile seems sadder.

"I wish you'd stayed last night. She was much better after a while and was asking for you."

I don't reply to her because I don't have anything to say. I know it's not Mom's fault that she's angry at me for what happened to my baby sister, and it's not her fault that she sometimes forgets me or confuses me with my asshole dad.

I know it's not her fault, and maybe I'm selfish for not sucking it up and taking every blow she throws at me, but I just can't sometimes.

"How are you?"

I only nod, and Capri doesn't push it, but I feel her eyes on me as she walks me to my mom.

She's in the backyard on a blanket near the pond. I take in her favorite yellow sundress she's in and she looks at peace. I hesitate before walking over because I don't want to ruin her day. I watch her from a distance for a while, but after a few minutes, I walk over before I change my mind and leave.

"Hey."

She looks up at the sound of my voice, and when she takes in everything in my arms, her smile widens.

"Oh! Is it someone's birthday?"

I settle next to her on the blanket but keep the cats close in case she flips out.

"It's *your* birthday, Mom." I hand her the balloons and gift, but she shakes her head like she's disappointed, yet she still smiles.

"It's not my birthday, sweetheart." She laughs softly as she plays with the string of the balloons. "You were never good at remembering it." She laughs again and I watch her smile, silently wishing she could always be this happy.

"I remembered this year."

She shakes her head again and cups my face. "You remembered, but you got the date wrong again, sweetie."

"If you say so," I give her a shrug. "It's your birthday. What do I know?"

She looks down when one of the cats meows, and I wait for her reaction, but she only lets out a soft gasp and reaches for one.

"Oh, these are beautiful." She smothers the smallest one, and when she kisses it, I'm suddenly grateful I got them cleaned before coming here. I let the other two out of my grasp and they make their way over to her. They climb her lap, and I feel myself smiling when she laughs again.

"Do you remember–" She laughs harder. "Do you–"

I feel a laugh bubbling in my throat as she struggles to contain herself.

"Do you remember when your sister tried taking the poor neighbor's cat home?" She laughs and laughs, and I barely blink as I keep my focus on her.

"We were walking home and she snuck up to their porch and just scooped up that poor thing."

I smile at the memory. Shanti attempted to catnap that cat every day that week and failed, but she was determined that day, at least as determined as a three-year-old could be.

When we passed the house, she tippy-toed all the way across their yard before grabbing the cat from behind. She got scratched across the face by the shit, and I almost killed it when she cried. Mom said it was unfortunate, but now she'll learn not to touch animals without asking. I guess she did learn, but her scar wasn't pretty.

Now that I think about it, it was definitely our fault for letting her do that, but it was cute watching her try to be sneaky. I genuinely didn't think the cat would scratch her since it's only ever been friendly, but I guess she scared it.

My mom suddenly pushes the cats off of her, and I pull them closer when I see her getting upset about something.

"Your dad was angry when he saw Shanti's scratch." She shakes her head, and when one of the cats makes its way back to her, she softly pushes it further, so I grab it and hold all three in my arms again.

"He doesn't know how to control his anger, Liam." She hugs herself as she thinks about him. My dad never put his hands on her, but his anger was genuinely insane to me, and it makes me feel like I can't breathe when I think about how I got that trait from him.

"You should take them back outside before he sees them." She glances at the cats, but I can tell she wants to hold them again.

"He won't be back for a while. They can stay a bit longer."

She asks me if I'm sure, and when I tell her I'm certain, her smile is back and she takes all of them onto her lap again.

"They are so perfect." She rubs one of their stomachs, and her words remind me of Sage before her meltdown in the shelter. That woman really is a headache, but I think I would've taken ten cats if she cried about it, and the thought makes my stomach turn. I don't know why I care so much about satisfying her, but I do, and it's unsettling.

"Did you let your sister see them?"

My eyes snap back to my mom, and she's watching me, so hopefully.

"Yeah." I lie, and her smile widens.

"How was she with them?" She looks down at the cats again and leans against her elbow. "The doctor says pets are beneficial for children with Down syndrome, but your father is against the idea." She shakes her head like she's annoyed with him, and I just want her to be happy again, so the words slip past my lips.

"He changed his mind. We're going to keep the cats."

My mom looks up at me with the brightest smile I've seen.

"For Shanti."

She leaps from where she is and wraps her arms around my neck. "How did you convince him?"

I tell her it took a lot of debating, but he caved after a while, which is probably the biggest lie I've ever told. When he was set on something, there was no changing his mind.

"Open your birthday gift." I push the gift to her and scoop up one of the cats when it walks off too far. I don't know if these things can swim, but I'm not going in that pond for either of them.

"It's *not* my birthday, Liam. You and Pri are very confused today."

We're confused? I bite back my smile because it's a dick move to laugh at her confusion, but she makes it too easy.

She looks over her shoulder and rolls her eyes at someone. When I follow her line of sight, my eyes land on Capri, who's watching us carefully.

"I know she's my best friend, but she doesn't listen very well. She keeps asking if I'm okay, and I've told her hundreds of times I'm *fine*." My mom looks at me for a response, and I glance at Capri before rolling my eyes.

"Tell me about it."

My mom covers her mouth as she laughs, and I smile down at her. Not even a minute passes before Capri makes her way over to us, and my mom sits up, but she looks guilty.

"How's it going over here?"

My mom glances at me and shakes her head, and I do the same before rolling my eyes again.

"We're *fine*, Pri. I don't need a babysitter." Her words are far from harsh but still laced with sarcasm.

"No?"

I glance up at Capri, and she raises her brows. "Liam sure does think so since he brought you here for your birthday."

My mom's head snaps over to me, and I have to turn away from her so she can't see me laugh.

I act like I'm clearing my throat before I look back over at my mom. "She doesn't know what she's talking about. It's not even your birthday." I shake my head and she agrees with a nod as she lays on her back with the cats on her stomach.

I bite back a smile as I glance up at Capri, and she laughs softly before walking off. I remind my mom to open her gift, and she doesn't tell me it isn't her birthday; she simply opens it instead.

"Is this a puzzle? I love puzzles!" She goes on about how she completed one with a thousand pieces the other day, and I'm not sure if I believe her, so I make sure to fact-check that with Pri later.

When she flips the box over, she stares at the picture the puzzle is supposed to make, and she runs her fingers along Shanti's face. "Where did you get this?"

"I had it custom-made."

She looks up at me with teary eyes, and I don't know what changed in the last few seconds, but when her tears start falling, I take the puzzle and hide it behind my back.

"I'm sorry. I didn't mean to upset you. Forget about–"

"No, I'm not upset. Here, let me have it."

I hesitate, but she urges me, so I give the puzzle back to her. I keep my eyes on her, and she keeps her gaze on the picture.

"She was so tiny."

I look down at the puzzle box, and my chest tightens at the picture of us in the hospital the day Shanti was born. I'm sitting on the bed with Mom and she has Shanti in her arms, wrapped in a white blanket. She was so tiny, Mom had to tilt her so you could see her face. I remember her being the smallest in the NICU. I refused to even hold her because she was barely bigger than my hands, and I was convinced I would crush her.

"She's getting so big, Liam."

I wipe my mom's tears, and she holds my hand on her cheek. "She's turning four soon, can you believe that?" Shanti would've been twelve this year, but I swallow the lump in my throat and smile at my mom.

"She said she wants a cat for her birthday. Do you think we're going to be able to hide these from her until then?"

My mom smiles again as she looks down at the cats. When her brows furrow, I catch myself and realize I already told her I showed them to my sister.

"She's a nosy kid." She laughs softly. "She'll find them. We can show her them and tell her it's an early gift." She nods to herself, proud of her idea, and I lean forward to plant a kiss on the top of her head.

We're in the middle of the puzzle when my phone starts ringing and I don't think of answering, but then I realize it's Sage and she must be out of the hospital.

"Give me a second, Mom."

She nods, and I walk a few feet ahead of her.

"Hello, Liam Leslie!" Sage smiles through the screen and she no longer looks like she was attacked by a beehive which is refreshing.

"Dory." I keep my eyes on her, and her smile widens, her pretty dimples popping.

"You know, I feel like you're calling me Dory because I'm calling you Liam Leslie, but jokes on you because I like the new nickname, and it's not going to make me stop calling you Liam Leslie." She holds her chin higher, and I raise my brows at her.

"Right."

She so clearly bites back as a smile.

"Well, if you enjoy being compared to a dumb blue fish–"

"She's–"

"She's not dumb, and neither are you." I finish for her, and when her face scrunches, I bite back a smile. "It *was* dumb for you to smother a cat when you're allergic to them."

"I *forgot* that I didn't have my medicine." She tries to defend herself, but she doesn't have a good case.

"Yes, Dory. *I* remember."

She burst into a laugh, and I shake my head at her. "I'll see you later tonight."

"Wait, do you still have the kittens with you?"

"Maybe."

"Can I *maybe* see them?"

I glance at the blanket and my mom still has all of them on her lap. I almost tell Sage no, but when I look back at the screen, she's watching me all hopefully with her big green eyes.

I let out a sigh and walk over to the blanket. "Let me see them for a second?"

My mom smiles up at me and gestures to her lap. I place them a few feet from her and give her my back before flipping the camera.

Sage awes at them and takes a few pictures through the call. "You're going to take them to the vet, right?"

"Sure."

"You mean yes."

"Sure."

"Liam Leslie!"

"Yes, Dory. I'll take them to the vet. Goodbye."

She makes me *promise,* and only after I do does she let me hang up. When I turn back around, my mom is watching me with a weird look.

"What?"

She shrugs and looks back down at the puzzle with a smile.

"I think you do know." I push, and she looks back up at me, her smile still present.

"Who was that?"

I tell her it was no one, but she only raises her brows at me accusingly. "I didn't know you were seeing anyone."

"I'm not." I grab the cat when it walks too close to the water again. I feel my mom watching me, but I don't look up and do the puzzle she's clearly struggling with. There's no way she did a thousand-piece puzzle.

"Is she your girlfriend?"

"No."

"But she's a friend who's a girl."

"I suppose."

"Hmm."

I look up at her, and I can't tell if she's humming at me or the puzzle since her eyes are on two pieces that clearly don't fit together.

"I suppose she's your girlfriend."

"She isn't, but you can suppose what you'd like." The cat walks off to the water again, and I scoop it up before bringing it to eye level. "I will let you *drown*," I whisper to it before planting it in my lap, and as if he understood me, he stays put.

"Do you like her?" *I like sleeping next to her.* I open my mouth but immediately close it again because even if she isn't going to remember this, I shouldn't say that. "I'll take that as a yes."

"Don't."

"Well, does Shanti like her?"

I go to tell her that they haven't met and aren't going to, but I think about her question. I think my sister would've loved Sage. She loved everyone, but Sage would've been good with her. She's kind and soft. She laughs easily, and Shanti liked making people laugh, but most of all, she's pure.

That woman could probably find the good in evil people, and her smile could make them want to be better while her tears would stop them from ever causing harm.

Sage is full of so much life, it would've been a lot to have them both in the same place. No room would've been big enough to contain the energy of the two of them, but it's a room I'd want to be in all the time if my sister was there.

I don't answer her, and she doesn't ask about Sage again as we complete the puzzle, but she's on the front of my mind the entire time, and I don't know how to feel about that.

Chapter Nineteen

SAGE

I PULL MY PHONE AWAY from my ear when I hear another call coming through, and my jaw slightly drops as Angie goes on. "Was there anything else—"

"No, that was all! Thank you, Angie! Vincent is calling. I'll call *right* back!" I hang up to answer Vincent's call. "Hey, Mr. Moore."

"Sage, how are you?"

I look around the room; although I'm alone, but I have no clue why he's calling me.

"I'm good, how are you?"

"I've been better. I'm not sure if you know, but I'm having a show at the end of next month, and there's been some hiccups."

I tell him I'm sorry to hear that before he goes on.

"I'm working on the last few pieces and tying up some loose ends with models. I had castings last week and was surprised you weren't there." His voice is accusing, and I feel like I'm in trouble, although I'm not sure why because I'm certainly not obligated to go to all of his castings, but I definitely wanted to be at the one he had last week.

"My agent was trying to get me a spot, but when she called, someone told her it was a private casting for certain models."

"Did Angelica tell them it was you calling?"

I tell him she didn't get the chance, and I can hear the mood change in his voice. Angie was also pissed when they hung up on her before she could even tell them who she was calling for.

"Thank you for telling me. I'll be sure they're dealt with."

I try to tell him it's okay to save this person, but he clearly made up his mind, and I'm sure he's going to fire them.

"Back to serious matters. Are you available the week of the twentieth to be in the show? The casting was to eliminate some girls since I had too many in mind, but I would still like you to be in it."

I don't even check my calendar, but I'll move whatever I definitely have that week for him.

"Yes, I'm free! It's in New York, right?"

He confirms and gives me the rest of the details, and when he hangs up, I literally scream.

I jump at the banging on my door and race over to check who's banging like the cops.

"Sage!"

I check the peephole before quickly opening it for Liam.

"Are you okay?" He looks around the room, and I look behind him to see who the heck was chasing him.

"Are *you* okay? Why do you look like you ran here?"

"I heard you screaming from inside the damn elevator like you were being murdered."

I laugh at his exaggeration and close the door behind him. "I'm fine."

"So you casually scream like a crazy person."

I tell him *why* I was screaming, but it doesn't look like that explains much.

"Maybe you are a crazy person."

"Liam, this is a *big* deal."

"I can see that, Dory."

"Like an actual dream come true."

I explain to him that I've been trying to impress Vincent since we were working on the photo shoot contest earlier this year. He watches me for a few seconds before closing the distance between us and planting a soft kiss on my lips. "Congrats."

I smile up at him and watch as his eyes glance down at my outfit.

"You're so pretty. Where are you going?"

"Thank you!"

He kisses my cheek.

"I'm going out for August's birthday. I didn't know you were coming over? What are you doing here?" I haven't seen him in a few days, so I'm glad he decided to stop by because I want to see pictures of the cats.

"Today's August's birthday?" He turns his head to the side as I nod with a smile. "It's your *twin's* birthday?"

"Yes." I let out a soft laugh, but he still looks confused.

"Why are you saying it like it's not also your birthday?"

"Because it's not." I walk to my room, and I hear Liam follow behind me as I explain. "I was born five minutes after twelve, so my birthday is tomorrow. August likes that he's older, although I feel like he pushed me out the way or something so he'd be born first."

I lay on the bed, and he flops beside me. "What are you doing tomorrow?" He wraps an arm around my waist before dragging me closer, his lips finding my cheek.

"My brother arranged a rooftop party downtown." I try to glance down at him, but he moves his face so he can smother my neck. "Do you want to come?"

He shakes his head softly before pulling away to look at me. "I can't, Dory." He kisses me softly. "But text me when you get home, and I'll come over to give you your gift."

I feel a smile touch my lips, and he kisses my cheek.

"What gift? You didn't know about my birthday until a minute ago."

"Obviously, I'm going to get something before tomorrow, smart ass."

I let out a laugh, and he buries his face in my neck again.

"When do you have to leave?" His voice comes out a bit muffled but I hear him just fine.

"He's going to pick me up in an hour."

He lets out a long breath, and I run a hand through his hair. He pulls my legs, so they're wrapped around him but doesn't say anything else.

"Are you okay?" I try to glance at him again, but he doesn't move.

"I'm just tired." He doesn't just sound physically tired but also drained... mentally.

"What's wrong?" I pull away more, forcing him to look at me, but he only shakes his head.

"Nothing you need to worry about." He leans forward to kiss me, but when he pulls away, he looks... sad almost.

"You can tell me, you know." I keep my gaze on him, and he buries his face in my neck again before letting out a sigh. I rub his back in circles, and he doesn't say anything for a while.

"It's just family stuff. I don't want to talk about it."

I nod in return and continue rubbing his back. "I'm here if you ever want to talk about it." I lean to kiss his hair. "You know that, right?"

He nods before pulling in a breath. "Yes, Dory." He kisses my neck before his entire body relaxes on top of me.

"Did you settle on names for the kittens?" I badgered him about keeping them when he came over the day he adopted them, and he caved *very* quickly.

He takes a minute to respond, and I think he's going to ignore me, but then he mumbles, "Periwinkle for the girl."

I feel a smile touch my lips, and I try to pull away to see if he's serious, but he forces his weight on me, and I let out a soft laugh. "You couldn't pay me to believe you came up with that on your own." I poke his side, but he doesn't move. "Who helped you name her?"

"Why does it matter?"

I let out a gasp and bite back my laugh when he sighs. "Are you naming my cats with other women?" I poke his side, and this time, he raises his head.

"No." He seems confused but also offended. He studies me for a beat as if he either wants to ask me something or confess something. I simply lay there and wait for him to make up his mind. He buries his face in my neck again and brings my legs around him. "My mom named her." His voice is just above a whisper.

"Aw, that's sweet! Okay, we can keep Periwinkle." I run a hand through his hair before hugging him tighter with my legs. "I still want to name the gray and black one Meeko."

He says, once again, that he hates that name but it's just because he hasn't seen *Pocahontas* and hasn't been graced with the presence of her raccoon.

"It'll grow on you." I tap his head. "We're keeping Meeko, and since Moon is their Godfather, it's only right we consider his request and name the third one Mars."

"I returned that one. He's a menace."

I try to sit up, but Liam forces his weight on me again, and I can't budge. "You did *what*?"

He doesn't move.

"Liam, please tell me you didn't really take him back there!" I feel my throat tightening, and he quickly sits up.

"Jesus, I was joking." He leans down and catches my lips with his. "Please don't cry. He's safe in my bed." He kisses me again, and I pull away with a smile.

"I thought you said they're too nasty to share a bed with you?"

"Well, you harassed me to sleep with them, so did I have a choice?"

I turn my head to the side as I smile up at him. "No, you didn't."

He shakes his head at me, and before he can respond, my phone is ringing.

My face lights up on the FaceTime call when I notice Helena's name. We've been mostly normal since we've been working together. It's kinda like whatever that argument was, never happened.

"Hello, babe." I tap Liam, and he rolls off me as I sit up.

She smiles at the phone before setting it up against something. "You look so beautiful! I love the birthday hair!"

"Thank you, thank you." I flip my hair over my shoulder with a smile. "What's up?"

"I'm just returning your call. You called me earlier?"

"Oh, right!" I get up from the bed and place my phone on my nightstand so she can see my outfit. "It was to help me style this dress. I couldn't decide on the shoes."

She tells me the ones I'm wearing are perfect, and I'm glad I switched them.

I study myself in the camera and run a hand down my frame. "How do you think I look?"

"Perfect."

My head turns at the sound of Liam's soft whisper, and I feel a smile touch my lips.

"You look great!"

I look back at Helena, and she watches me with a bright smile as if she really means that.

"Are you sure?" I turn to the side as I take in all of my curves. "You know I've been trying to lose weight, but I feel like it's not working." I've been following her meal plan to the T, but haven't lost any weight. I'm just hungry, which is annoying.

"Why are you trying to lose weight?"

When I look back over at Liam he's sitting up now as he watches me.

"Maybe it's your birth control." Helena pulls my attention before I can respond. "Remember when I was putting on weight with my old one?"

"Sage."

I don't turn back to Liam and grab my phone instead. "I didn't even think about that."

"Sage Loana," Liam voices again, and I can hear his short patience slipping, but he doesn't sound annoyed or angry.

I thank Helena with a smile before hanging up and turning to Liam. "Yes?"

"Why are you trying to lose weight?"

I shrug in response before sitting on the bed, but I feel him watching me.

"I think you do know why. Don't lie to me."

"I'm not lying…" I steal a glance at him, and he's watching me, but I turn forward again. "I just gained weight and want to lose it." I sort of shrug, and when Liam doesn't say anything, I turn to him.

"Who told you that you gained weight?"

"I did." And my best friend… and the mean comments under my post.

"When was the last time you even weighed yourself?"

I try to think, but I can't remember that far back.

"Exactly."

"Okay, you know I have a bad memory, but even my followers noticed."

"What are you talking about?"

I let out a sigh and open Famoura. When I click on my last post, I open the comments and hand the phone to

Liam before I even look at them. He sits in silence for a few
seconds, and I try not to look at him.

"You look hot in these pictures. *I* took these of you."

A smile creeps onto my face, and I turn to look at him.

"Fuck what everyone else thinks." He says it like it's so...
simple.

"Easy for you to say." I stand from the bed, but he grabs a
hold of my hand.

"What's that supposed to mean?"

"Only that you're unbelievably fit and don't post on social
media, so you don't have hundreds of hate comments body
shaming you. Of course, you don't care what people think
about you, but I get told things like that daily."

I let out a breath and a sense of relief washes over me
after getting that off of my chest. I posted that picture of me
in the prettiest dress a few days ago, and I've been fighting
back tears and resisting the urge to delete the entire post.

Of course, I got a lot of love on the post and my supporters are thankfully defending me, but I still see the bad
comments and it's becoming exhausting.

I keep my eyes down as Liam stands from the bed and
wraps his arms around my head. My arms immediately go
around him, and his hug alone somehow makes me feel
better.

"You're the most beautiful person I've met, beloved."

I pull away to look at him, but my vision blurs. "Really?"

"Don't cry."

I blink my tears away, and he leans in, planting two soft
kisses on my cheek.

"I'm sure you've met thousands of people as a professional baseball player. You-"

"And none of them are even a fraction of perfect as you."

I can't stop my tears from spilling any more. Liam cups
my face softly and wipes my tears with a sigh. "You're ruining your pretty makeup."

I laugh softly as I dab my face, but I know I'm going to
have to touch up my makeup. We settle onto my bed again,
and he pulls me into his embrace. "In how long do you have
to leave?"

I smile at his words before glancing down at my watch. "It's been... less than ten minutes since you last asked so-"

He pokes my side before telling me not to get smart with him. I try to squirm away, but he keeps me in place before hugging me again. I think he's going to start taking my clothes off, but he just lies there hugging me. I'm not complaining, not one bit, actually, since he seems like he needs a hug, but he doesn't normally show up without notice, and my heart hurts because it's clear something is bothering him. Not because he doesn't want to have sex with me. We can just hang out, but... something feels wrong.

I rest my face on top of his head before hugging him closer. "Can you please tell me what's up with you?" I whisper.

"It's nothing, Dory-"

"It's something, Lee." I rub his back and try to get up to pull away, but he doesn't move. "You seem sad; just tell me."

"I'm not sad, beloved. I'm just tired."

"Okay... well, you look mentally tired." I try not to worry, but growing up with a sister who battled depression her whole life, I'm a little worried.

He lets out a breath before kissing my neck. "I'm fine."

"Promise?"

He starts to nod, but I force him up. When his eyes meet mine he really does look tired. "I promise. It's not a big deal-"

"So it *is* something?"

He lets out a breath before rolling off of me.

"Wait, no. Come back. I'm sorry for badgering you." I try to pull him on top of me again, but he doesn't let me and sits with his back against the headboard.

"I need to go anyway-"

"Please stop." I grab him before he can stand and I crawl over to him. I straddle him instead, and he looks off to the side. "We don't have to talk if you don't want to. We can lay down if you're just tired."

His eyes meet mine, but I pull him to lie with me before he can voice a complaint. He feels tense at first, but I wrap my legs around him again, and as his arms come around me, he relaxes again.

I'm rubbing my hand down his back when I feel him kiss my neck.

"I just came from seeing my mom." His voice is just above a whisper, but he sounds numb again, so I lean forward to plant a soft kiss on his head.

"Is she okay?" I tread lightly and rub a hand down his shirt when I feel him tense.

"She's sick, Dory..." He holds me tighter.

"Is it like... terminal? Because I know amazing doctors, and we can-"

"There's no cure, baby."

I can barely hear his voice now, and I try to pull away, but he keeps his face in the crease of my neck.

He pulls in another deep breath before kissing my neck again. "I just need a break, Dory. She wasn't having a good day, and I'm going to go back later, but I *just* need a break."

"Okay. Just rest so you can reset." I kiss the top of his head again, and when I lay back down, I feel him relax again. We lay in silence for about an hour until my phone is ringing.

"That's my brother..."

Liam doesn't move, and I kiss the top of his head. As much as I don't want to leave him, I can't miss my twin's birthday...

"I need to go, babe, but you can stay and sleep if you want?"

He tells me he needs to go back to his mom, so he gets up. Before he stands from my bed, I cup his face and plant a soft kiss on his lips. "Thank you for opening up to me." I steal another kiss before hugging him, and his arms immediately come around me. "If it gets hard and you need more breaks, you can always come to me."

He only squeezes me tighter before we get up without a word.

I fix my makeup and grab August's gift, along with my spend-the-night bag since we're having a sleepover. When we get to the lobby, I stop when I realize Liam stopped following me.

He has his eyes on August's bright orange Lamborghini before looking over at me.

"What?"

"Nothing, go ahead, Dory. Call me tomorrow night." He doesn't make a move to hug or kiss me goodbye, but I tell him I'll call him before walking out and climbing into August's car.

"Hello, birthday boy!"

"Hello, almost birthday girl!"

I let out a soft laugh and lean over to hug him. Everyone else is already at the bowling place August wanted to go to, so we're the last two left.

When we walk in, it's clear Hazel rented the place out since it's just our friends. August *loves* balloons, and it's clear his girlfriend remembered that because every square inch is covered with huge balloon arcs.

The minute we walk in, they all yell in surprise, and I step aside so he can have his moment to shine since today is technically his, but like always, he grabs my hand, and we walk over to everyone together.

After saying hi to everyone, we start bowling, and it ends up being a competition between Sire and Vidia because they're insanely competitive.

"This reminds me of their first date," August whispers to Hazel and me, as we watch Sire and Vidia tease each other a few feet ahead of us. When Sire gets a strike, Vidia goes on about how he's cheating, and we break into a laugh before quickly hiding our faces when they turn to us. They still bicker like a married couple, but now it's just funny because it's clear half of it is just to piss the other off.

After a few games and about an hour at the arcade, we head to August's place and play a few games they set up. I hear a sizzling sound going off, and when I turn, August is walking in with a cake and sparkly candle, and I realize it must be twelve.

I rise from my seat as they sing Happy Birthday to me, and when the candle goes out, there's still one left for me to blow out, so I do and silently make my wish.

"Thank you, guys!" I hug them all, and my phone starts blowing up with calls and birthday wishes.

After a few minutes, I'm still getting messages and smile down at one in particular.

Liam Leslie

Happy birthday, Dory baby.

12:05 am

I heart his message, and a second later a few pictures of the kittens in birthday hats flood my phone.

I laugh quietly to myself as I heart all of the messages before thanking him.

Chapter Twenty

LIAM

"HOW OFTEN DO YOU GO out with her?" I keep my eyes on my mom as she brushes her hair.

"I try to take her out once or twice a week. She's a lot better outdoors." Capri sounds like that shocks her, but it makes me feel better about going out with my mom. I'm dragging Capri with us since this is the first time I'm stepping out of this house with her, but I'm trying to be positive, as Capri said I should be.

"Are you two ready?" My mom turns to us as if we're not waiting for *her*.

I smile down at her sassy ass before taking her hand. "Yes, Mom, come on."

We walk out to my car, and when I open the back seat for her so she can sit with Capri, she walks right past me and opens the driver's side.

"Yeah, no." I shut the door before kissing her head. "You wouldn't drive my car if it was your dying wish, Mom." I open the backseat door again as Capri breaks into a laugh.

"It's cute that you call your father's car *yours*, but you don't have your license, and he'll be very upset if you drive his car. Get in the back seat, Liam, and put your seatbelt on." She opens the driver's side door, and *again*, I close it.

"I do have my license and—"

"You do *not* have your license, Liam. In the back seat, or you can stay."

I can *stay*? She doesn't even know where we're fucking going.

Before I can voice another protest, Capri steps forward. "Here, why don't I drive and—"

"Fuck no."

"Excuse me?" My mom crosses her arms and sends me a stern look. "You're lucky I'm tired. Pri can drive."

I open my mouth to say she isn't driving my goddamn car, but my mom holds a finger up.

"Another word, and you'll stay. In the car. We have things to do." She climbs in the back seat, and I look over at Pri, who's smiling too damn happily.

"I've never driven a Rolls-Royce." She holds her hands out for my keys but I don't hand them over.

"And you're not going to."

She rolls her eyes before getting in the back seat and convincing my mom that I know how to drive. My mom is a backseat driver the entire time, and it reminds me of when she taught me how to drive, so I don't complain as we head to the mall.

After looking at a few stores, I'm still not sure what to get Sage for her birthday. I think of what she said about how things you can use make better gifts, but the woman is richer than me and has *everything*. I think of getting her makeup, but she has people who do her makeup, and I wouldn't even know what she uses.

I turn to my mom. "What makes a good birthday gift for a girl?"

A smile reaches her lips as she steals a glance at me. "Is this for your friend who's a girl but not your girlfriend?"

I falter for a beat before looking over at Capri. I didn't think she'd remember that. Capri doesn't answer my silent question, and my mom goes on.

"If you're confident you know her style well enough, maybe a cute bag will do."

I nod in thought as we keep walking.

"So you *do* like her?" It's clear she's teasing, and the smile I was fighting breaks through.

"Yeah, I like her, Mom." I shake my head at her when she smiles way to big.

When Sage kept asking if I was okay yesterday, I didn't want to ruin her day with my shitty problems. But then she looked at me like she was *so* concerned. These last couple of years, I haven't had anyone worry about me, but seeing the worry in Sage's eyes, I couldn't stop the words from pouring out of my mouth.

I didn't think it'd be that easy to talk to her. She just held me and *just* listened, and I felt good after talking to her. Capri always badgers me and tells me I shouldn't keep shit bottled up, but I didn't realize how good it felt to talk about it until I was in Sage's arms.

Chapter Twenty-One

SAGE

"**A**RE YOU NERVOUS?" MEL LOOKS at me through the mirror as I get my makeup done.

"No." I try to convince myself, and when I see Mel's face, I know I don't sound at all convincing. "Yes? Oh my God."

She laughs softly, and I join her, but even my laugh sounds nervous.

All month, I've been prepping for Vincent's show tonight. I've been nervous since he first called me, but today's the day, and I can't believe a whole month passed so quickly, but I'm ready. Or as ready as I'll ever be.

"I'm *so* proud of you, Sage." She smiles at me with such admiration, and I force myself not to cry because we're only halfway done with my makeup. "I remember when I first followed you on social media, before you were even a Magic Model, you talked about wanting to be a Moore Girl, and the fact that this is the *second* runway show he's invited you to?"

I feel my smile widen as she goes on. "He obviously loves you, and you're going to kill it tonight."

"No, literally." Cara pauses on my makeup, and when I look over at her, she also looks so proud.

"Thank you guys!" I pull Cara in for a hug before she continues.

I didn't count the first runway show I did for Vincent since it was through the agency, and he asked for every Magic Model. Then, when he invited me to his party, I brushed it off as him thanking me for modeling extra pieces at his show, but *now?*

Now, he's having a runway show in New York on the biggest stage in the state, and I've modeled here before, but I haven't walked this stage for *him* and I'm losing my mind.

We get back to my makeup and by the time I'm done, Helena is walking in with a coffee for me. "Why isn't your hair done?" Helena stares at me like I grew another head, and I can't help but laugh at her.

"I'm literally about to get it done, Annet is in the bathroom."

She nods before handing me my coffee.

"Move over." She literally bumps Mel out of her way with her hip, and my eyes widen at her in warning. "What?" She rolls her eyes at me in the mirror.

"That was *rude*, don't push."

She only rolls her eyes at me again, and when I glance at Mel, she pulls in a deep breath. I see her fist ball, but she thankfully walks away.

I was allowed to bring two friends with me, and the rest of The Core Eight couldn't make it, so I, of course, invited my best friend and Mel since we've been getting closer. Helena was annoyed that she was here but has been cordial for the most part. I don't understand why she doesn't like her, but she needs to stop being mean because Mel looks close to calling her out.

I paint a smile on my face and try to lighten the mood. "Are you sure I shouldn't have gone with the second hairstyle?"

Vincent surprisingly let me choose between two hairstyles since I was modeling two outfits and he couldn't decide so I of course had my best friend help me pick.

I am glad that Vincent let them tag along and also let me bring my own team to do my hair and makeup though, because knowing that *this* won't go wrong is what's getting me through most of my nerves.

"No, the style I chose is going to look way better with your second dress, trust me."

I nod in response, but I notice Mel turning her head to the side in the mirror.

"I still think the second one matches both dresses perfectly and—"

"She asked me." Helena cuts her off and Mel only laughs to herself before walking out of the room.

I let out a breath and turn in my seat. "Lena, can you stop being so mean to her?"

"What did I say? Did you not ask me?"

"I asked the two of you." I give her a pointed look, but she only shrugs before sitting on the couch.

When Annet comes out of the bathroom, she immediately gets to work and I decide on the style Helena chose, but send Mel a quick message.

> Babe, I am so sorry that she's being like that. I don't know what her problem is.

Mel Mel

> Don't apologize for her, Sage. It's fine, I just needed a second to breathe because I really don't want to ruin your big day and I'm going to punch her in the face the next time she says something to me.

I try to calm her down as I get my hair done.

After a while, we're done with time to spare, so everyone leaves as I get dressed. I try not to think about the show and listen to music to calm my nerves, but a guy comes to take me to the rest of the girls, and I realize this is it. I take a deep breath before standing from my vanity, but my vision blurs with stars as my blood runs warm, and I have to hold onto the desk to steady myself.

"Are you okay?" He's suddenly in front of me, and he grabs my arm to catch me.

I blink a few times as I stumble a bit. "Yeah." My vision clears, but I sit back down. "I'm fine." I try to get up again, and I feel weak but better.

"Do you want some water?"

I tell him I have a bottle, but he keeps his eyes on me. "Did you eat today? We have sandwiches for the models, we know some girls forget to eat with how busy these days get."

I have been busy today but I didn't *forget* to eat, if any-thing I've made sure not to. This event is way too important for me to look bloated, as Helena said, so eating was *not* an option. I'm fine. I've been drinking water and coffee. I'm fine.

"No, that's okay. I'm not hungry, but thank you."

"I wasn't asking," he says apologetically. "You looked like you were going to pass out, and it's Mr. Moore's rule that you have a meal before going on stage."

I try to tell him that I really am okay, but when he tells me I can take it up with Vincent, I shut up and walk to the kitchen with him.

He has me take a seat at the table as he gets me a Gatorade and a sandwich *with* fruit. I stare at all of the food, and I feel a knot forming in my throat, but I force it down because I cannot ruin my makeup over something this stupid.

I take in a deep breath and tell myself that I can at least eat the fruit. Compromising with eating one thing helps, so I chose the fruit and finished the whole cup.

I smile to myself proudly and get up to put the sandwich back.

"You have to eat the sandwich, Ms. Loana." He sounds like he honestly doesn't want to bother me and I know he's only trying to help and these are the rules for whatever reason but I really wish he'd walk away.

"If you pass out on stage and Mr. Moore finds out I saw you *almost* pass out before going out and I didn't have you eat, I'd lose my job."

I nod regrettably before looking back at my plate, and I feel the back of my eyes stinging.

"If you'd like something else, I can–"

"No, this is okay." I keep my eyes away from him as I sit back down. I close my eyes as I take a bite, and I don't want to, but I force myself to swallow it. He stays in the kitchen as he also eats, but I sense him watching me. I'm not sure if he's still just doing his job, but it feels like judging, and I want to crawl out of my skin.

I force myself to finish the dumb sandwich and rush out of the kitchen. I smile when I pass a few girls as I look for the bathroom. The minute I'm inside, a single tear falls.

"Stop it, Sage," I whisper to myself and force myself to get it together. I tilt my head down so my tears don't touch my face as they fall. When I look back in the mirror my makeup is, thankfully, still close to perfect.

Without another thought, I walk into one of the stalls and make myself throw up. That sandwich was like a footlong, and I honestly feel too full, so it's fine that I do this. I can't go on stage and throw up out there, that'll be a nightmare so I just get rid of what's in my stomach now...

I was *not* about to pass out. I get a little dizzy when I stand up too fast all the time, and I've always been fine. That guy just takes his job too seriously because I'm fine and—

"Are you okay, babe?"

I freeze at the knock on my stall. *I didn't lock the door.*

I flush the toilet as I tell her I'm fine because I *am*. I wait there for a few seconds, but she doesn't walk away, so I get this over with and walk out. When I open the stall I realize it's Allie, one of Vincent's models.

"Sorry about that." I give her a small smile and rush off to the sink.

"Is it the nerves?" She comes behind me in the mirror with a smile. "I used to get so sick before big shows like this, but you'll be great."

I thank her and leave before she can study me any longer and figure anything out.

When I start talking to a few of the other girls, I surprisingly feel way better, and I think it's their essence. All of the models here are Moore Girls, and something about them just... shines. I don't know how to explain it, but there is something different about Vincent's models.

"Let's take a group pic before we go on stage!" They all circle up, and I smile when some of them swap to be on their good side. They seem like such a family in terms of how they operate. It's like this with my girls, too, especially The Core Eight, and I'm not sure why, but I was expecting it to be different here, more formal, I guess.

"Sage, come on!"

My face hurts a bit with how big I smile, but I join in their picture, and when I look at all of us in the mirror, I realize, tonight, I'm one of them. I'm a model for Vincent freaking

Moore. This has literally been the dream since I had my first casting at nineteen, and I know he hasn't given me a contract or anything, but it feels surreal.

The opening music starts, and we all move around to make room for the first few models. They each go out one after the other, and when it's my turn, all of my nerves evaporate as I walk across the stage.

I keep my face stone cold as I focus on one point in the back of the room. A few people have their cameras out, but there isn't much flash and there also isn't a lot of cheering like our shows. At Moore events, everyone usually saves their cheering for the end as they clap here and there through the show and I don't know why, but it makes the events seem classier.

I make it backstage, and my eyes land on a girl who is frantically trying to fix her hairpiece.

"Can you help me with this?"

I rush to her and try to untangle her headpiece from her curls.

"Ugh! I hate when we have to change our hair between looks!"

I see her getting nervous, and I try to calm her down.

"You're okay." I gently pull one last curl. "There." I set the headpiece down and she lets out a breath of relief.

"Thanks, Sage."

I feel my brows furrow because I had no clue she knew my name, but I smile anyway. "Yeah, no problem, Jess."

She turns on her heels just as her hairstylist walks in. I walk over to my vanity, and I have to change into my next outfit, but just as I go to do so, I see a girl in tears.

"We have a problem." When I see *my* dress in her hand I think I forget how to breathe.

"What's wrong?"

She looks down at the dress I have to put on in a few minutes and just shakes her head.

"What—"

"Someone—" She burst into tears, and my eyes widen. Jess walks over in a hurry and snatches the dress from her. When she holds it up, I swear I could *die*. Everyone loses their mind, and shit hits the damn fan. I suddenly feel lightheaded, and I'm not sure if I say it out loud, but someone brings me water.

"Why is there a hole in her fucking dress?!" They hold the dress up again, and I look away from the opening because I have to wear *that,* and it looks like a freaking mess.

I go on stage soon!

Someone asks if she can just try to fix it, but she's crying and saying it won't work. One of my girls tells me to put it on, and I couldn't pull this off even if I tried because it's way too obvious that this slit on the side is not on purpose. It looks like I didn't fit in it and tore it.

"Dammit." Annet shakes her head at me. "This could've been covered if I did the second hairstyle on you." She sounds so upset, but this is definitely not her fault. She talks about trying to change my hair so it can hang down and cover this mess, but there's no time.

"This was perfect the last time she tried it on! What did you do?!" Everyone is yelling at the girl who brought my dress in, and she says she thinks someone cut it.

"What?" I shake my head, and everyone glances around the room.

Jess looks pissed as she turns to someone with a headset. "Check the cameras and find out who the hell sabotaged Sage's dress."

The girl rushes off, and I realize why Jess is Vincent's main model.

We ask her again if she can just sew it back together, but she tells us that there'll be a patch of diamonds missing, and I know she doesn't have time to put each bead back one by one because my music is starting.

"I need to go on stage," I finally say something, and everyone turns to me.

"What?!"

"You can't!"

"Sage, you—"

"I need to."

They tell me I can't, but all I can hear is the song playing, and I should be walking out right now. I glance around the room and grab a jacket. When I slip it on, I think everyone's soul leaves their body.

"You can't add something to Mr. Moore's look."

"He might kill you if you change the look."

"This jacket was already worn."

"Stop!"

Everyone goes silent, and I feel bad for yelling, but I can't hear my thoughts. "This was worn by one of the guys who walked one of the girls out, everyone was looking at her. They won't notice."

"Vincent Moore will."

Yeah, well, I think it'll be more noticeable if I don't go out there right this second.

I turn to the mirror. "Does it look good?"

Nothing.

"Yes or–"

"Yes," Jess agrees, and I walk out just as the beat drops. I should be at the end of the stage posing right now, and smoke appears at the spot I should be standing, but as if it was meant to go this way, everyone cheers as I walk down the stage.

I go off script since I'm already a few counts late. I stop in the middle of the stage and turn to the left. Some people are recording, and I give them a show before turning to the right and breaking the stone face I had the entire show, the glare everyone had. I smile.

I smile the rest of the show, and when people look shocked, I remember Vincent Moore's models don't smile, but it's too late, so I work it. If Mr. Moore is going to kill me, I may as well go out with a smile literally on my face.

After giving the middle of the audience my attention, I continue down the stage. When I make it to the end, I don't even glance at the man who might kill me, and my smile doesn't falter.

I pose at the end, and when I glance down at the sleeve of my jacket, I notice the model who wore it earlier didn't pull off the top layer. I pull the sleeve and the jacket is a completely different color. Everyone claps as I drop the top jacket at my feet.

I walk back down the stage, and instead of stopping in the middle, I continue, but I turn right before I leave, pose once, and disappear.

I don't only hear applause as I head backstage but cheering too, which is weird since it's not the end of the show yet. The last few girls go out, and a few minutes later, they're calling the designer on stage.

Everyone is mumbling things, and the room feels thicker as I change behind my curtain. Angie and Florence find me, and I guess someone told them what happened because they start reassuring me that it's going to be okay, but I don't think it will be.

It was a dream come true to model for Vincent not once but twice. I doubt he'll be giving me a chance like this again after what just happened, and it wasn't even my fault. I shake my head to myself as I slip my after-party dress on although I am *so* drained, I'll be going to my hotel room the minute Vincent is done yelling at me. I sit backstage as he thanks everyone and as he says goodbye I close my eyes.

"Where's Ms. Hale!"

I take a deep breath and tell myself to wait until I'm alone before I cry, but I don't think I'll be able to. When I open my eyes, I see Mr. Moore behind me in the mirror.

"What the *hell* was that?"

"She had—"

He puts a hand up and cuts Angie off. I expect her to yell at him, but she doesn't. No one says anything to help me, but I can't blame them. I take a deep breath and turn to him.

"There was a problem with the last outfit."

He says nothing.

"There was a tear on the side. It was my idea to add the jacket, and I take full responsibility for changing the look."

Nothing at all.

I blink away the stinging in my eyes as I go on. "I was already a few counts late when I went on stage, so I went off script. I'm sorry, but I figured the show needed to go on and—" I decide to just shut up.

He watches me carefully and I have no idea what he's thinking. "You decided to go over my head and break my one rule." He looks around the room "What's my one rule?"

"Don't change the look," all of the models say in sync.

"And you did."

I feel my throat tightening, and I look down at my feet.

"And they loved you."

My head snaps back up to him. "What?"

He lets out a scoff, but he doesn't look mad... he looks happy, and I'm so confused.

"You changed the look. You smiled at a Moore show, and they gave you a standing ovation in the middle of the show." He shakes his head and *smiles.*

I look around the room, unsure if this is one of those crazy smiles people give before killing someone.

"You broke every rule in the book, but you're Sage Loana. You're a Hale, so you may as well have rewritten them." He points at me. "*This* is what I like to see." He looks around the room and claps.

I didn't notice his team in here, but they clap with him.

"Any other model wouldn't have gone out there at all and certainly wouldn't have changed my look, but you took charge and owned the show." He takes my hand. "Model for me."

I blink once, twice, and he's still standing there.

"What?!"

Florence laughs and pulls my hand away from him. "Don't get ahead of yourself. She's a Magic Model, not a Moore Girl." She looks between the two of us. "She's *mine*." She looks ready to fight to the death for me, and I glance at Angie for help.

"You can be both."

I look at Mr. Moore so fast that I suddenly feel dizzy. "I don't let my girls work with other companies. If you're a Moore Girl, that's all you are because that's all you need, but if you don't want to pull your contract with Magic, I don't care. As long as you also walk for me."

What?!

Angie tells him I'll think about it, and he tells me to *take all the time I need.*

"Did I just get offered to be a Moore Girl?" I mumble to Angie and she starts making phone calls as Florence tries to get her off the phone, but I stay stuck in place.

Before anyone can say anything else, Jess is storming in with a crowd beside her. "We know who sabotaged Loana's dress."

I feel myself smiling at the way she calls me Loana as if we're besties, but then she moves to the side and glares at the girl beside her.

"Lena?"

Helena looks around the room like she was accused of murder, and I shake my head at Jess.

"This has to be a mistake, she–"

"We saw the footage. Go ahead and tell her your reasoning."

Helena doesn't move to defend herself, and I feel a lump in my throat.

Jess rolls her eyes before turning to Vincent and Florence. "She said she 'did it for Sage' and knew she'd get more publicity if she had an outfit malfunction which sounds like bullshit to me and–"

"Thank you, Jessica." Vincent cuts her off, and she quickly closes her mouth. He gives Helena a once over before turning to a very angry Florence. "She's one of your girls, so I'll let you handle her, but my lawyers will be in contact."

I don't move an inch as my vision starts to blur with tears.

"Get her off of the property," Vincent calls out before walking off, and his team follows. The minute he's gone, everyone is literally screaming.

I feel like my heart is going a thousand miles per hour and I turn to tell someone that I need a cup of water, but when they hand it to me, I completely miss it and it falls before I collapse beside it.

Chapter Twenty-Two

SAGE

"**Y**OU DO *NOT* NEED TO fly to New York, Sire. I'm fine."

He doesn't look at all convinced, but I put on a bigger smile for him. Angie, of course, called my brothers when I passed out earlier, and now they're on their way to the freaking airport.

"Stop saying you're fine, Sage!" August yells as he leans into the camera, and I don't laugh because it'll upset them, but really, they're being dramatic. I was overstimulated with the wardrobe malfunction– or sabotage... Then, being offered to be a Moore girl. I think I was going to pass out the minute Vincent gave me the offer, but when I saw Helena's face...

My stomach starts to turn all over again, and on top of all of that, I didn't eat all day, but I'm eating a whole bowl of cereal as we speak.

"Can you guys please turn around? I'll be home tomorrow. There's no point in coming to see me when you can see right now that I'm *fine*." I watch Sire look to the side, and I can't see what look August gives him, but when he turns back to me, I know I won.

"Fine, but we're picking you up at the airport tomorrow and I'm having your agent check on you throughout the night."

"What? Sire, I'm not a baby. I don't need to be checked on every few hours in the middle of the night. You–"

"Okay, so we'll see you in six hours." He reaches for the phone to hang up, but I quickly agree with his ridiculous terms.

August takes the phone next and at the soft look on his face, I know what he's going to say. "How are you feeling... you know, about your best friend being an absolute hater."

I pull in a deep breath before putting my bowl aside and slouching in the bed. "I don't even know what to think... I would've never done that to her, you know?"

August nods in understanding and offers me a small smile. "I know this isn't going to make you feel better, but Hazel said she's going to beat her ass on sight, so good luck with that."

"Oh my God." I cover my hands in my face, and when Sire says that Lisette said the same thing, I let out an exaggerated breath. They're both extremely aggressive, and I know what Helena did was messed up, but Lisette will actually beat her up every single time she sees her.... Like for years.

"How's Vidia doing?" I change the subject, and when August glances over at Sire, I know it isn't good. V's house recently got broken into, and it sounded *so* freaking scary. I went to visit her, but she was napping in Sire's bed, and she looked exhausted, so I didn't even wake her.

I hear Sire let out a sigh, and my heart hurts for them. "She's going to be okay."

I nod in response before Sire goes on.

"I didn't want to leave her alone, so I'm actually glad you're okay, but we're seriously picking you up when you land, and your agent–"

"Okay, Sire! I love you guys. Tell V I love her, and I'll pass by to check on her again." I hang up on him, and he immediately texts me, telling me not to hang up on him, but I only love the message.

A minute barely passes before Killian calls me and my friends were so right, he had a crush on me and he asked me out last night to get dinner after today's show.

Since he's a good friend of Vincent's, he's in New York this week, and we've been hanging out every day. It's been fun having someone outside of work to hang out with, and Killian is great company.

"Hello, love."

I smile to myself as I sit up in bed.

"Hey, Killian."

"I just got off the phone with Vin. He's obsessed with you."

My eyes widen as I put the volume up on my phone. "He was talking about me? What'd he say? Wait, did he bring me up first? Tell me *exactly* what he said!"

His laugh fills my ears before he spills the tea. "I just called him to see how the show went since I couldn't be there, and he immediately told me about what happened with you and how he admires that you even went on stage, which, may I add, is hard to believe since Vin can be very intimidating with his models. I'm surprised you had the balls to go on that stage with a ruined dress and a jacket he didn't approve of, *with* a smile on your face."

I laugh at how shocked he sounds, but now that I think about it... I can't believe I did that either. All of the girls were trying to get me to not go on stage, but I didn't consider that an option either.

We naturally keep talking about the show, and I'm glad he doesn't bring up Helena. He confirms our dinner date and I touch up my makeup after looking at the restaurant's menu.

When I go a day or two without eating, I just make sure to take a day to stuff myself so it cancels out, and it works for me. I know I passed out, but I was only out for maybe a minute. It was not a big deal.

I decide on what I think I'm going to eat when I get a text and I let out a laugh at his contact name.

Leslie

> Which Hilton are you staying at?

I reply, but before I can put my phone down, Liam replies.

> Omw.

> What? You're in NYC??

> Yes. I live here.

I almost ask a follow-up question, but remember he plays for the Yankees, and it makes a lot of sense for him to live here. I let him know what room I'm in, and by the time I pick out an outfit and finish getting dressed, I hear a knock on my door.

"Hey, Lee."

"Dory."

I feel myself smiling before pulling him in for a hug, but then my eyes land on who's behind him.

"Moon!" I move Liam aside and pull Moon in for a hug.

"Don't push me like that," Liam grumbles from behind me, and I bite my tongue so as not to laugh at how offended he sounds.

Moon's arms go around my waist as his laugh fills the hall. When we pull away, I notice Jordan behind him.

"Hey, Sunshine."

I smile up at him before pulling him in for a hug. "You guys can come in or—"

"They're not staying."

I turn to Liam who's standing in the doorway of my hotel room. "Moon just wanted to see you, and Jordan is his cheerleader." He keeps his gaze on them, and from the looks of it, he doesn't seem to like either of them very much, but they also seem like good friends? I'm not sure.

"I'm not his cheerleader. I also wanted to see your girl."

That gets my attention, and when I turn to Jordan, he's smiling at Moon.

I turn back to Liam, but he's still watching them. "She's no one's *girl*. You saw her. Leave." He grabs a hold of my hand, but before he can pull me into the room, Moon grabs a hold of my other hand.

"Wait! How did your show go today? You're on my entire feed, and people are going nuts about you and some girl who *sabotaged* your dress?!"

I let out a breath, and I can't believe that information got out so fast, but before I can respond, he goes on.

"I would've been able to see you in person if *someone* let me go with them." He points his words at Liam.

"You were at the Moore fashion show today?"

He only nods like it means nothing.

"Why'd you go?"

"To see his girlfri–"

"Shut up." He cuts Jordan off before he can tease him again, and then his eyes fall to mine. "The past month, you wouldn't stop talking about modeling in that show." He shrugs. "I went to see what the hype was about." He still talks like it was literally not a big deal, and maybe it's because he's not into modeling or fashion.

"Do you know what designer you went to see?"

He shrugs again.

"You spent God knows how much for a runway show of a designer you *don't* know?" I shake my head. "You have to buy tickets for his shows months in advance, how did you even get one?"

"I bought it off of someone."

"You–" My jaw slightly drops because I have no idea who in this world, in their right mind, would sell a Vincent Moore show ticket unless it was for– like half a million freaking dollars. "How much did you get it for?"

"Can't remember."

"Wasn't it a mil?" Jordan speaks up from the side, and my jaw drops.

"Why would you even *do* that?!"

Liam lets out a sigh and pushes off the wall like he's bored of the conversation. "I already told you; I wanted to see if it was worth all the hype you were making it out to be."

"Well, was it worth a *million* dollars?"

He watches me for a few seconds before nodding.

"Yeah, you looked pretty on stage." *What? He could've seen me on stage on freaking TV?!*

"You–" I literally cannot form words. I know baseball players make bank because my brothers blow through their checks like air, but a million on a fashion show Liam clearly doesn't even care about?

I study him for a few seconds, but he only watches me like this genuinely was not a big deal to him.

"Okay?" I shake my head of my thoughts and turn back to Moon and Jordan. "Are you guys sure you don't want to come–"

"They don't." Liam takes my hand again as he tries to pull me inside.

"Bye, guys!" I wave to them both as I walk backward.

"You were great today, Sunshine!"

"I'll talk to you later, Sunshine!"

"No, you won't." Liam shuts the door before they can even respond, and I hear both of them laughing on the other side. He rolls his eyes at the sound of their laughs, and when he looks over at me, his face seems to soften.

"You looked perfect on that stage." He steps towards me and cups my face before leaning in to kiss me. "I'm so proud of you." His lips are on mine again before I can respond, and I feel myself smiling against him.

His arms come around my waist as he pulls away, and I smile at him. "Thank you." I tippy-toe to give him another quick kiss, but he immediately deepens it and when his hands slip under my shirt, I pull him closer.

My hands roam down his stomach, and when I feel him through his pants, I smile against his lips.

"Did you miss me?" I tease, and he leans into my neck before humming in response. "We've barely been kissing, and you're like this?" I run my hand down his length, and he takes a step forward.

"It's only been a few days, but you must've *really* missed me."

When he goes still, I know he realizes I'm quoting him. He pulls away with a deep laugh and I stop moving as I smile at the sound he makes. His smile transforms his entire face when he laughs, his eyes are softer, and I don't know what happens inside of me, but his laugh triggers mine.

He smiles down at me, and I only admire him. *He's so pretty.* His *smile* is so pretty, and if me mocking him will make him laugh more, then I'll do it for the rest of my days. I don't mention how he should smile more since the last time I did, he wiped his smile clean. Instead, I simply kiss him before pulling away and saying, "You should take off my clothes." I take a step away from him, and his smile widens.

"I'm not going to be nice about it if you make me do it, and I remember you saying you like that shirt."

I glance down at my top, and he's right, so I take it off myself before he can rip it along with the rest of my clothes.

I stay in my underwear and bra, and Liam watches me like he's ready to *feast*.

"You can rip these." I shrug, and he starts stalking towards me, but I back away slowly. A playful look covers his face, and when my legs hit the end of the bed, he works his belt off.

He keeps his eyes on mine as he strips, and my heart races in anticipation. When he's completely bare, I try my hardest to keep my eyes on his face. His smile morphs into a smirk as his eyes cast down my body.

"You can look, you know."

I don't, and he laughs *at* me.

"Shut up."

He closes the distance between us and turns me around before leaning into my neck. "Watch that pretty mouth." He bends me over the bed, and I peek over my shoulder as he rips my underwear off.

"Oh, now you wanna see?"

My eyes travel up to his before I nod softly. He surprisingly doesn't tease me about it and only slips his condom on. When he slides into me, a loud moan slips past my lips. I watch him carefully as he loses control. His head falls back with every sound under the sun, and I love how vocal he is when he's in me like this.

"Hmm fuck."

I moan in response as he picks up the pace, and my back arches towards him. When his eyes meet mine, he immediately comes down on me. His lips are on mine, and when he grunts into my mouth, I return it.

"I *really* missed you." He kisses me harder before pulling away to lean into my neck.

"Like how much?"

A hand comes between my legs, and when he starts rubbing the right places, I melt into him.

"A lot."

I bite down on my lip as he moves harder against me.

"I was thinking about you a lot too." He kisses my neck softly. "Like at my game yesterday."

He leaves a trail of kisses to my ear. "And this morning... in the shower."

I bite down harder with every stroke he gives me.

"I thought of you on your knees for me."

"Mhm."

"And I imagined it was your mouth around my cock instead of my hand."

My jaw slightly drops, and before I can even make sense of his words, I'm falling apart under him. He finishes close after, and I let my eyes fall shut as his weight settles over me. Our heavy breaths fill the room, but instead of getting dressed when he pulls away, I climb under the sheets.

I keep my eyes on my phone as Liam walks over to the trash, and I notice I got a message.

Killian

> I'll be there in 20, love.

I check when he sent that and I have ten minutes to get ready. I glance over at Liam and suddenly feel guilty for going to get dinner with Killian after Liam and I just did... *that,* but Liam is constantly saying that I'm not his girlfriend when his friends tease him about it, and we also agreed this wouldn't become more.

"I have a question."

"I might have an answer."

I laugh softly, and Liam leans over to kiss my cheek. "What's your question, beloved?"

I bite back a smile at his name for me, but it adds to my confusion. "What... are we?" I hate asking guys this question, and I can see the shift happen in real time as Liam simply walks over to get his clothes. He doesn't necessarily look taken back, but his usual glare returns and the way his face was just softening with me is gone.

"Humans." His tone is dry and if any other guy had answered like that, I would've taken the hint, but I sense the joke under his bored tone and I need a straight answer because I've been getting mixed signals lately, and I don't want to lead Killian on if this is becoming more.

"Okay, so we're—"

"Not a we."

Okay. No joke under his bored tone there.

"I don't meet your standards, remember?"

Right... only he has been lately and just bought a million-dollar ticket to see me *look pretty* on stage. He also got me a freaking Birkin bag for my birthday, so I'd say he's exceeding standards just a bit.

"I said that months ago and—"

"And nothing has changed. We're just fucking."

Stop talking.

When he turns to look at me I send him a smile. "Right, I just have a date in a few minutes and wanted some clarification, but thanks, now I don't have to cancel." I slip out of bed and quickly get dressed.

"What *date*?"

"Dinner." I slip my shirt on and rush for new underwear.

"With whom?"

"You don't know him." When my pants are on, I keep my back to him and sit to put my sneakers on. I don't know why, because I'm used to his asshole attitude, but I haven't been on the receiving end of it in a *while,* so his words sting just a bit.

"You don't know who I know."

"You don't know him. Trust me." When I turn around Liam is still undressed and tries to say something, but someone knocks on my door before he gets to. I glance over at the door and go still.

"Get dressed!" I whisper, and Liam literally stands there. Naked.

"That's your date?"

"Most likely, yes. Please put clothes on and go to the bathroom or something."

"I'm not hiding in the fuckin—"

"Shh!"

"Do *not* shush me."

Killian knocks again, and I quickly grab Liam's clothes before shoving them into his arms.

"Please get dressed." I glance over at the door. "Coming!"

"You were coming on my dick a couple of minutes ago, too-"

I cover Liam's mouth, and I swear I feel him smirking.

"Get. Dre-"

"Sage, open the damn door! This is burning my hands."

"Angie?" I push Liam out of what her line of sight would be when I open the door, then answer it, and Angie is staring back at me with a covered plate. "Angie, hey. What's up?"

"I was instructed by your pain in the ass brother to check on you and bring you food."

"Oh, my goodness. Sire really called you?" I take the plate from her as I shake my head at how ridiculous that man is.

"Yes, and he wants me to check on you all night, so I'll be back."

"Angie, you do not-"

"I was already planning on it, so don't even try to tell me not to."

When I let out a sigh, she sends me a knowing look, but then pity washes over her and I feel bad all over again.

"Have you spoken to her?"

I shake my head and glance down at the floor. "She keeps calling, but I muted her. I have nothing to say to her."

"Good."

My eyes meet my agent's, and she nods approvingly.

"You're too nice for your own good, Sage. Don't let her guilt trip you, and do *not* forgive her. I've been telling you for years now that I felt like she's been secretly hating on you."

I don't say anything because she's right, and I don't want to admit that one of my closest friends was never my friend.

"You really scared us when you passed out earlier, Sage. I need you to tell me if we're having a rerun of last summer."

I steal a glance at her before my eyes fall to the plate in my hand, and I say a silent prayer that she doesn't ask me what I think she's going to ask because I can't tell her the truth, and I hate lying.

"Sage?"

"I really am okay, Ang." I give her a smile, but she shakes her head softly.

"What's *okay*, Sage? How are you doing with your meal plan? I saw they changed it."

I give a shrug, and when I see her concern grow, so does my nervousness.

"Angie–"

"Are you following your meal plan, Sage?"

I chew on my lip to stop myself from saying the truth and only nod.

"Are you sure?"

"Yes." My words come out strained, but when she lets out a breath of relief, so do I.

"Okay, good."

I smile at her, but she goes on. "Because, you know, after last summer, if you're following someone else's meal plan again, then it'd be deemed a concern of your physical and mental health, and you'd be forced to take a break from modeling."

I feel like I'm swallowing actual sandpaper, and I force my tears away because if I cry, I'm done for. I can't take a break from work right now. I might get signed with Vincent, and considering he has rules about his girls eating before going on *stage*, he'll never let me model for him if he hears I skip a few meals here and there. He'll make it a big deal along with everyone else.

"I know that, but I'm fine."

Angie keeps her eyes on me, and after a beat, she nods to herself and leans in to plant a kiss on my cheek.

"Good." She says she'll check on me before I fall asleep, and when I shut the door, Liam is, thankfully, dressed.

"You're the worst liar I've ever met." He looks *pissed*, and I almost open this door because I rather deal with Angie, but Liam doesn't have the power to stop me from modeling, so I stay put.

"What are you talking about?" I smile at him before walking over to put the plate of food down.

"You passed out today?"

I glance over my shoulder before confirming.

"How'd that happen?"

"It was after my show. I had an outfit malfunction that stressed me out, but then Vincent asked me to be a Moore Girl– I didn't tell you about that, actually. I'm, of course, thinking of saying yes, but I need–"

"You're getting off track, Dory."

I let out a sigh before turning to him and continuing. "I passed out after he gave me the offer. There was a lot of other stuff happening." I don't bring up my best– ex-best friend because I'm tired of the topic surrounding her.

He doesn't say anything for a second as he watches me. "Did you eat?"

"Yeah..."

"Sage." My name comes out like a warning on his tongue. "Did you eat before your show?"

"*Yes*. They make the models eat before going on stage."

He studies me for something else before folding his arms across his chest. "What was she talking about last summer and meal plans?"

"Nothing." I go to get my things for my dinner with Killian, but when I try to walk past him, he moves in my way. I look up at him, and he only stares down at me, neither of us saying anything.

"You're really going to make me ask you again?"

"Liam, that was a private conversion, not to mention none of your business." I move past him, but he grabs a hold of my arms before pulling me back to him.

"How come you're suddenly so defensive?"

"I'm not. You're just–"

"Let me see the meal plan you're following."

I pull my arm away from him before taking a step back. "Why?"

"Let me see it, Sage."

"Wh–"

"Sage Loana, enough with the back-and-forth. You told her you were following your meal plan, so tell me what the problem is."

I feel my tears building up, and I try to blink them away, but in an instant, something happens, and his entire expression shifts as he takes a step towards me.

"You're not following your meal plan are you?" His tone is on opposite worlds of his previous one and it only brings more tears to my eyes.

I don't say anything. I don't nod or shake my head. I don't respond at all and use every ounce of my strength not to cry, but the minute his hands cup my face I feel a single tear trek down my cheek.

"Dory..."

"Please don't tell her. They won't let me model, and I need to, Lee. *Please*." I squeeze my eyes shut, and all I feel is his arms as they come around me. I break into a quiet sob, and he doesn't say anything as he holds me.

When I pull away, he wipes my cheek softly. "You ruined your pretty makeup."

My broken laugh fills the room, and I walk to the vanity. Taking a seat, I take my makeup off, but I notice Liam watching me in the mirror.

"I need you to show me the meal plan you're following, beloved." His words come out so soft but somehow still hurt.

"I'll go back to following my own." I look at myself as I wipe away the last bit of makeup, but in the mirror, I see Liam close the distance between us. He kneels in front of me, and when I turn to look at him, I wish I didn't.

"Do not *lie* to me."

I try to respond, but he doesn't let me.

"No, I don't care. Don't ever lie to me, Sage. There's nothing on this earth I hate more than it, and it's beyond disrespectful."

"Okay... I'm sorry. I won't."

He rises to his full height and keeps his eyes on mine. "Show me it." He keeps his tone gentle, and I briefly close my eyes, but when I open them, he's unfortunately still waiting.

I get my phone and pull up Helena's meal plan. I keep my phone on my chest and turn to Liam. "You don't need to get upset." I try to calm him before he even looks at it because, while he denies it, I know he has anger issues, and he's totally going to blow this whole thing out of proportion.

"I'm already upset."

See what I mean?

"Let's not fight for the phone, Dory." He holds his hand out to me and I give it to him before flopping onto the bed. Grabbing my iPad, I scroll through my list of upcoming errands and events.

"Sage..."

"Hmm?"

"Sage, look at me."

"What?" I keep my eyes on my iPad and busy myself as I move some things around my calendar. I feel the bed dip before Liam turns my iPad off. My mouth feels dry, but I force the knot down.

"Sage, this meal plan is for someone who weighs at least one twenty."

"She weighs one ten on a bad day..." I keep my eyes on my iPad screen, and I can see Liam watching me carefully through the reflection, but I don't turn to him.

"And you weigh...?"

I feel my eyes burning again, and the bed dips as Liam lies beside me on his elbow. He tries to catch my eyes with his, but I look over to the side.

"Never mind that. It doesn't matter how much you—"

"Yes, it does."

"*No,* it doesn't. It doesn't matter this much, Sage. You're eating like someone who weighs *way* less than you. If you can't recognize how unhealthy that simply *sounds,* then this is an even bigger problem."

I keep my head turned, and when my eyes start to water, I let out a frustrated breath.

"This says *Helena* on it. Isn't that the hating ass bitch who fucked up your outfit tonight?"

I almost tell him not to call her a bitch but realize I shouldn't defend her.

"And I bet it was her idea for you to follow this shit? Sage, this is ridiculous. That girl clearly has it out for you. How long have you been following her meal plan?"

I almost shrug but remember how *passionate* he feels about lying and decide not to answer at all. I feel his fingers softly push my hair behind my ear, and I squeeze my eyes shut.

"I'm going to assume this hasn't been happening since last summer since you would've–"

"Been skinnier?" I turn to him now.

He watches me for a beat before shaking his head softly. "*Hospitalized*, Sage. You would've been in a hospital and you will be if you continue this."

I shake my head at how dramatic that sounds. I knew he'd be like this, everyone acts like this is the end of the world and they don't get it.

"I'm fine."

"You're not, though, beloved. You're sick."

"What?" I sit up on the bed, but he stays in his position as he looks up at me. "I'm not *sick*."

"You think this is okay?" He nods towards my phone and rests his head on his hand as he studies me.

"Well, I'm aware it's not the best thing, but–"

"But you think it's okay, obviously, since you're doing it and have done it in the past."

"Well, yeah, it's fine. I've *been* fine all this time–"

"You're sick."

"Stop saying that!"

"Sage, if you are convinced that it's okay to eat like this and you're doing it because you're not happy with how you look, then you're mental health is–"

"My *mental* health? You think I'm crazy because I want to go on a diet?!"

"I didn't say you were *crazy*." He gestures for my phone. "And that's not a *diet*. You're fucking starving yourself. Literally."

I don't move an inch, and he briefly closes his eyes before letting out a breath.

"You should go."

"Dory–"

"No, Liam, really. I'm leaving soon anyway, and I don't see why you care so much. You said it yourself, we're just fucking, and you already got what you came here for, so just go." I keep my back to him as I grab my purse, but in a quick move, he turns me to face him.

"You're seriously going to be like that with me right now?" He sounds hurt at first, but then he shakes his head, and I can see his anger settle. "I didn't come here just to fuck you, Sage, and it doesn't matter why I care; I just *do*, so how about you sit your ass down and eat whatever she brought you."

"I lost my appetite." I try to walk off but he grabs my arm and keeps me in place.

"*Find* it."

I snatch my arm back harder than needed, and I can see his temper rising. My feet are suddenly glued to the ground as he leans down so we're at eye level.

"I see you're bitchy when you're confronted, but let's not play the mean game because I promise you I'm going to win every time, beloved." He keeps his voice low, and we stare between each other's eyes, but I can see he's not going to be the one to back down, and it only makes me angrier.

I turn on my heel as I face the wall with my back to him, and he doesn't say anything else. When my watch dings, I glance down at it, and Killian tells me he's downstairs. I turn back around, but when I try to walk past Liam, he takes a step in my way.

"Where are you going?"

"My date is downstairs."

"Well, tell–"

"You wanted me to eat, right? I'm going to get food." I push past him, but I realize my mistake too late.

"What the fuck did I tell you about pushing me like that?"

"It won't happen again." I reach for the door as he calls out to me.

"Come over here!"

I walk out and quickly round the corner instead of walking ahead at the elevator. I hear my door slam shut a second later, and when I peek around the corner, he walks for the elevators. He looks up at the floor they're each on before turning. I lean behind the wall again, and a few seconds later, another door opens. Just as I look, the door to the stairs shuts, and he calls out to me. I head for my room again, and the second the door shuts, I lean against it.

I let my eyes fall shut as I let out a sigh, and I feel so *drained*. I know Liam is trying to help, but I don't need help, and he's wrong. I'm not sick. My mental health is fine. I'm *happy*.

I wipe away a tear just as it falls. "Ugh!" I throw my bag onto the bed before sitting on the ground with my face buried in my hands. "He's so– *ugh!*" I wipe my cheek, and I only get more mad that I'm crying *again.*

When my phone starts ringing, I don't even reach for it, but when I look at my watch, I see it's Killian and decide to answer.

"Sage, love. I'm downstairs. What room are you in?"

"Hey, Killian. I'm so sorry to cancel at the last minute, but I'm not feeling well and have an early flight tomorrow. Can we reschedule?"

He tells me it's okay and offers to keep me company, but I kindly decline.

I decide to get in the shower, and as the hot water hits my back, the shower fills with a soothing steam. I turn to let the water hit my face, but my vision suddenly blurs. I turn the water cooler before crouching down, and it takes some time, but this usually helps.

My vision goes completely dark, and I take a seat, but the cold water doesn't work, and I feel myself go limp.

Chapter Twenty-Three

LIAM

I DON'T HEAR ANOTHER SET of footsteps as I race down the stairs, and I have no idea how she left so damn fast, but both elevators were upstairs, and unless she went up for whatever reason, she had to have taken the stairs.

I call out to her but get no response, and I try not to get more upset, but she's being so difficult. This is why I don't make the effort to help people. Now I'm the bad guy for caring.

"Goddamn headache this woman is." I don't know how serious her obvious issue with eating is, but she's brushing it off like it's nothing, so for her sake, I'm going to assume it's not that bad and she only sometimes eats what's on that meal plan because there's no way she's following it to the T, she'd be hungry after every meal, and for my sanity, I'm choosing to believe she isn't completely starving.

When I make it out into the lobby, my eyes scan the room, but she's not in sight.

"Sage, love?"

I quickly turn but don't see her.

"I'm downstairs. What room are you in?"

My eyes land on some guy in an Armani suit, and I realize this must be her date. This man looks like he has the personality of a cardboard box, and whatever cologne he's wearing is way too strong.

"Of course, we can reschedule. I hope you feel better. What do you think you're sick with?"

I stop in my tracks before I walk off. *Sick?* I can't tell if she's telling him that so she doesn't have to go out with him, but a weird feeling settles in the pit of my stomach.

"I hope you feel better, love. Do you want me to go up to your room? We can order room service and..."

I don't bother sticking around for the rest of his sentence and head for the elevator. I don't know how she got back to her room when I walked out right after her, but I impatiently wait for the damn elevator. I press the buttons again, and when it finally opens, I feel like it takes forever to get upstairs. I rush to her room, but when I knock, she doesn't answer.

"Sage, please open the door." I knock again, but when I put my ear to the door, I hear her shower running.

I let out a sigh before leaning against the door and deciding to just wait, but that pit in my stomach only grows. I turn on my heel and knock harder.

"Excuse me. Did you need help with something?"

I turn to find a lady in uniform and a cleaning cart.

"Yes, I left my key inside, and my girlfriend is in the shower. Can you key me in?"

She barely even hesitates, which is concerning, but I walk in and sit at the edge of her bed.

A soft thud comes from the bathroom, and I rise to my feet. "Sage?" I head for the bathroom and knock on the door, but when she doesn't answer, I walk in.

When I see her limp body on the ground, I almost fucking pass out. "Sage!"

She's already stirring awake when I reach her, but I cradle her head in my lap and grab the towel beside us.

"Liam?"

"I got you; stay awake for me." I wrap the towel around her before lifting her.

"Lee, I'm–"

"Do not fucking say you're *fine*, Sage. You just passed out. *Again!*" I lay her on the bed softly before handing her a water bottle she had on her bedside. She takes a small sip, but when she tries to set it aside, I bring it back to her lips. "Drink the rest of it."

She doesn't fight me and downs the rest of the bottle. My heart is still fighting to get out of my chest, and I have to sit down to catch my damn breath.

"Why do you look like you just saw a ghost?" She fucking *smiles*, and the only reason I don't lose my shit is because that perfect smile somehow stops my damn heart. I let out a breath and only shake my head in response.

What the fuck am I doing with this woman?

I grab the plate of food they brought her earlier and place it on her lap. "Eat."

She glances down at the plate before glancing up at me. "Can I get dressed?"

I don't respond to her smart ass and take the plate so she can stand. She holds her towel close as she goes to get dressed, and once she does, she sits at the desk in her matching sports bra and shorts.

She starts putting a bunch of shit on her face, and I dead ass can't fucking believe her right now. "Are you doing your fucking skincare routine right now, Sage?"

"Of course I am."

Of course, she is? I open my mouth but immediately clamp it shut and grab her food and juice from her fridge. Walking over to her at the desk, I pull up a chair beside her before taking the top off her plate.

"Ridiculous skincare routine," I mumble under my breath as I cut her steak for her.

"What was that?"

I shake my head before scooping up some mashed potatoes and a piece of steak. I hold it out to her, and she turns her head to the side. "I can–"

"Open."

She sighs but opens her mouth as I feed her. She continues putting different serums and lotions on her face as I literally spoon-feed her. I bring her straw to her mouth, and she sips her juice with a smile. I almost roll my eyes at her, but she's so fucking pretty, I can't even be mad that she's acting so normal after just passing out.

When she's done with her skincare routine, she turns to grab the fork. "Do you want some?" She takes another bite, and I plant a soft kiss on her cheek before shaking my head.

"No, beloved. Finish." I keep my eyes on her as she glances down at her plate, and a weird look crosses her face.

"I'm sorry for the bitchiness... I don't think you only came here to have sex with me. I can tell you care about me, and I know you're trying to help."

When she turns her head to me, I kiss her cheek again. "We're not *just* fucking, so cancel the stupid date you rescheduled."

She leans back as she watches me, and I can see her biting back a laugh. "Does that mean we're also not humans?"

I roll my eyes when she laughs. I know what she's asking, but I don't know what we are. I meant what I said about not wanting to date her, and it worked out perfectly because I didn't meet whatever standards she had, but that was months ago, and now...

Now my dumbass got too close, and I feel like my skin is disintegrating when she cries, so I adopt nasty cats for her, and when she excitedly rants for *hours* about whatever fashion show she's in, I spend a fraction of my paycheck to watch her walk on a damn stage.

I care. I fucking *care*, but I can't. When I told her that we were *just fucking* I immediately wanted to take my words back, but I said that because it sounded a hell of a lot like she wanted a label on this, and it scared me. Everyone I ever cared about is either dead or forgetting about me and I'm the common factor in all three of their lives. When I get close, people leave. All of my friends do, which is why I stopped forming close friendships. Jordan has been the only one who has stuck around ever since college, but the rest of our group ended up growing apart. And even though I try not to care when people leave, this time, I do, and it's driving me insane.

"Finish eating." I give her a kiss before heading to the bathroom. I shut her shower off and stood there in thought.

This woman deserves so much more than my bad temper, but I'm too much of an asshole to let her date guys in Armani suits and bad cologne, so she's stuck with me.

"Fuck. I'm falling for her..." *I was just starting to like being alone...* "Jordan is *never* going to let me live this down." I shake my head at myself and walk out of the bathroom.

Sage gets up with her plate, but I stop her when she walks to get the trash.

"You're not done."

"Yeah, I am."

"Sage." I don't let her respond, and take the plate from her. "You barely touched your plate. Why don't you want anymore?"

She shrugs, and when her face falls, I feel a fist come around my heart.

"You need to finish all of it, Sage."

"*All* of it?!" She suddenly looks like the idea scares her, and I realize this is worse than I thought. I bring my hand to hers, and she tries to pull away, but I don't let her.

"Dory, it's not even that much, and I know you're not full."

She tries to convince me that it's a lot of food, but she's wasting her breath. "This is way more calories than my meal plan and–"

"But that's not *your* meal plan, Sage." I see the realization cross her face, and she takes a small step back. "Let me see your actual meal plan."

She shakes her head, but I grab her phone and hold it out for her to unlock.

Once she does, I find her meal plan next to the one she's been following. "Sage, this is perfect for your weight. What's the issue?"

She doesn't respond, and I set the plate down before settling on the bed with her.

"You need to follow your meal plan from now on, or don't follow it, but don't eat less than you should."

"But–"

"No, Sage. *No.*" I try my hardest to stay patient with her, but I refuse to debate or negotiate this. "Do not make me threaten to tell your agent, Sage. Trust me, if it's between your health and modeling, I don't care if you never walk another stage."

She keeps her eyes on mine, and they look *torn*. "Did you not just threaten to tell her?" Her voice lacks her usual joy, and it throws me off. She inches away from me, and I let out a defeated breath, knowing I fucked up.

"Dory–"

"I'll follow my own meal plan." She still sounds numb as she takes the plate from beside me. She doesn't make another sound as she takes the smallest bites of food. I study her for a minute, but I've never seen her this quiet, and it's killing me.

I lay beside her and plant a soft kiss on her thigh. "Please don't be mad at me." I glance up at her, but she keeps her eyes on her plate. When I kiss her leg again, she still doesn't budge. "I'm not the bad guy here, Sage. I only meant that your health is more important than modeling."

Nothing.

A small sigh escapes me as I lean against my elbow and draw small shapes on her leg. We sit in silence, and I steal a few kisses on her arm and leg, but when I hear her sniffling, I glance back up at her.

She has her eyes up to the ceiling and I briefly close my eyes before sitting up. "Tell me what's hard about this so I can help you, beloved."

"I just don't *want* anymore."

I almost give in and let her have her way, but I refuse. She barely ate any of it and if she passed out in the shower, then she clearly didn't eat much before she went on stage.

"I'm sorry, I really am, but I'm not letting you go to sleep hungry, Sage."

She squeezes her eyes shut, and I suck in my breath as I feel a pain in my gut. She presses her palms to her eyes like that'll stop her from crying, and I genuinely feel horrible.

"Come on." I pull her hand softly. "Let's finish it together."

She lets me take her hand away from her face, but when I see her watery eyes, it physically makes me sick. I lean forward and softly kiss her cheek. "You're perfect, Dory. Eating this won't change that."

She sniffles quietly, and I lean down a bit to kiss her neck. "You're flawless." I make my way lower and kiss her above her heart. "And pure."

I glance up at her as I kiss my way down to her stomach, but she still looks so upset. "Incomparable." I kiss her stomach again, and a small smile grows on her face, so I kiss the rest of her belly. "Pristine."

She laughs softly, and I smile at her.

"Are you running out of words?" She teases, but her smile is back, so she can bully me all she wants.

"Maybe." I kiss my way to her thighs, and she lets out a laugh. "Impeccable." I kiss her other thigh as she giggles. "Immaculate."

She laughs harder, and I resort to *things* that are as perfect as her rather than words.

"You're the sunset when it meets the ocean." I kiss my way down her left leg.

She sort of pouts, and I notice her eyes watering.

"You're beautiful." I kiss her again. "And you're insanely cute, like Periwinkle's yawn."

"Awe, stop it!" She covers her face, and when she shakes, I can't tell if she's laughing or crying, but I kiss my way up her right leg.

"You're Sunday afternoons."

She peaks through her fingers, and I can see her teary eyes.

"You love Sunday afternoons."

Yeah...

I pull her hand and kiss the back of it. "You're like..." I search my brain for the right words. "When you wake up two hours before your alarm goes off, and that relief you get when you realize you have more time to sleep."

She lets out a loud laugh, and I pull her into my arms, kissing her on the top of her head. "I can go on for hours, pretty girl. Eating this isn't going to change anything about you, so let's finish this meal, okay?"

She nods gently against my chest, and I kiss her head again before pulling away and grabbing her plate. I bring a fork full to her, and she looks like she might throw up, so I eat it instead.

I don't say anything else and eat a few more bites and after a while, she grabs the spoon. "Can I just eat the mac and cheese?"

"Sage–"

"There's a lot of mac and cheese, Lee."

I don't think she knows what a lot is, but I don't tell her that. This is bad. This is really bad, and I feel like a dick for how I was acting earlier because she isn't just being careless and skipping a few meals. She has a serious eating disorder, and I know she doesn't want her agent to know, but how can I not say something?

"Eat the mac and cheese with the steak, and I'll leave you alone."

"*All* of the steak?"

I don't answer her and stab a piece of meat. I take a bite out of half of it before giving her the other half, and she eats it without complaint.

"You *like* it, Sage. Try to finish; you're almost done."

She doesn't respond as she eats her mac and cheese, and it's like she's just trying to get this over with.

"You're doing so good, beloved." I kiss her cheek twice and hold her straw to her lips.

She takes a small sip before holding out a spoonful of mac and cheese to me. This is cheating, but she watches me like I might save her damn life if I eat it, so I do, and her smile is back. When she offers me another spoonful, I go to tell her *she* needs to eat all of the mac and cheese, but she's still smiling at me, so I open my mouth for her.

She looks down at her plate and her smile widens as she realizes we're almost done, and she's feeding me most of it, but she ate a lot more so I don't comment on it and get her to eat the rest of the steak.

"I really am full now." She turns her head to the side, but I follow her with the fork.

"It's the last piece, Sage."

She shakes her head, and I fight the urge to sigh and eat half of it. When I hold the other half to her, she shakes her head again. "Okay." I lean forward and bring my lips to hers.

"Look at how good you did." I gesture to the plate before kissing her again and she smiles over at me. "Finish your juice." I get up to get rid of the plate and she barely touched the mashed potatoes but finished the rest with my help. Considering I'm pretty full, I know I ate most of it, but I let her have this win.

When I walk back into the main room, she's lying on her stomach, kicking her feet as she scrolls through her phone. I keep my eyes on her, and when she laughs at whatever she's watching, it's like the last thirty minutes didn't happen. Her smile somehow makes the whole room seem brighter, and I'd do just about anything to keep her happy, but she cries when I make her eat. I'm not letting her starve herself, and it makes me feel like I'm dying to see her cry, but I guess I'm going to die trying to help her with this disorder.

I lay next to her on her bed, and she turns her phone to me. "Look at this!"

I watch an edit of her from today's runway show and I'm surprised by how fast her fans are. "How did they even get that clip of you? The show was just a few hours ago."

"I have no clue, but these people are talented." She goes through a few more edits and comments on all of them with a smile. I keep my gaze on her and take in a deep breath before nudging her arm.

"We need to talk."

She looks over at me, and I can see the worry in her eyes, but I quickly reassure her. "I'm not going to tell your agent."

She lets out a breath she must've been holding, and I study her for a beat before adding, "But you need to talk to someone about this. If you work on it with your brothers or someone else, then I won't say a word."

She watches me for a second before shaking her head, disappointedly almost. "An ultimatum? Really?" She moves to stand from the bed, but I grab her hand.

"Do you expect me to do nothing?"

"I–"

"Sage, you're putting your health at risk, I can't sit back and let you do that." I can't stand her brothers, but from all of the conversations I've heard of her on FaceTime with them for hours on end, I know they care about her. She clearly won't listen to me, but maybe they can get to her.

She shakes her head before looking back at her phone. "I'm not telling them. I'm fine."

"You're not fine."

"Yes, I am." She starts playing another video, and the way she dismisses me annoys the shit out of me, but rather than snatching the phone from her hand, I look forward and do the stupid breathing exercises I've been working on. When I look back over at her, she's smiling at her phone, and her pretty dimples ease more of my anger. It's clear she doesn't want to talk, so I let her have her way this time, but she's either going to work on this eating disorder with me, with her brothers, or she's never walking a runway show again.

Chapter Twenty-Four

SAGE

WHEN SIRE OPENS THE DOOR, he tells me to keep quiet but then immediately pulls me in for a hug. When we pull away, I look around for what we're being quiet for, but then my eyes land on Vidia on his couch.

I smile at how peaceful she looks compared to how restless she seemed when she was telling me about the break-in yesterday. When I turn back to Sire, his eyes are on her. I study him as he watches her, and maybe I just really want them to get back together, but he watches her like he wants to climb onto the couch next to her and hold her forever.

"How has she been?" It's been a little while since the break-in, but I know she isn't going to get over something like that overnight. Sire lets out a sigh and turns back to me.

"She says she's okay, but-" He sort of shrugs, and I can tell he's hurting.

"How are *you*?"

"I'm fine," he answers too quickly, and I give him a knowing look. "I really am, Sage. I've been talking to my sponsor, and Lis has also been checking in."

I give him a soft nod as I continue to study him, and he really does seem better than the last time I came to visit, so I choose to believe him.

I asked Lis to check in, and she said she was already doing that, which made me feel better. I know August, and I always tell Sire that he can talk to us about his addiction, but I also know he would rather talk to Lis about it since she gets it. I'm sure it's completely different talking to another recovering addict rather than me, someone who doesn't even drink and has never used drugs.

Both of those choices are my own, but I'd be lying if I said my siblings didn't play a part in it. Watching Sire and Lis fall into addiction at such a young age... changes the way I see things. They hid it very well for a while, but I found out eventually.

They've both been through so much, and watching them struggle to stay clean is the main reason I chose not to drink, and I'm certainly against all types of substances. It's for them, but also because I genuinely don't like alcohol or the way it makes me feel.

Sire tells me that V has still been struggling to sleep. "She just fell asleep a few hours ago, so I'm letting her rest."

I nod in return as we settle in the kitchen. He glances over at Vidia before his gaze settles on me. "Is Helena still calling you?"

"Yup."

He rolls his eyes as he sinks into his seat. "I know you already told Lis to drop it, but you should let her kick Helena's ass."

I'm already shaking my head at him, knowing he's being serious. "She's not worth the energy, Sire."

"Lis would love the excuse to let out some energy." He puts his hands up in mock surrender when I give him a pointed look.

"Please tell her to back off," I plead, and he simply nods.

"Hey."

I turn at the sound of that quiet voice, and Vidia walks over to me with a smile. I rise from my seat and close the distance before hugging her.

"Did we wake you?" I kiss her cheek gently and squeeze her hand.

"No, you didn't," she reassures me.

"Are you hungry?" Sire is already standing from his seat. "I can warm up some food for you."

I smile over at my brother, and Vidia thanks him before taking his seat.

"How is he?" I whisper to Vidia, finding it hard to believe he's as okay as he says he is after finding her the way he did the night of the break-in.

She pulls in a deep breath before glancing over at my brother and the way she smiles at her ex-boyfriend makes me think they already worked through their issues and got back together.

"He's okay... better, I think."

I nod in response and choose to believe them. My watch buzzes and when I glance at it, it's a message from Liam.

> Talk to your brothers.

> Please.

I exit his message but don't reply. He knows I was coming to see Sire before heading to work, but I'm *not* telling him about an eating disorder I don't have.

I feel myself chewing my lip as the thought runs through my mind, and when Vidia gets up to use the bathroom, I do a Google search.

What does an eating disorder look like?

With every scroll that passes, the room seems smaller.

Restrictive eating.
Avoidance of certain foods.
Purging by vomiting.

When I start reading through the scary health consequences, I shut my phone and stand on my feet.

"You okay?" Sire's concerned gaze focuses on me before his eyes dart to my phone. "If she's calling you again—"

"It's not Helena." I grab my bag as I muster up a smile, desperately trying to calm my breathing.

"I need to get to work." I turn to the hall before he can respond. "Later, V!" I call out, and Sire says something, but I rush out before I can hear the end of it. Refusing to be trapped in an elevator right now, I take the stairs, but my stomach turns with every step.

"I *don't* have an eating disorder. I'm fine." I keep repeating the words in my head, and by the time I get to work, I don't feel as sick, but I'm barely listening to anyone. Everything passes in a blur as I make it to my room and sit to get my makeup done.

"Hello?" Angie waves behind me in the mirror. "It's been five days since you've been offered to be a Moore Girl, and we haven't gotten back to Vincent."

I chew on my lip as I think, but there really isn't anything to think about. I'd be insane not to take his offer.

"Are you really going to leave us?" Lynn asks, and I turn at the heartbreak in her voice.

"No! Of course not." If I sign with Moore, I'm bringing my team with me if they're willing to travel twice as much.

"Sage, you can't turn down being a Moore Girl." Mel keeps her voice low, and I shrug in return.

"I didn't say that either..."

She smiles, and I can feel everyone's excitement buzzing. I turn to Ang, and she looks ready to make phone calls. "Was he serious about me being able to Model for both companies?" I hold my breath the minute the question is out.

Florence told me she thinks Vincent was just saying that to get me to sign with him, but Angie has been going back and forth with him and our lawyers, along with my mom. She's the district attorney but double-checks all of my contracts after my actual lawyer looks at them.

"I told him to put it on paper, and he did. Your lawyers are looking through the final contract." Ang sounds proud of herself, so she must've worked something in our favor with Vincent.

I only nod in response and finish my makeup, but I feel that everyone wants to say something or know what I'm thinking, but I already know what I want. I just need to see it on paper.

"Thank you," I tell Cara and Lynn as they add my setting spray. "I can dress myself today, can I have the room? I'll meet you guys after I take my pictures."

My team walks out, and I decide to call my mom after I'm dressed and the second she answers, both of our smiles grow.

"How's my favorite doing?"

I laugh softly at her. I think August and Sire, mainly August, would pitch a fit if they heard her call me that.

"Sire and Lis are doing fine." I tease and break into a laugh at how she rolls her eyes at me. I kid and say they're the favorites because mom is different with them. She doesn't actually treat any of us differently, but– I don't know. It's the way she looks at them. When we were kids, I'd catch her just watching Sire and Lis like she wanted to cry but, at the same time, was happy to have them under our roof and was willing to do *anything* for them.

Maybe she looks at all of us like that, and it's just a motherly look, but I can't help but feel like it's because they came from broken homes and made ours complete. She couldn't have kids after August and me, but then Sire and Lis joined us, and even as a kid, I saw how happy she was to have them around.

"So," I set up my phone and apply some lip gloss. I told Cara and Lynn not to add any until I was dressed. "Did you get a chance to look through the contract Ang sent?" She says she did, and as she explains, everything she says sounds really good until she continues.

"I read both contracts side by side, and there's only one problem, and neither Vincent nor Florence wants to adjust it."

"What is it?" I stop chewing my lip and fix my smudged gloss.

"Page seven on Moore's contract,"

I flip through it.

"It says you can't miss any Moore shows for another show. It doesn't say anything about missing other events he sets up if you're booked, but you can't miss a *Moore* runway show."

"Okay, that sounds fair, what's the issue?"

"Flip to page four on Florence's contract." I do. "She also says you can't miss a Magic Model show for another *runway* event, but she's fine with you not being able to attend other events she sets up for you *if* you are booked."

"Right..." I still don't see the problem and my mom notices that I'm lost.

"Sweetheart, if Vincent and Florence have a show on the same day, you can't attend both. You're one person, and even if you can somehow make it to both events, what if Vincent's is in Italy while Florence's is here in LA?"

"Oh..." Okay, this is an issue. "What are the chances they have a runway show for the company on the same day? I mean—"

"Sixty-three percent."

"How did you—"

"It's my job to know these things, sweetie." *Right*. "You shouldn't take the chance; talk to Florence; you've known her longer, and maybe you can get her to alter the contract."

"Okay." I shrug. "I think I'll be fine though, even if I end up needing to pick between both shows, I doubt the other person will be that upset, right?"

My mom looks confused. "Of course they will, Sage. I know you think these people adore you, and maybe they really do, but this is a business, they'll sue you."

My eyes widen. "What?! Sue me for missing *one* show? I've walked in shows for Florence with the freaking flu, and I just modeled five pieces for Vincent when I was originally supposed to do two, then modeled for him *again* with an outfit malfunction!"

"That doesn't matter, sweetie, but you should stop being so damn nice. If it's not in the contract, stop saying 'it's fine' and bending backward for people." She sounds like Angie. I let out a sigh, but before I could reply, someone is knocking on my door.

"I'll call you later, Mom. Thank you!" I send her an air kiss before hanging up and turning to my door. "Come in!" My door swings open, and giant bouquets come in one at a time. I can't see who's even carrying them as they fill my room with all of the flowers.

"Oh my goodness! These are so pretty." I hop down from my chair and walk over to one of the vases and they're so tall. Different people keep coming into my room and I'm *so* confused as to why there are so many flowers.

"There's eight more in the van."

"*Eight?*"

He turns from his coworker and smiles at me, almost apologetically. "I'm sorry, did we get the order wrong?" He glances down at his clipboard. "It was fifteen vases of peonies, correct?"

"I wouldn't know. Which brand sent these?" I glance over at the flowers, and the vases look like the ones Killian's brand usually sends me, but they've never sent this much, and if this is a mistake, I'm going to be a bit disappointed if I have to give them back.

He hands me a card before walking out for the rest of the flowers. I run my finger over the sealed wax, and before I break it open, I notice it's a kitten paw.

We're not humans. We're a we.

"What?" I laugh softly as I run my finger against the words. The last few vases come in, along with a bag of lunch, and I can't stop smiling. "Thank you!"

They shut my door behind them, and I immediately grab my phone.

"Dory."

I keep my eyes on Liam, and he just watches me like *nothing.*

"Lee." I wait for him to break and say something, but he only looks around his room, and I think he's *nervous.*

"Did you get my delivery?"

"Yes!"

He looks back down at the phone, and a smile grows on his face. "Is your answer also yes?"

"It would be if you had *asked.*" The room fills with my laugh, and when I look back at my phone, he's still watching me, but then Moon pops up behind him.

"I told him to put 'Will you be mine?' or something cute, but he put that corny poem, which doesn't even make sense!"

"It's not a *poem*. She knows what it means, now mind your business." He gets up, and I break into a laugh when I notice Moon and Jordan following behind him.

"It was my idea with the flowers!" Jordan starts. "I saw your post, Sunshine. I was the one who told him to make a grand gesture to officially ask you out!"

Liam slams the door on them, and I can't control my laugh.

I reposted a video a girl made about how her boyfriend asked her to be his girlfriend, and it was just a ton of roses on her bed with those big letters spelling out *Will you be my girlfriend?* but *this*. I look around the room again.

"It was barely their idea," Liam mumbles, and I smile down at him. "I would've sent them to your house, but I wanted you to be there when they delivered it, and I know you said you won't be home until later tonight, but they don't deliver after six, and I wanted you to get them today."

I laugh at how he rambles, and nervous Liam is my favorite. "Thank you."

His smile is back, but the second I take a picture, it's gone.

"Wait, let me get a better one."

"No."

"Please, come on." I hold the phone up so the flowers are in the frame as I smile. "I'm taking a screenshot. Smile."

He angles the phone up to the ceiling, and I burst into laughter.

"Liam Leslie!"

He mumbles, "Jesus Christ," before getting in the frame.

"Say, Sage Loana Hale is my girlfriend." I give him a bright smile that shows my teeth.

"Sage Loana is mine." He smiles with his teeth, and I know he's only mocking me, but he looks so cute. When I break into another laugh, his smile turns more genuine, and I take another screenshot.

"Did you eat?"

"You already asked me that." I bring my phone closer and open my camera to take a picture of all of the flowers.

"I asked at breakfast. It's lunch—come back to the camera; I'm talking to you."

"Wait, I'm taking a video of the flowers." I'm also thinking of posting the note, but a couple of million people are going to see it, and I, of course, don't mind, but I want that to be ours. When I go back to the call, Liam is still waiting for my answer.

"I just ate right before I did my makeup."

"What'd you have?"

"A taco."

He seems to be waiting for me to add more, but I don't.

"A singular taco?"

I nod, and he doesn't look pleased, but he doesn't comment on it. He keeps doing this. When he's not with me, he'll call and text all day, either reminding me to eat or asking what I had, and it's sweet, so I don't complain, but it's not fun having him watch me so closely.

When he *is* with me, which is a lot lately, he's feeding me all day. He doesn't force me to eat or finish everything, which is good, I guess, but I feel like I'm eating way too much. I tried to tell him that, but he keeps saying I'm actually still not eating enough, and after reading the articles from earlier... maybe he's right.

"Did you get the food I sent?"

"Yes, Lee."

"Go grab it so we can eat together." He sets his phone against something, and when I see the sandwich in front of him, a smile touches my lips. I grab the bag of food and find a sandwich similar to his, but mine seems to have less stuff in it.

"What is this?" I open it, but he quickly tries to stop me.

"It doesn't matter. Try it before you say you don't like it."

I roll my eyes at him, and he sends me a glare through the phone, which makes me laugh. I bring the sandwich to my nose as he takes a bite of his, and it smells okay, so I take a bite, and it isn't bad at all.

"What else do you have to do today?"

I tell Liam about the rest of my day, and besides my two photo shoots and a few meetings, I don't have much to do. We get lost in another conversation as he tells me about how the cats have been bothering him all day, and I laugh at how annoyed he sounds.

"You like it?" Liam smiles at me through the phone as I eat.

"I do, but I don't want to eat anymore."

"Sage–"

"I'm full!"

"Dory, I'm proud of how much you ate, but you can't be full. Please try *one* more bite."

I glance back down at it, and when the articles I read fill my head, I force myself to eat more. I blink the stinging in my eyes as I take a bite.

"Good job. If you really don't want any more, then that's okay." Liam tries to reassure me, but I feel my food coming back up, and it feels like acid in my throat. "What's wrong?"

I shake my head in response as I swipe out of the call and force the food back down. I know I shouldn't listen to Google, but reading about possible *heart* conditions as a result of constantly throwing up my food... I'm finishing this whether I want to or not.

"Is someone calling? Why are you on pause?"

I don't respond to Liam and quickly force the rest of the sandwich down. When I get back to the call, I plaster a smile on my face as I show him my napkin. "See? All done."

He watches me carefully before a crease grows in his brows. "You look sick... Baby, if you were really full, you didn't have to force yourself-"

"I'm okay, Lee."

Someone knocks on my door, and I'm glad for the interruption, so I let them in. Liam tries to get my attention, but I ignore him as Coral and Quinn walk in.

"Holy shit, who's the admirer?" Coral glances around the room.

I smile down at my phone, and Liam very clearly bites back a smile.

"Was this Killian again? Because, at this point, that man is in love with you."

My head snaps up to Quinn, and I try to tell her to stop talking with my smile, but she doesn't take the hint.

"Are you modeling for him today? If he asks you out again, maybe you should just give him a chance and–"

"*Killian* was your stupid New York date?" Liam grumbles. "When did he send you *flowers*?"

I glance down at him, and when I steal a glance at Quinn, she's looking between Coral and me with her brows raised.

"Yes, he was the New York date, and he hasn't sent me flowers in ages," I tell the girls before looking back at my phone. "And he's not in love with me. I also told him I wasn't interested." Both of those things are true, but Liam doesn't look like they make him feel any better. "Thank you for the flowers, babe. I'll see you tonight?"

"Mhm."

I pause with my finger above the hang-up button. "Don't *mhm* me, mister. I will see you tonight."

"Yes, ma'am."

I give him a smile as I nod before hanging up. I look back over at Quinn, and her eyes slightly widen. "I am *so* sorry. I didn't know you were on the phone. Is he mad?"

"No, it's fine." My heart aches at how nervous she seems. Quinn doesn't have the best experience with men, and I can see her fear for me growing, so I quickly reassure her.

"He doesn't care, trust me, he's not mad at me." He probably does care, but not as much as Quinn thinks, and she looks like she feels better hearing me say that.

"Who's the *he*?"

I look over at Coral, and she smirks at me.

"I'm nosy; you know I was going to ask." She puts her hands up, and the three of us break into a laugh.

"My boyfriend." It feels weird calling him that, but I smile at how it sounds.

"*Boyfriend?*" They ask for details, but I don't give them any and walk to the door. "Can we at least get a hint?"

"He plays for the Yankees." I'm not sure why that's the hint I give, but Coral pulls out her phone.

"Fellow celebrity? Okay!" Quinn snaps a few times, and I bite back another laugh as I shake my head at her.

"Shit, these guys are hot. I should start watching baseball." Quinn and I are a mess beside her as Mel walks over.

"What are we looking at?"

"Loana's boyfriend." Coral fills her in.

"Who is he?" Mel peaks over for a better look.

"That's what we're trying to find out."

I'm sure Coral will find out soon enough, and I don't care who knows, but it's funny to watch her spit out names as she goes through the roster.

"That Jordan guy is *fine*. Wasn't he in your project for the contest?"

I look over at Mel before telling her he was. "I could set you up with him!" They would be so freaking cute, and I think Jordan just broke up with the girl he was seeing. He seemed pretty bummed about it, but Liam said he was just being dramatic.

"Really?"

"Absolutely. I'll give him your number today."

The red in her cheeks deepen, and I give her a smile. Coral keeps throwing out names, and when she says Liam's, I look over at them.

"Not that one." Quinn leans forward as she swipes his picture away.

"Why not?" I ask with a soft laugh.

"He looks so mean. Like scary mean, and the guy on the phone said 'yes, ma'am' when you checked his attitude. Does this guy look like he'll let anyone, let alone his girl, put him in place?"

I bite back a laugh and leave them to guess as I walk over to the photographer.

"Do you think he'll text her?" I turn to Liam after sending Jordan a text about Mel, along with her number.

"Probably." He shrugs.

"Let's take pictures with the babies." I reach for my phone when I see the kittens yawning, but he grabs me, and I burst into a laugh. "How are you carrying me with one hand?"

"It truly offends me that you think I can't lift you." He still has me in his arms, and he carries me a few inches above the ground, and I glance over at him.

"How much *do* you lift?"

"I can lift *you*."

I try to tell him he can't, and he tries to prove that he can. He lays me on the bed and tells me to cross my arms and legs.

"Liam–"

"Just do it."

I let out a sigh and do as he says. Once I do, he grabs my ankles with one hand and my arms with the other. He lifts me from the bed, and I squeeze my eyes shut.

"Oh my goodness!"

He takes a few steps back before I feel myself going up and down. When I peek at him, he's looking down at me and brings me up to his chest again before kissing my cheek.

"Okay, we get it, you're strong."

A smirk grows on his face as he lifts me a few more times, kissing me between every lift. "I can do this all day." He brings his lips to mine and tosses me back onto his bed.

I can't wipe the smile from my face as I glance over at him, and he steals another kiss before someone calls him. I peek over at his phone, and it's his doorman.

"The food is here." He reaches over me for his phone before answering, and I hear them tell him he has a delivery downstairs. "You can let them up." He hangs up, and I try not to let my face fall. I told him I wasn't hungry, but he ordered takeout anyway, and now I'm stuck having to eat *again...*

I feel him watching me, but I keep my eyes on my phone.

"Do you want to eat downstairs or up here?"

"Neither."

I hear him let out a sigh before he tilts my chin up to meet his eyes. "You need to have dinner." He keeps his voice soft, but it only makes me feel worse.

"Mhm." I glance back over at my phone, but he turns my face to him again.

"What is it?"

I don't respond as I lay back on his stack of pillows, and he leans down to kiss me.

"Talk to me," he pleads.

I let my eyes meet his, and when I see the worry in his eyes, the words spill past my lips. "I searched up what an eating disorder is, and I'm scared, Lee. I don't want to die from this!"

His brows furrow as he settles on the bed with me. "You're not going to *die.*" His eyes bore into mine with so much certainty. "Stop believing everything you read, beloved."

I nod slowly, choosing to believe him. "What am I going to do?"

"First," he kisses me gently. "You need to try to eat but not *force* yourself," he adds firmly. "Whatever that was earlier on the phone can't happen again. Don't eat until you make yourself sick. It's no better, and it's why I don't force you to eat, Sage. I only ask you to try, and if you say you're full, I'll believe you. I'm sorry for before." He tucks a hair behind my ear.

I nod in response, stealing a kiss from him.

He studies me for a beat before leaving for the food.

An unsettling feeling washes over me, but I tell myself that I'll be fine if I eat and that nothing will change after eating this. However, my mind races with every comment I receive under my pictures about my body. Every article about me, picking apart my weight, pound by pound.

When Liam walks back in, the scent of the Jamaican food we got smells amazing, but I don't have an appetite for anything.

Liam doesn't serve anything on a plate and picks from the takeout containers instead, but I don't move to try any-thing. I know he's waiting for me, but I can't bring myself to do it.

"Try some." He serves some plantains on a plate. I tear off a small piece, and the minute I try it, my mouth waters, but I still don't *want* to eat.

I eat the rest of the plantains in silence, and Liam places a soft kiss on my cheek. "I have another surprise for my will-you-be-my-girlfriend gesture."

I turn to him with a smile, and he steals a kiss. "What is it?"

"I'm not telling you." He kisses me again, and I shake with a laugh. "Finish eating so I can give it to you." He gestures to the food, and I feel my face fall.

"I get rewarded for eating now?"

"*No*, I told you. It's a part of my be-my-girlfriend gesture, but I'll give you another reward if you want one for eating."

I muster up the courage and have a spoonful of rice before turning to him. "Give me a hint."

"No."

I bite back a smile as I study him. "There is no other surprise, is there?"

He shrugs, but I see the way he bites his cheek so as not to smile. "Finish eating, and I'll show you."

I can't tell if he's lying or not, and I don't eat much, but I pick a bit at the food.

"How's your mom?" I ask softly before turning to Liam. "Have you gone to visit her recently?"

He's been pretty open about her, but only when I ask. I'm still not sure what she's sick with, and considering it clearly takes a lot for him to open up, I haven't asked.

"She's good." He *smiles,* and I swear I hold my breath at the sight. "She's been having a lot of good days."

"That's so good to hear!" I smile over at him, and he leans forward to plant a soft kiss on my lips.

He gestures to my food, and I try a little more. He must be satisfied because he only asks me to eat all of the rice he serves me and doesn't tell me to have more when I leave some. Instead, he says, "Good job, baby," and kisses me slowly before pulling away to take the food down.

I'm lying on his stack of pillows when his phone starts ringing, and it's someone named Capri. I walk out of the room with his phone, and just as I round the corner, Liam reaches the top of his steps.

"Do you need something, beloved?"

"Someone's calling you." I hand him his phone, and he rolls his eyes, but when he sees who it is, his brows furrow as he brings it to his ear.

"What's up, Pri?" The furrow in his brows deepens before a panic covers his face. "Okay, slow down."

"Is everything okay?" I whisper, but it sounds like they are yelling on the other end, and he rushes past me before I follow him back into the room.

"I'm on my way." He hangs up before disappearing into his closet.

"What's wrong?" I peek into his closet from the bed as he pulls his hoodie over his head.

"It's my mom."

I sit up at the panic in his voice. "Is she okay?"

He grabs his helmet, and I realize he's taking his bike.

"It's raining. You shouldn't ride your bike." I walk over to him.

"I'll be fine."

"You look scared." I get up and grab his hand, stopping him from searching frantically. "You shouldn't ride your bike in this headspace. Let me drive you there."

"I promise I'm fine, Dory. I need to go." He kisses me gently before heading for the door.

"Please drive safe, Liam."

He rushes out.

"Text me when you get there!"

"I will, beloved." He sounds like he's already downstairs as he races out, and a pit grows in my stomach from how worried he sounds.

Chapter Twenty-Five

LIAM

"**M**OM?" MY FOOTSTEPS ARE LIGHT as I walk into the room, careful not to make any sudden movements. I'm practically holding my breath as everyone stares at her like the knife in her hand is a bomb. "What's going on?"

Her head whips to me, her eyes wide. I see the moment she recognizes me as her shoulders ease. "Liam!" She runs towards me with the knife, and I put a hand up before the nurses can tackle her.

She drops the knife just as she reaches me and wraps her arms around my neck. "Oh, thank goodness you're here. Oh, thank God." She smoothes my hair and kisses my head repeatedly. I hold her tightly, and I can feel her heart pounding against me.

Capri scrambles to the ground in a hurry and grabs the knife. She hands it to someone who rushes off with it like they are the bomb squad and it's going to explode. My mom says a prayer over us, and I keep my eyes on Capri, trying to figure out what the fuck is happening, but before I can ask, my mom pulls away.

All of the nurses still surround us with wide eyes, and I notice a needle in one of their hands, so I keep my hold on my mom so they don't touch her.

"Do you know where the baby is?" She searches my eyes frantically, and I look over at Capri, who now has her eyes on the ground like she can't even face me. "They keep saying there's no baby here, Liam. *Where* is she?" Her voice drips in desperation as tears start to form in her eyes, and I feel my jaw clenching.

I look back at Capri, and I might actually strangle her for even telling my mom that. I don't get why they don't just fucking entertain her. I don't care if it's not beneficial. Her flipping out like a crazy person isn't very beneficial, either.

I look back over at my mom and kiss her cheek softly. "She's sleeping, Mom."

She looks like she's holding her breath as she watches me. "Are you sure she's okay? When was the last time you checked on her?"

I swallow the lump in my throat as I give her a small smile. "I just put her down. She's fine, come, sit with me." I bring her to her bed and the crowd of nurses part for us like she's contagious.

"Leave us."

"Liam, they need to stay for–"

"Leave or we'll leave." My head snaps up to Capri and she looks like she feels horrible, but she's going to feel a hell of a lot worse before I leave this house. She avoids my eyes as she tells everyone to let us have the room, and they're reluctant, but do.

"Where'd you get a knife from?" I lean on my elbow on the bed as my mom starts braiding her hair.

"I keep one in here for emergencies. You know that."

She used to keep a knife in her room back at home but didn't anymore when Shanti learned to walk and open drawers, so she must have been stuck in some headspace when Shanti was really young.

"Where do you keep it?"

"I keep it where I always have it, Liam." She brushes me off and I glance around the room as I try to figure out where any other sharp weapons could be. "That's a sick joke Pri played earlier. I'm very upset with her."

"Yeah," I rise from the bed and start searching her dressers. "The knife show really gave that away." Everywhere I check comes up empty, and I decide she doesn't actually keep anything in here and got that one from somewhere else. Someone is getting fired today, and if it's Capri, then so be it.

"My brush is right there, Liam." She shakes her head at me as if she fucking asked for it, but I keep my mouth shut and hand her the brush. "Thank you, sweetie."

"Mhm."

She pauses with the brush to her hair as she turns to me.

"Are you upset with me?" She looks mad that I'd be mad and I quickly shake my head because the last thing I need is for her to throw a fit on me after I just calmed her down.

"No, Mom. Of course not. I–"

"Good because it's Capri who you should be mad at."

Oh, trust me, I am.

"I just wanted to see my baby, and she started going on in that condescending voice of hers about how there's no baby here and that Shanti was gone. Gone *where*?! HUH?" She yells out into the hallway, and I'm sure the entire block heard her.

"You're right..." I start off slowly, careful not to even move too much in case her anger grows out of my control. "That's a horrible joke."

She nods in response as she brushes her hair, and I feel myself relax when I realize she isn't going to flip her rage on me.

"But how about we don't pull knives on her?"

She huffs like I just asked her for the most absurd shit.

"Just punch her right in the face for me next time, got it?" I lay on my back with my eyes closed as she thinks about it, or whatever she's thinking about.

I don't think she'll actually hit Capri and even if she does, I'll deny ever encouraging it. She's sick, it's totally not my fault what she does or doesn't do.

"Where's the baby, Liam?"

I look over at her, and she's still brushing through her hair mindlessly. I *hate* lying. She always told me it was horrible to do, and I feel like shit every time I come to see her because I *always* have to lie.

"She's sleeping."

"Can you go check on her?"

"I just did."

"Are you *sure*?"

I let my eyes fall shut. Of all things, why does she have to remember Shanti? I get she was her baby, but she forgets *me* every other day, and I wish she didn't forget anything, but if she needed to forget something, I wish she'd forget her. This will all be so much easier for everyone.

"Liam?"

I look back at my mom, and she looks down at me with a smile. I blink away the stinging in my eyes as she brings a hand to my face. "You look tired, baby."

"I am, Mom." My voice comes out just above a whisper, and she lets out a sigh before lying on the bed beside me.

"How did your girlfriend like the flowers?"

I feel my brows furrow and I sit up on my elbow to look at her, but she only keeps her eyes on the ceiling as she plays with the end of her braids.

"She loved them." I have no clue how she continues to remember our conversations about Sage, but, of course, she remembers shit like this instead of what really happened to Shanti.

"What's wrong?"

I shake my head, not having the heart to tell her *she's* what's wrong since it isn't even her fault. "Nothing, Mom." I lay back down beside her, and she smiles at me knowingly.

She lets out a sigh before shaking her head. "I told you it's important to know her favorite flowers, Liam. Peonies are a great backup when you don't know a girl's favorite, but it's important to us girls that you guys know those things about us."

She just thinks peonies are a good backup because they're *her* favorite, but I don't say anything as she rambles on.

"Your father got me a gold watch the other day, and it was beautiful, don't get me wrong, but Liam," she gestures to all of the jewelry she's wearing. "I'm a silver girl, and I don't say this to be ungrateful, but it says a lot when men don't notice those things. Learn her favorite flower, and don't forget it." She points after her words, and I shake my head at her.

"You're right. I'll be sure to ask her what her favorite flowers are."

She nods with a smile, and a fist comes around my heart at the lost look in her eyes.

"I miss you, Mom." I feel my smile slowly fading, and a lump so big forms in the back of my throat, I physically can't swallow.

"Oh, honey." She whispers, and I wrap my arms around her tightly.

"I'm so sorry." *I'm sorry you're in here. I'm so fucking sorry Shanti isn't here.* "I'm sorry." I squeeze my eyes shut when they start burning and bury my face in her hair. She holds me close as she rubs my back.

"It's okay, baby. Whatever you did, we'll fix it."

I pull in a deep breath, and when she tries to pull away, I bring her back to me and hold her for another minute.

"Just tell me what happened, Liam. I won't be angry."

I shake my head softly before she pulls away.

"Nothing happened."

She lets out a sigh as she watches me. "Did you get into a fight again?"

When I don't reply, she shakes her head disappointedly.

"You *must* learn to control your anger, Liam. I tell you this all the time, and I'm going to keep saying it."

I keep my gaze away from her, but from the corner of my eyes, I can see her watching me.

"Look at how your father–"

"*Don't* compare me to him, Mom."

"Then don't act like him." Her words are soft, pleading almost, and it's the only reason I don't walk out. She takes my hand before kissing the back of it, and when I look over at her, she looks sad. "I miss you too." She hugs my side and I wrap an arm around her shoulder as I pull her in.

We pull away after a minute, and she looks up at me knowingly. "I know you too well, sweetie. What's really on your mind?"

I shake my head in response and try to muster up a smile for her, but my face doesn't budge. She keeps her eyes on me like she's waiting for an answer, and I still wish I could turn back the clock and go back to the age when she was able to solve my biggest issues, so I tell her something else I've been thinking about.

"I need to tell Sage something, but I don't know how she'll take it." I keep my eyes on the ground as I go on. "I don't

want to lose her, Mom. For the first time in a while, I feel...
happy. She's all I'll ever want in this life and maybe even the
next. I refuse to lose her. Even if that means I have to lie to
keep her."

"Oh no, don't lie, sweetie."

I keep my eyes on the ground because I can already tell
the motherly look she's giving me.

"Don't doubt her love for you. Tell her the truth, and trust
she'll stay."

She places her hand over mine, and I force myself to face
her.

"Do what you want, but believe this: if she doesn't hear
it from your mouth, her reaction will be worse than you
imagined."

I think of her words and feel my stomach turning at the
thought of Sage's reaction to her brothers hating me, but
my mom is right; I need to tell her. I just don't know how.

"I don't like it here, Liam."

I lean away a bit to look at her, and she keeps her eyes
forward. She told me this was her favorite place last week,
but she looks miserable in this second, so I get up and grab
her hand.

"Let's go home."

Her face lights up, and her smile is all I care about as
we walk out of her room. When we turn the corner, Capri
is slumped against the wall like she was standing there
the entire time. She quickly pushes off the wall and looks
between the two of us.

"Is she coming downstairs for dinner?" Capri looks between the two of us hopefully.

"We're leaving, Capri." My mom tells her as she holds her
head up high. "And we're no longer best friends. I don't
appreciate the way you joked about that earlier. Goodbye."

I nod at how mature she was about that because she's normally very petty. She pulls my hand as she walks forward,
and when I follow behind her, I can see the worry in Capri's
face.

"Is she being serious?"

"Of *course* I am! Why don't you ever take me seriously?"
She takes a sharp step forward, but Capri doesn't flinch.

"Yeah, Capri. Why don't you ever take her seriously?"

Capri looks over at me and sends me a pointed look as she turns her head. "This isn't funny, Liam."

"We're not joking," My mom starts. "Although *you* wouldn't know what a good joke is." My mom answers for me, and I bite back a smile at how offended Capri looks.

"Yeah, we're not joking, although *you*–"

"Liam."

I roll my eyes and turn more serious. "I really am taking her home." I walk ahead, but Capri gets in my way.

"Liam, think about this."

"He has."

She ignores Mom as she follows after us. "Liam, please. I know you're upset about tonight's incident, but *think* for a minute."

I don't answer her, and my mom walks ahead as we head down the steps.

"Liam, what are you going to do with her at home? You brought her here because of how much you travel for work. You–"

"*You're* still her nurse. Pack a damn bag, and I'll send you my address. She doesn't want to be here anymore."

"When she said that her first day here, *you* said she didn't know what she wanted."

I stop in my tracks, and when I glare down at Capri, she doesn't back down. "When I offered to move in with you, *you* said this was better for her, and it *is*."

I look over at my mom, and she wandered off to one of her friends. She whispers like she's talking shit about Capri, and I hope she tells all three of the other residents in here so they can all collectively hate Capri. It's a childish thing to wish for old people to hate and bully their nurse, but I don't care.

I think of Capri's words, and I hate that she's right. When I look back at Capri she crosses her arms at me. "You told her to *punch* me?"

I sense the joke under her tone, but I'm still pissed about what she told my mom.

"Maybe she should." I glance over at my mom, but she's still distracted. "You really fucking told her Shanti was dead?" I whisper now, although my words still seem too loud.

Capri's arms fall as she watches me, her eyes flooding with regret. "I'm sorry about–"

"When she asks you about Shanti, make up a fucking lie." I bite out, my built-up anger oozing out with every word. "If she asks about my asshole dad, *make up a lie*. If she thinks she can fucking fly, you ask her to show you, and when she flaps her arms like a damn bird, you act amazed. I don't pay you to try to cure her fucking Alzheimer's." I take a step forward, and she keeps her gaze on my heated one.

"I don't care if feeding her delusions isn't beneficial. I don't care about *anything*!" I snap.

She slightly flinches, and when she takes a step away from me, her face is blank. "I apologize, Mr. Walker–"

"Oh, don't start the Mr. Walker bullshit, Pri." I roll my eyes at her.

"I'll update you if anything else happens tonight, but I assure you, I'll make sure nothing does. We're working on figuring out how she came about getting the knife, and I'll report to you when we know more." Her voice is suddenly so... monotone.

She slightly bows her head, and I shake my head. "This is why I didn't want a young nurse. You're such a brat sometimes."

"I'll send you my best referrals if a new nurse is a path you want to take, Mr. Walker."

I stare at her for a minute, but she doesn't even blink. "You're fucking ridiculous." I walk away from her because I'm not dealing with this tonight.

"Liam, come meet my friend Susan." She makes me meet this woman every time I come, and I don't like her.

"It's nice to meet you, Leo."

I blink twice in her direction, and when she smiles, I look away. I know that old hag knows my name, and she's a horrible actor with even shittier humor. My mom laughs softly, and I almost think she's in on whatever joke this is. Somedays, I really do think everyone in here is faking it, but I don't voice my thoughts.

"Oh, Liam, I know I said I'd go see your new apartment, but our show is starting soon, and I don't want to miss it. I'll go after, but it's already getting late and–"

"It's okay, Mom."

She smiles up at me, and I kiss the side of her head before pulling her in for a hug. "I'll see you soon."

She barely hugs me as she rushes to the couch and gets comfortable as the show starts. I almost walk away, but she suddenly freezes and looks around for something.

"Mom, what is it?"

"Oh, Liam." She turns around and holds her chest. "I didn't see you there. Where's the baby?" She looks around again, but when she tries to stand, I stop her.

"I'll get her. Watch your show." I direct her back on the couch, and I watch her as she sings the theme song. The two other residents walk in, singing before sitting on the couch with my mom and Susan.

I take a seat behind her and stay for two episodes of whatever horrible show this is, but she looks fine, and I don't want her to even get reminded of Shanti by seeing me, so I leave without saying goodbye. When I turn, my eyes lock on Capri. I pull my gaze away from her as I head for the door, but just as I pass her, she walks out of the house with me.

"I really am sorry about telling her that. I've told her once before, and she didn't react like that; she remembered what happened and–"

"I don't *want* her to remember that day, Capri." I stop in my tracks as I turn to her. "You weren't there. You don't know what it was like to drag her off the floor as she sobbed for weeks when we lost Shanti."

"I know, but–"

"You don't though! When you lose your baby sister and have to take care of your grieving mother at seventeen, you can get back to me—actually, when your dad kills himself for what he did to his daughter, *then* you can get back to me."

"Liam–"

"My mom is getting a new nurse. Send me those referrals."

Chapter Twenty-Six

SAGE

I SIT UP IN THE bed as Liam walks in, and he looks *beat*. I force myself not to think the worst and chew my lip in thought as he slips his hoodie and shoes off.

He doesn't say anything for a few minutes, but when he slips into bed, I can't take the silence anymore. "Is everything okay?"

Rather than responding, he wraps an arm around my waist and pulls me to him like I weigh *nothing*. "I'm so fucking tired, Dory." He lays his head on my stomach.

His words pull at my heartstrings, and I wrap my arms around him.

"I just need a break," he mumbles, and I feel my throat tightening at how torn he sounds.

I kiss the top of his gently, and he squeezes me tighter. "Okay." I kiss his hair again. "I'll be your break."

He kisses my stomach in response, holding me closer.

"Do you want to take your clothes off?" I ask quietly as I rub my hand down his back.

A smirk paints his lips, and I shake my head at his dirty mind.

"I'm not in the mood for sex. Please don't tempt me because I'm exhausted, but I'll let you–"

"Shut up and just get comfortable."

He says he is comfortable, and it takes him a few minutes to gain the energy, but he lazily pulls his shirt off, and his pants follow soon after.

My eyes cast down his perfect body, and a sigh escapes past my lips as I marvel at the art on his skin.

He lays on my stomach again, and I study every perfect line of work on his back. I don't really care for tattoos and don't have any because of the pain and modeling but Liam makes everyone who has a tattoo look like a joke.

I glance at his face, and he looks so peaceful now compared to how lost he looked when he walked in here. I brush an eyelash off his cheek before kissing him softly.

When a smile appears on his face, I kiss him again.

"What are your favorite flowers?"

I feel my brows furrow at how random that was, but I answer anyway.

"Dahlias—or maybe hydrangeas." Both are so pretty, I can't begin to understand how they can form like that. Roses make sense in my brain, but hydrangeas? No clue how they're even real.

"Gold or silver jewelry?"

I laugh softly. "Gold? What's with the random questions?"

He shrugs. "Something my mom said..." He's quiet for a while before he adds, "Capri is my mom's nurse... *was* my mom's nurse," he starts randomly again, like his mind is on a hundred things at once, but I don't complain as he shares. "I just left after yelling at her and fired her which was stupid because she–" He shakes his head before going on. "Now I'll have to fucking say sorry, and I *hate* apologizing."

"Why'd you yell at her?" I wait for him to respond but notice he isn't going to. I have even more questions now, but I ask the only one that matters.

"Is your mom okay?" I feel him tense under me, but I wrap a leg around him and rub a hand in his hair. He pulls in another deep breath before pulling my shirt up and laying on my bare stomach.

"I hope so." He sounds like he's asking a higher power rather than answering me, and I don't say anything else as his breaths even out.

I reach over for my phone and reply to a few comments as he sleeps. As I keep scrolling, I notice I've been getting a lot of love lately, but then I realize I have *no* hate comments.

I keep looking through my post as I respond to my supporters, and I can't find one mean thing. It's good, of course, but weird. Even on posts where I remember seeing hate comments, there's nothing bad under my pictures.

"Are you hungry?"

I don't answer, and I know he heard my stomach growling, but I thought he was *sleeping*.

"Hmm?"

When I glance down at him, his eyes are still shut. "Not really." I move his hair again, and I think he actually is sleeping, but then he speaks up again.

"Do you want to try to eat?" He sounds like he's literally sleep-talking, and I can't help but smile at him.

"Go to sleep, Lee."

"The food is still downstairs." He lets out a small yawn before sitting up. "I'll get you some."

He makes his way out of bed, but I grab his hand. "What? No, you're going to fall asleep while walking down the stairs. I'll just eat in the morning."

"You can eat now *and* in the morning, beloved."

I don't usually eat much for breakfast if I have a big dinner and vice versa, but I don't say anything and let him crawl out of bed. When I get up after him, he tells me I can stay in bed, but I follow him into the kitchen. I hop onto his counter as he walks to the fridge. When he lets out another yawn, I shake my head at him.

"Liam, just—"

"No."

I shrug in response, although he can't see me.

"Do you want to try more of the food I got earlier, or do you want something new?"

I take a second to think, and I really don't want to bother him with cooking, but one thing comes to mind. "Can I have chocolate chip pancakes?"

He turns to me like he either didn't hear me or understand what I just said.

"For din—" He shakes his head. "Whatever you want, Dory."

A smile grows on my face as he gets everything he needs, but I speak up again when he grabs the chocolate.

"Maybe without the chocolate chips, though? How many more calories would the chocolate be?"

Liam doesn't answer me as he dumps a pound of them into the bowl. I feel myself smiling, but don't tell him I don't want to eat anymore, and it's not because of the chocolate.

I read somewhere that eating at night makes you gain weight, but I know he'll shut me down if I bring it up. I glance down at the tile but look back up when I remember something.

"My brother almost always eats breakfast for dinner, and I think he's rubbing off on me because I also had waffles the other night." It was also all I had that day, and Liam was upset even though he tried not to show it.

At the reminder of my brother, I turn my head in thought as I watch Liam. "Do you have any siblings?" I swear he freezes, but before I blink, he's back to mixing everything in the bowl.

I wait for him to respond, but it's clear he isn't going to. "You know, I feel like I don't know much about you."

"Is that so?"

"It is."

He adds the butter to the hot pan in silence, and I study him. "I feel like you were an only child. Don't take this the wrong way because I think you're a great person, Lee, but your meanness gives me the vibe that you never had to share your toys and always got your way. Only child or the youngest, for sure."

He doesn't respond as I go on. "Maybe it's because I'm comparing you to my siblings, and August is the oldest, by like thirteen minutes, but he's the sweetest. Then Sire and I are the middle ones, but he's younger and can definitely be a bit mean. Then there's Lis, and she's definitely an ass sometimes."

"Sire is *younger*?" He says, almost to himself.

"Yup." I bring my legs up and sit criss-crossed on the counter. I sit in thought, and when I don't add anything else, Liam steals a glance at me from over his shoulder.

"What?"

I shrug in thought. "I'm trying to think of whether or not they'll like you and—"

"Who cares?"

I try to answer, but he goes on.

"Don't answer. I don't."

The kitchen fills with my laugh, but Liam seems serious. "I care, *rude*. They're my brothers."

Liam pours a small circle of batter into the pan before turning to me and leaning against the counter. "You really care what they think about me?"

"Of course I do."

His face morphs with confusion but also like he didn't like my answer.

"What?"

He keeps his focus on me for a beat before crossing his arms. "What if they didn't like me?"

I let out a laugh because I could definitely see that being the case, but Sire doesn't like many people, and August likes everyone besides who *I'm* with. "Honestly, I don't think we'd be together very long if they didn't like you. They have a way of knowing when guys aren't good for me. The only boyfriend of mine they didn't scare away was also the only boy who never made me cry. He was the sweetest and would–"

"Yeah, I don't want to hear about your amazing ex." He turns again, and I bite back a laugh. "You wouldn't seriously break up with me if they hated me," he says it matter-of-factly, but he's wrong.

"Sure I would."

He turns around and looks pissed, but I don't get why.

"My siblings are the most important people in my life, and I care a lot about their judgment. I wouldn't be with someone they *hated*. I've stood with people they didn't *like,* but if they *hate* you, then you're the problem because Sire and August don't hate anyone. They're the best."

He stares at me blankly before rolling his eyes. "You're biased."

I laugh softly, but he looks off to the side now, almost annoyed.

"Maybe, but you don't even know them, everyone loves my brothers they're... well they're Sire and August." I shrug as if that says enough, but it sort of does. "And hates a very strong word, they wouldn't hate you."

He steals a glance at me and watches me for something but only shakes his head before turning back to the stove.

"Back to you," I start.

"Not back to me. "

"Yes."

He shakes his head and gets back to flipping pancakes.

"Where'd you grow up?"

"Earth."

I stare at his back, and I can imagine the bored look on his face. "Ha ha," I reply dryly, but he doesn't turn around. "Seriously, where'd you graduate from?"

"UC Davis."

I light up at his answer but then feel my shoulders slouch. "Oh... my brothers went to UC Faye, but I think I remember something about the two schools not liking each other." I almost asked what year he graduated, but I don't remember what year the boys graduated, and I doubt they encountered each other. Even if they did, I doubt Liam remembers.

"What about your family?"

He takes a while to respond this time, but he eventually does. "I have one, like most people do. These things don't matter, Dory." He tries to brush me off, but I don't let it offend me.

"I think your family matters a lot." I hear him let out a breath, but I don't understand why my curiosity is bothering him. "If you don't mind me asking–"

"I do." His words are cold now, and my mouth slowly closes. *Okay... now I'm a bit offended.*

I don't say anything for a minute or two, but the silence is killing me, so I hop down from the counter and walk over to him. He keeps his eyes on the stove, and I lean against the counter beside him with my arms crossed.

"You know if we're dating now–"

"What do you mean *if?*" He glances at me as he waits for me to answer.

"I mean, I should know more about you. Like your favorite color or food and–"

"I sleep with you every other night. My favorite color does not matter."

I feel my face scrunch as I wave in front of me as if I'd be able to wave away his ridiculous sentence. "Sex is not all a relationship is about, Liam, and I know that's how we started, but–"

"My favorite color and food is what a relationship entails?"

"I get the feeling you wouldn't *know* what a relationship entails."

He turns to me slowly, and I can't tell if he genuinely doesn't care about what's coming out of my mouth or if he's too tired to care.

He turns back to the pancakes without a word, but then it clicks.

"You never had a girlfriend before."

"Yes, I–"

"*After* high school!"

He doesn't respond, and my jaw slightly drops.

"Oh my God, I'm your first real girlfriend!" I'm at a loss for words, but Liam just flips another pancake before shaking his head at my epiphany.

"I don't think I want to date someone who doesn't have past experience." I think out loud and–

"I think the way I make you scream my name shows just how much experience I have."

"That–" Nothing else comes out, and when I shut my mouth, a smirk grows on Liam's face. "That is not the kind of experience I meant, mister."

"No?"

"No."

He raises his brows like he doesn't believe me and serves our food. "It's the only experience that matters." He walks over to the counter, but I'm stuck in place.

"No, it's not." I shake my head at him as he takes a seat. "I was this guy's first girlfriend in college, and it was *exhausting* teaching him how to be a boyfriend. By the time he was half as good, I was done with the relationship, and when I was literally on my way to break up with him, he sent me *a two-line* breakup text!"

Yes, I'm still annoyed about that because I had the decency to do it in person, and in the end, I didn't even get to do it first. At least it was mutual... sort of.

"Sounds like all the experience *you* have was bad. This is why I don't date. It's exhausting," He buries his face in his hands. "like now." He sounds exhausted, too, but I stop in my tracks. I notice him steal a glance at me before shaking his head softly.

"That's not what I meant; *you're* not exhausting. I just–" He runs a hand down his face, but I don't say anything as I grab my plate and take it to the couch.

"Dory..."

I grab my iPad beside me and get back to editing the thumbnail for last weekend's vlogs. Liam comes next to me on the couch and doesn't say anything, but I feel his eyes on me.

"Eat your food." His words are soft, but I only lean into the couch.

"Sorry I made you get out of bed to cook, but I'm not hungry."

"Dory–" He lets out a breath as if he really is tired of me, and I get up to go to bed. "Stop being like that, come here." He grabs my hand as I pass him and makes me sit on his lap. I keep my eyes on the screen as he kisses my cheek a few times and rubs my thigh.

"You're not exhausting." He kisses my neck before leaning his head on my shoulder. "I said 'like now' because I'm fucking tired right now. I'm not tired of you or our conversation."

He lifts his head from my shoulder and turns my head to kiss me, but I don't move an inch. He pulls away and looks between my eyes like he's offended. "Kiss me back."

He leans forward to kiss me again, and when I don't return it, he lets out a breath before kissing my cheek and leaning back on the couch. He's quiet for a while, and when I steal a glance at him, his eyes are shut. I try to stand, but he keeps his arm around my waist.

"Please eat." He sort of whispers before laying more comfortably on the couch, his arms still around me.

I grab my plate and eat two of the mini pancakes before putting them aside. When I get up, Liam doesn't grab me, and I realize he fell asleep.

Chapter Twenty-Seven

SAGE

"**I** LOVE YOU." I GRAB my phone and smile down at Mel.

"What did you do?"

She breaks into a laugh, and when she looks over at me, she still smiles innocently. "I didn't do anything." She looks up as she goes back to fixing something in her room. "I feel like we haven't hung out in a while, and I miss you."

I smile at her, although she isn't looking at me, and finish getting dressed. "I see you every day at work, Mel, but I get what you mean. I miss you too, we need to hang out, out of work."

While I see Mel almost every day, she isn't a Core Eight, who I spend most of my days with, but I'm going to try to get more photo shoots and other gigs with her.

I walk back to my phone when I'm dressed and check my calendar before I leave. I won't be back all day, so I need to take everything I need for the day. I'm on a time crunch since I wasted a bit of time coming back home after staying at Liam's place, so I grab my things a bit quicker.

When I put my watch on, all of my messages come through, but I notice one from Liam that I missed.

Lee

> I had to fly out this morning for my game but a coffee is waiting for you in that weird shop you like.

> Please make sure you try to eat something, beloved.

I like both messages before wishing him good luck at his game and grabbing my bag. I was a bit confused when he was gone this morning, but I'm glad he texted me instead of just disappearing, especially after whatever last night was.

When I let out a sigh, I notice Mel glance down at the screen. "I know that sigh. Don't tell me it's the very new boyfriend. How did he fuck up so fast?"

I laugh at her, but I love how well she knows me. "Ugh, I don't know, it's stupid." I head for the elevator, and she immediately tells me it's not stupid if I'm sighing and to just tell her, so I, of course, do.

"He said you were *exhausting*!"

"No! No, he didn't mean *me*. He was just tired and—"

"Wait, back up, why was he being so rude about you wanting to know about his damn life? Is he hiding a kid?"

I let out a laugh as I start my car. "A kid? Of all things, he's hiding a kid?" I glance down at my phone, and she shrugs.

"Matt had a kid." She brings up her ex she was just telling me about as if that proves anything.

"Matt was a pathological liar and is now in prison."

"Maybe this Liam guy will go to prison." She teases. "And are you sure that girl calling him was who he said she was?"

I roll my eyes at her because now she's just fishing.

"Why lie about her being his mom's nurse? That's insane." I also fully believe Liam wouldn't lie to me since he hates it so much.

"Whatever you say." Mel sounds like she believes otherwise, but I'm glad she doesn't voice her thoughts. "I still think he should be making the effort to open up to you, especially since you clearly care and rightfully want to know more about him."

"Yeah, I hate how distant he is sometimes." I chew my lip in thought as I pull up in front of the coffee shop. I ask Mel if she wants me to get her a drink before letting her go. When I walk into the shop, Rob and Cee Cee are watching me with matching smiles.

"Hello, stranger!"

I laugh softly as I close the distance between us and pull them both in for a hug. I was just in here a few days ago, but I haven't been coming in every day, and I can tell Cee

Cee is offended that I might be getting my drinks from somewhere else.

"How's your guys' morning going?"

"It was great until I walked in on this one," Rob nods towards Cee Cee, "making out with some girl in the storage closet," he whispers, and my eyes widen as I slowly turn to Cee Cee and she rolls her eyes at Rob.

"You're just mad because you don't have a girlfriend," she teases.

Rob's cheeks slightly blush, but before he can reply, Cee Cee turns back to me. "Speaking of, your boyfriend paid for your drink."

"Really? What'd he get me?"

"He said to let you pick." She walks around the counter.

I smile at the cute gesture, although Cee Cee and Rob rarely let me pay anyway.

"Well, in that case, I'll take anything with pumpkin." I also add Mel's order and smile as she starts making my drink. Pumpkin isn't in season, but they keep some for me since it's one of my favorites. As Cee Cee is making my drink, she reminds Rob of a note Liam made him write.

"Oh, he just wanted us to make you buy something to eat." He shrugs. "I told him I'd remember to tell you, but he didn't believe me."

I shake my head and get a croissant for the road.

"The note also says, 'Do not let her just get a damn croissant' so..."

I laugh as I imagine Liam's grumpy tone and get a bagel instead. When I get my drink I bring it to my lips and let my eyes fall shut at the perfect taste.

"Hmm, you're the best barista, Cee Cee."

She flips her pink hair proudly, and I drop two hundred bills into their tip jar. They both start telling me to take it back, but that's ridiculous, and I tell them so.

"Sorry, I have a delivery for Sage Loana?"

I turn on my heels and my eyes immediately land on a *huge* basket of pink dahlias two men are struggling to carry. I tell them that's me, and they put down the basket of flowers before having me sign.

I thank him with a smile, and when I look back down at the flowers, I notice an envelope with a cat paw print wax seal, and I gently break it open.

Thank you for being my break last night.
You're far from exhausting, Dory. You're my sanctuary.

I look back over at the basket, and I'm honestly surprised he even remembered what flowers I said I liked since he was half asleep.

"He pays for your breakfast *and* buys you flowers?"

I turn to Cee Cee, and she shakes her head with her arms crossed.

"Am I sensing some bare minimum groveling? Ugh, straight men." She shakes her head, and I laugh at how disappointed she sounds.

"It's cute, and this huge basket of flowers is barely the bare minimum."

She shrugs before going back around the counter. "They're flowers," she says as if that proves her point.

I chew my lip as I look back at the flowers but don't say anything. I take my bagel to go and, with Rob's help, take my flowers back up to my apartment before heading to work.

I find Mel in Quinn's room. After hugging both girls, I hand Mel her coffee.

"Did Jordan text you?"

She nods with a smile, and I feel myself getting excited. It's barely been a day, so I don't badger her for details and tell them I'll see them later.

When I walk into my room, I freeze at the giant basket of hydrangeas near my desk. "What the heck?" I bite back my smile as I walk over to them. They're freaking *gorgeous*. I touch them softly before leaning down to smell them, and they smell even better than I remember. When I see another envelope with the same wax seal, I quickly open it.

You were right. I never had a real girlfriend, but I'm glad
you're my first & you won't have to "teach" me how to be
a boyfriend. I know sex isn't all a relationship is:

**My favorite color is green. Emerald, like your couch.
My favorite food is New York $1 pizza.**

My favorite color is green. Emerald, like my eyes... I can't bite back my smile anymore, and I grab my phone. Someone knocks on my door and tells me my meeting with Florence is starting soon, so I text Liam instead of calling him.

> Thank you for paying for my breakfast & for the flowers!

I'm sure he'll know I got both baskets with the green heart I sent, and I rush off to my meeting with a smile.

"There's my favorite girl!" Florence pulls me in for a hug, and I silently hope that being her favorite will work out in my favor during this meeting. I look over at Angie, and she gives me a reassuring nod.

We all take a seat, and I pull in a deep breath before spitting it out. "I'm taking Vincent's offer." I keep my eyes on Florence, but her face is blank so I go on. "I want to be a Moore Girl."

She watches me for a few seconds before nodding and leaning back in her seat. "Well, you still have a contract with me and—"

"And I don't want to leave you, Florence." I watch her rough exterior chip away as her smile slowly reappears. "I sort of owe you a lot, if not everything I have, and I'm humble enough to admit it. My career took off when I signed with you, but you said you'd never hold your girls back, and I hope that's true."

She takes my hand with a smile. "Of course, I meant it, Sage. Do you know how proud I am that one of *my* girls is getting signed with Vincent fucking Moore?"

I smile at her appreciatively, and she squeezes my hand before kissing it softly.

"I feel like I raised you and the rest of The Eight when you came to me as baby models, and I'd hate to see you leave, and I'm so glad you're not, but I'll let you if you–"

"I don't want to." I notice Angie let out a sigh from beside us, but I ignore her. She thinks I'm going to be doing too much work for both companies since I'm already always booked with the events I get with Magic, but I know we can make it work, and I'll just do fewer events here and make it up with events I get with Moore.

Angie kicks my foot softly, and I get to the point of the meeting. I grab my current contract with Florence and turn to her.

"Since I'm signing a contract with Vincent, I was wondering if we can alter one thing in ours just so I can work with you both more easily." I smile shyly at her, but she's watching me more suspiciously.

"And what's that?" She crosses her arms again, and I pull in a deep breath.

"It says here that I can't miss a runway show, but–"

"Nope."

"Florence, let her finish." Angie sounds like she's warning her, but I give her a nod and silently let her know it's okay.

"Florence, Vincent's contract says I also can't miss any of his runway shows, and I doubt you two would have a show on the same day, but if you do and I sign both contracts–"

"You'd have to choose." She watches me carefully as I nod. "And let's say we do have a runway show on the same day. One here in LA for me and one for Mr. Moore in Italy. Who are you choosing?"

I feel like this is a trick question, and I know I should choose her or at least tell her I would, but I'd be breaking a contract by picking.

"She can't pick. That's why she's asking you to alter her contract." Angie saves me, and I'm glad she needs to be at all of my meetings. "We're not asking you to completely let her miss your shows because that's a ridiculous request, but we can–"

"I'm not altering the contract, Sage." She turns back to me, and I can literally feel Angie's aggregation growing. These two have some... bad blood from the past, but Angie usually gets me what I want and I love her for it, but I don't know if that will be the case today.

"Florence–"

"No." She cuts Angie off again before sliding the contract back to her and turning to me. "You're one of The Core Eight, Sage. I wouldn't let any of the others miss a show. The same goes for you. It wouldn't be a Magic Model fashion show without all eight of you. I already lost one girl, but it certainly won't be a show without you."

"I'm flattered you think so, but–"

"I don't *think* so, Sage. I know so."

My mouth falls shut as her eyes bore into my soul.

"You're *the* Magic Model, Sage Loana. I never admitted it publicly because I can't afford animosity between you girls, although there was clearly already jealousy between you and Helena because, let's be honest, while you girls were friends, jealousy sprouts in all of us, but *you're* the face of my company."

I don't know what to say, but when she turns to her laptop, I know this conversation is over. I glance over at Angie, and she ties her dreads back like she's ready to negotiate, but I know we're not going to be able to change her mind. Vincent also said this was a dealbreaker for him. What the hell am I supposed to do when they have a show on the same day?

When I get back to my room, I already want to go home, but I have so many things to do today, and I wish I had this meeting at the end of the day because now this is all I'm going to be able to think about.

I grab my things to leave and stick the card Liam sent in my bag. I have to be back here later, so I leave my flowers and tell Quinn I'll meet her in my car. We, along with the rest of The Eight, make our way to our interview, and when I tell her about my meeting with Florence, she tells me, "It'll work out," which isn't reassuring, but I doubt anything she could've said would've helped so I switch the topic.

"How do you think today's interview with Hollywood's It Girl is going to go?"

Quinn shrugs as we walk into the building. "Our last interview was almost exactly a year ago. I think it's going to be an update sort of thing."

I nod in response before turning to her. "Do me a favor?"

She's already nodding as she turns to me.

"If they bring up Helena, can you help me sway them away? I'm tired of people asking me about her." I tell her tiredly.

She grabs my hand, giving me a reassuring squeeze. "The girls and I already thought about that. We got you."

I give her a smile and turn as someone calls my name.

"Sage!" Coral calls, and the rest of the girls make their way to us. "We were trying to find our dressing rooms and got lost," Coral says shyly, and Stel shakes her head.

"She meant to say she wanted to look around and got us lost," Nin corrects her.

"Same difference." We all laugh at how freaking nosy Coral is, and someone finds us before taking us to where we need to be.

"Omg, did we all get flowers?" The girls walk into my room, and I already know they're not from the interviewers. I grab the card before they can and run my finger along the pawprint before breaking the wax open.

I grew up in Berkeley and it's one of the few places I love.
Along with New York, Greece, and by your side.
I agree with you, family matters, but I don't like talking
about mine, so I'll tell you about them another time.
For now:
Dad is gone.
Mom is sick.
I had a sister.

I keep rereading his note, and I can't tell if there's a typo on *had* a sister, but I really *really* hope there is because he said he's not ready for questions, but now I have a hundred more.

"Who are they from?"

I hold the note to my chest and muster up a smile.

Coral leans back as she eyes me suspiciously, but I tell her they're from my boyfriend, and she smiles at me knowingly. "Is it a dirty note?"

"What?" I break into a laugh, and she teases me about it the entire time we get ready. Liam must have looked at my schedule for today because there's no other way he'd know I'd be here today, but I certainly have no complaints.

"Are you guys done?" Coral asks Stel and Mace. When I turn to look at them, they giggle about something to themselves. I look back over at the other girls, and we all share a look. Royal mouths something I can't make out, and Coral and Nin start laughing. I look over at Quinn, but she only shrugs with a smile.

"Yeah!" Stel pushes Macey's hand away from her belly, and I smile as I look away from them. *They're totally hooking up, and I totally ship them.*

The interview goes smoothly. We had the same interviewer as last time, and she asked most of the same questions, at least as far as I can remember. Every time she tried to ask about Helena, the other girls, thankfully, swayed her away.

"The interviewer was totally hitting on you," Nin tells Macey, and Stel jumps up from her seat.

"I freaking told you!"

Macey tries to deny it but we all agree and it was very clear. "Okay fine, *maybe* she was, but she was hitting on you, too, and you were entertaining it, Stellamae."

I turn around at the use of her full name, and my eyes widen slightly because *no one* calls Stel by her full name.

Everyone else in the room must pick up on it because we all share a look, but no one says–

"Are you two fucking?"

My jaw drops at Coral's bluntness, but she sits there unapologetically. Stel and Mace look at each other for something, but no one says anything.

"Is that a no? Because the interviewer asked me for Stel's number."

"*Don't* give it to her." Mace bites out with her heated gaze on Stel.

A smile grows on Coral's face. "So you two are fucking like rabbits, got it." She gets up from her seat, and I bite back a laugh at her tactic and the other girls go on and on about how they knew it. Stel and Macey don't seem to care that we know as they bicker about the interviewer quietly a few feet behind us while we walk to the parking lot.

Royal helps me with my basket of flowers, and they barely fit in my backseat, but I'm definitely not complaining. He's making an effort, and definitely not the bare minimum.

I hug the girls and tell them I'll see them later before heading for a show I have with Elaine Wilson. I had a casting for her months ago and got the part. When I walk into the studio, her daughter is once again the first person to greet me.

"Sage!" She runs up to me, and I pull her in for a tight hug.

"Hello, Ms. Ebony."

She pulls away, and when she looks at me, her jaw is agape. "You remembered my name?"

I laugh at her before planting a soft kiss on the top of her head.

Her jaw drops before she looks up at me. "I'm never going to wash my hair." She hugs me tighter, and I break into another laugh.

"Don't say things like that, Ebony Mave." Her mom's voice pulls us apart, and she turns to me.

"Sage, you're early which means you're on perfect timing. Let me show you to your dressing room." She gives me another run-through of the show, and it isn't too long, which is why I was able to squeeze the interview before it and my other meeting right after.

When we reach my room, Elaine turns to her daughter. "Leave Sage to work."

When Ebony's head drops, so does my heart.

"Oh, it's okay. I'd love it if she'd stay with me." I smile at Elaine before glancing down at her daughter. "I don't like being alone during shows I don't know anyone in." My words are true, but I voice them for her sake.

Elaine keeps her gaze on her daughter. "Fine, but do not start trouble, Eb. I don't have time for your antics today." She warns, and after Ebony says she'll behave, we head into my dressing room.

"Wow, my mom is *such* a kiss ass. These flowers are obnoxiously huge."

I cannot believe this man. I walk over to the light blue hydrangeas and look for the note with a soft laugh.

I have a peanut allergy.
I despise honey.
Pineapples on pizza should be illegal; shoot me,
I don't care.
Babies are weird to me. They should know how to walk at
birth like every other mammal, grow up.
I have never been to Jamaica or Haiti, but we should go
together.

I laugh at how random these facts about him are.

"My mom must really love you."

I turn at Ebony's muffled voice, and she has a muffin in her mouth. I glance at *my* muffin basket and laugh at her. I'm sure her mom sent this one, but when I see the envelope and the cat paw, I glance back at the muffins and realize they're from the bakery I like to get them from.

Good luck on your show, beloved.
Please make sure you try to eat something.

I smile to myself and grab a muffin at his reminder because I only had half of my bagel earlier. I eat two of them before Annet and Cara walk in to do my hair and makeup for the show.

When I get on stage, the crowd applauds, but the girl in front of me trips and everyone lets out a gasp. There's more flash now, and I keep my smile in place but walk faster to help her.

I think her heel broke, but I don't look down. I grab a hold of her hand as we walk down the stage together. I let her walk in front of me when we reach the end of the stage and wave at her dress before clapping.

The crowd follows my lead and gives her a standing ovation. When she turns around, I see the gratitude on her face, and I only nod before reaching my hand out to her.

I help her back down the stage, and the second we're behind the curtain, she pulls me in for a hug. "Thank you *so* much!"

"It's not a problem at all, babe." I try to reassure her, but she starts tearing up

"That was so embarrassing." She shakes her head before covering her face in her hands.

"Babe, it's fine. I promise you, everyone is going to think that was on purpose."

She blinks away her tears, and I wipe the corner of her eye.

"Designers do stuff like that all the time, and girls actually fall for it. You only tripped a little. I promise it's okay."

I pull her in for another hug, and I stay with her for the rest of the show. Neither of us needs to go back on stage, and I think she feels better at the end of it because she stops shaking.

I remember the first time I tripped on stage, and I actually wanted to die. Like I thought my life couldn't get any worse, but when I cried to August about it, he told me I could've literally fallen on my face on live TV, and slightly tripping wasn't a big deal. I was still upset about it, but he made me laugh, and she's laughing at the end of my story, so that's a win.

When Elaine makes it backstage, I thank her again for having me, and she surprisingly thanks *me*. When I look over at her daughter, who's standing behind her, she kisses her hand before pressing it to her butt, and I have to act like I'm clearing my throat when I laugh in front of her mom, who she keeps calling a kiss ass.

I ask someone to help me with the flowers and muffins, and both baskets of flowers almost don't fit in my back seat, but after a lot of shoving and moving both seats up, I can close my door.

"Thank you again!"

Security tells me it's not a problem, and I drive back to MM Headquarters for one last meeting.

I glance around the table at the girls, and Stel and Macey are the only ones missing. We all meet with Florence once a month to go over our schedule and fit in things for group events and pictures.

Florence barely glances at me as she talks to the other girls, and I try not to let it get to me, but I really don't want her to be like this once I officially sign with Vincent next week. I already told him I'd take his offer, and it's practically set in stone, but he wants to meet in person, and since he had to be in Italy this week, we had to wait.

When the door opens, Stel and Mace walk in.

"Sorry, we're late." Stel keeps her eyes down, but her flushed cheeks and both of their swollen lips give them away way too quickly. I glance over at Florence, and she shakes her head at the two of them before they take a seat.

My phone goes off, and when I hear everyone else's buzz quietly, I know it's our group chat.

The Eight <3

Coral

> no fucking way ya just fucked before walking in here!
> BOLD ASF

I bite my cheek, and the girls all stifle their laugh. When I look over at Mace, she has a smirk on her face, but Stel's entire face flushes when our phones buzz again.

Royal

> That was you two I heard on the way here???

Mace

> you're full of shit. she was quiet… mostly

No one could hold their laugh anymore, and I think Stel kicked Macey from under the table.

"We can start this meeting whenever you girls are ready."

We all turn our phones off before placing them face-down on the table and turning to Florence.

"As you all know, we lost a model, and The Core Eight is down to seven."

I feel everyone glance at me, but I only keep my face neutral as she goes on.

"I was fine with leaving it at seven, but rumors about a replacement have been circling the media, so we may as well use the publicity now that eyes are on us. I wanted to come to you guys first since–"

"I vote Mel!" I blurt.

Florence bites back a smile, clearly at my excitement, before turning to the rest of the group. "She's a baby model and doesn't have the two years here to qualify. She–"

"Come on, Florence. That rule is kinda dumb, and while she's only been here a few months, she's getting us a lot of attention," Quinn voices, and I smile to myself.

"She's also getting into physical altercations with her peers." Florence counters as she reminds us that Mel fought Helena. It was apparently very messy, but I can't feel bad for Helena.

"She's also *not* sabotaging her best friend," Coral voices, and the room falls quiet.

"True," I voice, and Coral nods with a smirk.

While I haven't spoken to Helena, I'm glad Florence pulled her contract, and she isn't allowed on the property because, at this rate, I'm sure she'll pop up and force me to speak to her, but I refuse.

Florence says she'll think about making Mel one of The Eight and goes on about a few things she wants us to do as a group, but when she gets to scheduling them, I glance at when I have my meeting with Vincent, and I don't want to speak up, but I need to.

"Um, I can't do Tuesday."

She opens my shared calendar, but on the big screen, and I feel everyone's eyes on me.

"You're meeting with Vincent, as in *Moore*?" Nin's face lights up, but when she looks over at Florence's glare, her face drops.

"What is your meeting with him about?" Florence glances back at her laptop, and she asks casually, but we all know this is far from casual, and after this morning, I can tell she's upset with me.

"I'm taking his offer and meeting to sign the contracts." A few of the girls gasp, and when I look around the table, they look like *they're* signing with him.

"Oh my goodness! Congrats!" Nin starts before pulling me in for a hug.

"We *need* to throw a party. I call dibs on planning this one!" Royal grabs her phone and starts typing something. The rest of the girls congratulate me, and I thank them all before looking back at Florence, but she doesn't look at me.

"Alright, well, this is the only day that everyone else can do the photo shoot, so move your meeting or–"

"I can't." I laugh softly at how ridiculous that even sounds because she knows no one just *moves* their meetings with Vincent.

"So you won't be in it. Problem solved."

I open my mouth, but she shuts her laptop.

"Meeting's over. Have a good weekend, girls." She stands from her seat, and when she walks out, I'm still stuck in place.

"What's up her ass?" Coral looks around the room for an answer, but I don't try to think of one as I rush out of the room.

"Florence." I follow after her, and she doesn't slow down for me, and I know she's my boss and the freaking CEO, but she's never like this with us, especially not me. "I think that was very unfair. I can't–"

"Life's unfair, Sage. Don't be a brat about this."

"I don't think I'm being a *brat*. You–"

"Royal wasn't in the last group pictures, and she didn't throw a fit." She walks into the kitchen, and I follow her closely.

"Royal was on probation for missing the runway show!" I don't add how that wasn't her fault because she was stuck across the country. There was a storm, so she couldn't fly back on time, yet Florence still punished her.

"I'm being punished for no reason, and you said you wouldn't hold us back from opportunities. This is not very 'I'm so proud of you, Sage. You're my favorite girl' of you." I uncross my arms because I start to feel like maybe I am being a brat, but when she looks at me, I hold my ground.

"We both know this isn't fair and why you're being like this." I keep my tone soft and wish her pride would stop making her so mean. If I really can't be in the photo shoot with the girls next week, then fine, I'm not going to cry about it, but I might cry if this is how she's going to treat me every time I have to do something as a Moore Girl. I don't want to be in that kind of work environment.

"The photo shoot is happening on Tuesday, if your meeting ends early you can be there. If not, then you'll miss it, and it won't be the end of the world."

I bite my tongue and keep it between my teeth as we study each other.

"Am I clear?"

And her tone alone is what makes my tongue slip.

"Well, if I can't make it, I hope you still get the views you want without the face of the company." I don't walk away from her because that'd be rude, but her glare almost makes me run off to find Angie to fight this battle for me.

"I'm sure it will, and if it doesn't, we'll just find a new face for the company." She smiles tightly, and when I feel the back of my eyes stinging, I return the smile.

"Have a great weekend, Florence." I turn on my heels and rush into my room. I blink my tears away and don't let myself cry until I'm in my car. Stel and Mace put the basket of flowers I left here in Macey's car since it doesn't fit in mine, and while we drive to my apartment, I can't stop the tears. I tell myself I'm going to call Angie to deal with Florence, and I don't care if they argue; a part of me hopes Angie yells at her just a bit.

My phone dings, and the message pops up on my car screen.

Cee Cee

> You have another delivery from the straight man!

I laugh at what she calls Liam because while he's a straight man, I'm sure she means it as an insult. I love the message and text the girls before turning around. I was already planning on stopping by the coffee shop but changed my mind because of the mood Florence put me in. I have no clue how Liam knew I'd go there after work, but I have Mace follow me since the next basket will have to go in her car.

When I walk in, my eyes immediately fall on the purple dahlias.

"Two giant *lavish* baskets of flowers?" Cee Cee starts. "Maybe–"

"Five." I correct her as I grab the note. "And a muffin basket with my favorite muffins."

Cee Cee nods like she approves, and I'm not sure why, but I'm glad she does.

"Okay... maybe the groveling is like, two bars above the bare minimum."

I break into a laugh at how hard she is on him when she has no clue what he did, and I'm sure if a girl got her *one* huge basket of flowers, she'd be through the roof.

I do not have a middle name, but I like when you call me Leslie. ONLY because you laugh so damn pretty after saying it.
I prefer sunsets to the sunrise because I hate the mornings.
I don't like animals, and the cats are cool, but I think octopuses are cooler.

I put the note in my bag along with the others, and Cee Cee hands me a drink Liam also paid for. Stel takes one side of the basket, and I take the other. We drag it into Macey's car and squeeze it next to the other one.

When I get home, my doorman helps us fill the elevator with the baskets of flowers, and I hug the girls before thanking them. My doorman helps me drag the heavy flowers into my apartment, and when I lean against the door, one last basket of dahlias sits on my counter. I let out a soft chuckle as I walk over to read the note.

My flight lands at 9 pm.
Be ready for our date by 10:30 pm & you can ask all your questions to get to know me.

Chapter Twenty-Eight

LIAM

I HAVE NO IDEA WHAT'S wrong with me, but I might be sick. My palms are sweaty, and my stomach feels weird. It only gets worse the higher the elevator climbs to Sage's place, and it's ridiculous for me to be nervous about this date, so I must be sick with something.

My hand freezes at her door, and maybe it's because I've never been on a date or maybe because I want Sage to enjoy our date, but this is so damn hard.

I hurry up and knock, and I hear her yell on the other side of the door that she's on her way. I look down at the white roses in my hand and fix one that looks weird just as she opens the door.

My eyes land on her pretty smile, and I immediately lean in to kiss her. When I pull away to look at her, I slowly take in her dress. She's in emerald green and the color looks like it was made for her as the dress melts into every last one of her perfect curves.

"You are perfect."

She smiles up at me before flattening my button-up shirt. "You don't look too bad yourself, handsome."

I feel my face heat, and when she looks up at me, her jaw drops at something.

"Are you *blushing*?!"

"No, it's hot in here." I hand her the roses and unbutton the first few buttons on my shirt. Sage doesn't say anything else as she smiles down at her roses.

"You did not need to get me these for the date."

I look around her living room, and it's covered with the five bouquets I sent today, plus the fifteen for my be-my-girlfriend gesture. Her house smells like a garden, but I look down at her, and she's smiling around the room. I'll send her twenty lavish bouquets every day just to keep that smile on her face.

She sets her roses on her counter, but when her phone dings, I notice her face drop.

"What's wrong?"

She shakes her head, but I close the distance between us and lean down to catch her eyes with mine.

"What is it, beloved?"

When she lets out a sigh, I glance over at her phone and then back at her.

"My meeting didn't go how I wanted." She sounds like she's about to cry, and when I pull her face up to look at me, I realize her eyes are welling up. "She was being so mean and punishing me for taking Vincent's offer, but I didn't do anything wrong."

I pull her in for a hug, and she immediately melts into me. "This was that Florence lady?"

She confirms before telling me she's her boss, and I make sure I remember that name.

"It's gonna be okay; you'll have your way."

She pulls away and drags in a deep breath before putting on a smile, for I'm not sure who. "I don't think I will, but thank you." When she gets on her tippy toes, I lean down for her and kiss her softly.

"What did you have planned for our date?"

"You'll see." I grab her hand, and we head for the door. I grab it before she can, and she smiles up at me, but a second barely passes before her smile drops, and she looks past me like she's seen a ghost.

I turn around and take a step in front of Sage because the girl in front of us looks like a damn lunatic. It looks like she put on five pounds of mascara before dumping her face in a pool. She's in a sweatsuit with stains, and I think she's been wearing this for the last few days. Her hair also looks like she was fighting her brush.

"Do you know this girl?" I mumble to Sage, but when I glance at her, I see tears building in her eyes.

"Sage—"

I shut the door on her face before grabbing Sage's hand. "Who is that? Do you want her to leave?"

She only nods, and when she pulls in a deep breath, I think she physically can't let it back out.

I plant a quick kiss on her forehead before opening the door again, just a bit so she can only see me as I keep Sage covered. "Leave."

The girl looks up at me like *I'm* the one who shouldn't be here. "Who the hell are you?" I glance at the bruise under her eye before giving her a once-over.

"Who the fuck are *you*?"

She pulls in a breath before rubbing her nose on a nasty-ass napkin in her hand, and I inch away from her, although there's plenty of space between us.

"I'm her best friend. I just—"

Sage suddenly swings the door open, and I wrap an arm around her waist because with how quickly she moves, I think she's going to attack the homeless girl in front of us.

"You are *not* my best friend, and you never have been, Helena."

It suddenly clicks who the hell this chick is, and I let Sage go because this girl deserves to get her ass beat, and my money is on Sage.

"Sage, I am so sorry about what happened. Can you please just let me explain?"

"You're sorry for *what happened*?" Sage shakes her head, and I hate how hurt she looks. "You mean you're sorry for trying to ruin the biggest day of my career because that's what happened."

Helena keeps her eyes on Sage, and I swear it's as if she's forcing her tears out. "I did it for you, Sage. I was trying to help you, why can't you see that?" She takes a step forward, and I wrap an arm around Sage before pulling her a step back because this girl actually sounds manic with the way she tries to justify this.

"That doesn't even make sense, Lena! You know I'm not one of those models who self-sabotage for attention, and even if those were your intentions, you should've come to me with the idea before cutting a hole in my fucking dress five minutes before I needed to go on fucking stage!"

My eyes slightly widen because I've never heard Sage curse. I like this side of her; I just wish she didn't have to be hurt for me to see it. I realize she has a slight accent that slips as she yells, and I bite back a smile as I watch her.

"I don't even care about the dress. I don't care that it was a Moore show. It was the fact that *you* did that." She shakes her head again, and I see her lip trembling.

"If it was anyone else, *anyone* else, I would've brushed it under the rug, but you–" She pulls in a deep breath before trying again. "We started this together. At nineteen, it was just you and me, and then you—I would've never–" Her voice breaks, and I think my heart does too. "I would've *never* done that to you."

A single tear treks down her cheek before she walks away. Helena grabs her arm, and I grab hers. "Do not fucking touch her." I push her hand away, and Sage escapes for the elevator as I turn to Helena. "If I so much as see you on this *street,* I'll drag you out myself. Let this be the last time you even *think* of her damn name."

I shut the door, and she slightly jumps before I walk past her and get into the elevator with Sage. She's quiet until we get to my car, but it's clear she's trying not to cry.

"I'm sorry–"

"Do not apologize, Sage. That was not your fault, and if you want to cry, then go the fuck ahead."

She looks up at the ceiling of my car as she blinks her tears away. "I don't want to ruin my makeup. She isn't worth it."

I give her thigh a reassuring squeeze, and after a minute, she pulls in a deep breath and turns to me.

"Do you want to talk about it?"

She bites her lip, and I know she does. "I used to *dream* of becoming the greatest model to ever walk a stage. I'd dream of winning it all, and every time, in every dream, Helena was by my side, winning with me."

She shakes her head before glancing out her window, and just as she does, we watch Helena walking for her car.

"I loved her like a sister, and she tried to humiliate me on my biggest day."

I glance over at Helena, and she walks with her head held high like she has no shame in what she did to my girl.

"Do you want me to run her over because there's still time, and we can make it look like an accident?" I turn the car on, and Sage grabs my hand before filling the car with her perfect laugh.

"Are you crazy?" She laughs harder, and I lean over before kissing her dimples.

"No, but I'd do some pretty crazy things for you."

Her eyes meet mine, and not a single tear is in sight.

"Ready?"

She nods in return, and I give her a soft kiss before driving off, but just as we pass Helena, I put Sage's window down.

"What are you—"

"Fuck you! Hating ass bitch!"

I speed off, and Sage's jaw agapes. "That was so—"

"Don't say it was mean because she—"

"Funny!" She breaks into a laugh. "Did you see her face?"

The car fills with our laughter as I drive us to our date. I let her play her horrible music, and she dances in her seat with a smile.

When she puts the music down, I steal a glance at her, and she's watching me with an innocent smile. "So..."

"So..." I keep my eyes on the road, but a smile tugs at my lips when I hear her giggle next to me.

"You love Greece?"

I take a slow breath and force myself not to sigh so she doesn't misinterpret it. I told her I love Greece and that was the same card I told her about Shanti...

I asked her not to ask about it, but my last card also said she could ask whatever she wanted tonight, and I appreciate how subtle she tries to be.

"I do." I bring my hand to her thigh before giving her a soft squeeze. "I think I'd like Jamaica or Haiti more, though." When I look over at her, she only nods, her smile still present, and I'm glad she understands that I don't want to talk about it.

She asks about my time in Greece, and as I tell her about it, I make sure to stay away from the topic of *who* I was there with, but she, of course, asks, and when I cringe, she notices.

"Oh gosh, you were being a whore out there, weren't you!" She laughs, and I'm glad this is her reaction, although I wasn't expecting her to be weird or jealous.

"I was..." I sound like I'm in trouble, but when I think about the shit I did there, I'd probably be in trouble if she knew, and she didn't even know me at the time. "But that's not why I love Greece, and either way, I'm your whore now."

She fills the car with her laugh, and I steal a kiss when we get to a red light.

"Why octopus?"

I kiss her cheek one more time before I continue driving. "I just always thought they were cool as a kid. Three hearts, eight legs." I say with a shrug. "And they only live maybe five years instead of an insanely long time or ridiculously short time. They're cool."

"Five years is a pretty short time to live."

In comparison to humans, I guess she's right.

"Yeah," I pull in a deep breath, and it's not as hard as I thought it would be to continue, so I do. "I always liked them, but I think they remained my favorite animal because my sister liked them. We went to an aquarium, and when she touched one, she lost her fucking shit."

I laugh at the memory. "She kept saying 'octo' like a broken record. We practically lived in the aquarium that week."

Sage laughs softly from beside me. When her laugh sobers, I steal a glance at her, and she grabs the hand I have on her thigh. She studies my tattoo, and it's dark in here, so she uses the front of her phone for light, but I can see her connecting the dots in her head as she analyzes the octopus tattoo on my hand.

"I thought none of your tattoos had any special meaning to them?" She turns to me, and I offer a small smile as I glance back at the road.

"Those are for my sister. None of the others mean anything, though."

She kisses my hand and then kisses my forearm where my bigger octopus tattoo is, and with how tender her lips are on a part of me that's so special, I never want her to stop kissing me.

The rest of the drive, we sit in a comfortable silence as her music plays.

When we park, she looks out the window, and her eyes light up. "Oh my God! The El Captain theater? I've always wanted to come here." She looks over at me and quickly kisses me. "Are we watching *Lady and the Tramp*?"

She sounds way too excited, and my face drops. "No... Do you want to watch that?"

She looks back over at me and her brows slightly furrow. "Oh, I don't mind what we watch." She shakes her head softly, but now I feel like this is ruined. "I just asked because that's what they have on their signs?"

I glance out the window and see pictures of dogs eating spaghetti everywhere. "Because that's what they're showing, but I rented the place out for us to watch something else, but if you want to watch that, I can tell them, and I–"

"Liam." She laughs at something before taking my hand. "It's okay; we can watch whatever you pick."

"Are you sure? Because–"

"Yes!" She laughs again, and I don't know what's so funny, but my eyes fall on her smile before I kiss her.

"Why do you seem so nervous?"

I pull away, and she clearly bites back a laugh. "I'm not *nervous*. What is there to be nervous about? It's a *movie*."

"It's a date... Probably your first real one." She teases, and I roll my eyes before slipping out of the car, and she laughs behind me. I grab her door for her and take hold of her hand as we walk to the theater. I look over at her to watch her reaction, and I can see her excitement growing at the *Princess and the Frog* theme everywhere.

I had them change their entire theme from the ugly dogs to this because I wanted Sage to have the full experience. I'm glad I didn't just have them play the movie because she marvels around the room like a kid on Christmas.

"This is my *favorite* movie."

I smile at her.

"Like ever—besides *Finding Nemo*."

"I know."

"How?" She asks, as if she doesn't walk around her apartment singing the entire soundtrack, but I reply with a shrug and her smile only grows.

"Do you want to get something to eat?"

She surprisingly says yes, and I think it's because she just wants to get a picture of the Mickey-shaped pretzel, but I make her order some food.

"They only have junk food, Lee–"

"You can have a cheat day, Sage."

She lets out a sigh as she looks at the menu.

"If you want something else, we can order something to come over here."

"No... I don't want to do that." She glances at the menu again, and it's clear she doesn't want anything.

I plant a kiss on her cheek before leaning into her ear. "You don't have to finish it, beloved. Just try something."

She takes a deep breath before forcing a smile and looking at the cashier. "Can I have a hotdog and fries?" She kept her voice light and her smile intact; you'd never know that was a struggle for her.

"Good job, pretty girl," I whisper in her ear before stealing a kiss and ordering my food, along with popcorn for us.

"Is it a four-D movie?" Sage takes the glasses from the lady after thanking her, and when she says it is, she hurries into the theater as if the movie will start without us. A minute or two after we sit, it starts since we're the only ones here, and Sage is recording the live pianist.

"This is so cool."

I laugh at how she whispers when we're *alone*. She looks like a kid who was told they could have ice cream for dinner with how happily she sings every song and says every line with the characters.

I only ever watched this movie once, years ago, with Shanti, so it's like I'm watching it for the first time, and it's even better having Sage say half the lines and giggling beside me.

"Oh, oh, this is my favorite song." She sings along with Tiana, and I spend the whole time watching her rather than watching the movie.

When the VooDoo man comes on screen, Sage watches with wide eyes as if she can't miss a second.

"When I watched this as a kid, I was amazed that Lawrence kept calling Naveen Sire, you know because that's my brother's name, but then I learned it's what you call a king." She turns to me. "Isn't that cool?"

No. Her brother isn't a damn king.

"Mhm."

She turns back around and tells me this is her favorite part and to pay extra close attention, so I do.

"And I got friends on the other side." She makes her voice deeper.

I lean into her ear. "He's got friends on the other side."

She loses her shit and is surprised I know this part, but it's honestly the only song I know since she sings it all the time.

"Shake my hand," Sage says and holds her hand out to me. "Come on, babe, won't you shake a poor sinner's hand?" She nods for her hand, and I have no idea what's happening, but I take her hand just in time, and she tilts her head back.

"Yes! Are you ready?"

I break into a laugh at how much of a damn character she is. She sings the rest of the song before we sink into our seats to watch the rest.

"Oh, this is my favorite song." She whispers to herself, and she says this about every other song that plays, but I don't tell her that. "Look how she lights up the sky."

The ceilings light up with stars, and one shines brighter than the others, like on the screen. Sage looks up again, and the star rivals her eyes. "I adore you. I love you." She looks over at me and puts her hands up in defense like the frog. "Just translating." She laughs as she says the lines with Naveen, but I physically can't look away from her.

God, she's so pretty. She's literally perfect.

My heart suddenly races as a heat wave washes over me, and my eyes travel along every inch of her face. Her dimples deepen as she sings, and a fist comes around my heart.

"And I love you, Evangeline," she whispers, and when pink spotlights light up the room, she lets out a soft gasp. "Ou, can we dance with them?"

I blink, and when I look at the screen, the frogs are danc-ing under a pink light. I hate dancing, but she's watching me hopefully, so I rise to my feet, and we dance.

The lights around us change on cue with the movie, and Sage looks like this is all she has wanted in her entire life. We sway softly, and I watch her as she watches the ceiling change colors.

I love her.

I clear my throat and look away from her because it's starting to physically hurt to look at her. I don't know what the hell it's like to love someone, but I don't think I'm sup-posed to say that shit on the *first* date. I *do* know, right now, I never want to be apart from this woman, and I desperately need for her to always have this smile on her face.

The lights cut, and shadows scurry around us. When I turn to the screen, a shadow grabs one of the frogs, and Sage pulls me back to sit down for the rest of the movie.

Chapter Twenty-Nine

LIAM

"THAT WAS SO MUCH FUN!" Sage walks into her apartment, and I follow close behind her before she sinks into the wall. "I wore my cute heels, though, and my feet hurt." She tries to take them off, but I grab her hand when she stumbles.

"Here." I give her my phone to hold and kneel down to take her heels off. I unwrap the string around her calf and kiss the mark it left her. When I slide her first heel off, I kiss her foot softly before grabbing the other one.

"So sweet."

I glance up at her, and she has my phone pointed at me. "Are you recording me?"

"Mhm." She puts her other heels on my chest, and I shake my head at how she smiles behind the camera. I start unraveling the string around her calf but glance up at her dress and slowly push it up.

"What are you—"

I drag my tongue along her inner thigh, and she shoves me away with a laugh when I try to push her legs open. "Stop that!"

I look back up at her, and the phone is suddenly nowhere in sight. "What happened to recording?" I tease, and when I hear her laugh in the video, I know she caught me on camera.

"Well, now I can't post this." She shakes her head with a smile, and I take her second heel off before lifting one of her legs onto my shoulder.

"Why not?" I push her legs further apart as I kiss my way under her dress.

"Liam, what—"

I can only imagine her face when I tug at her underwear, and I'm sure she's looking everywhere but me. "Liam." She whispers now, and I feel myself smiling as I kiss her heat through her underwear.

"Hmm?"

She moans in response, and with one more tug, her underwear snaps right off. I let it fall to the ground as I slide my tongue exactly where she likes it.

"Liam, you look really hot on your knees for me, but let's go to bed." When she tries to move me, I keep her in place, and she doesn't voice another protest as I work my tongue along her folds. She tastes *heavenly*, and I can stay here on my knees for her all night, but within minutes, she's coming over my face.

When I glance up at her, she's trying to catch her breath with her head tilted up to the ceiling. I know little to nothing about relationships, but I *do* know you shouldn't say those three words I was just thinking after the *first* date. I don't know what clicked, but being around Sage altered my brain chemistry.

This woman consumes my every thought. The only place I want to be is in her presence, and the only thing I want to do is satisfy her. Whether that be on my knees, adopting cats, or watching her walk in million-dollar fashion shows.

"If you pull out a ring, I might need to decline." She laughs softly, and I have no clue what she's talking about, but I can't pull my gaze from her pretty smile.

"What?" My eyes bore into those green ones, and I just decided she's somehow prettier from this angle. I should be on my knees for her all the time.

"You're looking at me like you're going to propose. Get off your knees." She laughs again as she takes my hand, dragging me to my feet.

"Why would you say no if I did?" I don't mean to sound so offended, but a part of me is.

"We only accept big gestures, Lee. I don't see 'marry me' spelled out on a billboard." She walks past me, and I can't help but smile at her insane standards, but I'll climb the moon to reach them.

"Billboard proposals are all you accept?"

She looks like she's thinking before she shakes her head. "No, I was kidding. If it's something small and intimate, I'll accept it, but I want a photographer there."

I follow close behind her as she walks for her room but then she glances at her wall full of pictures before adding, "And my siblings. They need to be hiding somewhere."

I want to be with her for every second, dare I say forever, but her siblings will not be *anywhere* near us. I almost voice that but quickly remember our conversation from last night. I genuinely don't think she'll break things off with me if she finds out her brothers and I can't stand each other, so I just need to rip this bandaid off.

When we make it to her room, a playful grin plays on her face, but I pull her in before ripping her clothes off. "I want to apologize for last night." I plant a kiss on her nose before wrapping my arms around her waist. "I don't like opening up... I never had to, so this is new to me, but I promise I'm going to try with you, Dory, because I want to let you in."

A smile touches her lips, and I steal a kiss before continuing.

"My mom had an episode and flipped out on her nurse, and I know her bad days don't excuse my bad attitude, but it was still fresh, and when you started asking about my family, I shut down, but I shouldn't have. I should've communicated with you, and I won't brush you off like that again because you don't deserve that, so I'm sorry. You're *not* exhausting, Sage, and I'm sorry for the attitude."

I hate apologizing. It never came easy to me, but as I stand in front of this woman, saying sorry is like breathing, and I swear to myself that I won't hurt her again and have to apologize more in my future with her.

"Thank you for that." She kisses me slowly, but I regrettably pull away to tell her one more thing because if I want to be with her, she needs to know the truth, and my mom was right; she'll be more upset if she hears it from someone else. It'll hurt more, and I never want to hurt her again.

"Dory." I hold her hand, and as I look down at her, she looks so damn happy. I hate that I'm about to crush that spark in her eyes. "I need to tell you something, beloved."

Her brows slightly pull together as I pull her to sit with me on the edge of her bed. "Why do you look like that? What's wrong?" She asks warily.

I try to offer her a smile and tell her it's nothing she needs to worry about, but that'll be a lie.

SAGE

I FEEL MY HEART SINK at the worry on Liam's face. "Is it your mom? Is she okay?" I squeeze his hand a bit tighter before he shakes his head gently.

"She's okay; I just need to talk to you about something, but before I tell you, I want you to know that my intentions were pure, Sage." He shakes his head, clearly lost in his thoughts. "Well, not *pure* since I wanted to sleep with you from the moment I saw you in that lingerie set, but I saw your sweet smile and innocent soul first, then the way you said please made me want to give you the sun and moon, but nothing between us had to do with your family, I swear, Dory, and-"

"Wait," I stop his quick rambling as my brain catches up. "What about my family?"

He looks down at where our hands meet before visibly growing anxious.

"Lee, what is it?" I ask again, getting a bit scared now.

"When you asked if I knew your brothers, I didn't tell you the whole truth, Dory."

I feel my brows pull together as I watch him, but his eyes don't meet mine. "You lied?" I try to pull my hand away, but his grip tightens as he looks up at me.

"I didn't *lie*. I just didn't tell you everything..."

"That's lying." I pull my hand away harder. "You always go on and on about how disrespectful it is to lie, and you've been lying?"

He looks like he regrets saying anything which makes me more upset. "What's the whole truth?" Whatever he wants to say clearly isn't good since he has that look on his face.

His shoulders drop before he turns to me. "I met your brothers in college. We went to rival schools."

He watches me carefully, but I'm clearly missing something. "That's it? You already told me you went to UCD. I didn't think you knew my brothers, but I thought the rivalry between those colleges was over something silly. Either way, that was years ago; why lie to me about that?" My mind races with a hundred other questions as his worry grows.

"Because your brothers and I aren't the best of friends, and it's more than college rivalry."

"Okay... what does that mean?"

He shakes his head now as he grabs my hand. "It was stupid, Dory. They did some fucked up shit, I did stuff back. It's dumb and doesn't matter. I just wanted to tell you because I realized today that I want to be with you for a very long time, and I didn't want you to hear it from someone else."

I watch him for a beat, but if whatever happened was so dumb, he wouldn't have lied. "Tell me what happened, and let me decide what matters."

"Sage-"

"Tell me, Liam," I say more sternly. After needing to confront Helena tonight and now hearing he's been lying to me for months, I'm done playing nice when it's clear no one cares enough to return it.

He keeps his eyes on me, and when he realizes I'm not backing down, he gives in. "Your brother tried to create peace between our schools, specifically between the baseball teams."

I don't ask which brother since I can guess who put in that effort.

"I guess he thought the rivalry between past classes was dumb, and at first, our schools didn't want to go with it, but most of us came around. I was hanging out with your brothers a lot, playing scrimmages, practicing, racing with Sire on our cars and with August on our bikes."

"You were *friends*?" I almost don't believe him because it's so rare for my brothers to fall out with any of their friends.

"What happened?" I almost ask what he did, but I don't want to place blame.

"When the season started, they were winning games left and right. There was foul play involved, so we flipped the tables."

My brain tries to make sense of what that means, but that doesn't make sense. "I highly doubt my brothers were cheating in a sport they were recruited by the best college to play."

He looks offended now as he leans away to look at me. "You think I'm *lying*?"

"I never said that, but I know my brothers and-"

"And you know me."

"Not as well as I know them, and you've been lying to me," I counter, and as much as it hurts me to say it, it's true.

He lets out a scoff as he faces forward. "They were cheating, and no one was doing anything about it, so we made sure they went down for something else."

I watch him for a minute, but he's being serious. "That genuinely sounds so silly. What do you mean you *made sure they went down*?" I try to voice another question, but he continues.

"We suggested they throw a party, but as athletes, we weren't allowed to smoke and drink. One of my teammates took pictures of them and sent them to the dean, but while I was there, I may have picked a fight with August-"

"You *may* have?"

He ignores me. "We knew Sire would jump in if August was getting jumped, so one of my teammates hit him and stepped away once Sire joined in. They filmed the short minute of your brothers jumping me to send to the dean before my team... jumped them."

I wait for him to tell me he's joking, but he sits on my bed with a serious face. "Do you even hear yourself?" I stand from the bed as he looks up at me. "You set them up? All for a dumb baseball game?"

He *rolls* his eyes at me. "It meant more than that. Nothing ever happened to them since your parents paid off the school."

I open my mouth to counter but remember the boys getting in trouble, and everything makes sense now, given the full story. "That was *you*?" I say, thinking out loud as memories of August's rants about this from years ago come back. "They were going to get kicked out of school for that. Not just benched from a few games. *Why* would you do that?"

His brows pull together as he focuses on me. "No, they weren't."

"*Yes*, they were. I was there, and if they had scholarships, they would've lost them because of you." I watch Liam, unable to believe he'd do that. Sire and August were offered scholarships but didn't take them because they wanted kids who needed them to have them, but that all would've been gone over a dumb game because of Liam.

He looks like he thinks of something before he shakes his head at his thoughts. "I didn't know that, and either way, they're not saints. They jumped me multiple times after that."

"You jumped them first! Why don't you sound the least bit remorseful?"

"I'm aware that it was wrong, but-"

"No, there are no buts." I put a hand up, stopping him from trying to justify this, but I stop myself from making this into a bigger fight when I feel myself getting angry. "This is all so dumb." I shake my head at myself. This doesn't deserve my energy, at least not right now.

The tension in his shoulders eases as he stands from the bed and grabs my hand, but I pull away and take a step back. "I'm still upset that you *lied*, Liam. Go home." I have no idea what he thought my reaction was going to be, but I certainly don't want to share a bed with him tonight.

He looks as if I just said I never wanted to see him again, and I'm genuinely surprised he really thought I'd forgive him that easily.

"You said it yourself that it's disrespectful to lie and that you hate it more than anything, yet you've been lying to me for *months*." I cut myself off as I realized something. "A few months ago, you came here with a black eye." I take another step back as the pieces fall together. "That was Sire who you got into a fight with, wasn't it? I didn't think you guys were *still* fighting? And you've just been sleeping with me like nothing? Do you know how stupid that makes me look?"

I nearly yell now, and his face drops.

"Get out."

"Dory-"

"No, you're such a *hypocrite*, Liam. Get out. Right now." I walk out of my room, and he follows me into the living room. The smell of all of the flowers wraps around me, and I shake my head at how ridiculous this is. When I open the front door, Liam doesn't walk out.

"I don't want to leave." He watches me like I should really take his request into consideration.

"Well, I do want you to leave, Liam." I keep the door open, but he doesn't budge.

"I'll sleep on the couch," he tries to negotiate, but I shake my head at him. "Please?"

"No, sleep in your own bed. I don't want to be near you."

He tries to say something, but I beat him to it.

"Do you not understand how much it hurts that you casually came to my house to sleep with me after busting my brother's lip? You really expect me to believe you didn't get with me simply out of spite or some sick payback?" I blink my tears away, forcing myself not to cry, especially not in front of him.

I see his face morph into anger now as he closes the distance between us. "Don't ever say that. That's not why I got with you. I have way too much respect for you to-"

"But not enough for you not to lie to me?" I let out a scoff as I step away from him. "Did your friends know?"

When he doesn't answer quickly enough, I have my answer.

"So you all just treated me like an idiot."

"That's not-"

"Liam, get out, or I'll call my brothers to get you out. *Leave*." I look away from him and force myself to keep my eyes forward. For a minute, he stands there watching me before walking past me.

"I'm sorry, Dory."

I hold my head up as I keep my tears at bay, and when he walks out, I let the door shut.

Chapter Thirty

SAGE

"WHERE'S HAZEL AND V?" I give August a hug, and while I know I didn't do anything wrong, it feels wrong hugging him, knowing what Liam told me last night. I haven't spoken to him all day, but he sat outside my door all night and tried to talk to me this morning before I left, but I told him I needed space. I don't know when I'm going to talk to him, but it's not now.

August kisses my head before pulling away. "Hazel is down on the boat releasing an otter for work, and I think Sire mentioned something about Vidia having a meeting at work, but he sounded weird about it."

Before I can question him, Lis comes up beside us. "Is this the Grammys or an AA meeting?" She takes in my outfit before pulling me in for a hug, and I let out a soft laugh.

"We're going somewhere after this, and I just wanted to wear my outfit now." It's a cute dress, but I also wanted to spend the rest of the day with Sire. This way, I won't have to leave to change for the rooftop place we're going to.

Today's Sire's one-year soberversary, and when he came by to tell me earlier, I literally screamed. He's been working *so* hard to get to this, and I'm immensely proud of him. He *also* told me what happened between him and Vidia and why they broke up back in college, but I'm so glad they're officially working on getting back together.

"Where are we even going because you're being all top secret about it, and I don't like those bougie ass places you always take us to," Lis complains, and I laugh at her.

"She's just accustomed to the trenches."

I turn at the sound of Sire's voice, and all of us break into a laugh before I pull him in for a hug.

"We were neighbors in those *trenches*, asshole."

"Maybe, but which of the two of us made it out first?"

"Because these idiots adopted your pathetic ass, don't make me go there." Lisette points at Sire at the end of her threat, and surprisingly, he doesn't bother her anymore.

The two of them grew up on the other side of town from August and I, and it definitely wasn't the best part of town, but we all went to the same school, which is how we met.

I let my eyes focus on my brother, and when he smiles, my chest suddenly feels heavy. "I'm so proud of you, Sire." I pull him in for another hug and squeeze my eyes shut when I feel them stinging.

"Oh my God. She cries for everything. Sage, stop; we said there won't be any crying today." Lis sounds annoyed, but Sire immediately tells her to leave me alone, which I appreciate because I didn't agree to this no-crying deal, and I'll definitely be shedding a few tears.

"I love you, Sage." When we pull away he plants a soft kiss on the top of my head before wiping away a single tear that escaped. "Seriously though, no crying."

I laugh softly and blink away my tears. "Fine!"

Our parents trickle in soon after, and the meeting starts.

"This next chip is also for three hundred and sixty-five days sober."

I start recording since this is Sire's sponsor on stage now.

"I know I shouldn't say this because it might boost this man's already huge ego," The crowd laughs, and when I look over at Sire, he rubs his eye while not so discreetly flipping off his sponsor.

"But I'm most proud of you. People in your position usually throw money at their problems or ignore them completely because they have that privilege, being that they're wealthy, but you put in the work, and I think the teenage version of yourself would be most proud so keep doing it for him."

There's no use stopping the tears now, and when I steal a glance at Sire, he blinks rapidly as he keeps his tears at bay.

"I now present this bronze chip for one year sober to Sire Griffin."

I'm still recording like a proud mom as Sire walks up the stage, and the family stands to clap for him. He looks so content, almost like this is just another day, and he couldn't care too much, but I know how hard he's been working to stay clean this last year, and I know he's proud of making it.

The minute I get the chance, I make everyone give him his gifts, mainly because I love gifts and want to see what he got.

"Socks?"

Lisette smiles proudly as Sire holds up the gift he gave her.

"What do they say on it?"

"Sober AF." Lisette still has a smug smile on her face, and Sire burst into a laugh.

"You could've done worse. Your gift is going to be easy to get now."

"No gift is worse than socks."

"There's always worse." They share a laugh, and I have no clue why they gift each other bad gifts for their soberversary, but I love all of their inside jokes.

"Okay, open mine."

Sire takes my gift, and I wait excitedly as he unboxes it. When his eyes land on the snow globe, he immediately looks over at me.

"Sage, I said we couldn't cry."

I fight my tears to stay at bay, and he clearly does the same as he tries not to look at his gift.

"Look at the picture."

He turns his head to the side, but I urge him to look at it. When he does, a smile creeps onto his face before he pulls me in for a hug.

"What is it?"

Sire lets August take the snow globe as he keeps his arms around me.

"This is a picture from the first time you made a year sober?"

I pull away to wipe my tears and smile down at the picture.

We look like babies in this. We were eighteen, and Sire and Lis were just sixteen. We threw the biggest party the first time Sire made a year sober, and he begged me not to because he doesn't like the attention, but he deserved to be celebrated. It was also Lis's soberversary and she almost didn't go to the party, but Sire dragged her to it since he had to be there.

"It's the perfect gift, and it'll be perfect for the collection." Sire kisses my forehead before taking the gift back from August.

Snow globes have become our thing. It started with the first one I gave him on Christmas when we were kids. I felt bad that he had fewer gifts than August and I. We hadn't adopted him at the time, and our parents didn't know he was going to be spending Christmas with us. He only had a few gifts, so I gave him a snow globe I got for Easter, and he loved it so much; he said it was his favorite gift ever, and since then, I get him snow globes whenever I have the excuse to.

"Okay, at least open my gift before you say hers is perfect."

We laugh at my twin's jealousy, and Sire opens August's gift. It's a pair of very expensive headphones, and it's a nice gift since I know Sire mentioned he wanted these. I think mine is still better, but Sire nor I mention it.

I spend the rest of the day with my siblings, and it only makes me realize how much I miss them. The boys spend way more time together than with me and it's mainly because they're literally neighbors, but it makes me miss being young when we all lived together and didn't have our own lives.

When we make it to the rooftop place I booked, Liam calls me so I slip to the bathroom to answer.

"Hello?" I keep my voice hushed, although all of the other stalls are empty.

"Dory, hey." He lets out a small breath as if he was informed I was harmed and he needed to hear my voice. "Where are you?"

"Why do you want to know, Liam?" With my phone connected to my headphones, I put my phone down as I apply more lipgloss.

He's quiet for a second before he says, "I miss you."

I shake my head before rubbing my lips together to spread the gloss. "You saw me this morning."

"Well, I still miss you. I don't like this space stuff."

"I don't like being lied to and made out to look stupid. Have a good night." I try to hang up, but he quickly stops me.

"You know I didn't get with you out of spite, right? I wouldn't do that to you, Sage, I swear. I wanted you for you."

I focus on myself in the mirror as I think of his words. I give myself a once over, and no matter how much my brain tries to pick me apart, I know those weren't his intentions.

"I know, Liam. That doesn't take away from the fact that my brothers don't like you."

"So you're going to break up with me because of them?"

I can hear the shift in his tone as he gets upset, and I chew my lip in thought. I know they fought a few months ago, but I have no clue how much my brothers truly dislike him. They clearly don't *hate* him since I haven't heard about it.

"Sage," he calls when I don't answer.

"No, Liam, maybe not, but you didn't need to lie and loop your friends in on it." I haven't spoken to Jordan, but Moon has tried calling me. I forgot I was mad at him, so I answered, and he told me that he told Liam to tell me. He said, "It's not my fault he's a liar," which I guess is true. It was Liam's job to tell me, not Moon's.

Someone walks into the bathroom, and I offer them a bright smile as I grab my phone. "I need to go." I hang up before he can respond and head back to my siblings.

Chapter Thirty-One

SAGE

"**S**AGE, IT'S GOING TO BE okay!"

I pull the blanket off my face and look over at August.

"Really, gorgeous?" He mumbles before lifting her off of the counter with ease and reaching whatever she was trying to get.

"I could've reached it had you given me another second." She grabs the cookies from him, and a smile tugs at my lips.

"You're going to fall, angel. Just ask me to help you."

Hazel is already walking away from him with the box of cookies, and August only smiles as he watches her.

"You don't know that it's going to be okay." I sink further into their couch, and Hazel flops on the other end.

"This Florida girl sounds like a bitch." She picks up her phone, and I can't help but laugh at how horrible she is with names.

"It's Florence." I remind her once again. I have my meeting with Vincent today and, of course, I came to see August first to make me feel better because I also have another meeting with Florence.

Angie spoke to her, and I was told there was a lot of yelling, so I won't be surprised if I'm no longer a Magic Model by the end of the day. She technically can't fire me since we have a contract that I haven't broken, but she's released girls in the past.

"I don't really care," Hazel voices, and when August sits between us, she swings her legs onto his lap. "She's being a hater, just like that Holly girl. I don't like her."

I stifle a laugh at her name for Helena. "You don't like anyone?"

She glances over at me for barely a second before looking back at her phone. "I like everyone in this room." She shrugs, but I sit up in my seat.

"Really?!"

Hazel is far from affectionate, at least with everyone but my brother. I can count on one hand how many times she's said she loves me, and all of those times, August or I told her to tell me.

When I hear the front door open, I turn just as Vidia and Sire walk in, hand-in-hand. It's good to see them happy together. I wasn't *trying* to be nosy, but August told me why Vidia missed Sire's soberversary, and I know Sire was pretty upset. That was a few days ago, though, and I think they're simply tired of fighting for the last four years because they made up pretty quickly.

Liam and I haven't made up, though; we're in a weird space. He keeps coming to my house to see me and apologize. I got three more bouquets and they were gorgeous, but I don't want flowers. I want to know how bad his relationship with my brothers is.

My heart races whenever Liam walks into a room; I know what he did was messed up, and I'm mad he lied, but I can forgive it if my brothers do. I want to be with him, but not if my brothers absolutely hate him. I couldn't do that to them. I just don't know how to bring it up to Sire and August.

"I take back what I said. I do not like everyone in this room," Hazel teases, pulling me out of my thoughts.

I stifle a laugh, and Sire shakes his head at our brother's girlfriend.

"I literally just walked in."

"Walk back out."

The room fills with everyone's laugh besides Sire's. He flips Hazel off, although she isn't sparing a glance at him.

I rise from the couch to hug Vidia, and the minute she's in my embrace, a whiff of her vanilla perfume hits me. "You always smell so freaking good."

"Thanks, babe!"

I give Sire a hug before returning to my seat, and Vidia sits next to Hazel.

"Seriously?"

I glance at the end of the couch, and Sire looks between the girls. I'm assuming he wants to sit next to his girlfriend, but there's clearly no room for him in that corner.

"Leave us alone, Sire. Can't you go away for five minutes?" Hazel lays her head on Vidia's lap and with her legs still on August, she's sprawled out comfortably.

"No, I want to sit with her. Move down."

"No."

Sire looks over at Vidia, and when she shrugs, he looks like she just told him they need to break up again.

"Fine." He flops next to me, and I try not to be offended by how upset he is to sit with me instead.

August wraps his arm around my shoulder before pulling me into him. "Both of your meetings are going to be fine, Sage. Even if the worst case scenario happens with both of them, everything happens for a reason and—"

"That's bullshit."

We turn to Sire.

"I really hate that saying. Everything happens for a reason? There should be no reason for why a lot of fucked up shit happens in this world," he voices his words casually, but I can't help but think about his childhood, and he's right. No reason is good enough for what he went through with his bio mom or a lot of other bad things in this world, so the motto is a pretty bad one, but I get what August was trying to say.

"Florence isn't firing you, and Vincent is going to be so sweet during the meeting." August plants a soft kiss on the top of my head, and I smile up at him. "And if he isn't, Sire and I will have a nice chat with him."

I glance over at our brother and he has a smirk on his face. I shake my head at them but genuinely appreciate them more than anything.

"Vid." Sire has his eyes on Vidia now, and when I look over at her, she's playing with Hazel's curls. "Are you seriously not going to sit with me?" *And he says August is clingy.*

I bite back my laugh, and Hazel sighed so loudly that I'm sure the neighbors heard.

"Come, I'll sit on your lap, mi amor."

Hazel sighs again, obnoxiously loud, and this time, we all laugh, but Sire stands with a smile and settles back down with V on his lap.

Hazel has to readjust herself and sighs while doing it. I know she's just doing it to mess with Sire, but his reaction is what kills me.

"Shut up already, she's mine."

"She's literally not, though." Hazel plops her head onto V's lap again, and she returns to playing with her curls. "I tell you this every day, she's *my* wife."

"No, the fuck she isn't."

Hazel shrugs, and I watch them as if they were on TV. "Ask her what she was doing this morning before work."

August looks down at Hazel before laughing quietly, and Sire only looks between all of us before glancing back at Vidia.

"What were you doing?"

"She was in bed with me," Hazel answers for her, and Sire shoves her head off of Vidia.

"You fucking wish." When Sire wraps an arm around V protectively, she lets out a laugh, and I keep my gaze on her. Vidia is one of the most beautiful girls I know, and her laugh is somehow more beautiful. Even now, with her curls in a loose ponytail and in my brother's oversized hoodie, she's just... beautiful.

I glance down at Hazel next, and they really are two pretty best friends. Hazel looks airbrushed perfect *every day,* and she doesn't even wear makeup. My nieces and nephews are going to be adorable.

"You okay?" August slightly moves his arm that's still around me to get my attention and I smile up at him.

"Yeah," I pull in a deep breath before leaning into him again. "You're right. Both meetings will be fine." Being with my twin will *always* bring me comfort. Even on my absolute worst days, a simple text from August somehow makes my day better, and there has to be a scientific reason behind the whole twin bond thing because I'm certain I could be dying, and a hug from him can save me.

"Ugh! I have to leave soon, but I don't want to." I hug August, and he rests his head on top of mine.

I stay with them for a few more minutes, and I can't bring myself to ask about Liam, so I rush off to meet with Vincent. We're discussing over coffee, and I really wanted Angie here, but she was busy, and since she already read through these exact same contracts, she doesn't *really* need to be here unless anything new is brought up.

When I reach the coffee shop he chose downtown he's already sitting outside and stands when he sees me. "Sage, how are you?" He plants a soft kiss on both of my cheeks, and I smile at him before sitting.

"I'm good, how about you? Your flight just landed last night, right?"

He tells me about his recent trip back home, and at the reminder of all of the traveling he does, I grow more excited because I know as a Moore Girl, I would also be traveling twice as much as I already do.

When we start discussing business, it goes smoothly and feels so easy, almost too easy, but once I hand him the contract I had for the last week, it's officially set in stone.

"Words can't express how pleased I am that you're now one of my models."

I feel my entire body flush as I return his words and thank him. I've been modeling for a while now, but I never fail to get shy when people compliment me. It always feels surreal that this is my life.

"As we discussed over the phone, you will be flown to Italy for a month to learn the ropes as a Moore Girl. All of my girls go through a similar training."

"Yes, I'm so excited to go! You also mentioned a show that will be happening while I'm there?"

He looks like he just remembered as he looks for something on his laptop. "Yes, I know it's so soon, but you'll be in that show. That actually brings me to what I needed to share with you."

He types something into his laptop before my phone dings. It's a link to a calendar for the next month, and it's *loaded* with everything I need to do while I'm in Italy. I'll be busy almost every day while I'm there, but it only excites me.

I text August to let him know the meeting went perfectly with Vincent. I thankfully get to do the photo shoot with the girls since Florence pushed it back by an hour for some reason, but when I walk into her office, I think I'm holding my breath.

"Sage, hey."

I send her a smile although, I'm not sure what's happening. We haven't spoken since she basically said she would be replacing me, yet today she's genuinely smiling in my face and rearranged the photo shoot she said she won't rearrange... something is up.

"Hey." I take a seat in front of her, and she finishes typing something before shutting her laptop and sliding a folder towards me. "What's this?"

"Our new contract." I freeze with the folder halfway open as I study her. "I'll save you the trouble of reading it all, although I'm sure your damn agent will be sure to read it three times every day before you sign it." She rolls her eyes, and I'm glad Angie isn't here because she *hates* it when people do that.

"You can miss a Magic Model show if the time conflicts with a Moore show, but you can't miss three in a row, and you can't miss our anniversary shows." Her last part was a given, and I wouldn't miss those, not even for Vincent.

"Thank you, but I'm a bit confused, Angie said–"

"Your agent wasn't the reason I changed my mind."

I'm only even more confused, but she's looking at me as if I should know what she's talking about.

"Your boyfriend came to see me? Or should I say, demanded."

My. Jaw. Drops. I'm stuck for a second then immediately start apologizing for whatever the hell Liam threatened her with because I won't be surprised if he dognapped her German Shepherds and threatened to snap their poor necks. Florence *laughs* as I blurt out an apology and I must be dreaming because *what* is happening?

"He really didn't tell you he was coming to meet with me?"

I shake my head, and a smile grows on Florence's face.

"What is it with athletes and their arrogance? Is it all the money they make? Because your brothers also waltzed into my office just a few months ago when you had the flu and demanded I let you miss the show. The common factor with all three boys is the sport they play."

I actually cringe at the reminder of Sire and August doing that. I was so sick but adamant to be in the show. They made it their mission to tell Florence to let me rest, and me missing one show wouldn't kill her, but she certainly acted like it would kill her, considering it was an annual show I would've been missing, and those are *huge* for us. Agencies around the world know not to plan anything for that day because everyone comes to watch us.

"I'm sorry, I'm still confused. What exactly did Liam say?" When he came to see me the last few days, I talked about my worries about the contract headaches since he asked. I even cried about it, but I wasn't expecting him to talk to the damn CEO. I might actually die to know what got her to change her mind because not even Angie could get her to cave, and everyone caves for Angie.

"He asked me how much money I'd be losing if you didn't model in a show for me. I did the math, and as I said, the majority of our audience come for you, and I told him how much it'll cost the company not to have you."

I wait for her to add more, but she doesn't. "And?" I don't see where this is going...

"He doubled the cost of losing you if given the possibility you were to miss my show for Mr. Moore."

I feel my eyes squint as I focus on her lips because I can't seem to comprehend what came out of her mouth.

"He. Did. *What?*"

She says it so casually. Like this was just another business deal for her, and I guess, in a way, it was. I'm sure this was all a bribe in his eyes. Either way, we make *millions* at just one show... how much did this cost him?

I WASTE NO TIME GOING home since Royal is throwing my congrats party tonight, but I text Liam to meet me here, and it takes him five hundred years for whatever reason. I'm already ready for the party by the time he knocks on my door.

"Dory."

"Hey." I look up at him, and I love that even though I'm 5' 10, he's still taller than me with my heels on. I watch him as he drinks in my outfit, and a small smile tugs his lips.

"You look perfect."

I thank him before his smile widens.

"How was your day, beloved?"

I step into my apartment, and he follows me in before we settle on my couch.

"You went to see my boss?" I turn to him.

He shakes his head as he lays back on my couch.

"I told her not to tell you," he says more to himself. When he looks over at me, his smile grows, but it looks sad. "I told you you'd have your way."

"How much?"

"None of your business."

"It's all of my business. How much money did you give her?"

He lets out a soft sigh as he rubs my thigh, but he doesn't make a move to answer me, and I move his hand from my thigh. "Hello?"

"I don't remember." He rubs my leg again.

"Tell me."

"Couple million, I don't know, but it was way less than what you're worth." His eyes meet mine and he watches me with such sincerity. "I would've paid triple what she asked for. You're priceless, baby."

"Liam—"

"Stop asking."

I tilt my head to the side, and he mirrors me. "How much is a *couple* million to you because a couple is like two or three." When he doesn't answer, I feel my brows raise. "You paid more than that?!"

"Shh, why do you always get so shocked when I spend a bit of money on you? Didn't you just officially become a billionaire a few days ago?"

I smile at his reminder. That's also what my congratulations party is for, although I didn't really want to celebrate that bit. I found out through social media that I'm officially a billionaire, and I didn't even believe it at first, but it's true, and it just adds to how surreal life has been lately.

"Yes, which is why I'll be paying–"

"No, the hell you're not."

"Yes, I am, and bribing my boss isn't going to get me to forget that we're not on the best of terms."

His brows furrow now as he watches me. "I didn't do that because you were mad at me." He looks genuinely confused as he watches me. "You and I both know I would've done that if you weren't mad at me, so don't think for a second that I did that to win you back." His voice is stern, the weight of their truth looming in the air.

"Then why'd you do it?"

"You were crying," he says as if that's reason enough.

When I first slept with this man, he didn't even have the decency to walk me back to the bar or open a single door for me. *I knew under all that gruff attitude, there was this thoughtful person.* It's not even the cost, but the thought behind it that makes this so much more important. He went completely out of his way, and my tears surely put a pretty dent in his bank account. I know he didn't do it because we're fighting because he sits here and watches me like this is all he wants out of life. Me.

"I hate seeing you upset," he goes on. "Now you can have the best of both worlds with both agencies just like you wanted." His eyes fall on my lips, and I watch him have a million different thoughts.

"You just said we're not on good terms, not taking *space*. Does that mean I can kiss you now because it's been five days?"

I bite back a smile at how he sounds as if he's been suffering.

"Sure, but only if you tell me how much you paid her."

"Seven million," he quickly answers, and before I can react, his lips are on mine. He kisses me slowly, like he's trying to savor the moment.

When he pulls away, I keep my eyes on him, and my heart aches and flutters all at once. While he lied, he's exceeding those standards I once told him he didn't meet. The way I feel about him has nothing to do with the money, but everything to do with the way he makes my heart skip several beats when he walks into a room, but I refuse to tell him that now because I don't want him to think I'm forgiving him for spending some money on me.

"I'm paying you back." I stand.

"You better not."

"I am, and I need to get to my party."

"You're not, and I'll drive you there." He gets up and grabs my hand, pulling me out before I can counter.

We walk down to his car and make it to the hall that Royal booked. I glance out the window and freeze at the sight of my brothers. "What a coincidence that we all got here at the same time."

I turn to Liam, but he doesn't say anything.

"I should go in…" He was *supposed* to come with me, but we both know that can't happen. I let out a disappointed breath, and I hate that I'm hiding this from the boys. "What if we just tell them right now?" I look back out the window, and both August and Lisette's nosy selves are trying to see into the car, although it's blacked out. I stifle a laugh, and I appreciate how easily they can fix my mood without trying.

"That isn't going to go well."

I turn back to Liam, and he offers me a sympathetic look.

"Do they really not like you that much?"

When he doesn't answer, my heart sinks.

"I should go." I grab the door as he calls out to me.

"Congratulations again. I'm so proud of you."

I mumble thanks as I force a smile and catch up with my siblings, Hazel, and V.

Chapter Thirty-Two

LIAM

T HE SECOND I WALK THROUGH the door, all of the nurses
turn to look at me, only to quickly glance away, as if
looking at me would set off some nuclear bomb. I'd be lying
if I said I didn't feel like shit for yelling at Pri the other week.

As much as I wanted to be at Sage's party, her brothers
were there, and I wasn't going to make her choose who she
invited. My mom needed me to come see her, so in a way,
it worked out that I couldn't go, but I wish I could be there
to celebrate her accomplishments.

Capri gives me a single nod before walking right past me,
and I fight every urge in me to not walk away, but I follow
after her instead.

"How's she doing?" "A lot better. She had a full one-eighty
from this morning." She busies herself with preparing a
plate for someone, but she's clearly trying not to look at me.
"My apologies for not updating you."

I roll my eyes at how formal she's being. "Don't worry
about it."

She doesn't reply, and I lean against the counter beside
her. "You a waiter now, too?"

She adds more food to the plate but doesn't spare a
singular glance at me.

"No smart response?" I tease, trying to get something out
of her, but she doesn't budge.

"My smart responses are unprofessional. You won't have
to worry about them anymore." She moves to the fridge
and I shake my head at her.

"Can you stop this weird monotone robot shit?"

"What do you mean?" She keeps her eyes in the fridge, and I look into the living room to find two other nurses watching us.

"You never replied to the email of my referrals. Do you mind letting me know when exactly your mother's new nurse will be assigned because I need to look for other jobs and–"

"You don't need to look for other jobs. You're her nurse." I keep my glare on the nosy girls in the living room, and after a few seconds, they turn away. When I look back at Capri, she's already watching me.

"Okay." That's all I get as she grabs the plate and cup of juice, but I step in her way before she walks off.

"Are you really going to make me do this?"

"Yes." She answers so damn fast, but I shouldn't be surprised. She shakes her head to move her auburn bangs from her face, and she looks mad, but I can see the hurt behind her eyes, and all that rings in my damn head is Sage reminding me to be nicer to people.

"Sorry." I glance off to the side, but in my peripheral, I can see Capri shaking her head.

"Okay." She goes to walk off again, but I let out a sigh before blocking her path.

I feel like my throat is closing as I try to find the words, and I don't know why apologizing is so damn hard for me, but this is torture.

"I shouldn't have yelled at you, Pri. I know you were trying to help, and I lost my temper... again, but I shouldn't have."

She keeps her gaze on me, and I swear her freckles pop out more when she's upset, but she better not give me a hard time because, frankly, that's the best she's getting from me today.

"Your mom talks about that temper of yours quite a lot, but I never believed her until I was on the receiving end of it."

"Would you believe me if I said I was working on it?"

"No," She counters, and I shake my head at her.

"I won't yell at you again." I really have been working on my anger. The stupid breathing exercises don't work all that great, but I can try not to yell for a while. She keeps her eyes on me like she genuinely doesn't believe me, and I hate how hard she's making this, but I know I deserve it.

"You're my mom's primary care provider. You spend more time with her than I do and practically live here with her. We shouldn't be on bad terms."

When she lets out a sigh, I know I won a part of her over. "I might start charging you extra for having to deal with your asshole attitude."

"Send me the bill." I give her a shrug as I walk into the living room, and she laughs softly behind me, but I wasn't joking. If I knew she'd accept cash apologies, I would've come in here with a check instead of torturing myself with sorries.

My mom isn't in her usual seat in the living room, and it's dark out, so I'm sure she isn't by the pond. I head for her room but stop short when I hear a piano playing. I peek into the music room, and there she is, playing Beethoven with her eyes closed.

She gets to the end of the song, and I walk over to the piano. She still has her eyes closed, and I place my hands over the keys before transitioning to her favorite song. I'm sure she was going to play it next since she always played it after this song, claiming the end of this one flows perfectly into the one I play now.

I keep my eyes focused on the keys, and I haven't played a piano in years, but it's muscle memory for this song.

"Wow, who taught you to play so beautifully?"

I miss a key, and it throws off my entire rhythm, so I just stop. When I look over, she's watching me with a warm smile, but I know that look in her eyes, and I wish I hadn't come to check on her.

"You did." I remind her, but she only looks confused, and a pit grows in my stomach. At least once a week, she forgets me, without fail, but every time my mom looks at me like she really can't recognize me, I get sick all over again.

"Were you a student of mine?" She turns her head to the side like the angle will make her recognize me, but it's clear no bells ring. She never had a job but taught kids to play piano in her free time simply because she loved it. "Sorry, you're all grown up now. I barely recognize you."

"It's me. Liam." I watch her, desperate for her to remember me, but she only gives me a small smile.

"Right, how have you been?" She laughs softly, and I know she's just pretending to remember, but I appreciate the effort. I just wish I hadn't seen through her act.

She turns back to the piano and plays something I don't recognize, but I don't say anything as I sit beside her and watch her play. All I can think about as the melody fills the room is my childhood. She would sit at the piano for hours as I sat there on the rocking chair, watching her play with Shanti in my arms.

My focus shifts to Sage, as it has been the last few days. I keep asking her if we're broken up, and she keeps saying we're not, and she's just upset that I lied, but it sure does feel like we're broken up. She's distant, and I know when she talks to her brothers and they tell her just how much they hate me, it's over. I'm done lying to her. I told her they didn't like me, but she wants to hear it from them. After seeing her looking out my window at August like he was her fucking world, like he rotates the damn earth for her, it made me hate him more, and I know it's stupid, but I *hate* their bond.

She talks about her brothers all the time, and if she didn't love them so damn much, my life would be easier, but they're her brothers, and I need to figure out what the hell I'm going to do.

"Oh, don't cry, honey."

I look up as my mom rubs my back, and when she sees I'm not crying, she looks a bit embarrassed but still smiles at me sheepishly. "Trouble in paradise?" She offers me a warmer smile and I let out a sigh before leaning against the piano.

"Sorta."

She smiles at me before pressing a few random keys.

"When did your late husband tell you he loved you?" I keep my tone light as I watch her closely in case the mention of him sets her off, but she surprisingly remains calm, and I let out a breath.

"A couple of months into our relationship." She smiles at the reminder, and it's rare that she speaks well of this man, so I listen closely. "We were on a carnival date. I kept nagging him about wanting to go on the Ferris wheel, but he was afraid of heights."

She laughs softly, and I smile at the thought of my dad being afraid of anything. My dad was good to us when he wasn't angry. My mom was good at keeping his temper in line, and honestly, I think she believed she could fix him or something, but he would just have these erratic episodes whenever something pissed him off. When I feel myself growing that mad, I remind myself that I swore not to be like him, and it's the only thing that calms me from tearing apart rooms the way he did.

"He gave in after I begged, and when we were at the top, it stopped, as it normally does." She peeks a glance at me. "He didn't know that bit." She laughs again, and if I could wish for anything on this earth, I'd wish he was always that romantic man she fell in love with.

"He squeezed my hands with his eyes shut and said, 'You are so fucking lucky I love you,' and it was like my world stopped." She lets out a long breath before looking at the piano, and a sad look casts over her.

"Then he killed our baby."

I feel my blood run cold, and she stares at the piano keys like she's going to rip them apart.

"Mom—"

"My son has his temper." She turns to me, but it's almost like she sees right through me, and my heart sinks at her words.

"He tears apart his room when he's angry, just like his father did at that age." She shakes her head like she's so fucking disappointed. I haven't been that angry in a while. I resort to punching bags now, mainly because I got tired of having to clean my room after an episode.

"I pray every night that his temper never forms into the monster within his dad."

"It won't." I don't even recognize my own voice, and I have to look away from her lost eyes. I'm not sure how long we sit there, but she plays a few more songs as I drown in my thoughts.

When I run a hand through my hair, my mom looks back over at me with a smile on her face.

"What's wrong?"

Everything.

I shake my head in response and try to muster up a smile for her, but my face doesn't budge. She keeps her eyes on me like she's waiting for an answer, and because I still wish I could turn back the clock and go back to the age where she was able to solve my biggest issues, I tell her about Sage.

"Sweetie," She gives me a knowing look. "You shouldn't have lied."

"I know that, Mom."

Her brows furrow as she gives me a once-over.

"I'm not your mom." She shakes her head again, and she watches me. "Please don't call me that." She looks like she's getting upset, so I don't push her.

"Sorry, you just remind me so much of her." I swallow the lump in my throat as I try to distract her. "Do you have any advice?"

She turns back to the piano as she thinks or tries to remember something, but she never answers.

Chapter Thirty-Three

LIAM

"**W**HY ARE YOU SMILING LIKE that?"

I try to wipe my smile, but it's no use. "Because Griffin is mad."

Jordan breaks into a laugh, and I shake my head at him as I finish putting my gear on. We're playing against the Hale brothers today, and they are losing by a shit ton. Sire is the captain and takes their losses so personally.

I get that this is our job, and I want to win, too, but *God*, that kid is dramatic. He's letting his emotions get in the way, and it's interfering with the way he's pitching. Usually, when I piss him off, it bites me in the ass because he channels his anger and pitches ten times better, but now? He's throwing horribly, and I know he's going to be swapped out soon.

I doubt they can catch up at this point, but pissing him off a *bit* more will make him play worse and guarantee our win.

"You look like you're plotting." Jordan eyes me suspiciously, and I grab my glove.

"Maybe I am." I slip my helmet on before stepping onto the field. I glance over at the big screen, and when I see Sire is up to bat next, I shake with a soft laugh.

"Liam, give me a heads up right now if we're going to fight."

I roll my eyes at how dramatic he is. "I'm not dumb enough to fight at our game. Coach was a dick the last time I fought Griffin on the field." I couldn't play for the rest of the season. We were nearing the end, but still, the end of the season was the best part, and I missed it. Either way, I'm on thin ice with Sage. No way I'm going to put my hands on her brother.

I get in my position behind home plate, and after Jordan throws me a few warm-up pitches, Sire comes up to bat. As a catcher, I watch every batter, and I know all of Sire's flaws by now. I hold two fingers between my legs, and when Jordan nods in response, I get into position.

Sire takes a swing, and when he misses, I can't help but laugh. I toss the ball back to Jordan, and Sire glances back at me but surprisingly doesn't say anything.

I signal for another curve ball, and when he misses again, I genuinely can't help myself. "This is embarrassing, Griffin."

"So is your bitch."

I rise to my full height before his entire sentence is even out of his mouth. In a swift move, I flip my helmet off, and he takes a step towards me.

I hear the umpire calling for us to back up from each other, but when a smirk grows on Sire's face, my tongue slips. "It's not very nice to speak of your sister like—"

My words are cut off by his fist, and I stumble back, pulling every will of strength I have not to hit him back because I *know* Sage will tear me a new one, but he hits me again, then *again*, and reflex takes over.

I don't stop swinging, and after being pulled apart too soon the last two times we fought, I definitely don't hold back. When he stumbles, I realize Jordan hit him from behind, and it was definitely a cheap shot, but I don't stop as he loses his balance.

"Are you fucking *dumb*?"

I turn at the sound of August's voice, and he knocks Jordan on his ass.

With my head turned, Sire takes another swing at me, and a metallic taste fills my mouth.

"You son of a bitch." I grab a fist full of his jersey and hit him back, but in a quick move, he flips us and punches me back.

"ENOUGH!" Someone must've pulled Sire to his feet, but he drags me with him, and with a punch to the gut, he lets me go.

"It's *every* other fucking game with you three!" My coach shoves me back, but I push his arm away. "I said *enough*!"

"Fuck you, Walker!" Sire takes another swing at me, but I quickly dodge it, and with his coach dragging him away, he wasn't going to reach me.

"Shut the fuck up, Griffin." I spit out the blood in my mouth, but just as I look up, August hits me in the mouth again. I punch the side of his face before we're pulled apart again.

When Sire lunges at me, I take another swing, and he doesn't get to hit me back as August catches him. "Sire, let's fucking *go*!"

I let my coach push me back as Sire tries to fight August off.

"In the dugout, Walker, or—"

"Listen to your bitch, Griffin!"

My coach pushes me again as Sire tries to get out of his brother's grasp.

"You're lucky I don't let him break your mouth!" August shouts as they make it across the field, but I got the last hit, so I don't give a shit about whatever else they yell about.

Both teams are on the field, but after more yelling from the umpire, everyone heads for the dugout. When my coach shoves my back again, I stop in my tracks.

"Stop. Fucking. *Shoving* me." I turn to him slowly, and he looks just about pissed enough to hit me, but I'd love another excuse for a fight.

"Get your ass in the dugout *now*."

"Do not touch me."

"Now!"

"Lower your tone." I take a step forward, and I immediately get pushed back. I almost swing again until I realize it's Jordan.

"Are you fucking insane?" He steps between our coach and me and walks me backward. "The brothers are one thing. Coach *Finn*? Did Griffin give you a damn brain injury, or are you actually insane?" He whispers now, and I turn on my heels instead of responding and head for the dugout.

No one says anything to me as I start taking my gear off and tossing it aside. I'm clearly not playing anymore, and I honestly don't give a shit. I spit out some more blood, but my mouth fills again.

"You seriously need to stop fighting those guys at games. You're going to–"

I turn to my teammate, and he's smart enough not to say anything else, but then my coach storms in.

"Pack your shit!"

I turn to my coach and gesture to the bag in my hand. "What does it look like I'm doing?"

He tosses his clipboard aside before stalking towards me. "That smart mouth of yours is going to get you kicked off this team someday."

"So–"

"Liam."

I pull in a deep breath and look over at Jordan, and he shakes his head ever so slightly. "Don't."

"No, go ahead, Liam."

I direct my glare back to our coach, and when I swallow more blood, I'm not sure if it's because I was punched in the mouth a minute ago or if it's from how hard I bite my tongue.

"Nothing to say?"

I let out a scoff, but just as I open my mouth, Jordan steps in front of me, blocking my view from our idiot coach, who's about to get punched in the damn throat.

"Breathe, Liam."

My hands start to shake, and I pull in another deep breath at his reminder, but I can feel myself growing hot all over again.

"You need to calm down." Jordan keeps his voice low, and when he takes a step towards me, I know it's because he wants me to put more distance between myself and Finn, so I back away as he moves towards me.

The umpire walks into the dugout, and as soon as our eyes lock, I know what he's going to say. "Liam Walker and Jordan Rhodes, *out!*"

I turn for my bag and pass Jordan his, without a word. My coach tells me he'll deal with me later, and I know I'm automatically suspended for the next few games, but I'm sure he'll muster up some other consequence for me.

I head straight for Sage's place, and I want to change out of this damn uniform, but I want to see her more. I doubt her brothers told her about this so fast, but I want to tell her first. As I walk into her building, her front desk guy stands up to greet me, but I keep walking before he can speak to me.

"Oh–" He closes his mouth.

I press the elevator, and he clears his throat from behind me. "Sage isn't here."

I let out a long breath before turning to him. "How long ago did she leave?"

"This morning."

I ask if she mentioned what time she'll be back because she usually tells people random shit like that, but he says he doesn't know, so I call her as I head for my car.

The phone rings for a while, and when I get her voice-mail, I immediately call back, but it goes directly to voice-mail this time. I glance down at my phone and almost call again because I'm certain she had nothing planned today, but maybe she's on the phone, so I text her and tell her to call me before heading home.

As I step out of the elevator, I pull my phone out and start recording. Mars has been trying to scare me, and I want to show Sage because it's the cutest shit ever. He's usually in the kitchen, so I make sure to make some noise so he knows I'm home. As I walk into the kitchen, he jumps out from behind the counter and meows so softly as he hops onto my foot.

"Ah!" I fake my surprise, and he hops around before running off. I shake with a soft laugh before sending Sage the video. After getting some pictures of all three of the kittens eating, I also send them to her, but she doesn't respond, which is weird because she's quick with her responses, especially for the cats.

I call her again and it rings twice before I get her voice-mail. "What the fuck?"

I decide to take a shower before I think the worst, but as soon as I'm dressed, I call Moon.

"Should I play the damn lottery?!"

I roll my eyes in return, and his laugh spills through the speaker as I flop onto my couch. "Are you with my girl?"

"Nope. I was going to meet up with her later, but she canceled on me."

"Call her and ask what she's doing." I scoop Periwinkle into my arms and lay her on top of me, but then Meeko starts scratching my damn couch for attention, so I bring him up with us.

"No need, I know what she's doing."

I wait for him to tell me, but a second passes, and he's silent.

"Well, enlighten me, Moon."

"Oh, she's with her sisters."

I hang up on him and call Sage back, and this time, she answers.

"Why the fuck are you ignoring me?" I ask innocently, although the annoyance slips into my tone. *There's no way she saw that fight so quickly.* "And don't even say you aren't, Sage Loana."

She's silent for a beat, and it sounds like she's on mute because she's too quiet. "Can you state your name for the record?"

I feel my brows furrow because that is *not* Sage's voice, and there's some ruffling in the back, then some hushed laughter.

"Who the fuck is this?"

"I asked first," Whoever this is goes on.

"I don't give a shit. Where the fuck is Sage?"

"Oh, you are *rude.*"

I let out a breath, but she continues before I can tell her to give Sage the damn phone. "Can you just tell us if you're Mr. L or Mr. K who texted her that dirty message?"

"Lisette!" *That* sounds like Sage now, and I think they're fighting because there's more background noise.

"Mr. who? Sage, I swear—"

"No one texted me!" Sage screams, and I'm certain she's fighting for her phone now.

"Where are—" They hang up on me, and I call back, but she sends it to voicemail *again.* I feel myself growing more annoyed, and when I call back, she either turns her phone off or blocks me, but either way, I grab my helmet and storm out.

Chapter Thirty-Four

SAGE

"**Y**OUR BOYFRIEND IS RUDE. I don't think the boys will like him." Lisette *smiles*... like the boys not liking Liam would be the best news ever, but it *won't*. It's *not*, and the thought of them knowing...

"If you tell August or Sire–"

Vidia's door opens, and the boys stroll in.

I glance at Lis and then back to the boys. "Hey–"

"Your sister's a whore!"

"OH MY GOD!" I cover my face with my hands and sink into the couch as Vidia laughs, but I might be sick.

"Stop fucking calling her that, Lisette," Sire bites out, and they go back and forth. I tell Lis I'm allowed to *mingle*, but as soon as the words leave my mouth, I tune them out because I can't *think*. I glance back at my brothers, and when I see the cuts on their faces, on top of knowing who put them there... my stomach turns.

I wanted to go see Liam's game today since my brothers were also playing, and it's safe to say that it went horribly. I didn't even recognize Liam in his gear since we got there late. When Vidia referred to him as Walker, I refused to believe she meant my Walker, but she did. This drama between him and my brothers is clearly worse than I thought since Vidia knew they apparently hated each other.

"Be grateful we stopped beating up your *and* her boyfriends a long time ago." Sire's words pull me out of my thoughts. *You just did beat him up...*

"Sage's last one was actually decent; that new guy you had over did not wash his hands after using the bathroom, and he was mean to you." August defends the only one of my exes they liked, but Lis scoffs from beside me.

"Wait until you meet *her* new one," she mumbles, and Sire picks his head up from Vidia's lap to look at me. His eyes bore into mine as if the words *I'm dating the man you hate* were written on my forehead, and I feel my tears building again.

"She's joking." Vidia glances at me before turning Sire's head back to face her, and I let out a breath of relief. "What was that on the field today?"

I keep my gaze on Sire, but he only lets out a sigh, and it's August who unintentionally makes my heart feel like it just shattered.

"Walker is such a fucking bitch, that's what happened."

Hazel tries to clean a cut on his eyebrow, and I shake my head at all of this.

"He always wants to fucking talk shit. I'm going to knock his damn teeth out the next time I see him," Sire adds on, and I squeeze my eyes shut.

"Don't you think this rivalry between you guys is getting old? It's been what? Six years?"

I steal a glance back over at Sire just as Vidia moves his hair from his face, and an ugly bruise is forming in his cheek.

"Seven." He corrects her, and my heart sinks.

I bite my lip to stop it from trembling and put on a smile for my brothers and the girls, but I just want to go home.

"I have to go." I grab my things, and I'm on autopilot as I walk out, but V stops me as I reach the door.

"You okay?"

"Yeah... I just forgot I need to film a video today, so I won't be able to post it on time." I put on a smile and my words aren't completely a lie. I didn't film my weekly girl talk today because I wanted to watch Liam and my brothers play... I wish I had just stayed home, and today never happened.

"Okay..." She opens the door for me and we step out together. "If you're worried about your brother finding out about Mr. Chocolate and peanut emoji, just know I'll make sure to tell Sire to leave you alone, and he'll tell Lis to fuck off."

I let out a soft laugh at the reminder of Liam's contact name. After he told me he was allergic to peanuts I added the emoji to his name, and the other week, it was clear he didn't like chocolate, so I just made the two of them his contact.

I feel my smile falling but reassure Vidia that I'm okay, and after she hugs me goodbye I head for the elevator. I turn my phone back on to call a ride and the second I do a few messages come in, and then Liam calls me again.

He's not going to stop calling, and I need to find a ride, so I mute him before calling a car. The entire drive home passes in a blur, and when I step out of the elevator, Liam turns to me. When he sees my face, it's clear he knows I know what happened.

"Dory, I am *so* sorry."

I let out a scoff as I scan his bruised face. "You keep saying that, Liam, and every time I think I want to forgive you, you mess up again."

He shakes his head as he closes the distance between us. "You saw that fight; he hit me first."

"Do you hear how childish that sounds? He wouldn't hit you for no good reason, Liam."

He shakes his head in disbelief, this time as he watches me. "You're not even going to place an ounce of blame on them? Can they truly do no wrong to you?"

"I never said that."

"No, but all you keep saying is how *I'm* wrong."

"Because you are!" I step away from him, tears blurring my vision. "This isn't fair, Liam. *You* wanted to sleep with *me. You're* the one who wanted the friends-with-benefits thing. You're the one who asked *me* to be *your* girlfriend. Why is it that *you* wanted this, and *I'm* the one who gets hurt?"

His eyes soften, but his face blurs as my throat tightens again. "The last thing I wanted was to hurt you, Dory."

"But you *did*. It was clearly still on your list, just the last thing." I move past him, and he quickly wraps an arm around my waist. "Let me go."

"Sage, I swear I never wanted this."

I try to push him away, but he doesn't let me.

"Sage, *please*." Desperation seeps into his voice. "Tell me how to fix this, and I will."

"There is no fixing this." I force myself not to look at him as I try to push him off and reach my door. "We're done. We did the apologies and cute gestures last time, but we're not doing it again. You showed me the kind of person you were twice before, and this is the third time. I've learned my lesson. You're a liar. You can't open up to me, and your anger blinds you from what's right and wrong. I don't want to be with you."

"No, no, Sage, wait." He keeps his grip on me, trying to get me to stop and listen, but I'm done listening.

"Get off!"

His hands drop as my voice rings through the empty hall. "Please," he begs again.

"Leave," I tell him one last time as I reach my door, but he grabs my hand. When I turn to deny him, he drops to his *knees*.

"I am *so* sorry." He grabs my hand, and his touch must paralyze me because I can't pull away from him.

"I should've told you I knew your brothers. I should've told you we hated each other, and I was *going to* tell you sooner, but I was scared of losing you."

I shake my head softly as I look down at him... on his knees for me. "You already did." My voice is just above a whisper, and I try to pull my hand away, but his grip tightens before I notice tears forming in his eyes.

A single tear treks down his face, and a lump forms in my throat at how broken he looks, but he broke me first, so I don't let myself cry for him, but my vision begins to blur.

"I shouldn't have done what I did to them." He shakes his head. "It was wrong. I know that, but if you want me to build a time machine and go back in time to take it back, I will, Sage. I'll go back and be best fucking friends with them."

I don't say anything, although I don't think I'd be able to form any words if I tried. Instead, I try to turn to my door, but he grabs me with both hands.

"Tell me what you want, and it's yours, Sage." He blurts as he realizes that he's running out of time. "I'll mop the fucking ocean for you. I'll sweep the sand on every beach, Sage. Name anything in the world, and it's *yours*."

I try to tell him I don't want anything from him, but my watch buzzes, and it's a text from August.

Ugly Twinnn

> Hey! You left all the new clothes you bought at Sire's place but I'm taking it up to you. Heading in the elevator now!!

"Liam, stand up." I quickly glance back down the hall.

"I can make anything in the *universe* yours. If you want something on the moon, I will buy NASA and have them fly me there within the hour, Sage."

"Liam–"

My eyes land on the elevator, and he's almost on my floor.

"I want you to stand up. *Now*."

He rises faster than light, and we escape into my apartment.

"You need to hide," I blurt.

"What?"

I jump as August knocks on my door.

My eyes snap open before I look at Liam frantically. "That's August. Go to my room right now."

He rushes off, but I remember August might go in there since he brought my shopping bags.

"Wait!" I whisper-shout. "Go in the closet in my makeup room."

He disappears without a word, and my heart is in my throat as I turn for the door. I take a deep breath to calm my nerves. When I open the door and see August's smile, I genuinely feel like the last five minutes didn't happen as his arms come around me, and it adds to the twin theory. He can fix everything.

"Hey, ugly twin." I squeeze him tighter and stifle a laugh as he tries to pull away.

"You *will* stop calling me that," he demands, although he laughs.

Hazel walks in from behind him, and when I open my arms out to her, she doesn't look amused. "You saw me ten minutes ago."

I paint a smile on my face with my arms still open, and when August nudges her, she rolls her eyes and lets me hug her.

"What are you guys doing here?" I glance at my makeup room and force my nerves to settle.

"Sire and Lis are a damn headache," Hazel grumbles, and I bite back a laugh as she walks to my couch. "I really like Lis, but her and Sire together are like *four* toddlers."

August and I share a laugh as he takes my bags to the couch. When he turns to look at me, his shoulders slouch. "Were you crying?"

"No." I force a smile, but he sees right through me.

"What's wrong?" He closes the distance between us before wrapping his arms around me.

"I was just worried about the fight you guys had today." *That's not a total lie.*

"Don't worry about that, Sage. We're fine." He kisses the top of my head, but with the opening, I finally ask about Liam because I want to hear his side and know how much he hates him. "He's just an asshole."

"Yeah, but why do you guys not like each other so much?"

We settle on the couch as he tells me the story, and it's just as Liam said. The only difference is that I was right, and my brothers weren't cheating; Liam's teammates only thought they were.

"He and Sire bump heads more often than he and I do because Sire is petty and likes to hold grudges. I don't care anymore. He's an asshole; we should move on, but when he says slick shit, he gets punched for it. Like today."

"What'd he say today?" I ask although a part of me doesn't want to know.

August rolls his eyes at whatever it is. "It was something about sleeping with you or dating you. I don't know, but Sire punched him before he could finish his sentence." He laughs, but I feel my face heat, and it hurts me more that

Liam rubbed that in their face... maybe I really was just a way to get at my brothers.

I muster up a smile and grab the bags he brought over. "I'll be right back." I head for my makeup room, and as I open the closet door, Liam stands from his seat on the floor.

"Is he-"

"What'd you say to Sire for him to punch you?"

He doesn't hesitate to tell the truth. "He said my girl was embarrassing, and I told him not to talk about you like that."

I shake my head at him, knowing he didn't say that to defend but to make him mad. "August is still out there, but you can just walk out and go home."

He looks confused now as he watches me. "He'd see me?"

"I know that, but there's nothing to hide since we're no longer together. Go home." My voice breaks, and I hate that it does. He walks over to me, but I walk backward. "I mean it."

"I'm not giving up on you." He stalks towards me.

"You threw it in my brother's face that we were together. You're really going to stand here and tell me there wasn't a single thought in your head that entailed-"

"*No*, Sage." He stops me before I can say it again, and my back hits the wall as he closes in on me. "You think too highly of your brothers if you believe I'd spend time thinking about them enough to plot sleeping with you. I actually tried to stay away from you because I didn't want this exact same problem, but then I fell in love with your damn dimples and perfect smile, Sage. I fell in love with you. *All* of you. I'm in love with you, and it has absolutely nothing to do with either of them."

His scent mixed with his words and the small space between us are all too much at once, and I can't bring myself to say anything.

"I love you," he says one more time. I shake my head as I look to the side, but he leans down and catches my eyes. "I do."

"You're a liar."

"So tell me what it is I'm feeling, Sage. Tell me how I feel about you because every time I so much as hear your name, my heart feels like it's doing backflips. Every time I see you cry, I feel like my skin is disintegrating, and the only reason I don't fucking die for hurting you is because I'm going to die trying to fix this. If that's not love, then *tell me* what it is because I've never loved anyone, and I fucking adore you."

He brings his forehead to mine, and I nearly hold my breath, willing myself not to admit that I fell for him too, and he hurt me anyway.

"You need to leave," is all I can choke out.

He cups my face, forcing me to look at him. "Tell me you don't love me, and I'll go."

I open my mouth, but he goes on.

"I can't promise I won't be back, but tell me you don't love me, and I'll let you have this last night of peace before I beg you for the next ten years to take me back." He looks between my eyes like they're his life support, and it forces a weight in my chest.

"Just go, Liam." My voice falls into a whisper, but he doesn't seem to have lost a sliver of hope.

"If you're mad I lied, then fine. If you're hurt because you *think* I just used you, then I'll prove you otherwise, but I think we both know you're just scared of your brothers." His words are bitter now, pulling me away from him.

"I'm not *scared* of them or anyone."

He looks down at me for a beat before walking out without a single word. I follow after him, but his quick pace carries him out of the closet faster than me.

"What are you doing?"

"If you're not scared of them, you won't care if your twin knows about us."

He walks out of my makeup room before I can even think to stop him. August and Hazel have their backs to us but turn at the sound of our footsteps. I watch August's smile drop before the confusion hits as he looks between us.

"What-" He cuts himself off as he slowly stands from the couch.

"Your sister and I are dating. We've been together for six months."

"We've been dating for a *week*." I correct him. "We *met* a few months ago for my contest, but I broke up with him."

"No, she didn't." Liam tries to correct me.

"Yes, I-"

Liam turns to me now as he cuts me off. "No, you did not, Sage. We're not breaking up."

"We're not together, Liam. I said we're *done*. You don't get to decide when or if we get back together." Neither of us breaks eye contact, challenging the other.

"Wait, is this real?" August's voice pulls us apart. He's still looking at Liam as if he appeared from thin air, and I guess he sort of did. "What is happening? Why are you here?" He shakes his head. "How did you get *in*?"

I cover my face in my hands, a headache forming from previously trying not to cry. "I didn't know you guys didn't like him, but I broke up with him today, and it's over."

When I look back up at August, he still looks confused. It takes him a second, but the pieces fall together in his head before he turns to Liam. "How dare you rope my twin sister into our issues?" August walks towards him, but I stand in front of Liam because I refuse to let them fight again.

"I didn't rope her into anything." Liam counters. "Look, I know you don't like me, but I love your sister, so tell her you don't care if we date."

"I *do* care." August's face scrunches as if he can't understand a single syllable Liam is forming. "You're not a good person."

"You don't even know me." Liam practically spits out. "Do you think I'm a bad person, Dory?"

I don't get to answer as August replies before I can in disbelief. "Who the hell is Dory? You don't even know her name. Get out of here! Did you *break in*?!" August grows more frantic as he pulls me away from Liam.

I try to de-escalate, but neither of them lets me get a word.

"Do I look like a threat to her life?" Liam rolls his eyes as he tries to grab me, but August actually karate chops his arm and grills Liam from head to toe.

"Uh, yeah. You do, actually."

Hazel stifles a laugh from the couch, and I don't bother asking her to help. I step in front of the two of them before Liam hits him back. "Both of you stop." I turn to August first. "He's *not* a threat to my life, and he's not a bad person," I reassure him.

He looks like he can't understand me, but after I give him the Cliff notes of the last few months, he watches the two of us, and I watch all of the stages of grief fall on his face one at a time.

"You *love* him?"

I never said that, but when I don't deny it, understanding washes through his face.

"Do you want him to leave?"

"Dory-"

"Let her speak, Walker," August cuts him off, and Liam surprisingly doesn't say a word as I think of my options.

I know August said he no longer cares about what Liam did to them. Liam was also wrong; I'm not scared of my brothers. I just know what it looks like when you continuously forgive someone, and they keep apologizing with no changes. Three times, Liam had to ask for my forgiveness within less than a week of our dating.

"I don't believe you got with me because of my brothers, and if you did, I'll leave that to them to deal with, but if you want me back, Liam, you need to change. Apologies without action feel a lot like manipulation, so no more nice flowers or four-D movies. I don't want it. How about you learn to get your temper in order and learn to be more open with the woman you claim you love? Until then, I don't want to speak to you."

I see the realization settle in his eyes at the seriousness of my words. It's clear he knows he can't just say we're together, and that'll be it.

He nods slowly, and when I see a gloss cover his eyes, I need to look away.

"I meant what I said about not giving up on you, beloved." He closes the distance between us and presses the lightest kiss on my cheek. He takes one step away, and that single action nearly crushes my heart. "Try to eat something tonight, pretty girl."

And that's all he says before he walks out, taking a small piece of me with him.

Chapter Thirty-Five

SAGE

I TAP MY STEERING WHEEL nervously as I watch my brothers, their girlfriends, and Lisette all sitting around the table. We come to this bakery/cafe whenever we all want to meet up, so I asked them to meet me here.

Being that I'm leaving for Italy today, I wanted to talk to them. I know myself, and I'm not going to want to eat, let alone hold down a meal, especially with all of the fittings I'm going to have, but after hours of contemplating last night, I know I can't do that for the entire month I'm there. I can't afford to get sick in another country, and if I pass out and someone finds out *why*...

I think it'll just be easier if I tell my family now; this way, I can leave before they freak out, but I can also call them whenever I need to talk.

I keep my eyes on all of them, and when August smiles down at Hazel, I smile to myself at how happy they look and decide to hurry out of the car. I force myself to keep walking before I can chicken out, but when Lisette notices me, I know it's too late.

"The queen finally decided to grace us with her presence." She rolls her eyes playfully, and I let out a soft laugh.

"Hazel has been here for fifteen minutes?" August looks around, confused, before looking back down at his girl-friend with a smile, and she immediately leans forward to kiss him.

"Sorry, I'm late." I take a seat next to my sister, and they catch me up on what they are talking about, but my mind races with how this is going to go, not to mention last night's horror show. August hasn't told anyone anything, but I told him to break it to Sire once I'm on the plane so I can avoid *that* reaction.

"You okay?" August smiles over at me, and I paint a smile on my face before nodding.

"What's wrong?" Sire questions, and I should've known that he'd notice.

"Nothing..." I feel the entire table watching me, and I want to say what's on my tongue, but I can't form the words.

"Hey," Lis elbows me, and I turn to find her watching me with a smile. "I know that face, just say it so we don't have to hold you captive all day. I need to feed my turtle."

I let out a soft laugh, and when Sire tells her we don't care about her turtle, she throws a piece of bread at him and the entire table erupts with a laugh when it hits him dead in the mouth.

Vidia gets up to use the bathroom, and I follow after her. I'm thankful for the excuse to leave before they keep asking me what's wrong.

When we walk in the bathroom, my eyes land on a huge mirror, and I pull Vidia to take a picture with me. After posting it and tagging her, I tuck my phone away and she goes into one of the stalls as I touch up my makeup.

"Hey, V?"

"Yeah?"

I pull in a deep breath as my eyes scan my frame. I love my outfit, but when I stare at myself for too long, I start to pick myself apart. I shake my head and turn away from the mirror.

"What does an eating disorder look like to you?" I don't know why I ask her, of all people but I do. She's a physical therapist, and while she isn't a doctor for stuff like this, I still want to hear her take on it.

"Eating disorders look different in different people."

I wait for her to add more but she doesn't. When she exits the stall, her eyes meet mine, and she suddenly pauses. "What's wrong?"

I shake my head and turn back around. She comes up next to me and washes her hands. "There's anorexia, which is when someone thinks they're overweight, but are underweight. They'd have a strict eating pattern and a fear of gaining weight."

I chew my lip in thought as she goes on.

"There's bulimia. When someone eats large amounts of food in a certain time frame. They usually purge, like make themselves vomit, to compensate."

It's all exactly like the article I read...

"Then there's pica. A disorder that causes people to eat things like dirt or cornstarch."

I shake my head at myself.

"There are many different ones. Honestly, I think anything associated with an unhealthy relationship with food can be seen as an eating disorder."

I feel the back of my eyes sting, and my nose starts to burn, but I only nod in response as I keep my back to her.

"And that's not a bad thing." She comes around, and I force a smile. "There's nothing wrong with having an eating disorder." She watches me like she knows everything in my mind, and I hate that I can't paint a better fake smile.

"It's not a good thing..."

She smiles, but it doesn't seem to reach her pretty honey eyes. "Working on it is all that matters. I'm proud of you for simply asking about it. I think that means you want to work on it."

I let my eyes fall shut, trying to stop my tears from spilling.

"What are you thinking?" Vidia keeps her voice low, and I force myself not to fall apart.

"I just feel so... worthless sometimes. The entire world has its eyes on me, and I'm deemed the prettiest model by *millions*, but-" My voice breaks, and her arms quickly come around me.

"I get torn down by so many people every day, and I try not to let it get to me. I've been doing this for years, so I'm used to it, but it still hurts, and when I stare at the mirror for too long, my brain decides to listen to those comments that tell me to starve for a week."

I can't stop the tears as they start, and when I feel another pair of arms around me, I pull away to see Lisette holding me. "Fuck those comments."

I let out a broken laugh and they both hold me tighter. When I pull away, they both watch me like they don't see me a fraction differently, and I wish I had said something sooner.

"You're *not* worthless," Vidia starts, and I notice a crease growing in Lisette's brows.

"Sage, you're supposed to be the put-together one." Lis shakes her head, almost in disbelief. "Sire and I are supposed to be the fuck ups, *we're* the addicts. I'm the one with crumbing depression, and August has possibly the worst case of ADHD I've seen."

I burst into a laugh, and I'm so glad she walked in here. I'm certain she came after noticing something was wrong.

"All of the Hale siblings are just fucked, huh?" She has a smile on her face, but I can see the pain behind her eyes. "You are *not* worthless. You're actually a billionaire. You're worth more than our loser millionaire brothers."

I give her a weak smile, and Vidia laughs beside us.

"We'll work on the eating disorder." Lis nods firmly, and I feel my eyes watering again. "Okay, no, I'm not the mushy sibling. You know this."

I can't help but laugh as she backs away from me like my tears will kill her.

"I already used up all my niceness. I'll help you, but we're not going to cry about it and comfort each other. Go to your brothers for that."

"You ass," Vidia mumbles before pulling me in for another hug. "You *can* tell your brothers, you know." She squeezes me, and I nod to myself.

When the door opens, we pull away to find Hazel.

"Now, why would ya leave me out there with those two?" We all laugh, but Hazel looks serious.

"Sire is so annoying." She rolls her eyes, and when Lisette agrees, Vidia and I are a mess of laughter.

"My boyfriend is not annoying. He probably asked you *one* question you didn't like." Vidia shakes her head as she looks over at Hazel.

Hazel sends her best friend a glare before turning to the mirror to fix her hair. "I told him you're a good kisser, and the asshole threw his dirty napkin at me."

I laugh quietly at her grumpy tone. Hazel is constantly telling Sire that she's kissed and even slept with Vidia, and I'm certain it's a joke, but Sire believes her since Hazel is always flirting with Vidia to piss him off.

Vidia laughs softly before we walk back to the table.

"Gorgeous, look at this," August calls out to Hazel the second we're in his view as he balances two cups *full* of juice on his forearm.

"August–"

"I think I can do it standing."

We all try to tell him not to, and the second he tries to stand, the cups fall from his hand and shatter. My jaw slightly drops, and I'm glad we're sitting outdoors because at least the mess isn't *in* the bakery.

"My bad!"

We all sit at the table, and Hazel grabs August's hand as he tries to clean up the glass. "*Dejalo.*" She shakes her head, and he looks like he feels horrible, but I hear Lisette laughing from beside me.

"Why do you look like you didn't know the cups would break?"

August turns to the table like a child in trouble. "Honestly... I didn't think they would shatter like *that.*"

We tell him it's *glass,* and I can't help but laugh now. Sire shakes his head silently, and I'm certain he tried to warn him before we came out here.

"It's *fine,*" Hazel whispers to August, and I feel myself smiling when she kisses his hand. "They're just dumb cups, who cares?"

"Yeah, but I feel bad..." August whispers back.

"It was an accident. We'll buy them a hundred more. They were ugly anyway; you did them a favor." She shakes her head, and I can tell her words make my brother feel better.

August tells her something I can't hear, and Hazel rolls her eyes like she's bored of the conversation. Her attitude reminds me of Liam's grumpy mood. I shake my mind of him and smile to myself when Hazel reassures my brother again. "I'll tell them I broke it."

August's smile is back, and I shake my head at them silently with a smile. They're so freaking cute. They've been dating for *years* now but still seem so in love. They're always in their own world, and I love their relationship, especially because I know my brother is obsessed with her.

"Were you crying?"

I glance over at Sire, and when his eyes scan my face, I remember I didn't fix my makeup. I pull out my mirror and beauty blender, touching up my tear treks.

"What happened?" Sire glances around the table, and when my eyes land on Vidia beside him, she smiles encouragingly.

I take a deep breath and swallow the lump in my throat. "I'm going to tell you guys something, but I don't want you to overreact, and you have to swear on Mom's life that you won't tell another soul, especially not my agent."

I keep my eyes on the table, but I can feel everyone watching me.

"I swear." August quickly agrees, and I feel a smile grow on my face. He didn't need to swear it. It's our twin rule that we're on each other's side no matter what, so I knew he wouldn't say anything. The twin rule trumps everything.

I was talking about Sire because he's *overly* protective, and if he thinks Angie needs to know about this, he'll tell her.

When I look over at him, he's watching me carefully. "What is it?"

"Swear—"

"Sage—"

Vidia nudges his arm before shaking her head. "Swear it."

He looks between her eyes and it's as if he's in a trance because he simply nods his head in agreement. "Fine. I swear not to tell a soul. Why were you crying?"

I nod my head and work up the nerve to spit it out. I start with how I've been following Helena's meal plan, and my brothers immediately tell me how much smaller she is than me and how bad that is, but Vidia tells them to let me finish, and I'm glad I told her first.

"And sometimes..." My vision blurs, and I look down the road, past all of the concerned eyes on me. "Sometimes I go a few days without eating, *but* I make sure to eat a big meal after I do that..."

No one says anything, and I wipe my tears, forcing my voice to stay strong. "And sometimes-" My voice breaks, but I clear my throat and get the last of it out. "Only before my fittings or runway shows do I need to make myself throw up, but I *don't* do that often, I swear."

I drag my eyes to August, and I'm not sure what I was expecting, but I'm surprised when he nods like this isn't bad news at all. "Okay," he starts, "So what do we need to do now? How do we help you? What do *you* need?"

I let out a laugh, and it turns into a quiet cry.

I feel a hand come over mine, and when I look up, Sire is holding me softly. "We got you," he nods softly. "We don't need to figure it out right now, but we will."

I give him a soft nod, and both boys come around the table to hug me. It feels like this *isn't* the end of the world. Like, I'll be fine.

"What time is your flight to Italy?" I let them know it's in a few hours, and I can see the worry on my twin's face. "Maybe I should go with you–"

"August–"

"It'll be fun!"

"And you'll be a helicopter twin. I need to be able to do this on my own. I told you guys because I wanted to be able to call you guys whenever I needed to, but you don't need to follow me across the world. That's–"

"Very reasonable."

I turn my head at August; he only mirrors me, pulling a laugh out of me. "I appreciate your concern, August. I really do, but you don't need to be concerned and follow me around." I take his hand in mine. "I want your support, but I don't need you to come to Italy with me."

I'd love him there, but I wouldn't be able to breathe if he went solely to babysit me. August kisses my head before deciding to stay behind. When I look over at Sire, he also looks just as ready to come with me.

"Promise me you'll–"

"I–"

"*Promise* me you'll call if you need us. If you're struggling to eat or want to make yourself throw up. Just call us, and we'll do whatever you need." Sire holds his pinky out to me, and I smile up at him, linking my finger to his.

"I promise." I kiss my thumb, and he does the same before we press them together.

They sit back down just as the waiter comes, and when he asks me what I'd like to order, I feel my siblings watching me, but when I look over at them, the boys and Lis only smile encouragingly.

I order a sandwich and, thankfully, get lost in a conversation with everyone before my food gets here. Once everyone's order comes out, I wait a little while before I start to eat, and after I take a bite, Lis squeezes my hand reassuringly, and that small action makes me feel better.

Chapter Thirty-Six

SAGE

"**H**OW'S IT GOING FOR YOU? Are you all settled?" Vincent takes a sip of his tea, and I glance at the view behind him, still unable to believe I'm *here*. I've been to Italy before, but I'm here for *him*.

"Yes! I'm doing great, thank you so much again for everything." I knew I would have accommodations, but Vincent got me a personal driver for the entirety of my stay, and I was able to choose between a house or a hotel. I chose a hotel since I wanted to be in the city, and they had a spa plus a ton of other things I couldn't pass up.

He goes through everything we have planned for just this week, and I try not to let it overwhelm me.

My entire team gets here tomorrow, so Vincent's crew will be doing my hair and makeup for today. I'm glad Angie was able to fly with me, though. The flight was nearly fourteen hours long, and I slept for a lot of it, but I don't like flying alone.

"And then today will just be the first interview with our publicist. I emailed you and Angelica the details, but she's going to be writing about your first week here, so you'll meet with her every day for the first week."

"That sounds great. I forgot to ask, but I'm sure you know I vlog on Famoura, and I was just wondering what I can and can't post?"

He lets me know what are no-go's, and I write them down in case I forget, then ask him to also email them to Angie so she can be on top of my posts.

"That should be everything for this week." He closes his laptop and folder. "My crew is waiting for you at the headquarters."

I get up to hug him goodbye and thank him for breakfast, although I barely touched my food. My stomach just feels... off.

Marco, my chauffeur, opens the door for me, and I thank him before climbing in and texting Angie to let her know I'm on my way to Moore headquarters. A few minutes after I hit send, my phone starts ringing, and when I notice it's Moon, I feel myself smiling, but it falls when I realize a possibility as to why he's calling.

I don't know how things with Liam will turn out or if I'll even speak to him again, but maybe a month here will help me forget him.

When the call ends, Moon calls back, and I start to feel bad because he's still my friend, so I answer. "Hey, Moon pie." I muster up a smile, but it turns more genuine when I see how happy he is that I answered.

"Sunshine!"

I laugh softly, and Jordan peaks his head into the frame. "Hey, Sunshine."

"Hi, Jordan."

Moon backs the phone a bit so they're both in the frame, and I realize they're in Liam's penthouse, but I keep my smile intact.

"Are the kittens there? I miss them so much." I haven't seen them in a while, and a video of Mars scaring Liam, along with a picture of them eating, was the last thing I saw, but I'm probably not going to see them for a while or ever. They turn the camera to face them, and I get a few pictures of them.

Someone clears their throat before Moon mumbles something, and then the camera is switched to face him. "So..." He smiles *too* innocently. "How's Italy?"

"It's good. I've only been here a few hours, but I love it." I've been practicing my Italian, so getting around hasn't been that bad, but a lot of people here speak English, and Marco is also nice enough to translate a lot for me.

"That's nice..." Moon looks over at Jordan, who smiles weirdly. "So..."

What is going on...

"It must be so beautiful over there. What part of Italy are you in?" *That's* what this is about. I shake my head at them and almost laugh at their non-subtlety.

"Who wants to know?" I turn my head with a smile, and they both laugh, but it's clearly forced.

"*We* asked, duh! We miss you. We were thinking of visiting."

"Mhm." I keep my eyes on them. "Is it just going to be you two who will visit?" When they look back at each other, I shake my head before letting out a soft sigh.

"Look, you guys, I think it's cute that you're trying to help your friend, but we're broken up, and I honestly don't want to see him. If you genuinely want to see me, then I'll tell you what hotel I'm in, and you can visit next week when I'm really settled here, but I don't want to see Liam."

I force my voice to stay steady and act like I at least mean that but in reality... I don't. Of course, I want to see him, and I hate that I do since I was the one who sent him away, but I really want to see him.

Moon and Jordan give me a sympathetic look, but I smile a bit bigger.

"I really do want to see you, Sage." Moon sounds sincere, and I tell him I'll send him my hotel information next week, just in case Liam finds a way to get it out of them. While a part of me wants to see him, the other part just can't.

LIAM

"ALRIGHT, I'LL TALK TO YOU later then, Sunshine."

I watch through the phone as Moon waves goodbye, and Jordan says bye next.

"Later!"

My chest aches at the sound of her voice, and when I hear the call end, I sink further into my seat. I didn't think you could miss someone who's alive *this* much, but I do.

My bones ache, and I don't know if it's for her or because I sat uncomfortably on this jet for twelve hours. I just landed in Rome, and I didn't even know she was leaving for Italy today until Moon mentioned it. I literally dropped everything and had my pilot do the same to get me here. I haven't slept since Sage broke up with me. I can't think. I can't eat. I clearly can't sleep. I can barely fucking breathe, and I just want *her*.

Sage said she doesn't want me to speak to her until I change, and I'll obey that wish. I won't speak to her, but I need to be closer to her, even if we sit in silence. I signed up for anger management therapy the minute I left her house because I knew she was right. I had my first meeting this morning, and my therapist does not agree with my choice to come here, but I do not care.

I landed in Rome twenty minutes ago when I realized there are over two hundred cities in Italy. She might not even be here, and I might lose my mind before I search every city and find her, but at this rate, I'm ready to lose my mind.

"We tried..." Moon looks over at me through Jordan's phone, but I toss my phone in front of me and I bury my face in my hands.

"I'm sure you can narrow down where she is..."

"How, Jordan? Please tell me."

He's silent for a while as I search my brain for a possible solution. "Maybe I can track her phone." She stopped sharing her location with me, but I have a friend who can find her for me. This is the same friend I'm paying to keep the mean comments and DM's out of Sage's account, I'm sure he can find her for me.

"That's an invasion of her privacy," Moon starts. "She's going to be more upset if she finds out."

Jordan agrees, but I don't admit that he's right. As I get another idea, I sit up and grab my phone. She's here for that designer, which means she'll be wherever he is.

After making the guys check her social media because I can't remember the designer's name. After a few minutes, they get his name. He lives in Venice, Italy, which narrows it down a lot. I tell the pilot we need to get on the move, and before we even take off, I find his headquarters in a town in Venice. *Perfect.*

This place is still huge, but I have better luck searching one town than searching the entire damn country. I'm on the plane for another hour, and I should've researched first, but I told my pilot to just fly to Italy, and when he asked me where I told him I didn't fucking care. I just needed to be closer to her.

I can never sleep on flights, but I certainly can't sleep on this one. I don't know how many times I pace the plane, but my feet hurt by the time we land. I was smart enough to bring my bike, so the minute I'm off my plane, I ride into the city.

It's already five by the time I make it to his headquarters, and I was expecting something similar to Magic Model's office, but Sage wasn't joking when she said this Vincent guy was a big deal.

His headquarters look like a fucking *town.* It's gated on all sides, and as I drive around, I know I won't be getting in here even if I paid someone or offered them my jet... I know because I just tried that.

"No bribes! *Partire!*"

I don't speak fucking Italian, but I take the hint and slip my helmet back on. After moving my bike, I stand a safe distance away and wait for her, but cars come in and out, and I have no clue what she's driving or if she's even here and the sun is starting to set.

"Fuck." I speed off and search for nearby hotels instead. After maybe another hour, thunder sounds through the air, and after a few bolts of lightning crash through the angry skies, it starts to pour. I really should not be riding my bike in this weather, but I'm still fucking desperate, so I only slow down a bit as I search every hotel in town and bribe anyone with ears to tell me where the hell my girl is.

Chapter Thirty-Seven

SAGE

I MOVE MY FOOD AROUND with my fork, but after another bite, I can't stomach it anymore. I hate that this is so hard for me. The last few weeks haven't just magically been easy, but I've been eating a bit more. One full meal a day, sometimes two on good days... this is my first meal today besides the coffee and croissant I had with Vincent, but after he reminded me that my fitting was tomorrow... I lost my appetite.

I press my palms to my eyes. "It's going to be okay." I try to convince myself to take another bite, but when I look at my plate, I feel sick. I rise from the bed and walk over to the window. I stare down at the city, and listening to the rain for a few minutes seems to calm me.

I try to think happy thoughts, and only one thing comes to mind, so I grab my phone. I check the time, and it's seven AM in LA, but I know both boys need to meet with their coach about their suspension, so I call anyway. The group FaceTime call rings, and August answers first.

"Sage! What's up?"

"Hey, ugly twin." His smile slightly drops, and I burst into a laugh.

"Fuck you."

Sire joins the call just as he voices his words, and when I act like his words hurt me, Sire glares at my twin. "Don't talk to her like that."

August lets out an exaggerated sigh before flopping onto his couch. "She started it!"

"I don't care."

I let out a laugh, and when Sire turns more serious, my smile slowly fades. "So you and Walker aren't getting back together, right?"

An awkward silence fills the air as I take a minute to respond. August told me that he broke the news to Sire while I was on the plane ride over here, and I've tried texting and calling Sire, but he hasn't been answering until now.

"I don't know yet..."

"What is there for you to know?" He snaps. "He lied to you and has been messing with us for years. Why would you even *want* to date him?"

His question is clearly rhetorical, so I don't answer him.

"Whatever." He hangs up before I can respond, and I sink into my bed.

"He hates me." I bury my face in my pillow.

"He doesn't *hate* you. He's just upset, but he'll get over it if you really do love Walker, which I still can't grasp since that man has zero redeeming qualities besides his *awesome* bikes."

I do love him. I'm just too scared to admit it out loud.

I let out a frustrated breath, but when I sit up, my eyes land on my plate, and I just want this whole year to be over already.

"What are you thinking about, Sagey?"

I smile at August's name for me, and he only ever calls me that when he knows I'm sad.

"How mad was Sire when you told him about me and Liam?"

When August scratched his neck, I knew it was bad. "Well, um... we went by your house to water your plant since you had forgotten, and Walker was outside your door for some reason and... well, Sire kind of beat him up."

I feel my heart sink as my face drops. "Please tell me you're joking."

August shakes his head, and I let my head fall.

"If it makes you feel any better, Liam didn't fight back."

"That makes me feel worse, August." Feeling a headache forming, I rub my temples. "*Why* would he even do that?"

"He's convinced Walker only slept with you to piss us off." August shrugs like he also believes that. "Don't get me wrong, you're an amazing person, Sage, and you're beautiful; I mean, duh, you're my twin."

We both let out a soft laugh before he continues.

"Any man would be lucky to be with you, and we don't think there was no other reason he got with you, but he's an asshole, and until proven otherwise, I'm convinced it was all out of spite."

I don't say anything in response, and when my eyes land on my plate again, I change the topic. "Can you please tell Sire to join the call again? I called you guys because I wanted company while I ate."

August nods in understanding before he texts our brother, and a minute later, he joins the call again, but he still doesn't look happy, and I feel my face fall again.

"Okay," August starts. "Lose the attitude, Sire, because you're making my sister feel bad. Don't make me drive to your house this early in the morning. She didn't know Walker was a dickhead, and we can't help who we fall for. So put on the best performance of your life and act supportive because her happiness comes before all else."

Sire doesn't look pleased, but August sends him a knowing look, and surprisingly, he doesn't fight him on it. "What are you eating, Sage?" Sire voices sincerely, and I flip the camera to show them my plate.

August hums in return, and I watch as he rises from his seat. "I'm hungry." He walks into his kitchen, and I chew my lip as I turn the camera back to me and lean my phone in front of me.

"Yeah, so am I. Vidia made those Red Lobster biscuits again last night–" Sire looks around for something. "She messed them up again, but I told her they were better and ate one. I actually think I might get food poisoning."

I stifle a laugh at how quiet he's being as he walks into his kitchen to serve breakfast. Vidia is a good cook, but she apparently can't get these biscuits right. I know they are Sire's favorite, though, so I'm sure she's going to keep trying.

My brothers casually get me to talk about my day as they serve their breakfast. I move my dinner around with my fork as they sit to eat.

"So you like it so far?" August asks before biting into his food.

"Yeah, I love it. Everyone is so friendly, especially at work." I keep my eyes on my plate but look back up at my phone when they don't respond. They're both watching me carefully, and I try to smile, but it looks like I feel worse than I do.

"Talk to us, Sage." Sire urges, and I let out a long sigh. I try to form the words but can't get anything out. A second later, it looks like Sire's typing on his phone, and after a minute of August telling me I'm going to be okay, Lisette's pretty face pops in, and she looks half asleep.

"What's up, bitches?" Her groggy voice sounds through the phone as she rubs her eyes.

"Lissy bear!" I smile over at her, and she rolls her eyes, but she has a small smile on her face as she complains about my nickname. I know she secretly likes it.

"Are you having a hard time, Sage?" Lis asks so straightforwardly, but I shouldn't have expected her to be soft about this like my brothers are. She watches me the way she watches Sire when they talk about his addiction, and it reassures me that she'll be able to help.

"Yeah..."

"What are you thinking when you look at your plate?"

I glance back over at all of the food, and I feel like every grain of rice and piece of fish is screaming at me. "It's just too much. I saw how many calories this was on the menu and–"

"Okay, we're doing this one step at a time. Okay?"

I let out a sigh and give my sister a nod. She tells me to get a second plate, so I do.

"On the second plate, you're going to serve a small amount. It doesn't have to be a lot, just however much doesn't scare you."

I nod to myself as I start serving the plate, but I feel my eyes stinging.

"You're doing good, Sage, just–"

"Why are you crying?" Lis cuts off August, and her words aren't harsh, only like she genuinely wants to know, so I swallow the lump in my throat as I answer her.

"I don't know, I just—I don't want this to be so hard, but it *is*."

I watch my siblings, and Sire nods. The look he gives me makes me feel like he knows *exactly* how I feel. "It's going to be hard for a while, but I promise you, Sage, it's going to feel *so* much better and more rewarding on the days that don't feel as hard."

I nod in return and blink away my tears as I finish serving the small portion that I feel more comfortable with.

"However much you served is great, Sage," August reassures me. "It doesn't matter how much or how little it is."

I pull in a deep breath and Lis walks me through my first bite. She tells me not to think about how much food is on the other plate or how many calories are in the small portion I serve. My goal for *now* is to just finish this part, and I do.

"Good job!" August beams.

"I'm so proud of you, Sage." Sire goes on, and I smile at the phone as I wipe my tears.

"This feels so stupid." I let out a broken laugh before wiping another tear. "I'm an adult. I should be able to–"

"Don't do that," Lis warns. "I'm an adult. Is it stupid that I want to actually die at every minor inconvenience?"

I don't answer.

"Because that's not an exaggeration. On my bad days, my depression actually makes me want to die when I *finally* gain the energy to get out of bed after two days, then I serve myself a bowl of fucking cereal, and when I go get milk, I realize I have none."

Sire laughs quietly, and when she calls him an asshole, I smile at their bond, but August and I watch her with soft, identical eyes.

"How are *you* doing?" August voices.

"This isn't about me." Lis quickly tries to brush him off, and when Sire chimes in, she literally ignores him. "Come on, Sage, let's try again. Serve yourself another small amount, and don't look at how much is left on the other plate."

I do and finish another small portion, but as I keep serving myself more, it only gets harder.

"I don't want anymore." I shake my head as I watch the next portion, my stomach turning.

"Okay, that's fine—" August is cut off as Lis chimes in with her tough love.

"Why not? You just said after the last bite that you weren't full."

"I am now."

"You're not. What changed?" She pushes, and I feel my throat tightening.

"Lis, she did great. Leave her–"

"Sire, you texted me to join the call and help. I'm helping. Shut up or leave."

He surprisingly doesn't say anything, and I bury my face in my hands, knowing neither of the boys are going to help me out of this. Lis asks me again what's wrong but I don't answer as I cry silently. They wait, and it feels like forever, but they sit in silence as I get myself together and blurt out what's been on my mind.

"They're taking my measurements tomorrow! I *can't* eat all of this food. If my measurements are bigger than my last fitting, I'm going to *die*."

"Do *not* say that, Sage."

My stomach turns at the worry in August's voice.

"Sage."

I keep my face buried as August calls me.

"*Sage.*" Sire tries to get my attention now, and I let out a shaky breath before looking back at my phone.

"I promise you," Sire starts. "Eating that plate won't change a *single* thing."

I start shaking my head, but August continues for him.

"It won't, Sage. You won't gain a singular pound if you finish that plate. I promise."

I keep my eyes on my plate but look back up when August calls me again.

"Trust me." He nods encouragingly, and I pick my head up and take another bite. I squeeze my eyes shut as I force it down, but as I bring another spoonful to my mouth, I quickly turn my face away before dropping the spoon.

"Okay." Lis nods with a small smile. "You're done. Good job."

I cover my food before taking a few gulps of my juice, washing away the sour taste in my mouth. The boys voice their encouraging words, and I smile through the phone before thanking them and wishing them a good day because while I'd love to keep talking to them, I feel drained.

August and Lis leave first, but from the look on Sire's face, I know he wants to say something.

"I'm sorry for before," he starts gently. "I just can't stand Walker, and I hate the thought of him even looking at you, but August is right; we can't help who we fall for, and you're an adult. You're also very smart, and you know your worth. If you really do love him, it won't be the end of my world, but I'm telling you now, I'm never going to be his friend." He adds that last part more harshly. His eyes bore into mine and I can see the finality in them.

I nod in understanding, reminding myself not to push my luck. They've hated each other for nearly ten years; that isn't going to go away overnight.

"I love you, Sage."

"I love you more."

We end the call, and his words reassure me that he isn't going to hate me for whatever I decide to do with Liam.

I get up from my seat but freeze at the note of paper on the floor. I know it's not mine, so I grab a shirt to pick it up in case this is some sort of trap and the paper is laced with something. I know that sounds ridiculous, but my dad has scared me into being extra precious ever since I started traveling alone.

When I flip the page over and see the name *Dory* written on it, my worries fade.

I'm not sure if this counts as speaking to you but I couldn't be so close and not say anything. I booked the room across from you and I'm staying with you for the rest of the month. We don't have to speak, but if you need me, knock on my door anytime, beloved. I know you miss the cats, and I didn't want you to be alone, so Moon lands with them tomorrow, and they're also staying for the month.

I love you. Have a good night, my perfect girl.

I glance over at the door, and when I see a shadow of feet from the bottom, my heart aches at how close he is. I walk over to the door quietly, and as I look through the peephole, there he is, soaking wet from the rain and holding his helmet. I think he's listening out for me, and I bite back a smile at how ridiculous we both probably look.

"Thank you," I voice, and his head snaps up so fast, I'm sure he just gave himself whiplash.

A smile spreads across his face as he kisses his fingers and presses them to the peephole before disappearing into his room.

Somehow, one letter made my whole night better.

Chapter Thirty-Eight

SAGE

"SO, WHAT'S UP WITH YOU two? Because it looks like you're together but... not talking or having sex." Moon goes still before turning to me slowly. "You guys aren't secretly having sex, right?"

"What?!" I break into a laugh at how disgusted he looks.

"I laid in both your and his bed. Please tell me you're not having sex, Sunshine." He shoots up from the bed and quickly grabs Meeko.

"We're not having sex! We're broken up."

One of Moon's hands shoots up in surrender as he holds Meeko in the other. "Hey! You can be having break-up sex."

"We're not!" I tried to convince him for the last time, and he let it go.

"Fine, but I need some sort of update because you told me he was on his *knees* for you and that was hard to believe. Now, he's actually listening to you and not speaking to you. It's weird seeing him so... in love. It's like you can tell him to jump off of a roof, and he'll ask which one."

I let out a laugh, but he's not totally exaggerating. It's been two weeks that we've been in Italy and Liam hasn't said a singular word to me, but he's being perfect in everything else.

"Is he still sending you breakfast every morning?"

"Yup." *With cute notes.*

"And he's still waiting for you outside your room every morning at the crack of dawn just to walk you to your car and give you lunch?"

"Uh-huh." *With even cuter notes to help me eat lunch.*

"Hmm." Moon settles onto the bed with me again, lost in his thoughts. "Maybe his therapist is brainwashing him."

I break into a laugh, but he remains serious. I didn't believe it for a second that Liam was in therapy, let alone anger management, but he is, and he's apparently sticking to it. "These things aren't out of character for him."

I can say for certain that Liam would've been doing all these things to make sure I was eating if we were still together because he did, but rather than his handwritten notes, he used to text me throughout the day. His logic is that paper messages mean he's still not speaking to me, and I like the notes too much to tell him they are, in fact, a form of communication.

Moon lets Meeko onto the floor with the other kittens before turning back to me. "Maybe, but carrying you bridal style as he walks through a puddle with his thousand-dollar shoes? *That* is out of character for him."

I cringe but also smile at the reminder of yesterday. "He didn't want me to get dirty before work."

Moon looks at me as if I'm crazy, but I didn't ask him to do that for me. I was going to walk in a trash bag since there was no way around the puddle, but he just carried me once I said I was running late.

"Okay." Moon hugs the pillow as he lays on his stomach to continue our girl talk. I absolutely love that Liam flew him here on his jet because his company is making my stay here so much better. "I know you're standing your ground, but you're standing on a mountain on your damn tippy toes, Sunshine."

"I am not."

He gives me a knowing look, but I don't say anything.

"Well, what's it going to take for at least the no-talking strike to break because I honestly would've folded once she let *Mel and Jordan* use his jet to come see you after you mentioned you missed them." Moon looks at me more carefully. "You know those two definitely slept together on his plane right? Liam let that happen for you! Give my guy a break."

I tilted my head back with another laugh. "They did *not* sleep together on his jet." I asked Mel after Jordan was teasing Liam about it, but he was only trying to upset him. Surprisingly, Liam barely gave him a reaction, and I think whatever he's doing in therapy is working because all he did was tell Jordan to leave him alone after walking away when he normally would've cursed him out and threatened to hit him.

"Wait, aren't Jordan and Mel *so* cute together? I was so right about them!" I'm a genius matchmaker because they shared a room for the weekend they were here, and Mel told me all about *that*, and I'm so happy I got them together.

"Yeah, they're going to make cute babies, now back to Liam." Moon brushes me off.

"Oh my goodness." I throw myself onto the stack of my pillows. "Did he offer you a car again to help him?"

He glances off to the side at a fake camera before looking at me. "Maybe?"

We both erupt into laughter as I toss a pillow at him.

"He misses you, Sunshine."

I let out a sigh as he turns more serious and pull one of my pillows closer.

"He really wants to win you back, and if you aren't going to take him back, at least make it worth our time and get him on his knees in front of me so I can record before you send him away for good."

"You're a horrible person!" I shove him with a laugh, but then he turns serious again.

"I have to ask–"

"Do you?"

He tilts his head at me. "What's it going to take, Sage? Because he almost gave up his plane just to *find* you, and I believe the therapy thing is working. I think he actually likes it."

"He did *not* try to give up his jet."

Moon nods, and I bury my face in my pillow. He thankfully doesn't press me again, and I take a second to think, but there isn't really much to think about.

"I meant what I told him, and I'm glad he's in therapy for his anger issues, but I don't know when we'll get back together. I can consider it at the end of the trip. Jordan says his suspension ends next week. If he leaves without me, then I guess that'll be my answer."

"You and I both know he's not leaving without you." Moon rolls his eyes at the possibility. "His coach is going to give him hell, though. Are you going to make him choose between you and his career?"

"No," I explain, "I would never expect that of him. He'd just be missing one game; I go back home in time for his next one. If he can't miss *one* game and take some yelling from his coach, then that says a lot." He was the one who said he'd buy NASA and go to the moon if what I wanted was there. This is far from that.

"You're standards are insane." Moon shakes his head as if he's amazed at me.

"It's the bare minimum!" I defend myself. "My brother quite actually called his coach to quit the team just to try to prove a point with his girl, not even get her back."

Moon thinks about it for a second before nodding. "Okay, yeah, I see why your standards are so high, but your brother is Sire Griffin. Liam is an *amazing* player, but he's in the hot seat with his coach and always has been."

"And why's that?" I ask a question I already know the answer to.

"Because of his anger issues and—" Moon cuts himself off as he realizes my point.

"Liam is constantly bumping heads with his coach, him missing a game will for sure cause a fight, and it's not necessarily a setup, but I know Liam is going to choose me and have to get yelled at by his coach. How he reacts to that will tell me if he really did at least try to get his temper in order." I explain.

I guess you can say it's a test, along with whether or not he decides to open up to me about *anything* that's a hint of personal because, as his girlfriend, I want to be able to talk to him about those things. I still don't know what happened to his sister or what his mom is sick with, and I'm not forcing him to tell me everything, but he should be willing to try, and he has yet to. Mainly because I set the no-speaking strike, but I'm going to give him the option to open up to me.

"You can't tell him." I force Moon to act like this conversation never happened, and when he does, I flip the conversation to him. "Did he tell you anything about Capri?"

Moon sighs at the sound of her name and looks up to the ceiling. He claims he fell in love with her, although he only saw her picture on Liam's phone when she called him.

"He's given me *nothing*." He sits up as he remembers something. "I should tell him you told him to tell me!" He shoots up from his seat as he races for the door, and I'm hysterical as the door shuts.

Chapter Thirty-Nine

LIAM

"**I** WANT TO DISCUSS YOUR triggers, Liam," Rose, my therapist, continues. "Your family seems to be one of them, but can you think of another instance where you got really upset?"

"When people annoy me." *Like now.*

Anger management therapy hasn't been the worst thing ever. I've been doing it for three weeks now, and it definitely got easier. I just hate how much she wants to talk about my family.

"Have you ever lost your temper with Sage?"

I look up at her, my brows slightly pulled together, and she only watches me through the video call as if the way I simply breathe will tell her my answer. "I've gotten *mad,* but I never lost my temper with her. Why are you asking me that?"

"What does mad versus losing your temper mean?"

"Losing my temper is like storming off to break a punching bag with my bare hands. She's never made me that mad, and I don't think she ever can."

"Why not?"

"Because I love her?" My head tilts slightly to the side as I study her. "Where did you say you got your degree from?" I scan the diploma on the wall behind her, but it's too far for me to read it.

She stifles a laugh, and I'm not sure why because I was genuinely asking.

"Let's circle back to the root of your anger."

"I don't want to talk about this anymore." I can actually feel the pressure in my temples intensifying.

"It was a big step for you to tell me about how both your dad and your sister passed away, but the last week, I've been trying to bring up your dad, and it ends in you hanging up on me, yet you keep answering when I call back. That shows me you genuinely want to get your anger under control."

"I do." I shuffle in my seat uncomfortably.

"That's good. When you booked your first appointment with me and filled out your questionnaire, you said you wanted to start anger management because you didn't want to be angry around your kids. Is Sage pregnant?"

"I fucking hope she is," I mumble, but she hears, and a smile touches her lips as she writes in her notebook. "Unfortunately, she isn't." I don't even think of the possibility.

"Why are your future kids in thought when you join these calls?"

"I don't want them to grow up seeing my bad temper," I say the obvious.

"Yeah, but why them? Why don't you want your friends or Sage to see your bad temper? Why the kids?"

"Because they're *kids*, they don't need to see that."

"Does Sage need to see it?"

"No, but that's different. She's an adult, and she understands. Either way, she's another reason I'm here. I don't want her to see how angry I can really get."

"But why not the kids?" She presses, and her poor listening skills are starting to annoy me.

"I don't want to lose my temper with them." *I'm losing my temper with her.*

"Why? Kids can get annoying, I'm sure you'll yell at them sometimes, all parents do."

"Well, I don't want to."

"You don't want to yell at them? Why?" She goes on, and I feel my annoyance growing. "Yelling isn't the worst thing and-"

"Killing them is." I snap, and when her eyes meet mine, she looks satisfied with something. I realize she *wanted* me to get mad. "What's the point in this shit?" I bite out.

"Do you think you're capable of killing someone?"

"Aren't we all?"

She nods gently as she writes in her notebook, and I hope she picks up on my sarcasm and isn't writing, *this man is crazy, make sure to call the cops once you hang up.*

"Do you think you're capable of killing your kids, Liam?"

I keep my eyes on her, and my mind goes over all of my episodes. All of the times I tore apart my room in high school, the baseball bats I snapped in half in college, the punching bags I break now... I think of all of that, and then I think of Shanti, and I've been angry around her. I've come home furious multiple times, but every time I entered her presence while I was mad, it just faded.

"No, I don't think I am, but you psychologists think killers are both born and made, so what does that say about me? Am I fucked because my dad's a murderer?"

"Do you think you are?"

"Yeah," I answer so quickly it scares me. "But I refuse to put Sage through what my dad put my mom through, so I'm here. If you think I'm screwed, though, just let me know now so I can be sure to stay far away from her."

"We're all capable of killing someone." She shrugs. "What do you think the root of your anger is?"

I bury my face in my hands as I rub my temples. Her words repeat in my head once before my answer comes to me. "My dad. I hate that I'm like him."

"Are you though?"

"Well, I'm here, aren't I?"

"Exactly."

I look up at her, and she isn't writing in her book anymore. Instead, she studies me.

"You're going to tell me to figure it out on my own, aren't you?"

When she smiles, I know that's exactly what she's going to say.

"We're running out of time, so let's discuss some strategies for when you feel you are getting mad. You said the breathing exercise you read about doesn't work, so we can skip it. I want you to verbalize what you *want* to do when you're mad and think about the consequences of that. Once you realize how bad it sounds to, let's say, punch someone in the face, you can resort to other things."

"Like what?" I ask instead of telling her I don't see anything wrong with punching people.

"That's for you to figure out." She smiles just as her alarm goes off. "Feel free to text me if you are in a situation where you lost your temper before our next call."

I tell her I will and hang up when there's a knock on my door.

I look through the peephole, and it's only Moon. I walk away, but he knocks again.

"Sage doesn't like it when you're mean! Open."

I roll my eyes and grab the damn door. He keeps using Sage against me. Last week, he did it to get information on Capri, and I genuinely thought Sage wanted to know, so I sat here for an hour and talked about my mom's nurse with him. I can't believe I didn't notice sooner that he was lying.

When I open the door, he's laughing. "Whipped." He covers his words with a cough as he walks in.

"What do you want?"

"I just need my hoodie." He walks over to the couch before slipping it on. "I'll see you later. I have to go meet up with Sage."

"Where are you guys going?"

"The arcade in—"

"I want to come." I grab my jacket, but Moon stops walking before turning to me.

"You don't even like arcades?"

"Sure I do."

"Jordan and I invite you to Dave & Buster's all the time and—"

"I don't care for the arcade, Moon. I want to go because Sage will be there. If she was going to sit in the lobby and sort through her junk emails, I would want to go down there and watch her. You are here simply to help me. Why didn't you think to invite me?"

"Because—"

"I already know your answer is going to piss me off, and I'm minimizing my yelling to once a month. I'm not wasting it on you so how about this, she wants you to stay here. I still need help with her. If you actually do what the hell I brought you here for and invite me out with you guys and get her to *talk* to me, I'll genuinely buy you a car."

He studies me, but I'm not kidding, and I see the moment he realizes that. "Any car?"

"I'll get you two if she has a full conversion with me tonight."

"Let's go." He finally shuts up. I follow behind him without a word and pet the cats goodbye, but then I wash my hands in case I get the opportunity to touch Sage.

When she opens her door, her face lights up at the sight of Moon, and I hate that her smile falters when she sees me. If she hates me, I need to know, and I need to know soon because I said I wouldn't leave without her, but if she genuinely hates me and doesn't want me here, I'll consider leaving her alone.

Moon elbows me and I don't punch him in the back of the head because I no longer have the energy. "Change your face," He whispers before turning to Sage. "I want Liam to join us. Do you mind?"

She barely glances at me as she shakes her head.

We walk to the elevator in silence before Moon turns on his heels. "I left my phone. I'll meet you guys downstairs!"

He rushes off, and when I turn to look at him, he winks at Sage. I look back over at her, and the way she chews on her lips tells me she wants to say something, but she doesn't. It isn't until we get inside the elevator that she turns to me. "How's your mom doing?"

I'm stunned for a breath before I shake it off and answer her. "She's okay." I nod a few times like an idiot. "I spoke to her yesterday."

She nods in return, but before whatever this is ends, I add. "You look pretty. I love your hair." I'm almost certain she's wearing her natural curls, and I love it when she does.

"Thank you." A smile touches her lips and it makes the entire elevator feel hotter, or maybe I'm blushing, I don't know but I don't even care.

She turns to me again, and it's embarrassing how eager I am for her to speak to me again. "Do you mind me asking what she's sick with?"

I feel my previous eagerness fade at her question, and all it does is unpack sour feelings. I glance forward, and almost out of habit, I prepare myself to ride down in silence, but I actually want to talk to her about it since I've only been focusing on my anger with Rose.

"She has Alzheimer's." I turn to Sage, and her face slightly drops as she watches me. "She didn't recognize me the night of your party and kept getting upset that I called her mom." Like the first time I told her about my mom, it doesn't feel so hard. I just need to teach myself to come to her about it rather than her having to probe me about it because I *want* to tell her. I just don't know how.

"I'm so sorry, Liam." She grabs my arm, and her touch alone makes every ache in me feel better.

"She's been sick since I was in college. Some days, she's really good, and other days, she's trying to stab her nurse." The elevator suddenly feels smaller, but Sage gives my arm a reassuring squeeze, and her smile lifts the weight off my chest just a bit. "Her nurse is great, though; Moon also thinks so."

She lets out a soft laugh, and I'm grateful the topic is lighter. The doors open before she can add anything, and when Moon walks in, I realize neither of us has pressed any of the buttons.

He watches Sage, and when I turn to her, she only nods.

"What are you guys doing?" I look between the two of them, but they both shrug, and they're both horrible liars. I decide to threaten not to get Moon a car later so he'll tell me.

By the time we get to the arcade, we realize they don't have a parking lot, so they go in without me as I look for parking nearly forever. When I finally get in, it's thankfully not too crowded, but I texted Moon asking where they were, and he didn't respond, so I'm stuck searching for another ten minutes.

I finally spot Sage from across the room, and three guys are talking to her. I let out an annoyed breath and tell myself not to get upset over something so dumb, although they're so shamelessly checking out her titties.

"His English is no good."

"No, don't be silly! His English is great." Sage laughs softly, and the two guys behind the one who's talking to her say something I can't understand, but I'm sure they're talking about her with the way their eyes roam her for too damn long.

"Beautiful." One of them says as he gestures to Sage and I have to actually hold my hands behind my back not to grab him when he takes her hand and leans in, and kisses her dimple. *My* dimple.

"*Grazie!*"

They cheer as if a two-year-old can't say thank you in Italian, and I decide I hate Italy and their friendly men. The one I'm going to punch first, given the chance, gestures to the game in front of Sage.

"Pink?" He points at the huge pink dolphin, and when Sage confirms that she wants it, I almost push past them and pay for it, but he hands the girl his ticket, and when she hands him three baseballs, I let him embarrass himself first.

Only one of the balls hit the pins, but he needs to knock over all three towers to win. He gestures for her to wait, and when he gets three more balls and misses, his friends laugh and take a turn. The second one misses all three horribly, and they push him away, which makes Sage die of laughter. I don't know what the hell is so funny about this, but even Moon laughs, and I'm not buying him a goddamn car after this, let alone two.

I take a step forward but remember what my therapist said. "I want to punch all of the guys in the fucking throat," I verbalize and quickly realize this isn't working because I don't see what's wrong with that.

Then my eyes land on Sage, and I think about her reaction to that, and she'll be upset. I let out a breath and think of what I can *resort my anger to.*

When the guy next to Sage pays the girl another ticket, I walk over and take all three balls from her.

"*Mi scusi?*"

I ignore him as I throw the first ball into the tower of pins, and they crash so hard that one pin hits the second tower which makes it fall. I throw the second ball at the last tower, and it falls just as quickly. The girl hands me the dolphin, and I turn on my heels.

All of the boys stare at me, and I shove the last ball into the chest of the one who kissed her before wrapping an arm around Sage's waist and walking away. *Hmm, I guess my therapist was onto something.*

"That was a bit unnecessary..."

"Punching them in the throat would've been unnecessary. Be happy you got a dolphin in peace."

She pushes my arm off of her as she turns to me. "We're going back to no talking."

I shove the dolphin into her arms before she can walk off, the remainder of my patience slowly evaporating. "Fine by me; one more thing, though. You may *think* we're not together, Sage, but you're not available. *Nothing* about that was funny, so stop giggling at every man who looks at you because I don't have any more coping strategies in me tonight."

She looks confused about my last part before she *rolls* her eyes. "I'm very available."

"Sage Loana—"

"I'm *available* for any man I *want*."

I glance over at Moon and silently tell him to tell me this is a joke and another one of his ways to piss me off, but he only puts his hands up in mock surrender before taking a few steps away, and I lean down so I'm at eye level with her.

"That was me playing nice, beloved. There's still plenty of time for me to turn around and put him in a coma for kissing you, so watch that pretty mouth of yours and do not test me."

When her chest falls and rises faster, I know she's mad. She shakes her head before whipping around, but I grab her arm and turn her back to me before she storms off. "And you're not available. Don't make me fuck the thought out of you."

She snatches her arm away before shoving the dolphin back at me. "Stop being ridiculous, Liam." She crosses her arms now. "I thought you were working on your anger?"

"I *am*, and I'm improving, so stop pissing me off."

"Stop being a possessive *caveman*. I just wanted to be friends with them." She walks off before I can tell her they certainly wanted to be more than friends, but I let her leave this time.

"Really?" Moon voices from beside me, and I drag my eyes away from her back to look at him.

"What were they doing that was so funny?" He opens his mouth, but I beat him to it. "You're not getting a damn car." I shove the dolphin into him before I walk past him to catch up with Sage, and he says I technically had a conversation with her, but I ignore him.

Sage ends up walking away every time I get too close, even if she's in the middle of a game, so I take the damn hint and watch her from a distance.

One of the guys comes back to her, and he must be the first brain-dead person who can walk and talk because he's a fucking moron. He puts a hand on his chest as he gestures between Sage and me. When she shakes her head and puts a hand on his arm, I realize he must be apologizing.

I let them talk, but when the conversation gets too long, I walk over, and he leaves before I can reach them. "What'd your little boyfriend say?"

Sage turns to me and crosses her arms. "He feels *horrible*, Liam."

I watch her for two seconds before rolling my eyes. "You were supposed to say he isn't your boyfriend."

She sends me a pointed look, and I lean against the game behind me. "He could be feeling a lot worse."

She shakes her head, almost disappointedly, so when she tries to walk off, I catch an arm around her waist and drag her between my legs. She keeps her arms crossed and looks off to the side like a damn brat, but I wrap both arms around her waist and lock my hands behind her.

"Let me go."

"I'm sorry."

She shakes her head, and I pull her closer. "I'm *sorry*, Dory."

"You said that already, and I said we're no longer speaking."

I sit there in silence and wait for her to look at me, and when she does, I can't help but smile at how pretty she is. "Can I have a hug?"

"What?" She uncrosses her arms and tries to move my hands, but I keep her in place.

"Please. I'll go say sorry to him. Just let me get a hug."

She watches me like she's confused, but I sit in silence for her answer. "Weren't you just mad?"

"Just a bit. May I have a hug?"

Her eyes squint like she can't understand me.

"This is the longest I've touched you in over three weeks. I think I'm touch-deprived, Sage. I miss you. I need to resort to other things when I'm upset, and this is me resorting to you. I just want one hug, and I'll go kiss his ass."

She looks between my eyes, and when she shakes her head, I think she's going to say no, but she wraps her arms around my neck, and I immediately pull her closer.

I bury my face in her neck, and she smells so good. I squeeze her a bit tighter, and it's like moving for the first time after sitting still for years. I stand up straight and slightly lift her off the ground, but she doesn't say anything.

With my face still in her neck, I steal a few kisses, but after the first three, she squirms away. "Stop that." She pulls away, and I kiss her neck one more time before letting her go.

She fluffs her curls as she avoids my eyes, but I watch her carefully. After a beat, she nods to the side. "Go."

I fight every fiber in me not to roll my eyes as I push off the game and walk off to Ed, Edd, and Eddy. They whisper amongst each other as I approach them and stand a bit straighter. I try not to glare, and the smile from hugging her slowly appears.

"Hey."

They look at each other before looking back at me. I feel the words knot in my throat, but when I look over at Sage, she's watching, so I force them out. "My bad about earlier." I can't seem to form the word *sorry,* so that's the best they're getting.

"No worries, I apologize. We no see she married. She wears no ring."

I feel a smirk grow, and I only give them a nod before walking away. If a ring is what it's going to take for every other guy to stop dropping their jaws when she walks into a damn room, then she's getting one tonight.

"What'd they say?"

"He said not to worry about it." I shrug, and she studies me for a beat before glancing over my shoulder. "Can I have another hug?"

She looks back over at me before shaking her head. "No, and we're still not speaking." She walks off, and I push off the game before walking after her with a smile.

Chapter Forty

SAGE

I QUICKLY WIPE MY TEARS as it falls. I've been rereading all of Liam's letters *all* day. It's our last week in Italy, but ever since I said we were back to no speaking terms at the arcade, he's been sending me actual letters. Everything has been nearly the same between us other than that, but with every letter, my heart sinks for him. I hate that he's suffering, but I am, too, and when I remember he's the reason for my pain, I continue to ignore him.

When I hear my door opening, I'm pulled out of my thoughts and touch up my makeup.

"You look hot."

I glance at Moon in the mirror, and he nods like he's agreeing with himself.

"Thank you!" I look over his outfit before nodding in return. "You look so cute!"

"*Cute?*" He says it like there's something wrong with the word then looks down at his outfit.

"What?"

"Nothing." He shakes his head. "You ready?"

"Yup." I get up and grab my bag before leaving, and I expect Liam to be outside my room since he's been tagging along with us, but he isn't here.

"Do you want to tease him about us going on a friend date?" I turn to Moon, and I'm actually surprised when he shakes his head because he never passes up the chance to mess with Liam.

"I think he fell asleep. He's a monster when awakened."

I let out a soft laugh, but my shoulders slightly drop since a part of me was hoping he'd join us tonight, even if we sat in silence.

I muster up a smile and remind myself that we're already broken up.

Moon and I decide to walk down to the boats since it's nice out. I've wanted to go on a gondola ride since I arrived in Italy but haven't had the time. When we reach ours, I quickly take a video of it.

"*Benvenuta.*"

I smile at the tour guide and thank him as he holds a hand out to me to climb in. Another man is holding one of the paddles, but he keeps his back to us as he fixes something.

I turn to Moon but glance back at the dock when I notice he hasn't climbed on yet. "Come on."

"I'm actually not going with you." He tucks his hands in his pockets before smiling, and I slightly sit up when the boat starts moving.

"What are you talking about?"

"You're going to have fun, trust me."

I laugh nervously as I glance at the two *men* I don't *know* behind me. "I'd have more fun with you." My face turns more serious. "Get on the freaking boat, Moon."

"I'll see you later, Sunshine!" The boat gets further, and I stand before grabbing the top of it.

"Moon, I'm going to kill you!"

He *laughs,* but this seriously is a horrible joke, and I feel myself start to panic.

"Say the words, and I'll kill him for you."

I whip around so fast that the gondola slightly rocks. "Liam." I let out a breath of relief. "I thought I was being kidnapped."

"I'm sure you did," he says unamusingly, and I can't help but laugh. "You look..." His eyes cast down my frame before a smile touches his lips. "There should be a whole new word to describe you."

I feel my face heat as his eyes bore into every inch of my skin like he's trying to memorize me. "You really are perfect, Dory." He whispers now. "Completely without fault."

I look between his eyes, and with the way he watches me... I think every cyberbully could try to tear me down and fail because his words seem to put a force field around me.

"I love it when you say that."

"I'll tell you every day if we stop the no-talking thing." A smirk plays at his lips before he adds. "We can sit here in silence, but I want to talk to you about something."

I give in and say, "Silence would be awkward for the entire ride."

A smile spreads across his face as we sit down. "I spoke to your brothers."

"You what?" I pull away to look at him, but he seems completely serious.

"I got Moon to send me August's number from your phone. I spoke to him, and he said he's over what happened between us."

Yeah, he told me that a while ago.

"So I got him to talk to Sire," Liam starts carefully.

"No, you did not." I almost don't believe him until he goes on.

"I was wrong about you being afraid of your brothers. I see now that you just didn't want to hurt them by dating someone who did something messed up to them, but after a month of both August and me harassing Sire, he came around. I'm going to be very honest with you..." He starts carefully.

"Uh oh."

He stifles a laugh before explaining. "I *did* threaten him so he wouldn't call you about it because you've been so stressed with working over here, but they'll be here for your show on Saturday, and you don't have to lie to them. I'm not implying we're getting back together, but you don't have to be stressed about Sire completely hating me."

As I look between his eyes, I have to bite my tongue to stop myself from telling me I don't even care about how Sire feels at this point. I'm half as miserable as he is, and it took me long enough to realize being apart is hurting more than what he hurt me.

"How's therapy going?" I ask instead, honestly wanting an update.

He looks down at the water as he answers. "She wants me to figure out how I'm not like my dad, but I don't see how I'm not. I get my anger issues from him. She said I shouldn't place blame, and instead, call it the root of my anger, but he's the reason for—well, everything."

"And she thinks you're different from him?"

He only nods in response, and I know his dad isn't in the picture because of the note he sent with my flowers last month, but I know nothing else about him.

"I have a gift for you." He swiftly shifts the conversation as he grabs a bag beside his feet. "And this isn't a please-take-me-back-because-I'm-miserable gift. I just saw it and thought of you."

I let out a quiet laugh as I took the bag from him. I recognize the brand and when I take the box out of the bag, my jaw slightly drops at the way the entire charm bracelet seems to shine. My fingers run along every charm and I let out a soft gasp when I notice one is actually glowing a soft green.

I notice it's a firefly, and when I bring it closer to read, it says *you light up my life.* As if on cue, Me Belle Evangeline starts playing, and my head snaps up. I look around, and beside us on another gondola is the small band that plays in town.

"Stop it." I look back over at Liam, and he's already watching me with a smile. "I love this." I try to remind my brain that I'm not supposed to fall for his cute gestures, but screw my mind. I get to fall tonight, even if I don't tell him.

"Look at your charms."

I glance back down at the bracelet, and he scoots down to sit closer to me. I break into a laugh when I notice the Dory charm, and it's so freaking cute. "Very creative."

"I tried."

I keep my gaze on the bracelet. "Is this supposed to be us?" I lightly touch the girl and boy holding hands and playfully roll my eyes as I look back up at Liam.

"No, it's a twin charm." He gestures at it. "It's you and August."

I let my smile break through as I look back down at the charms. My finger runs along the A, L, and S, and I shake my head softly. "August, Lis, and Sire?" I peek over at him, and he only nods.

I take in the bracelet, and I don't think I could've gotten charms to describe myself better than he did. There's a gold Christmas tree, my favorite holiday. A paw print for the kittens. An emerald stone, my favorite color, and birthstone. My zodiac sign. A Jamaican and Haitian flag. A pumpkin right next to a coffee.

When I see a particular one, I take the bracelet out of the box for a better look and glance back over at Liam. "Is this a snow globe?"

He nods softly. "To represent you and Sire's bond."

It takes everything in me not to hug him, and I look back at the bracelet to stop myself. Every other charm is a location. The LA one makes sense, but then there are ones like Paris, Brazil, and Italy, and I realize they are all places I've been to.

"How'd you know all of these?"

"I took Moon's phone and looked through your travel playlist on your account." My travel playlist is incredibly long, so I'm sure he meant he just looked at the locations, but still, he got all eleven.

"Thank you." I wrap my arms around his neck and he wastes no time before pulling me closer and with the way he holds me, I believe what he said the other day about being touch-deprived.

I try to pull away and he holds me for a few more seconds before letting go. "Want to wear it now?" He sounds so hopeful, even if I didn't want to wear it, I can't say no to him.

I hold my wrist out, and when he clasps the charm bracelet on, it's a perfect fit. I shake my wrist and move the charms over. "Half a heart?" I turn the charm, and when I glance up at Liam, he only nods but doesn't explain the meaning of this charm.

He asks about how my day was, and I immediately tell him about the sweetest old lady I met today who helped me finish my meal. Liam seems to want to know how all my days have been, apparently because he asks about what I did yesterday and the day before that. I tell him my days are mainly filled with work for Vincent and preparation for the big show.

The band beside us plays the same song the entire ride, and I have no complaints because I can genuinely listen to it for hours on end. When they get to my favorite part again, I turn to Liam.

"I adore you," he says before I can. "I love you."

"Just translating." I put my hands up in mock surrender as I finish for him, but he doesn't add that part, and as he watches me, I actually can't look away. My hands fall, and I don't know if there are any animals in this water, but if a whale were to jump out from beside us, I wouldn't even notice with how Liam watches me.

"My perfect girl." His words are strained, and he looks off to the side as if he suddenly can't breathe.

"Are you okay?"

"No."

I look over at what he's looking at and notice we're nearing the dock soon... a part of me is bummed that the last half hour passed so quickly.

"Can we pretend we're still together?" He turns to me now. "Just until we reach the dock."

"Liam–"

"*Just* until we reach the dock, Dory."

I glance back at the dock and we have maybe a minute. I don't let myself think about it since I can't see what two minutes will change. "Fine."

He sits at the end of the gondola, and when he spreads his legs, I know all too well what he's asking. I shake my head at him before getting up to sit on his lap. He guides my arm around his neck before wrapping his arms around my waist, and I softly laugh at how quick his movements are.

The second his face is in the crease of my neck I melt into him and a second barely passes before he softly kisses my neck.

"Liam–"

"We're still pretending." His nose rubs against me softly, and I let my eyes fall shut as he kisses his way to my jawline. "I love you." His cool breath kisses my lips, and I don't move a muscle.

A chill runs down my spine as his nose nuzzles my jaw, and then there's that soft kiss on my cheek that I missed *so* badly.

"I'm *so* in love with you, Sage Loana." His arm tightens around my waist, and I wrap another arm around his neck. "From the moment I saw you crying over nasty cats, and I adopted all three of them, I knew I was done for."

I bite back a laugh, and when his lips graze mine, I suck in a breath.

"From our first date, I knew I loved you, but I'm sure I fell long before that. Probably when I started spending a shit ton of plane fuel to fly back to LA directly after *all* of my games and literally losing sleep just to be with you."

A smile touches my lips just as his hand cups my cheek. "Please say something." His voice is so quiet, I almost don't hear him over the music.

I squeeze my eyes shut as I rub my nose along his. "You're lovable, Liam." I bring up what he said in one of his letters that nearly tore my heart. I slightly pull away to look at him, and he keeps his eyes shut tight as he shakes his head gently.

"I only want to be loved by you, Sage." He leans into me again, resting his forehead on mine.

I feel like my mind is at war, but I give in and say what I've been wanting to tell him for a while. "I love you, Lee."

His lips meet mine, and when I pull in a deep breath from my nose, it's as if this were a true love's kiss because something deep inside of me awakens.

His grip around me tightens, and I realize the boat has just stopped. I try to pull away, but he doesn't let me. "Wait," he begs before his lips are back on mine, and when his tongue slides into my mouth, I don't *want* to stop pretending.

I pull away and as I look between his eyes, I never want to look at another man. I tried to stand my ground all month, but I knew for a while now that I was going to take him back because I *do* love him. More than I've loved anyone.

"You better not make me regret this, Liam," I warn breathlessly.

A smile spreads across his face as he quickly kisses me again.

"I *mean* it." I pull away so he can see me. "We're humans, we're going to make mistakes, but don't let one of those end in me being hurt because I swear on my twin's life, I won't speak to you again the next time you hurt me. I don't deserve that."

He cups my face before tucking a curl behind my ear. "I'll let your brothers gut me alive if I hurt you again, Sage."

"Oh, they didn't need your permission."

He lets out a deep laugh, and I think I fall in love all over again.

Chapter Forty-One

LIAM

"**A**M I TALKING TO A damn wall! Are you injured or not?" Coach Finn yells again through the phone, and I put him on mute as I do the strategies I've been working on with Rose.

"I want to tell him to fuck off." I take a deep breath as I identify why that'll be wrong. "He's my coach, I need to respect him." I remind myself.

"Walker, so help me God, if you're not at the next game-"

"Don't-" I cut myself off because threatening him for threatening me would be very wrong. I realize I'm still on mute and decided this doesn't count. It's me resorting my anger to other things. "Don't fucking threaten me. I'm not going to be at the next game because I just got my girl back yesterday, and I'm not leaving her. *Yes,* I am injured. I'm still recovering from a broken heart!"

He doesn't hear a word, but I hang up on him and surprisingly feel so much better. "Wow." I smile to myself as I decline his call. "Therapy is great." I'm about to text Rose since I've been looking forward to the validation, but I decide to tell Sage instead.

I got to sleep in her room last night, and after a month apart, I didn't want to leave her side, but I needed to take this call. Just as I open the door, Moon tries to knock.

"Go away." I try to shut the door on him, but he puts a hand on the door.

"Don't be rude, Sage doesn't like it."

I try to walk out, but he grabs me. "I wouldn't go there if I were you." He looks over at Sage's door as if he just saw her putting together an evil plan for world destruction.

"Why not?" I keep my eyes on her door.

"I just ran in here to escape Sage. She was being mean, then started crying because she was being mean, and I got scared. It's a shit show in there."

"What are you talking about?" I look back over at him at the mention of her in tears.

"I don't know. I think she's on her period."

I stare at him for two whole seconds, but he just pets my cat nonchalantly. "Don't tell me you told her that."

"I wish I didn't. She got more mad and then cried more. Something is wrong with her."

"Why didn't you get me? She's not on her period, you idiot." I shake my head at him before turning back to the door.

"How do you know?"

Because she gets a pimple on her cheek when she's on her period and she had it last week. I booked her a spa and got her chocolate-covered strawberries, pretzels, and marshmallows. It was a bundle, and I obviously needed to get them all for her.

"This is why you're single."

"So were you up until twelve hours ago? Thanks to me, by the way."

I turn to him very slowly, and he's already standing from my bed and putting distance between us.

"Do not be here when I get back." I walk out and knock on Sage's door. I can hear her let out a sigh, and I bite back a smile. *She sounds like me.*

"Oh–" Her brows slightly furrow, and I'm glad that sigh wasn't for me.

"Are you okay?"

When she lets out another breath, I know she isn't, and I just want to hold her as she tells me what's bothering her so I can make it go away.

"Not really, but it's fine. I'll–"

"It's not fine. Tell me what it is, and I'll fix it."

She watches me for a few seconds, and I move an inch to lean forward and kiss her cheek. She's so pretty. She looks even more beautiful in this moment with her bonnet and her oversized hoodie. My eyes slowly roam her face, and when she starts talking, her dimples appear and I kiss them one more time.

"You can't fix it. I'm just stressed about the runway show." She shakes her head before covering her face with her hands. "I tried on one of my dresses today, and it didn't *fit*. I actually wanted to die, like-"

"Don't say that." I pull her in for a hug, and I feel her go still, but I don't let go. "I wish you saw yourself the way I see you, Sage." I pull away just a bit so she can see me. "Don't ever say that again," I tell her more sternly.

"That was very sweet, but I didn't mean *actually* die, Lee. Just metaphorically."

"Well, I don't want you to want to metaphorically die, so don't say that. If your dress didn't fit, then the idiot who made it needs to make sure the measurements are right because I'm sure it had nothing to do with you."

She looks up at me with a sad smile. "They *did* read the measurements wrong, and Vincent fired them, but I didn't know that at the time, and his entire team was there, and it was *humiliating*." She covers her face again, as if she actually wants to disappear off the face of the earth, and I pull her hands away.

"Yeah, for the idiot who can't read numbers. Don't be embarrassed that they couldn't do their job."

She turns her head to the side, and I mirror her. "That's not why I was embarrassed..."

"There's no other reason you should be."

She smiles up at me, and I kiss her.

"Have you eaten?"

Her smile disappears, and when she avoids my eyes, I have my answer. "Did you at least eat breakfast at work?" She didn't want to eat the room service I got her but said she'd eat at work. When she doesn't answer, I have to force myself not to let out a sigh.

"Sage-"

"I just *couldn't,* Lee. I've been doing *so* well these last few weeks. I swear I have, but I weighed myself, and I *gained weight*." Her eyes widen like the thought alone is her biggest fear.

"Dory, that's because this is the first time you've been eating healthy. You're not going to gain fifty pounds in a month. I'm sure it was probably two pounds."

Her eyes cut to the ground, and I know I'm right.

"I knew I had my fitting today, and I was so nervous the outfits wouldn't fit, so I didn't eat yesterday and–"

"You didn't eat all day yesterday *or* today?" I look between her eyes, and she looks beyond torn. Her eyes fall to the ground again, but I tilt her chin so she can see me. "You *can't* do that, Sage."

"Liam–"

"What if you pass out again, Dory?" I shake my head at the thought of how scary it was to find her in the shower like that last time. "No. You can't do that, let's go." I grab her hand, and when she asks where we're going, I tell her we're getting food.

She tries to object, but I don't listen, so she tries stalling by taking her bonnet off at the speed of a sloth before fixing her curls with a pick.

"Your hair looks perfect, Dory."

She blatantly ignores me, but I let her fix her curls for the next five minutes and nearly nothing looks different and we both know that.

"I can wait all day, by the way." I tease, but her face falls. I walk over to her and plant a kiss on her lips. "You know I'm not going to force you to eat, let's go *try*."

She nods to herself before I drag her to the restaurant downstairs. She grows quiet as we're seated in a booth in the far corner. They bring out bread and butter, but she doesn't touch it, and I don't push her to.

"How was the rest of your day?"

She only shrugs, and when I see that look in her eyes, I take her hand in mine.

"You're fine, Sage."

She shakes her head and tries to pull her hand back, but I don't let her. When her eyes meet mine, there's a shine in them, and I wish more than anything that it wasn't from her tears.

"You don't understand how humiliating that was today." She shakes her head, and I hate that she's beating herself up.

"The dress barely made it past my thighs, and after *squeezing* into it, we couldn't get the zipper up, and I just looked... horrible." She looks like she might be sick, and I walk around the table to sit next to her instead, and she immediately melts into me.

"On top of that, I had to walk out of the fitting room, in front of maybe *ten* people, and they looked *so* judgemental and–" She covers her face and only shakes her head as if she was reliving that moment all over again.

"Sage, it's *not* your fault the dress didn't fit you. It's not like you gained a hundred pounds from the last time they got your measurements. You gained *two* pounds. That doesn't make a difference in your dress size. They quite literally made the dress too small. How–"

"That's not the *point*, Liam. I don't care that the dress didn't fit. Outfit malfunctions aren't the end of the world. It's the fact that those people looked at how big I was in the dress, and their stares alone told me they thought Vincent was making the worst choice in hiring me. Like I wasn't worthy enough to be their model. Like I wasn't pretty enough or skinny enough; like I'm just not enough and–"

"Stop it." I pull her in closer, and I feel her pull in a deep breath. She shakes her head softly against me, and I kiss the side of her face.

"You're more than enough, Sage. You're *more* than pretty enough. You're—you're fucking ethereal, and it doesn't *matter* if you're not skinny. That shit doesn't matter. I'd give anything for you to see that."

I shake my head as I pull away so she can see me. "I'd gouge my own eyes out and give them to you if it'll make you see yourself the way I see you."

She smiles up at me, but it seems forced as if she's tired.

"Tell me what you need so I can make you feel better, Dory."

She lets out a defeated sigh before running a hand down her tired face. "I just want everyone to never look at me again."

I give her a small smile and wish I could make that happen. "I'd do anything, but that's a bit impossible, baby. I think you're like one of the top ten most famous people on this planet."

She lets out a soft laugh, and I kiss her perfect dimple. "Do you not want to model anymore?"

She sinks into her seat before grabbing up a piece of bread and picking it apart. "I want to model. I love modeling... I just don't love what it comes with." She shakes her head at something she just thought. "I wish the world wasn't so mean."

"The entire world isn't mean." I nudge her arm, and she turns to me. "Sage, you have hundreds of *millions* of people who love you. If you loved yourself a bit more, the world wouldn't be able to tear you down."

"I do love myself." She sounds certain, and I'm sure that's partly true. For the most part, Sage is the most confident person I know. Most days, you'd never guess she tears herself apart, especially not when she doesn't hide her body and wears what she wants.

But on those other days... on the days she doesn't eat and rereads all of her hate comments. Deletes her pretty pictures or changes her outfit. *Those* are the days she needs to love herself more, but until she can, I'll love her enough for the both of us.

"I was doing so good." She rips apart a piece of bread before tossing it into the basket. "I was eating multiple meals *every day,* and when I didn't want to eat, I asked for help. I'd call my siblings to eat with me, and it didn't feel so hard."

I smile at how far she's come, and I wish she'd call me when she needed help, but I'm glad she's finally talking to someone.

"I haven't even made myself throw up in a while, but then today happened, and it feels like such a huge setback." She takes a bite of the bread in her hands, but I falter at her words.

"What?"

She turns to me, and she looks confused for a second before it hits her.

"I didn't know you were making yourself throw up? When was this?" I pull away to look at her, but she avoids my eyes.

"I haven't purged in a while." She shakes her head. "I didn't want to talk about it; my siblings knew, but... I just didn't want to tell anyone else. It took a lot for me to simply tell them, so please don't be mad–"

"I'm not mad that you didn't tell me, Sage."

Her eyes meet mine.

"I'm mad I didn't notice. I'm mad at whatever I did that no longer made you feel comfortable enough to come to me or–"

"No, Liam. It had nothing to do with you." She looks between my eyes, but I don't say anything. "I promise... you're the one who made me come to terms with my eating disorder. I just—I didn't want *anyone* to know, and after I told my family, I didn't have it in me to tell anyone else."

I nod a few times and try to convince myself that this has nothing to do with me or the way I fucked up with her. Instead, I say what matters. "I'm so proud of how far you've come, Sage. Today wasn't as big of a setback as you think, even though you skipped some meals. You acknowledging it is a big first step."

She holds her head a bit higher as she nods to herself, and when the waiter comes, I smile proudly as she orders her food with grace. Even if she's faking until she makes it, I know she's going to get there eventually. *She's got this.*

When the food comes, she nods to herself a few times, convincing herself of whatever is on her mind, and I love how hard she's trying.

"You're doing so good." I kiss the side of her face, and a small smile grows on her face as she turns to me.

"You know, it makes me feel so good when you say things like that."

A smile touches my lips, and I remind myself to keep praising her. She takes a few small bites of her food, but after getting a taste of everything, she must realize that she's hungry because she slowly eats more.

Jordan calls me, but I decline it, and then Sage's phone starts ringing. I roll my eyes but don't waste my breath telling her not to answer because I'm sure she isn't going to listen. "Hi, Jordan."

"Hey, Sunshine. Is Liam there?"

She looks over at me, and I shake my head no, but when she forces a smile, I know she's going to rat me out. "Of course, he is." She flips the phone to me, and I roll my eyes at her before looking down at the phone.

"Tell me what happened!" Jordan is staring at me like I just escaped an insane asylum. "Coach just tore *me* a new one because you hung up on him mid-lecture? Why am I always getting in trouble for your bad temper?"

"What is he talking about?" Sage looks between the two of us.

"Coach called me after I told him I was missing the next game, and you're *not* getting in trouble for my temper." I'm in no way letting him take away this win from me. "I didn't even say anything to him."

Sage looks as confused as Jordan as she watches me. "So what'd you do?"

"My therapist says I need to resort to different things when I'm anger, so I sat there in silence, and that worked for most of the call, but then he started pissing me off, so I put him on mute and yelled at him, then hung up." I smile down at Sage, and she looks confused before a small smile grows on her face.

"I'm so proud of you!"

"Thank you!" I can't help but smile at her praise, but the moment is interrupted by Jordan.

"What the hell?" He stares at me in disbelief. "I have *never* seen you smile like that or say thank you that enthusiastically. Sunshine, what is he on?"

I flip him off before hanging up, and Sage breaks into a laugh.

"Block his number, please."

She laughs harder, and I smile down at her.

When she pulls away, she simply looks up at me in awe. "I love you."

I feel my eyes slightly bulge before a heat runs down my entire face, and her eyes light up at something.

"You're blushing," she whispers, and I don't even bother to look away.

"You should only say those three words for the rest of the day." I practically beg.

She breaks into a laugh, and I pull her into my embrace.

"I wanted you to open up to me, and you have," she starts. "I had to ask about your mom and therapy, but you told me, and you added a bit about your dad on your own." She gestures to her phone. "And you didn't lose it on your coach even though you hate when people yell at you. I asked you to try, and you are. You're also clearly doing this for yourself, which I think is very important."

My face hurts from how hard I'm smiling. "That last part sounded like my therapist."

"I think I like her." She holds her head up as she looks at me more seriously. "Thank you for becoming the better I deserve."

She closes the distance between us, and I want to kiss her forever, but she pulls away. "What are you going to do about your game?"

I shrug in response. "My team will be fine. Plus, I don't even like them."

She softly shakes her head. "You don't like anyone."

"Nope. Just you."

She laughs again before I bring her in for another kiss.

Chapter Forty-Two

SAGE

I LET OUT ANOTHER SQUEAL before pulling my brothers in for a hug, and they fill the room with their laugh. They arrived in Italy two days ago, but I'm still excited that they're here. I knew they would be here, especially since my first show as an official Moore Girl is tonight, but I missed them *so* much.

"Can I please get a sneak peek at what you're wearing tonight?" August begs once again.

"No!" I let out a laugh at how persistent he is. The minute I told him I'd be in this show, he wanted to know the theme, what color I'd be wearing, *what* I'd be wearing. August is hands down my biggest supporter, and I usually always give him hints as to what I'm modeling, but I want tonight to be a surprise.

Sire laughs when his shoulders slouch. "It'd be better not knowing," he reassures August.

"Let's place bets on what color she's going to be in!"

We turn to Lis on the bed, and I shake my head at her with a smile. I don't say it, but I'm certain she also has a gambling addiction.

"Five thousand dollars; she's in white."

I am.

"You don't have five thousand dollars." Sire covers his word with a cough, and when Lis throws a pillow at him, it hits him dead in the face, and we all break into a laugh.

I flop next to Vidia on the couch before leaning my head on her shoulder, and she wraps an arm around me. She and Hazel, of course, came with my brothers, and I realize how much I also missed them.

When someone knocks on my door, August rushes to get it, and I don't exaggerate, he actually runs, and I'm not sure why he does, but I burst into a laugh watching him race against no one.

He opens the door wider and two people walk in with our crates of food. We didn't have time to go to the restaurant downstairs since the girls are still getting ready so we ordered room service and a part of me is glad we did.

With my first show as a Moore Girl being tonight, I really didn't want to eat, mainly because of nerves, but I had to force myself to eat breakfast this morning. I wanted to throw it all up but refused to. Everyone in the room with me has been such a great distraction, though.

August brings my plate to me, and Lisette flops on the floor in front of us. They dig into their plates, and I move my food around silently.

"Want to try some of mine?"

I look up at the sound of Sire's voice and smile as he holds his fork out to Vidia. She tries it and clearly likes his pasta. When she looks down at her plate, I silently laugh because I know she wants his food, and he said she would, but we all know she's too stubborn to admit it.

I take a bite of my food as I watch them, and Sire smiles down at her before eating more of his pasta.

"Admit it, and I'll let you have it." He teases, and I bite back a laugh before trying some of my chicken.

"Shut up." Vidia rolls her eyes at him and eats her food but she looks so unsatisfied, I start to feel bad.

"Don't be stubborn, my love. Just say I'm right."

She ignores him and only flips him off. My brother shakes with a laugh before swapping their plates, and when Vidia smiles to herself, he steals a quick kiss before she digs into his pasta.

My watch buzzes, and when I glance at it, I see it's Liam.

Lee <3

> Try to eat something and good luck on your show tonight, pretty girl. I'll see you later. Enjoy the day with your annoying brothers.

I let out a quiet laugh as love the message before exiting it.

When I look back up, August is smiling down at me. "I can't believe that's really a thing."

"I can't believe you guys have been in contact all month and trying to get Sire on board."

August laughs before Sire turns to me. "The only reason I'm on board is because August said you really love him, but I still think he brainwashed your ass, so I'm keeping a close eye," Sire grumbles, and I bite back a laugh.

"What'd Liam say to you?" I ask what I've been dying to know.

"He called me *every day* for nearly twenty-eight days and said *let your sister be happy and accept that she loves me.*"

I wait for him to add more but he doesn't. "That's it?" I look between August and Sire, and they both nod before Sire goes on.

"Well, he also threatened to kidnap you, which was bull-shit, but yes, he said that every day, sometimes twice a day, and when I blocked him, he used apps to call me. I finally gave in because August joined in and showed up at my house every day, but I still don't like the guy, so if he breaks your heart, I'm breaking his neck." He eats a spoonful of food as August smiles proudly beside me for winning that fight.

"Thank you." I nudge his arm, and he nods.

"Are you nervous about today?" August nudges me back, and when he glances down at my plate, he only smiles at how much I ate, and it makes me feel better.

"Insanely nervous. Us new girls are lining up at the end of the show, and I had a dream I trip, and we all fell like a freaking domino effect." I cringe at the reminder of last night's nightmare. We've been practicing so much for this show, and if I ruin it, I will actually disappear from the world.

"Is that the worst-case scenario?"

"Is the worst of the worst." I shake my head at the thought of it.

"So if you don't trip and knock over everyone like a domino effect, then the show went perfectly. Right?"

I smile over at August before nodding and remind my-self that it'll be fine and if the worst-case scenario doesn't happen, it was perfect, no matter the other hiccups.

After a few more bites of my food, I glance at how much is left, and I *can* finish it.

"Don't think about it."

I glance up at Lis and she's watching me with a pretty smile. "You can push some aside if you want." She extends her plate out to me. "*Only* a little."

I smile down at her, and when my eyes start burning, she rolls her eyes at me. "Oh my God, please don't cry." She quickly pulls her plate back like my food is suddenly contagious from my tears.

I break into a laugh, but then Sire throws something at her before telling her not to be an asshole, and I only laugh harder.

"You don't have to finish it, Sage, but you'll be fine if you do, and we know you can." Sire gives me an encouraging smile, and I nod in response. We all get lost in another conversation, and I'm grateful no one pushes me, but I eat more, and when I finish my plate, I get a group hug. Even Lis and Hazel join, which they never do willingly. They all squeeze me a bit tighter, and I'm reminded of how grateful I am for all of them.

Before I know it, I need to meet up with my team and get ready for the show. I hug everyone goodbye, and they head to where the event is taking place.

My hair is already ready, so we do my makeup, and my nerves start to settle in.

"You're going to be great." Cara voices, and I nod in response before pulling in a deep breath. "Someone put her playlist on."

A smile touches my lips and I love how well she knows me. Someone puts my pre-show playlist on and I think of the worst-case scenario speech August gave me. I keep telling myself that if *that* doesn't happen, it was a great show.

"Okay," Cara says after a few songs before putting my setting spray on. "Are you ready?"

"No?" I laugh nervously, and someone is knocking on the door. Angie lets them in, and when I see it's someone with a headset and clipboard I know I have to go soon.

"Mr. Moore wants you dressed."

I nod in response, and my outfit crew starts rushing around to get all of my things. *This is it.*

I get in my first outfit, and I'm sure I dissociate as they work my jewelry and shoes on because I'm suddenly walking backstage with the other girls.

"There she is!"

I look up at the sound of Jess's voice, and after all this time, I'm still a little shocked that I'm friends with her. She's Vincent's best model, and the second time I modeled for him, I was shocked she even knew my name, but since I came to Italy, she's been by my side the entire time.

"I think Vincent is favoring you." She crosses her arms playfully as she shakes her head and looks down at my dress. She laughs softly and pulls me over to take a picture with me.

"Hey, I want in!" Allie rushes over, and I wrap my arms around them as we pose for a picture.

I turn at the sound of a gasp and go still. "Have we been... replaced?"

I break into a laugh and rush over to Quinn and Coral for a hug. "Oh my God! What are you guys doing here?!" When I see the rest of The Eight behind them, I physically have to hold back a scream so the Moore Girls don't think I'm completely insane.

"Oh my *God!*" They break into a laugh before joining in on our hug. "You guys are going to make me cry!"

"Don't!" They all yell in sync before bursting into a laugh. "You know we wouldn't miss this for the world, Loana." Royal voices, and I pull her in for another hug. I love my girls.

"I'm sorry," We turn at the sound of Jess's voice. "We need a video, like right now."

I laugh softly, and all of us do an outfit check. We're literally all wearing Vincent, but Jess was right, and it came out so cute.

"We're on in twenty! Essential personnel only!" The girls say goodbye, and I feel ten times better about going out there.

LIAM

"THERE SHE IS!" A GIRL from beside me whispers to the girl she's with, and it's as if the entire world stops when Sage walks on stage. She modeled a few different outfits tonight, and every time she came out I was somehow more amazed by the way she so gracefully walks the stage like she owns the *world*.

She lines up with a few of the other new girls, but Sage has my undivided attention. She stands in the middle, and they clearly saved the best for last because she's stunning. I can't tell if it's just the lighting and the material of her dress, but she physically shines, and I think it solely has to do with her smile.

This is the same dress they fucked up, and she thought she looked horrible when it didn't fit her, but it certainly fits her like a glove now, and I can't see how she'd ever think she'd look anything resembling bad.

I find myself standing as I applaud her, and after a beat, a few people around me stand with me. Before I know it my entire section is standing as Sage walks down the stage one last time, and then the entire stadium rises for her. As she walks back up the stage, she glances at the crowd, and she keeps her face stone cold, but I can see the shock in her eyes as the crowd gives her a standing ovation before the show even ends.

The other girls disappeared sometime between the time I was watching Sage and when she disappears last, the lights go out, and the crowd is still roaring for her.

"Yeah, Sage!"

I glance at the front of the stage, and when a few people start cheering her name, I have no doubt in my mind that those are her siblings up there.

I shake my head but can't help but feel good knowing how supportive they are. The designer makes his way out, and the crowd cheers for him, but I disappear to find Sage's room.

I had to bribe some girls and reassure them a hundred times that we're dating and I'm not a crazy stalker but after a while, I get in her fitting room and it's scary how much money can buy you but I chose to believe the pictures I showed her as proof is what got her to open the door and not the stack of cash she counts as she walks off.

After a few minutes of waiting, the door swings open and I rise to my feet. She's frozen for a second but then a smile touches her lips and I waste no time closing the distance between us. "How did you get in here?"

I wrap my arms around her waist as I rise to my full height again. "Some possible illegal ways but I wanted to see you." I feel her smile into the crease of my neck and the ache I've somehow developed in all of my bones from not seeing her all day, disappear.

"To say you were amazing on that stage would be disrespectful to you."

She pulls away to take her flowers and a beautiful smile is on her face. "I was *so* nervous, Lee."

If I didn't know her, I wouldn't have believed that. "You didn't look nervous at all." I look between her green eyes and I'll do anything to keep the happy look in them. "You were perfect, beloved. I'm so proud of you."

Her smile somehow widens and I swear the whole room seems brighter. My eyes are glued to her smile and I couldn't look away even if you put a gun to my head.

Chapter Forty-Three

LIAM

"**S**MILE."

I glance over at Sage and her smile is the only reason I obey. "Good, now keep that smile intact."

I let out a sigh, and the second she turns, my face drops.

"Liam Leslie." She warns.

"Jesus Christ." I smile for her and she shakes with a silent laugh before knocking on Sire's door. The night of her show we all went to her after-party but Sage said it was awkward and she wants me to bond with her brothers so here we are... to bond.

"Hey, babe." Vidia pulls Sage in for a hug after complimenting her dress. After spending the night with them all in Italy, I realized this was Sire's girlfriend. I vaguely remember her from the few times she was at our baseball games in college.

"Me? Look at you!" Sage pulls away and gives her dress a once over. "Sire was right, blue is so your color, V."

"Thank you!"

Sage moves aside, and Vidia's eyes land on me. "Hello again." She gives me a small smile, and I feel Sage watching me, so I return it. I look around their apartment as she lets us in, and their huge floor-to-ceiling windows catch my attention first.

When I glance over at the couch August is sitting there with a girl in his lap. Her blonde fro covers her face, but I immediately recognize that it's his girlfriend, Hazel, I think her name was.

The door closes and August glances up at us with his usual bright smile. "Sup, Walker."

I give him a single nod. "Hale."

Hazel looks up at me and barely spares me a glance before turning to Sage. "You look hot." She nods in approval of Sage's dress before looking back down at whatever they're watching and I think I like her the most. She isn't as nice as everyone else and clearly isn't going to pretend to like me or bother me at all.

"Hello, cutie!"

I turn at the sound of Sage's voice, and she bends over to pet a *huge* dog. I walk over to her and pull her dress down when it rises too much.

"You said this dress was fine when you bend over?"

Sage pulls her dress down more and looks over her shoulder at me like she's in trouble. She gives me an innocent smile and I shake my head at her.

"Maybe it's a little short, but it's cute!"

"True."

She laughs softly, but the dog starts growling, and I quickly pull her closer. I take a step back before pushing Sage behind me, and the dog keeps its eyes on me.

"What's wrong with her?" Sage voices as she tries to get closer to the dog, but I keep her behind me.

"Maybe she doesn't like him."

I look up at Sire and he only leans against his kitchen counter with his arms crossed. Vidia walks over and shoves Sire before looking at her dog.

"Athena, heel." The dog stops growling and sits but keeps her eyes on me like she's ready to attack. "Sire, what did you tell her?"

"I have no idea what you're talking about, beautiful."
Fucking liar.

I keep my mouth shut, and Vidia crosses her arms before squinting her eyes at Sire, who returns the look.

"You said you'd be nice." Vidia reminds him.

"I said I'll try." Sire points out.

"Try harder and leave my dog out of it. I'm not cooking all this food for you guys to be fighting."

He lets out a sigh and turns back to the dog. "Athena," The dog turns to him on command. "Go ahead." She runs off after being released and grabs a toy before taking it to August.

When I look back at Sire he still has his eyes on me. I don't say anything, and Sage walks over to him first. "Nice to see you too." She clearly doesn't sound happy, and the only reason I don't punch her brother for making her feel bad is because I promised Sage I would be on my best behavior.

"You know I'm happy you're here, Sage." He pulls her in for a hug before kissing the top of her head.

"I'd prefer if you'd also be happy about who I brought with me." When they pull away she keeps her eyes on him as he turns to look at me. He doesn't say anything, but Vidia clears her throat from the stove, and he rolls his eyes before looking back at me.

"Glad you could make it." You'd think he had a gun to his head, but with the way his girl watches him, he may as well. *Whipped bitch.*

I don't reply and glance over at the dinner table instead.

"Excuse me, mister?"

I let out a sigh and look over at Sage. She crosses her arms, and I keep my eyes on her. "Thanks for the invite." I force out before glancing over at Sire and he has a smug smile on his face.

"You are *so* welcome."

Asshole.

I try not to show how annoyed he made me in less than five minutes since I'm sure he'd find it satisfying. Instead, I look over at Sage and her smile makes me feel better. She hugs Sire before walking over to me and grabbing my hand to guide us into the living room, where we flop onto the couch with her twin.

I hear someone walking behind us, and just as I turn, Lisette shoves Sage's head so damn hard, she almost falls over.

"Ouch?!" Sage fixes her hair as she turns to look at her sister.

My eyes land on Sire as he takes a few long strides and shoves Lisette into the couch way harder than what she did to Sage. "Stop hitting her," He warns.

"You see!" Lisette points at Sire, but he walks off. "You baby her! If I hit August like that, you would've laughed."

"Don't be so rough with her, Lisette. I'm seriously not going to tell you again."

Lisette mocks Sire, and I bite my cheek before turning back around. She's my favorite out of Sage's siblings for sure.

She flops next to Sage before laying her head on her lap. "I can't put into words how happy I am that you're dating someone Sire hates. This *truly* brings me joy, I wish I would've thought of this." She shakes her head like she's in pain.

Sage shakes with a laugh as we look down at her sister, and she tells her, once again, that we're not dating purely to piss Sire off.

"Maybe I should date someone he hates, too." Lisette glances over at me now, her head still on her sister's lap. "Do you have any brothers?"

"No."

"Cousins?"

"None you want nor does Sire know of."

"Hmm..."

Her brother joins us on the couch, and I make sure to keep my gaze off of him, and Lisette continues to fuck with him. "My dear brother."

"Leave me alone."

I bite back a smile, and I'm so glad Lisette doesn't leave him alone.

"Would you rather I sleep with someone you hate or one of your close friends?"

"I would rather you sew your lips together."

"Close friend it is; who are your best friends?"

"August."

Lisette is quiet for a second, and when I look down at her, she's staring at Sire like he's speaking a foreign language. "Besides him– ew!"

Sire breaks into a laugh, and I glance over at August for his reaction, but he's rubbing his girlfriend's feet and staring at her with a smile as she scrolls through her phone mindlessly.

Sage voices that she wants water and I pull her back onto the couch before kissing her cheek and getting up to get it for her.

I walk into the kitchen but stop short as I walk past Vidia. "Can I grab a water bottle for Sage?"

"Yeah, go ahead." She shuts the oven, and I turn for the fridge. When I grab a bottle, I turn and stop in my tracks as I watch Sage's smile. She sits next to Hazel now, and when Hazel turns her phone off, August smiles as his girlfriend entertains whatever Sage goes on about.

"You two are cute."

I glance over at Vidia, and she's watching me with a small smile. "You can't take your eyes off of her. It's cute." She shrugs before heading to the table with a few plates, but I decide to follow after her.

"How come you're being so nice?" I grab some of the plates from her stack and mindlessly help her make the table because my mom's voice is ringing in my head, and I feel like a shitty guest for not doing something.

Vidia didn't talk to me much in Italy and was glued to Hazel or Sire's side, but now she's telling Sire to be nice to me, and I'm confused as to why she cares.

"Well, you're a guest in my home. It'll be rude to treat you like shit."

"Your boyfriend should take notes."

She laughs softly, and when she looks into the living room, I think her eyes sparkle when she looks at Sire. "Sage was so stressed about her brothers hating you." She shrugs. "I know what it's like having the people you love hate your person. It gets exhausting, and I don't want that for her, so if she wants to be with you, I'll keep Sire in line."

I study her for a beat, and I have no clue who didn't want her to be with Sire since everyone is obsessed with them. Paparazzi and fans have been constantly sneaking pictures of them ever since they were spotted at some lantern festival, and I don't follow either of them on social media, but I still seem to scroll across a picture of them.

"Thanks."

She laughs, and out of the corner of my eye, I notice Sire turning to look at her from across the room.

"I did it for Sage, not you."

"Yeah... thanks."

Before she can respond, her boyfriend is by her side. He kisses her temple before wrapping an arm around her waist and taking a step away from me. "I said I can make the table."

"It's fine, Liam already helped." She brushes him off like it really was no big deal since it *wasn't* but Sire sends me a glare. "Oh my God, do you want to remake the table, mi amor? I'm sure you could do it better than him."

Sire smiles down at her before squinting his eyes. "Smart ass."

She laughs softly and rushes off with Sire on her tail.

When I hear Sage's voice, I look over to find her leaning over to pet the dog again. I shake my head at how much her dress rises, and you can't see anything, but either way, I walk over and pull it down.

She leans back up with a smile, and I pull her in for a hug. I already feel my energy draining, and we haven't even been here that long, but there are just too many of them. I have no idea how I'm going to last the whole night talking to everyone.

"You okay?" Sage looks up at me and I give her a nod before giving her a quick kiss.

"Can we leave after we eat?" When her shoulders slouch, I kiss her cheek and tell her to forget it. "We can stay however long you want."

"We were going to play a game after dinner."

That sounds like torture. "Fun." I give her a smile, but her knowing look genuinely makes me laugh. "What game?"

She shrugs before telling me August chose, and now I'm certain it'll be torture, but Vidia calls us over to the dinner table before I can respond. Lisette sits at the head of the table after Sire voices he wants to sit there, and she's *officially* my favorite out of Sage's siblings.

August and Sire end up sitting next to each other with their girls across from them. Sage sits next to Vidia, and the only options left are across from her, next to Sire, or next to her at the head of the table, so naturally, I chose the ladder.

They talk about the upcoming holidays, and I eat in silence or watch Sage whenever she comments on something. She didn't serve a lot of food on her plate, but she laughs, and eats like she isn't going to have a hard time with this meal, so I don't comment on it, especially since she had such a good breakfast.

The topic of holidays lands on New Year's, and I eat in silence as they go on about throwing a big party since this is the first New Year that Sire and Vidia are together, and I don't know what they're talking about since I could've sworn they've been together since college, but I don't question it.

"What do you think, Lee?"

"Hmm?" I glance up at Sage, and she nods towards the table.

"The color theme for this year's New Year's. I said green, white, and gold."

I tell her that will be cute, but a crease grows in her brows as she turns her head to the side.

"It doesn't seem like you agree." She laughs softly, but I only shrug in response.

"Do you not like New Year's or something?"

I know Sire is just trying to get under my skin, so I don't reply, but Sage keeps her eyes on me, so I give her my response. "I don't celebrate New Year, but I think the colors you chose would be great."

"Why don't you celebrate New Year?" Sire voices, and he *severely* needs to stop talking to me.

"I just don't."

"Why?" He pushes.

"I don't see the point in counting down and screaming for a new year. We get a new one every twelve months without fail, no need to celebrate it."

"I disagree." Sage smiles at me but is clearly confused. "It's a day to celebrate our year's worth of achievements and welcome a new chapter."

"I disagree," I mumble, but, of course, her brother hears.

"What do you think it represents?"

"Nothing."

"Well, it's a holiday." Lisette sort of laughs as if I'm wrong.

"It isn't for me."

"Why?" Sire digs once again.

I drop my fork and pull in a deep breath. When my eyes meet Sire's, it's obvious he can tell he got under my skin, and I almost get up to walk away, but Sage puts her hand over mine, so I turn to look at her instead.

"It's the anniversary of my sister's passing. I don't celebrate it."

Her face drops, and I think every person stops chewing because the room becomes eerily quiet. I knew that would get them to leave me alone, so I don't care about how bad they all suddenly look for bugging me.

Sage gives my hand a soft squeeze, and I turn back to my plate.

"I'm sorry for your loss." August voices first, and I only nod in response as I finish eating, and I'm glad they don't talk to me anymore. *I should've led with that.* I know it's bad to pull the dead sister card, but Sire was being annoying, and Shanti would've found it funny. She always laughed in awkward situations... her humor as just a toddler always amazed me.

Sage and I offer to help clean once we finish eating, but Sire and Vidia tell us they got it, and it's really just Sire who cleans everything for his girl.

I get up to go to the bathroom, and when I hear Sage's heels clicking after me, I slow down for her. She walks into the bathroom with me, and a smirk grows on my face as I turn to her.

"Your brother will be pissed if we have sex in here." I take a step forward. "Are you going to let me have that satisfaction?"

A smirk grows on her face as she shakes her head at me. As I reach for her, she pushes my hand away. "You know that's not going to happen."

"I had to try." I shrug before leaning against the sink, and I see the sympathy in her eyes as her smile fades. "Why are you looking at me like that?"

She pulls her bottom lip between her teeth, lost in thought before closing the distance between us and wrapping her arms around my neck. "I'm sorry about your sister."

I don't say anything and simply wrap my arms around her waist and bury my face in her neck.

"How old was she?"

I let my eyes fall shut and hold her a bit closer. "Three." I feel her go still, but I give her a squeeze, and she holds me tighter.

"I'm so sorry, Liam."

"Stop saying that." I kiss her neck before pulling away, and the sad look in her eyes is the reason I didn't want to tell her about my sister. "Don't cry. Your makeup took way too long to ruin so soon."

She laughs softly before blinking up to the ceiling and I kiss her cheek softly. My phone starts buzzing and I let out a breath at the ringtone. I ignore every call besides Capri and Sage, so I gave them separate ringtones and as my phone keeps ringing, I'm only a bit happy about the possibility of needing to leave.

"Are you gonna get that?" Sage pulls away, and I grab my phone. It's a Facetime call, which is weird, but I answer, and Capri's face appears on the screen.

"In case you also have Alzheimer's and forgot what tomorrow means, it's the day after today."

I briefly close my eyes as I realize my mistake. "Shit, my bad, Pri. I swear I forgot I even told you I'd be there today. I needed to come to this dinner for my girlfriend and—"

"This is why I told you to add it to your calendar."

"I don't have one."

"Which is why I told you to make one. Do you listen to anything I say?"

I almost tell her no, I, in fact, do not, but then there's a high shriek, and the phone is snatched out of her hand.

"Liam!" My mom looks beyond ecstatic to see me, and I feel ten times worse than I was for not going to see her for today's family night. After my month in Italy, I saw her as soon as I could and spent the day with her, but she keeps calling and saying she misses me, which is weird because she never cares to call me.

"How are you, my sweet boy?"

I glance up at Sage when she laughs quietly, and I roll my eyes at her.

"Oh, are you with someone?" My mom tries to look around as if that would change her perspective through the *phone*.

"No, I just–"

"Please tell me Sage is with you!"

A smile pulls at my lips, and I genuinely can't grasp how she constantly remembers her.

"She is but–"

"Let me see her!"

I don't know why she's yelling, but I don't turn the phone to Sage. "Mom, she's busy–"

"Liam." She gives me a pointed look, and I glance up at Sage, who's smiling shyly.

"You told your mom about me?" She whispers and I feel my face heat. Her jaw slightly drops and I give her my back. "You just blushed!" She pokes my back before turning to get in front of me but I turn again.

"I just had the best idea!" Mom shouts again. "Bring her over. I can cook, and she can meet everyone. We're playing music and I'm going to perform soon, hurry!"

It's a talent show over there, and by performing, I'm sure she means she's just going to play the piano, but she smiles at me like she's about to go on a Broadway show, so I tell her I'll be there.

She lets me end the call, and when I look over at Sage, she has a beautiful smile on her face. "When you'd tell her about me?" She clearly bites back a smile, and I shake my head at her with a smile of my own.

"Officially, when I was trying to figure out how to ask you to be my girlfriend. But she had an idea of you when I brought the cats to see her." It was my annoying friends who saw Sage's post about the girlfriend proposal, but I naturally asked my mom what she thought, and she had the idea to give her peonies. "Do you want to come with me to see her?"

Her eyes light up, and I think I have my answer. "Are you sure?"

I'm not, but my mom is having a good day, which may not last long, and I want Sage to meet her eventually, so I give her a nod and grab her hand.

Just as she opens the door, Sire walks out of the room across from us. He looks between us before walking over.

"My bad about earlier. I should've just left you alone after you said you didn't celebrate New Year's."

His apology throws me off, but when I glance over his shoulder, I see that his girlfriend is watching us.

"You'd jump out of a window if she said so, huh?"

He glances over his shoulder and Vidia gives him a bright smile as she turns her head to the side and I'd be a liar if I said she wasn't beautiful.

"Possibly... Yes." He keeps his eyes on her, and Sage stifles a laugh from beside us, and every last one of my cells reacts to the sight of Sage's smile.

"I really am sorry for your loss, Walker."

I look back over at him, and his sincerity is hard to believe, but I do. "It's fine, thanks for the invite." I force out before walking past him with Sage who is smiling too big for such a small gesture but I know she desperately wants us to get along.

I thank Vidia for the food before we say goodbye to the rest of Sage's family. I'm glad this dinner went well because it was important to Sage.

Chapter Forty-Four

SAGE

"**I**F SHE STARTS FLIPPING OUT about something, you could leave the room and let the nurses and me handle it."

"Okay." I nod, more to myself, and Liam's face is really hard to read as he focuses on the beautiful house in front of us. "Are you sure you're good with this?"

When we had dinner with my brothers in Italy, they were asking questions about Liam that I couldn't answer, and while some were absolutely absurd and Sire was just being over-protective, I couldn't even answer anything about his family.

I told Liam that bothered me since I'm family-oriented, and he told me he'd tell me about his family, but as I'm about to meet his mom, I'm very nervous, and it has nothing to do with the fact that she has Alzheimer's but because I'm scared she won't like me.

"Are *you* good with this?"

I glance over at Liam, and he *laughs* at me. "What is funny?"

"You're nervous about meeting my mom?" He laughs harder and I cross my arms at him.

"Oh, I want to see you meet my mom *and* dad because they remember what you did to their son and are not as forgiving as their children."

His smile instantly drops as he studies me. "That's not funny."

I bite back my smile, which earns me a glare.

"Do I seriously have to meet them?"

"Of course you do! Why would you even ask me that?"

He lets out a breath before turning to the window. "Let's go," He mumbles, and I let out a soft laugh as he climbs out and grabs the door for me.

When we walk in we're met with a beautiful nurse. She has long red hair that falls down to her waist and pretty freckles all over her face and arms. "Hi, I'm Capri."

My eyes slightly widen as I take her in again, knowing who she is. Moon has been talking about this girl's beauty since he first saw her, but I definitely underestimated him because she is gorgeous.

"It's so nice to meet you. I'm Sage."

"I know, you're all this boy seems to talk about lately." She pulls me in for a hug, and I laugh when Liam tells her not to call him a *boy*. "Let me know if his mom doesn't show you any embarrassing pictures of him, and I'll do the honors."

"No, you will not. Go away." Liam wraps an arm around me, and I bite back a laugh as he guides me further into the house.

We pass two other nurses but the house seems empty for the most part. It isn't until I hear the music and laughing that I realize where everyone is. We walk into a room filled with instruments. A few nurses in scrubs sit around four older ladies who are with, I'm assuming, their family. One of them turns to us as we walk in, and from her face alone, I know she's Liam's mom.

Even if she didn't have his blue eyes and blonde hair I think I could still tell this was her. Liam is her spitting image.

"Liam! I didn't know you were coming!" She rushes over to us and when she pulls Liam in for a hug he briefly closes his eyes and my heart aches at how happy he looks to simply hold her.

"I wasn't going to miss your performance." He pulls away, and she smiles up at him. "Capri tells me you haven't been practicing, cocky if you ask me."

She laughs before shoving her son playfully. "I didn't want the competition to hear me. Lucy copied me at the last talent show." She looks off to the side at an older lady in a yellow cardigan before rolling her eyes.

"What an asshole," Liam adds, and my jaw drops.

"Hey," She swats her son's arm. "Watch your mouth. She's a bitch but only I can say so, young man."

"My apologies."

She doesn't seem to pick up on his obvious sarcasm as she nods in approval.

"Mom, this is my girlfriend, Sage."

I smile sheepishly as they turn to me and she lets out a gasp as she takes my hands and gives my frame a once over. "You're beautiful!" She immediately pulls me in for a hug.

"It's nice to meet you." I voice, and she squeezes me a bit tighter.

"The pleasure is all mine." She gives me a sweet smile. "Have you met the baby?"

She watches me hopefully and I give her a smile before glancing over at Liam. He keeps his eyes on his mom, almost like he doesn't want to look at me. "She did, you were right; Shanti loves her."

I see the pain in Liam's eyes as he lies and I realize now why he hates lying so much. His mom's laugh pulls my eyes to her, and I give her another smile.

"Did she play peekaboo with your hair?" She laughs again, and I force myself to smile.

"She did, she's so cute. God bless her." She thanks me and before she can say anything else someone is calling her over. I let out a breath and when I turn to Liam he's still watching her.

"Sorry about that. I should've warned you that she might—"

"Don't apologize for things you can't control, Lee." I take his hand, and he finally lets his eyes meet mine. "Are you okay?"

He only nods in response, but I make him say it.

"Yes, Dory."

I give him a nod, and we walk over to his mom. The Lucy woman they were talking about is up to *perform* and we sit around as she walks over to the piano.

Liam's mom lets out a scoff, and when I turn to her, both she and Liam shake their head at something. Liam bites back a smile and looks over at me to explain. "She was talking shit about her all week and complaining about how she knew she was going to play something on the piano."

He glances over at his mom, but when he realizes she isn't listening, he goes on. "She thinks only people who know how to play well enough should use it."

I bite back a laugh and we watch as Lucy starts. She plays beautifully but misses a few keys and Liam's mom sure does notice. "Amateur." She mumbles to Liam and my eyes slightly widen at how mean she is.

"Tell me about it." Liam rolls his eyes as he entertains her, and I have to bite my tongue not to laugh at them. When Lucy finishes, we applaud her, but Liam only sits there unamused, and his mom claps slowly, and it's very dramatic.

"Aria," Capri warns, and she only puts her hands up in mock surrender. "We are here to support our friends."

"And I have been supporting my *friends.*"

Capri gives her a warning look and I have no idea why she doesn't like Lucy but I can't take this seriously.

"Yeah, Capri. Lucy isn't her friend. She doesn't have to support her." Liam keeps his voice low and with the poor lady being across the room with a hearing aid she doesn't hear them but I still feel horrible.

"Liam." I kick his foot, and he clearly fights back a smile.

"Why do you like making my job so hard?" Capri looks at Liam like she's genuinely confused, and he only laughs at her. "Aria, it's your turn."

His mom rises proudly and walks over to the piano.

"What was that about?"

Liam shrugs before wrapping an arm around me. "My mom is kind of mean. It's fun to join in on it."

I elbow him, and he glances down at me.

"What? It's not like we're actually bullying these people for their lunch money or something."

"You're horrible."

He tells me his mom is worse but I surprisingly don't doubt it. I lean into him as we watch his mom play the piano, and I know I thought Lucy was good, but she really is an amateur with the way Aria plays. Her hands move so gracefully across the keys and she doesn't even look at a music sheet as she plays.

The song grows more intense and it's as if she is telling a story with how the tempo speeds. I feel myself growing anticipated as I watch her hands fly across the keys only for her to slow down again. I glance up at Liam and he's watching his mom like it's the first time he's heard her play.

When the song finishes, we stand to applaud her, and she only sits there with a proud smile on her face. "So, who won tonight's talent show?" She voices, and Capri lets out a sigh from beside us.

"We're all winners."

Aria rolls her eyes before walking over to us, and Liam wastes no time as he leans over to her. "She's just saying that to make everyone feel better. Clearly, you won."

"That's what I'm saying." She rolls her eyes and I can't stop myself from laughing at them. She ends up calling Capri over and I feel bad that she has to deal with these two for a living.

"I won't tell anyone. Just tell me who really won." Aria urges.

Capri watches her for a beat before glancing over at Liam and shaking her head. "You won, Aria. With your years of experience, that wasn't even a question."

She hums proudly before nodding to herself. "Liam, you should play a song."

"No, thank you." He counters, not even giving her suggestion a thought.

"You haven't practiced all week, Liam. How do you expect to be ready for the musical if you don't practice?"

I'm not sure what she's talking about, and I'm not sure if anyone else does, but we don't question her.

"I don't need prac–"

"Liam." She gives him a warning look and I feel my brows raise at how quickly he shuts his mouth. "Practice for an hour then you can go out with your friends."

"Mom–"

"Now."

He looks over at me, and I nod for the piano. "Listen to your mother, Liam."

A smile grows on his pretty face. "Oh, don't fucking—"

"Excuse me?" His mom steps in front of him with her arms crossed. "Don't speak to her like that."

I smile at him from over her shoulder. "Yeah, Liam. Don't speak to me like that." I try my hardest not to laugh, and he looks like he's going to make me pay for this, but it's too easy.

"You can forget about seeing your friends for your language. Go practice for the musical." His mom flops onto the couch but keeps her eyes on the piano like she's planning on watching him practice.

"You're so lucky she's watching," Liam mumbles as he passes me, and I break into a laugh.

He sits at the piano before glancing over at his mom, but she only nods, and he lets out a sigh before he turns back around. I'm not sure what I was expecting, but when he starts flipping through the music sheet in front of him and *actually* plays, my jaw drops.

"He can play the *piano*?"

Capri laughs from beside me, but I can't shake off the shock. "He was in the Winter musical every year from sixth through twelfth grade. That's what she was talking about before."

"He was a *theater* kid?"

Capri tilts her head back with a laugh and I also laugh at the idea. There's *nothing* wrong with being a theater kid. I actually think it's cool, and everyone who can play an instrument is superior, but it's hard to imagine *Liam* as a theater kid.

"Oh, don't let him hear you saying that. He almost fired me when I said that. He was *not* a theater kid. He only played the piano in a few musicals."

I turn to Capri, and she smiles over at me.

"His words."

We share another laugh and I get out my phone to record him play. He plays one song for a solid three-ish minutes and it's like he went somewhere else as he plays. His mom ends up getting up and giving him tips about a mistake I couldn't even hear.

She makes him do it again, and he has to restart twice when he messes up, but he gets it. I clearly don't have a musical bone in my body because it sounds the same every time he plays, but he gets her approval once he finishes.

"And you said you didn't need to practice." She rolls her eyes. "Shanti can play better than that."

"That's hard to believe since she can't read a music sheet yet, but okay." Liam rolls his eyes, but I can tell they're joking again.

"You know," His mom turns to him with a smile. "I think she's going to have perfect pitch."

I feel my smile slowly fade at the hope in her eyes, and I hate that she lost her baby girl.

"You thought the same for me."

"Yeah but Shanti is just perfect, she'll have perfect pitch." His mom nods like she's certain, but Liam looks offended now.

"Wow, she's *just perfect*? What am I?"

She quickly realizes her mistake and hugs Liam, but he rises from the piano. "You know that's not what I meant. You're perfect, too, sweetie."

"Nope, she's your favorite, I understand." He walks off, and she laughs at him as she turns back to the piano. When he reaches me, I smile up at him, and when he turns his head to the side, I know he can see right through me.

"If you're going to get sad every time she brings up my sister then we may as well leave now."

"No, I'm fine."

He lets out a breath before pulling me in for a hug, and we sit on the couch while his mom plays another song.

"You were a theater kid?" I glance up at him, and when he closes his eyes, I let out a laugh.

"Capri is fired."

"She didn't even say anything."

"Bullshit."

I only laugh harder and he pulls me closer before kissing the side of my face. I force him to show me pictures and he says he doesn't have any so I call over Capri.

"She doesn't have any." Liam tries to get out of this, but it's no use because I'm determined.

"Of course I do." Capri flops next to me and pulls out a phone that clearly belongs to his mom since the lock screen is Liam holding a baby girl.

"Wait, let me see that."

She tilts the phone back to me, and I swipe down to look at the lock screen again. Liam is in trunks by a pool, and he looks so different without all of his tattoos. He only had one on his arm, and I realize this is his first tattoo, the one he hated.

"What was that tattoo supposed to be?"

"I don't even know." He shakes his head disappointedly, and I break into a laugh before looking back down at the picture. His sister is sitting on his knee in a bright yellow bathing suit, and they look so happy.

"It was her birthday."

I glance over at Liam, and he has his eyes on the phone.

"I almost drowned because she jumped into the deep end, and I was struggling to swim while trying to hold her." He shakes his head, and I smile at him.

"I held her above my head as I was underwater, and when the lifeguard finally grabbed her after I was about to pass out, she was fucking *laughing* at me."

"The lifeguard?!"

"No, my sister. I swear she did that shit on purpose."

I break into a laugh, and Liam joins beside me. "She kept walking on the edge to scare me and would pretend to jump in, just to see me lose my shit."

He smiles at the memory, and I only laugh harder. "She sounds hilarious."

"She was." He pulls in a breath, and I feel my smile start to fade as I look back down at the phone. Liam kisses my cheek before taking the phone from me. "If I show you pictures from the musical, you have to promise not to send them to yourself."

I cross my fingers before giving him a smile. "Promise."

He studies me for a beat, and I keep my smile in place. "Let me see your hands."

I burst with a laugh before burying my face in his chest.

"You're the worst liar I've met." He tickles my side, and I laugh harder as I try to squirm away.

"Let me have three pictures of you as a kid."

"No."

"Two."

"No."

I give him a bored look, but he returns it. When I notice his mom making her way over to us, I give her a smile as I wave her over. "Aria, I was just asking Liam for some baby pictures, and he said he didn't have any?"

"I'm going to–"

His mom cuts him off before he can finish his threat. "I have plenty. Here, let me see that." She reaches for her phone, and I snatch it from Liam and hand it to her as she sits next to me. She shows me *way* more than I wanted to see and sends me all of her favorites, which are almost all of them.

Liam's entire face turns red more than once, and when I tease him about it, he says he's hot and not blushing.

"Sure you are."

"Shut up."

I bite back a laugh as he pulls his hoodie over his head. I almost turn back to his mom, but my eyes land on the necklace around his neck. I reach for it and a smile touches my lips at the Dory charm he's wearing.

I move the charm between my fingers, and there's also half a heart next to it. I glance down at the charm bracelet he gave me, and next to my Dory charm is the other half of the heart he's wearing.

I bite my cheek so hard I'm surprised I'm not bleeding. When I look back up at Liam, he's already watching me. "How long have you been wearing that?"

"Since I bought it."

I glance between his eyes and with the way he watches me I feel my entire body flush. I turn back to his mom but can't seem to wipe my smile.

We spend the rest of the night with his mom, and Liam seems to be holding his breath more the later it gets, but his worry is for nothing because she seems fine the entire time. She tries to get me to spend the night and voices how Liam can't share a room with me, and I have to bite my tongue so as not to laugh at the way Liam teases her.

"She likes sharing a room with me."

His mom sends him a glare before her brows raise. "Do not tell me you've been having *sex* in my house, Liam."

He bites back a smile before kissing her head. "Of course not, mom. I'm a virgin."

A snort escapes me, and he sends me a teasing grin.

We hug his mom goodbye, and I smile at how light he seems on the drive home. His hand lands on my thigh as we pull up in front of his penthouse, but he turns to me before stepping out.

"Do you want to know about my sister?"

A smile touches my lips because he's trying. "Only if you want to tell me."

He tells me he does, but it takes him a minute to find the right words.

"She passed away really young... she was three."

I feel my breath get caught in my throat, but I only hold his hand and hold my emotions back as he goes on.

"She was being fussy all day and would only let me hold her." He shakes his head at something before facing forward and glancing out the window. "It was New Year's Eve and everyone was raving about this party some girl was having." He's quiet for another minute and I bring his hand to my lips before kissing him softly.

"My mom asked me to stay, but I wanted to go to that stupid fucking party."

I force the lump down my throat, but he sounds like he's in so much pain. I almost tell him he doesn't have to finish his story, but he looks like he needs to as he goes on.

"Shanti started crying when she saw I was leaving, and I felt bad leaving her, but I thought she'd settle down after a while." He shakes his head before his eyes fall shut. "My dad-" His voice breaks, and I blink away the stinging in my eyes.

"You don't have to finish, Lee," I whisper, my mouth still against his hand.

He takes in a couple of breaths before shaking his head. "He had really bad anger issues." He looks over at me now, and it's a little dark in here, but I swear I see tears forming in his eyes, and it breaks me. "If you thought I had anger issues, his was out of this fucking world. He'd black out and rip things apart."

I don't like where this is going.

"She kept crying and crying, and he snapped."

I go still, almost afraid to breathe.

"He hit her once, right on her tiny head, and just like that, I lost my sister. I'm pretty sure he blacked out since he looked shocked as they put him in the back of a police car... he killed himself a few days later. " He brings his other hand to my cheek before wiping my tears. "If I didn't go-"

"Uh uh." I cut him off before grabbing his other hand. "Do *not* blame yourself for that, Liam. Absolutely not."

A bitter smile touches his lips at my tone, and I lean forward to kiss him.

"Nothing I can say can bring her back or make you feel better, but it wasn't your fault, and you are *not* your father. You have some... slight anger issues."

He laughs softly before wiping his cheek.

"But you sure as hell do have control over it. You're even in therapy!" I remind him. "You're not like him."

Clarity fills his eyes, and he lets out a scoff.

"What?" I cup his face.

He holds my hand as he shakes his head. "It's something my therapist and I were talking about... I've been so angry at myself for being like my dad, but I'm not him." He says it as if he's just realizing that now.

"Of course you're not, Liam."

He looks between my eyes, tears welling in his again. "It feels like that sometimes... Like I was just as responsible for killing her."

I shake my head and wrap my arms around him when another tear falls. "You're not a bad person for going to that party." I pull away for a small kiss before leaning my forehead against his. "You're not a bad person in general. You're perfect, and before you disagree, don't waste your breath because you're perfect to me. You're loveable, Liam. You're worthy of love and everything else you could wish for."

"I only want to be worthy of you."

"You are especially worthy of me." My lips meet his, and I tell him I love him in a different way.

Chapter Forty-Five

SAGE

"H OW LONG HAVE YOU BEEN doing this?" I turn to Liam and he keeps his eyes on the road as he drives to the Yankee Stadium.

When he told me he had an event this weekend, I cleared my schedule to come with him simply to see him interact with the kids. He's giving a tour of the stadium to kids with disabilities, and this is the last kind of event I expected him to host.

"I've been doing this twice a year since I was signed with the Yankees."

I smile at his words as he goes on.

"It's for my sister..." He keeps his eyes on the road and I can see his shield go up, like it took a lot for him to simply say that but I hold his hand and give him a reassuring squeeze, silently urging him to continue but he doesn't.

"Did she have a disability?" I keep my tone light, and when he pulls in a deep breath, I can tell he's just trying to find the right words, so I don't push him.

"Yeah, she had Down syndrome." He suddenly looks so lost, and it hurts to see how torn he is as he talks about her. "She was born prematurely, and I was so scared that she wasn't going to make it out of the NICU, but then she did, and... my whole world turned upside down."

He turns to look at me, and a soft smile touches my lips. "I bet you were a great big brother."

"I thought you were certain that I was an only child or the youngest?" He teases and I immediately remember my words from a month ago. "What was it you said? I'm mean and seemed like I never had to share my toys?"

I laugh softly before pushing his hand away, but he reaches for me again with a small smile. "We had a fourteen-year age gap, so you were sort of right, I never had to share my toys with her, but she loved to eat off *my* plate, even when we had the same fucking thing."

The car fills with my laugh, and he glances over at me with a small smile. After a beat, a sad look washes over his face, and he's quiet for a minute before saying, "I just wish she was here sometimes."

He sounds so... desperate. I feel my nose burn as my eyes tear. "Oh, Liam..."

He keeps his eyes on the road but I notice him force the lump down his throat.

"She would've been so proud of everything you've done." I kiss the back of his hand and he looks out his window as he nods silently. We get to a red light, and when I turn his face to mine, I swear my entire soul is crushed by the sight of tears in his eyes.

He blinks them away and before I can voice any comforting words he brings his lips to mine. "Don't say sorry."

I smile against his lips and kiss him harder. Someone behind us honks, and when I pull away, Liam leans in again and kisses me one more time.

I hold his hand for the rest of the drive, and by the time we make it to the kids, they're all here, and they are *so* freaking cute. Some of them run to Liam, and I didn't peg him as the type to be good with kids or like them at all, but he bends down and hugs all of them.

"How is everyone doing today?" He looks around at all their excited faces and a few of them waste no time to go on a tangent about how they're doing.

"And my hot dog had *mustard* in it!"

I glance down at the little boy in a wheelchair and smile at the shock on his face.

"Is that good or bad?" Liam asks before lifting another little boy when he keeps pulling on his arm.

"It was great! I *love* mustard!"

We laugh at his excitement, and Liam tells him we'll get him more mustard before he starts the tour. Their parents are with them, and I can see how happy they are to see their kids so excited.

"What's everyone's name?"

The little boy in the wheelchair is the first to answer as he screams his name. "Kyle!"

I let out a soft laugh, and all of the other kids share their names before the tour starts. All of them ask an insane amount of questions as we start walking, and a lot of them have nothing to do with the stadium or baseball, but Liam answers them all patiently. Considering he's someone who is insanely impatient with adults, it's like watching a different person as he interacts with them.

One of the kids has Tourettes, and when she has her tics while Liam is explaining something, the other kids clearly get distracted.

"Would you be *quiet*?! He's talking!" One of the boys turns sharply.

I feel my eyes slightly widen as I take a step forward. "Oh— that's not—"

Liam calls the little boy's attention before I can finish my sentence. "Bren."

He turns to him, and from Liam's look alone, he shuts his mouth, but I don't feel too bad. I know he's a kid, but he's been mean to the other kids the entire tour. Rather than his parents trying to correct him or, at the very least, apologize for him, they're on their phones, taking pictures of Liam and the stadium. I'm sure his outbursts are a result of them completely ignoring him.

"Remember what I said about being kind on the tour?" Liam reminds him. "Nora can't control her tics so let's be kind and *not* tell her to be quiet."

The little boy apologizes and Nora seems to shrink as everyone looks at her so I hold my hand out to her and nod towards the huge mirror behind her. She takes my hand and her mom smiles at me appreciatively as we walk a few feet away from the group.

"Did you pick out your outfit on your own? I love your dress."

She studies herself in the mirror, and a smile touches her lips as she runs her hand down her dress. "Thank you!

Mommy–" She has a tic, and I give her a few seconds before trying again.

"Mommy helped and–"

I wait for this one to pass, and she lets out a breath before going on.

"And I picked my shoes!"

I glance down at her red rain boots and laugh quietly. "I love them!"

She taps her heels together, and her mom laughs quietly from behind her. When I glance back at the group, they start walking again, so I take her hand and catch up to them.

We make our way around for another half hour. In each room, Liam set up an activity for the kids and I'm surprised he's able to keep their attention for so long. Before I know it, we make our way to their favorite part, the field.

There's just enough of us to play a small game so we moved up all the plates since the kids would get way too tired running all the bases and I pitch to both teams as Liam squats behind home base and catches. They made Liam put his gear on and it's hilarious seeing him in full gear with seven-year-olds running around him.

When my watch starts buzzing I glance down at it and notice Angie is calling me. I hit the automated message and tell her I'll call her back before throwing the ball, and Kyle hits it pretty damn hard.

Liam shoots up, and I laugh at his excitement as he pushes his wheelchair at *full* speed.

"Liam, slow down!" I only laugh harder as he ignores me.

Kyle is dying of laughter as Liam gets him to second base before the other kids can even figure out who to throw the ball to.

When my watch buzzes again, I let one of the parents pitch and walk toward the middle of the field to answer Angie's call.

"Hey, Ang, is everything okay?" She normally doesn't call back to back once I decline her call so I try to listen closely as the kids yell behind me.

"Are you sitting?" She sounds excited, and I feel myself growing nervous.

"No?"

"You want to sit for this."

I bit my lip in anticipation and take a seat in the middle of the field. A few of the kids tell me to stand and get in position but I tell them I'm taking a break as Angie goes on.

"You were invited to New York's fashion week."

I wait for her to add more but she doesn't and I let out a soft laugh. Being that Florence is a designer and always a part of New York's fashion week, I'm always there, along with the rest of The Core Eight.

"That's it? Angie, I get invited every year. I thought–"

"And Milan."

At that, my eyes widened just a bit. I was invited to Milan's fashion week last year, but since I'm a Moore Girl now and Vincent's name is *branded* in Italy, I was kind of expecting that.

"And London."

"*And* London?" My heart rate picks up just a bit, and after she tells me Jade Marine, *the* designer, invited me, my jaw is on the floor.

"And by Colette Dubios... in Paris." She sounds like she's smiling ear to ear, and I go still.

"Colette Dubios?" My jaw drops before I quickly pick it up. "You're joking." I wait for her to tell me she's messing with me, but she's quiet on the other end. "Angie, tell me you're joking!"

She laughs, but I need to stand now.

"I was invited to all four locations?" I don't let her answer as I let out a scream. "I was invited to all four locations!" I'm quite actually jumping with joy when Liam runs to me.

"What is it?" He looks around the ground before lifting me. "Is there a bug or something? What's wrong?" He keeps his eyes on the ground and makes sure to keep my feet away from whatever he thinks I'm yelling about.

I let out a laugh before throwing my arms around his neck and wrapping my legs around him. "I'm going to fashion week!"

"You always–"

"In all four locations, Lee!"

"I don't know what that means, but we're happy–"

"YES, WE'RE HAPPY! AHH!"

"Well, now I'm also deaf, so thank you for that!" His laugh fills my ears before he puts me back down on my feet, and I grab hold of his hand before running in place excitedly.

"Yayyy!" All of the kids run over to us and scream excitedly, and I break into a laugh.

"Why are we screaming?" One of the kids covers his ears before looking over at his dad, who hands him his noise-canceling headphones, and Liam tries to get everyone to settle down so he doesn't get overstimulated, but *I* can barely settle down.

"Did we win?"

Before we can answer him, one of the kids screams, "Yes!" and they all start yelling again and I'm crying from how much I laugh.

Liam looks over at me with a smile and gives up on trying to calm their excitement. "Look at what you started." He shakes his head with a smile before leaning in to kiss me. "I'm so proud of you, beloved. You're going to be the biggest fucking star."

I smile up at him before throwing my hands around his neck.

"Fuck!"

I pull away and we both look down at Nora and when she curses again I realize it's one of her tics. I cover my mouth and shove Liam but he immediately turns to her mom.

"I shouldn't have said that around the kids. I–"

"Don't worry about it!" Her mom laughs softly before soothing her daughter's hair. "That was one of her tics long before you said it, no thanks to me."

We laugh softly, and when Nora says it again, she covers her mouth and apologizes, but Liam crouches down and pulls her hand away from her mouth. "Don't apologize for the things you can't control."

She smiles up at him before wrapping her little arms around him. My ovaries are screaming when Liam hugs her back with a *smile.*

When he pulls away and looks up at me, I'm still watching him in awe. "I love you."

A crease grows in his brows before his smile reappears, and he stands to his full height. "Do you?"

I laugh softly before wrapping my arms around his neck. "Of course I do, Lee."

He smiles *so* damn big I can't help but laugh.

"I love you more." He brings a hand up to cover our face, and I'm confused at first, but then he leans in to kiss me, and although he tries to cover us, I still hear some of the kids shout, "Ew" and "Yuck" before they all run away, leaving Liam and I hysterical.

Chapter Forty-Six

LIAM

Three months later

"**D**ON'T GET MAD WHEN I say this, but..." August looks around my private jet before turning to Sire. "I think his jet is better than ours."

I bite back a smile and lean back in my seat before Sage scoots closer to me.

"That's why I've been telling you guys to fly with us." She smiles over at her brothers, and I steal a kiss before laying back down.

"Yeah," Lisette looks around while nodding. "You guys are bougie, but this is extra bougie." Lisette starts opening my drawers, and I don't tell her not to touch my shit because I'm sure it'll be a waste of breath.

We're on our way to Milan from New York, and Sage just carried the entire fashion week on her back, *solo*. I may be biased, but she's on every tabloid, and the people seem to agree that she looked the best these past few nights.

The last month has been extremely hectic for her. All four designers who invited her flew out someone to get her measurements and everything else they needed for her. Sage could've easily canceled on one of the designers, but they made all the required accommodations and clearly desperately wanted her there.

"Are you hungry?" I kiss the top of her head before readjusting her bonnet.

"I am, but we just ate..." She keeps her voice low as she glances around, but no one is paying attention to us.

"So? You can eat again."

She looks up at me with a smile, and I stand to grab the food we packed. As I walk past August, he lights up as he glances at the plate in my hand.

"I didn't know we had more food?"

"It's for your sister."

"But–"

"No."

Sire tells me not to be an asshole, and I ignore him. I can hear them both laughing behind me when I roll my eyes, and I know they're fucking with me on purpose.

As much as I hate to admit it, they're not the worst people on the planet. Sire barely speaks to me unless he wants to fuck with me, but I've learned not to let him piss me off. August, on the other hand, is so damn friendly. He constantly wants to tell me something or show me something I don't care about. The only reason I entertain him is for his twin.

I hand Sage her plate, and she smiles at me before turning to August. "Here, we can share."

He shoots up from his seat, and I shake my head at them. He takes a few spoonfuls of her food and a bite of her chicken before I shove him away.

"Let her eat."

He leaves her alone and I watch her quietly as she eats in peace. She's been doing so good but I know a lot of that has to do with her siblings. Being in all four locations for fashion week put a bit of stress on her and she had a breakdown. After the tough love speech her sister gave her she's been putting on a brave face but I can tell she really is better.

She purged once before the first night in New York Fashion Week, but she felt horrible after a very long talk, and after keeping a close eye on her, she hasn't done it again.

I turn my head at the sound of a soft laugh to find Vidia and Sire whispering about something. She shoves him away before laughing harder.

"You're so arrogant." She teases, and Sire pulls her closer.

"I'm *confident*, and confidence is key." Everyone laughs at him, and I shake my head before turning back to Sage. She dances in her seat as she eats. I laugh softly before kissing her cheek.

"My perfect girl."

She smiles up at me, and I wipe the sauce from the corner of her lip before kissing her.

After about an hour in the air, August is officially getting on my nerves. I should've let them take their own jet, but Sage so badly wanted us all to fly together.

"How tall do you think this is?" He raises his arms and when no one answers him he doesn't seem to notice. "Do you think this is taller than our jet?" He turns to Sire who only shrugs and keeps his eyes on the movie he and Vidia are watching on her laptop.

August starts walking around again, and if I didn't know it was impossible to burst with energy, I'd expect him to do so any second now.

"Can he not just sit?" I mumble to Sage and her shoulders slightly drop as she smiles at her brother.

"He has ADHD. He's not too good on plane rides."

I mumble an apology to her for being bothered by him because I'm sure he can't help it.

"August," Hazel sits up and reaches her hand out to him. "Come help me with this." She hands him a Rubix cube and I can tell it's just to keep him busy but her effort is sweet and it's all he focuses on for the next half hour but then Lisette starts next.

"My ass hurts from sitting, let's go see what's back here." She's already walking to the back of the jet, and Sage shoots up from her seat to follow behind.

"Come take a picture of me." Vidia rises next and forces Hazel out of her seat. They walk into the bathroom, and it's pretty nice, so I see the appeal of wanting pictures in my mirror.

With the girls being gone, I glance over at the boys and Sire is still watching the movie as August still tries to solve the Rubix cube. With how focused he is, I think the plane can crash right now and he wouldn't notice.

"I have to ask you guys something." I wait for them to turn to me, but neither of them does. "Don't make me repeat myself."

A smirk grows on Sire's face, and I think he pauses his movie, but he doesn't turn to me.

"What?" August glances between the Rubix cube and me. "I have a question, listen."

He places it aside before giving me his attention, and Sire turns to me slowly, clearly unamused.

I glance behind me and when I hear that Sage sounds pretty far, I turn back to her brothers. "I'm proposing to your sister." I keep my eyes on them and Sire looks as if he doesn't understand English and August is lost for a second before I see his excitement settle in.

"When?!"

"Keep your voice down." I shake my head at him and check if Sage is coming, but she still isn't in sight, so I turn back around. "I'm doing it at the end of our trip."

New York had Fashion Week first, and we're on our way to Milan now, but London is next, then–

"In Paris?!"

I tell August, once again to keep quiet and now I regret telling him because I'm not sure if he can keep a secret.

"Yes."

My answer only excites him more, but when I look over at the stick in the mud, Sire doesn't react.

"You guys haven't even been together for a year."

"Your point?"

Sire rolls his eyes at my tone, but I don't say anything as he explains. "Don't you think it's too soon to propose?"

I try to figure out if he's genuinely asking or if he's just being an asshole because he doesn't want me to marry her, but Sage is mine, whether he likes it or not.

"I didn't think there was a timeline for when you should propose. I'm marrying her eventually. Why prolong the inevitable?"

Sire only watches me for something but I don't add anything else and August speaks up from beside him. "Maybe you should talk to her first, are you sure she wants to get married?"

I let out a scoff before shaking my head at him. "You and I both know your sister wants to dress up in a huge white dress like a princess and get married in a damn castle."

August nods but thinks of something else. "Well, what if you guys want different things? You should discuss that before marriage."

"I want whatever she wants."

"What if–"

"I don't *care*, August. I want to marry her. I want a private wedding, and I'm sure she wants a big one so she'll have the biggest wedding known to man. I want kids now, and she wants to wait, so we will. I want her to take my last name, but she's *the* Sage Loana Hale, so I'll take yours instead and become a fucking Hale too. Whatever she wants, she's getting it so long as I get her in return."

They both nod slowly before Sire turns his head to the side in thought. "Are you asking for our blessing?"

I roll my eyes at how full of himself he is. "Are you her father?" I don't care for Sire's blessing. I would've guessed he knew that by now.

He squints his eyes at me before a smirk reaches his lips. "*Did* you ask our dad?"

"Yes."

I can see the shock on his face even though he tries to hide it, but I'm not fucking with him. It took a little while for her parents to warm up to me, and I still think they aren't my biggest fans, but they want their daughter to be happy, so when I asked her dad at dinner a few weeks ago, he said yes. Not that I wasn't going to marry her if he had said no, but out of respect for their family, I let him think he had a say in it.

"Wait, so what's the question you wanted to ask?" August voices now.

I get up and grab my bag before tossing them both boxes. They each catch one, and when they open it, August's jaw drops, and Sire nods silently, but I can see he's amused. They glance at the ring the other is holding, and both of their eyes slightly widen, more so August's.

"You got her *two* rings?!"

"Shh!" Sire and I snap synchronously before they turn to me.

"I was indecisive." I nod towards the rings in their hands. "I hate to admit it, but you guys know her a bit better–"

"Just a bit?" A smile plays on Sire's face, but I ignore him. "Just pick one."

They glance back down at the ring, one pear-shaped and the other emerald-cut. My mom was adamant that I know whether or not Sage wears gold or silver, and while her jewelry is versatile since most of them were gifts, she's a gold girl, so the rings are also gold and covered in white diamonds on the band with a twenty-seven-carat diamond in the center.

"What are you doing with the second one?"

I only shrug in response since I haven't thought about that yet. I can't really return them since it'll be past the thirty-day mark from the day I bought them when we get back to the States. I'm honestly thinking of letting her have both; that way, she can switch between the two to match her outfits or something.

August is looking at the rings in awe, and when he moves them side to side, I know he's watching the way they shine in the light.

"Pick one and give them back before she comes out here."

They close the box and glance behind me before meeting my eyes. "Emerald-cut." Sire tosses the box back, and I put it back in my bag before taking the second one from August.

"Why?" I glance over at Sire, and he leans back in his seat.

"She tagged along with me when I was buying a promise ring for my girl a few years ago. I remember her mentioning how perfect emerald-cut engagement rings are."

I nod to myself and almost grab the ring to look at it again, but I'm too nervous that Sage will come back out and see.

"It doesn't matter though."

I look over at Sire, and his eyes are already on me.

"She'd wear a ring pop candy with a smile on her face if you proposed with it."

August laughs softly from beside him and agrees before Sire goes on. "She loves you, and I know I give you a hard time, but I can see you love my sister." He shrugs. "I know you don't give a shit about my blessing, but I'm not against you becoming my brother-in-law. Sage always has a smile on her face, but she seems even happier when you simply walk into the room or call her on her phone. As long as that never changes, I'm happy you guys are happy."

I feel a smirk tug at my lips, and he immediately rolls his eyes at me and looks back at his movie. "Careful, Griffin," I start. "You said we wouldn't be friends, and that sounds like we're a step in that direction."

He fakes a gag, and when August genuinely gags, I shake my head at the two of them and get up to find Sage. When I pass the bathroom, I think Vidia and Hazel are still there. They're whispering, and I'm certain they're talking shit about something, but I keep walking to the back.

When I hear her laugh, I realize the room door must be open. Just as I turn, I see it is and peek into the room to find her lying on the bed with her sister.

"Lee! I was just talking about you!"

"Were you?" I flop on the bed beside her and lean on my elbow to look at her.

"She was just talking about how she wants to break up with you."

My head snaps over to Lisette so damn fast I give myself whiplash. "The fuck are you talking about?" I rub my neck before sitting up, but she only shrugs, so I turn to Sage. "The fuck is she talking about?"

She crosses her arms and just stares at me, but I'm so confused.

"What did I do?"

Her face softens, and I clear my throat from how weak my voice sounded just now.

"You did nothing! Why are you believing her?" Sage laughs before pulling me in for a hug, and I must've been holding my breath because when her arms come around me, I don't feel as lightheaded

"I was *kidding*. Why do you look so damn pale?" Lisette *laughs*, and I don't flip her off because I'm sure she'd try to hit me, and I won't hit her back, but I will lock her in the damn bathroom for the next five hours if she touches me.

"Your brothers are calling you." They aren't, but Lisette lets out an annoyed breath and leaves us. When I look back at Sage, she's already watching me with a perfect smile. I wrap an arm around her waist and pull her on top of me before laying on my back. "What were you saying about me?"

Her smile widens before she kisses me. "I was just telling her that I love you."

I feel a smile spread across my face and I catch her lips with mine. "I love you way more." I kiss her again before she can respond and sigh softly against her. "I feel like we haven't been alone in *days*." My hand slips into her shirt, and I rub her back as she rests her head on my shoulder.

"Ugh, I know." She kisses my neck softly as she plays with my hair. "I have a meeting as soon as we land, but I'm all yours tonight." She promises.

I wrap my arms around her as I hold her closer. "You're mine every hour of the day." I remind her, and when she pulls away, a pretty smile plays on her face.

"Very true." She leans in, but I pull away before her lips land on mine.

"Is it true?" I ask, and her brows pull together.

She pulls away so she's sitting up. "Of course, it is." She says as if it were a no-brainer, and I bite my cheek not to smile.

"What was it you said in Italy?"

She looks confused before the realization crosses her face, and she shrugs with a guilty smile. "I have no clue what you're talking about, mister."

"No?"

She starts shaking her head before I flip us over so I'm on top of her, and she lets out a shriek as I hold her hands above her head. "What was it you said in Italy?"

She shrugs again as she bites back a laugh, and I bury my face in her neck to bite her. She squirms and laughs under me, and a smile reaches my mouth at the beautiful sound of her laugh. I pull away to watch her and wish I could marry this woman right now on this plane. She consumes my every waking thought, and I know it sounds so damn unhealthy, but I have no clue what I'd be doing on this earth if she wasn't in my life. She is everything to me.

"You're so lucky you have these pretty dimples." I kiss her cheek as I let go of her hands.

"Why am I lucky?" She kisses my nose, a bright smile still playing on her lips.

My hand slips into her shirt before I steal a kiss. "Because I was going to fuck you until you really did forget ever saying what you said, but now I just want to kiss you softly."

My lips are on hers before she can reply, and when her tongue slides into my mouth, and her legs wrap around my waist, I almost take back what I said, but she pulls away first. "I don't think I want to be lucky."

A smirk touches my lips, but as I reach for her pants, she puts her hand over mine. "Later."

"Now."

She starts shaking her head no as I nod yes in return.

"My brothers are right outside. Are you crazy?" She whispers now, but that didn't even pass my mind.

I take a second to think and it doesn't take much longer to make up my mind. "I don't care. Take your clothes off, please."

She also looks like she's thinking about it, and a smile grows on my face when she glances at the door. "We have to be very quiet." She whispers again, and I kiss her neck.

"I make no promises." I bring my hand between her legs again, and she closes them.

"Liam!" She whispers, and my dick is hard solely from how nervous she is of getting caught. She shakes her head at herself, but a mischievous look plays in her eyes. "Go lock the door."

I quickly rise from the bed before locking it, and when I turn back to her, she still has her clothes on. I throw my shirt aside, and in the few steps it takes to get to her, I'm already bare for her.

"Are you going to make me rip your clothes off, or are you going to get it?"

She shakes her head at me as she pulls her shirt over her head, but as she reaches for her pants, I pull on the middle of her bra, and it snaps like a twig.

"I was going to get it!"

"You took too long. Take your pants off and lay on your stomach."

She does as she's told with no hesitation, and I smile down at her as she watches the door nervously. I kiss my way up her back before leaning into her ear. "This is your last chance, Sage."

I bring a hand between her legs and rub her clit. "They'll hear us no matter how hard you try to keep quiet." I kiss her cheek softly, and she's dripping for me. "Say no." I push two fingers into her entrance. "Tell me to stop."

She lets out a soft moan, and when she turns her face to me, she brings her lips to mine. I waste no time sliding into her, and the minute I do, she moans into my mouth.

I pull away and suck on her neck as I fuck her. She tries her best to keep quiet, and her efforts are cute, but I pound into her a bit harder, and she fills the whole room, maybe the whole plane, with her moans.

"I think Sire heard that." I kiss her cheek and notice she's biting her lip now, so I fuck her harder.

"Liam!"

My whimpers mix with the sound of skin slapping together, and when I glance back down at her, she's burying her face in the sheet. I kiss her neck again before pulling away so I can turn her around.

"Do you remember what you said in Italy?" I keep my gaze on her, and she looks away with a guilty smile on her face.

"I said a lot in Italy." She wraps her legs around me, but I untangle myself from her, and I tease her with my fingers instead, and she squirms under me impatiently. "Liam, *please.*" She keeps her voice quiet now, but I don't give her what she wants.

"Take back what you said."

"I take it back." Her back arches to me, and I can't help but smile at how easily she gives in. "I didn't mean it." She wraps her legs around me again, stroking my cock softly as she brings me closer to her needy pussy.

"I was never available for anyone else but you." She lifts her hips, trying to close the distance between us, but I hold back as I watch her struggle under me.

Her eyes meet mine, and she lets out a frustrated breath before she drops her hips to the bed again. "What do you want?"

"What are you willing to give?" I bring my tip to her entrance, and she keeps her eyes between us as I play with her.

"Anything." Her voice is breathless now as she arches her back to me again, but I bring my hand to her waist and push her down.

"Careful, pretty girl," I warn.

Her eyes meet mine.

"Anything can mean a lot of things."

"Liam, enough with the games."

A soft laugh escapes me at her anger, and I bury my face in her neck. "Are you mine, Sage?" I bring my hand between her legs as I kiss her neck gently.

"Yes, Liam. I'm yours."

I pull in a deep breath, soaking in her words as I bury myself in her. "Say it again."

"I'm yours, Liam." She kisses me behind my ear, and I'm a mess as she whispers sweet nothings to me.

When we finally pull apart, she has a smile on her face. "That was your best performance yet."

I pull away, genuinely offended. "*That* was the best?"

She laughs as she lays on top of me. I kiss her head and wrap my arms around her. "I fucking love you." I kiss her again, and she pulls away to look up at me.

"I love you more."

I smile at her words but shake my head. "Trust me, Dory, that's impossible."

SAGE

"*SAGE LOANA HALE IS THE* It Girl *in New York, Milan, London, and, after tonight, Paris. Do we have ourselves another Josephine Sloan in the making?*"

My jaw drops at how casually they get on the radio and compare me to the greatest model who ever walked a stage.

I think I'm far from Sloan's status but nonetheless flattered, and I can't stop smiling.

"You were perfect tonight, beloved."

I turn to Liam with a smile I can't seem to wipe from my face. He tells me how perfect I am after every show I have, and I believe him every time.

"*Ms. Loana was a pleasure to work with.*" I put the radio up more, and Liam rests his hand on my thigh as he drives. "*She's the sweetest person I've ever met. She's the purest soul and immensely professional. It was an honor to have her model my designs in this season's Fashion Week.*"

I let out a shriek in excitement, but none of this feels real. Designers are usually prideful and don't get on the radio to thank models, but *the* Colette Dubios talks about me like she's known me for years, and I hope this means I get to work with her in the future.

Today was the last day of Fashion Week. Milan and London went perfectly, and while the last few weeks have been crazy, they were more fun. Especially New York, since I was with my girls from Magic and Milan with the Moore Girls.

I glance out the window and smile up at the Eiffel Tower. I've been to Paris a few times but love it a bit more every time I come. It isn't as nice as the pictures make it seem but it's not the worst city and I always get cute pictures.

At the reminder, I turn to Liam. "I hope you know we're not leaving until we get the best pictures."

We haven't posted each other on social media, and August had the idea of taking pictures in front of the Eiffel Tower as our hard launch. Of course, I loved the idea and forced Liam to agree. He caved pretty fast and even got us a photographer.

Liam doesn't reply, and when I turn to him, he only smiles, but I swear his cheeks blush, and I don't tell him because he'll look away, and he looks so freaking cute when he's nervous.

"They're just pictures, Lee." I laugh softly and kiss his red cheek. He nods in response and rushes out of the car. I watch him carefully, and he seems to take a deep breath before running his palms on his pants and getting the door for me.

When I step out, I steal a quick kiss, but when I grab his hand, I feel how sweaty they are. "Are you really nervous about these pictures?" I laugh again. "It's not like an actual photo shoot, Lee. It's just to post on Famoura."

"I'm not nervous." He swallows, and it seems nervous to me, and I feel bad for laughing. If he's nervous about these pictures, he won't last a day as a model.

He pulls my hand, and we walk in front of the Eiffel Tower. I glance around, and it's weird to see the place so empty. Liam got them to shut the street down because there was no doubt that everyone would be swarming me, especially since I've been on every TV and billboard in the city for the whole week.

"Did the photographer call you?" I don't see anyone, but Liam only shrugs.

"Maybe she's late."

I shake my head and bite back an *I told you so*. He was adamant on hiring someone *he* wanted, and I tried telling him I knew plenty of great photographers, but he didn't listen. I don't care enough to be upset, so I watch the Eiffel Tower as the lights turn on. I let out a gasp when they shimmer a beautiful emerald green because the lights are never green but it's so pretty and reminds me of why it's my favorite color.

"Look at that."

I turn at the sound of Liam's voice, and when I see a few fireflies lighting up the night, my jaw drops. "Oh my God! I've never seen fireflies here before." I watch them in awe as more and more fly around us.

A quiet violin starts, and I recognize the song far too quickly. "Okay, *what* is happening?"

Ma Belle Evangeline starts playing, and there's no way it's a coincidence that this song starts when a bunch of fireflies appear, but it feels like I'm right in the middle of my favorite scene in *The Princess and the Frog*.

"Maybe it has to do with that?" Liam points behind me, and when I turn to the Eiffel Tower, a poster unrolls, and my jaw drops with it when I read the huge *Will You Marry Me?* sign.

"Sage."

I squeeze my eyes shut before the tears can start, and when Liam takes my hand, I shake my head, more to myself.

"Beloved, please look at me."

I pull in a deep breath and force the tears at bay, but the minute I turn to Liam and find him on one knee, I'm a mess.

"Sage–" His voice breaks, and he squeezes his eyes shut before looking down. "Fuck, I bet your sister *ten* thousand dollars I wouldn't cry."

That sounds just like Lisette. I let out a laugh and pat my cheeks, trying not to ruin my makeup, and I'm so glad I let Vidia and Hazel convince me to wear waterproof mascara. *They knew? How long have they known?*

Liam pulls in a deep breath before trying again, and when his eyes meet mine, I barely blink. My favorite part of the song comes and he says the lyrics just in time, "I adore you. I love you, Sage."

I let out a soft laugh, which turns into a soft cry as he continues.

"You light up my life, Sage. I used to crave being alone. I don't like people, but then... you fucked up my brain chemistry, and I don't ever want to be cured."

I blink away my tears to clear my vision and wipe his cheek as he continues.

"My *soul* aches to be in your presence, and I don't just *want* to spend the rest of my life with you, but I need to. I need you to be my wife. I need you to be the mother of my kids. I need you, Sage, and I need to be everything you want me to be."

"Every cell in my body calls for me to give you what you want. Whether that be three nasty cats from the shelter or letting you call me Leslie so you could fucking smile."

I break into a laugh, and he kisses the back of my hand.

"Say yes, Sage. Let me make you my wife, and I'll make you the happiest you could ever be. Or the proudest. Anything. Anything you want is yours, my offer to mop the ocean and sweep the sand off every beach is still standing but say yes. Marry me."

"Yes!" My laugh turns into another cry as I throw my arms around him. "I do! I will! I want to marry you. Yes, yes, yes!"

He laughs before standing, and I keep my arms around him and wrap my legs around him.

"I was so damn nervous I forgot to show you the damn ring." I laugh at him, but when he opens the box, my jaw drops at the *gorgeous* emerald-cut ring.

"It's perfect."

"*You're* perfect." He slips the ring on my finger before planting a soft kiss on my lips. "And you're my fiance." He kisses me again. "My soon-to-be wife."

I let out an excited squeal and when I turn to the side the photographer is here. My head whips around at the sound of cheering, and I notice everyone making their way to us. My siblings, their girlfriends, Jordan, *Moon*.

I turn back at Liam and he's already watching me. "You wanted your big gesture billboard proposal with a photographer and your brothers." He kisses me. "You got it."

He remembered.

"How'd I get lucky enough to end up with you?" I can't pull my eyes from his, and everyone reaches us and congratulates us, but it's as if it's still just the two of us.

"I should be asking you that." His lips meet mine before he buries his face in the crease of my neck. "My perfect girl."

The End

Epilogue

LIAM

One year later

I QUICKLY CLIMB OUT OF the car and before I can make it to Sage's side she's already out. She grabs a hold of my hand and gives me a reassuring squeeze as we walk for the house and I've never been one to pray but as we make our way closer, I silently pray my mom is okay. Capri just told us to get here fast, but I'm losing my mind.

"It's going to be okay." Sage squeezes my hand and I pull in a deep breath before walking into the house. My eyes scan the room and I spot Capri's red hair and Moon laughing in front of her.

"Pri."

She whips around, and when her smile doesn't falter, I let out a relieved breath.

"Hey, guys!" Moon pulls Sage in for a hug, but I keep my eyes on Capri.

"Liam..." She looks between Sage and me, and I don't know what the fuck the suspense is about, but it's killing me. Just before I tell her to spit it the hell out, she says, "Your mom is lucid."

I go still, and I can see Sage turn to me in the corner of my eyes.

"What?"

"She's lucid. She remembers... everything. It may not last long, maybe a few hours or the whole day. Maybe she'll be lucid for the week if we're lucky, but I called you as soon–"

"She remembers?"

Pri barely finishes nodding before I pull Sage with me to find her. I stop in my tracks when I see her in the backyard, skipping rocks in the pond.

"Are you okay?"

I look over at Sage, but I can't seem to form any words.

"Do you want to go alone or–"

I quickly shake my head, no, and she holds my hand a bit tighter. "Okay... I would say you can take your time, but the last time she was lucid, we didn't make it here in time, so I think we should go."

She keeps her tone light, and I can't help but smile at her. I take in another breath before Sage leads us out, and I'm so grateful she's here. When we reach the pond, my mom has her back to us, and Sage softly clears her throat.

When her eyes meet mine, it's as if she's seeing me for the first time in years, and I realize she really is in there. I immediately pull her in for a hug, and she holds me incredibly close.

"Oh, my sweet boy."

I squeeze my eyes shut at the sound of her voice, and I feel her kiss my shoulder softly. When I pull away, I smile down at her and wipe her tears.

"Hi, Mom."

She smiles up at me and pulls me in again. I don't know how long we stand there but when we pull away I notice Sage wiping her tears and she isn't discreet about it although I know she tries to be.

I pull her hand before kissing her cheek, and I make sure to keep her close. My mom looks between the two of us, and when I see the tears building in her eyes, I have to look away. I focus on Sage instead, and when she smiles at my mom, it does something to my heart.

"Capri filled me in just a bit before you got here." My mom takes Sage's hand and smiles so big at her ring.

I figured when she's lucid, she'd remember everything, but Capri explained to us the last time this happened that she might still be confused when piecing together the past and the blurriness of the last few years.

"When's the wedding?"

"This December." Sage goes on excitedly.

She was stuck between a summer or winter wedding, but after seeing a wedding photo shoot in the snow, she was sold on the idea, so now I get to freeze my ass in a few months on our wedding day, but I'll do it with a smile on my face.

I watch them get lost in a conversation and I'm so glad my mom was able to meet Sage, really meet her.

"The wedding sounds like it's going to be beautiful. How's everything... else." She looks between the two of us. "No babies?"

Sage's eyes slightly widen and I let out a soft laugh when she turns to me for help.

"No, Mom. No babies, *unfortunately*." I point my last word at Sage as I wrap an arm around her waist and rub her belly. She seems to shrink as we both look at her accusingly, but I pull her closer before kissing her temple. "You know I'm kidding, beloved," I whisper in her ear before turning to my mom.

"She wants to wait a little while. She's exactly where she wants to be in her career so we're going to let her have her time to shine before I make her take a break to have my kids."

Sage smiles from ear to ear, as she does every time I say anything along the lines of *her having my kids*. I understand why she wants to wait, and she promised me we'll have a kid in four years *tops*, but I'm not holding her to it. It'll happen when it happens.

When my mom looks over at me, a sad look crosses her face, and she tries to put on a brave face, but I see right through her. "Promise me you guys will record the wedding. Not just the traditional wedding video but everything else. I don't want to miss anything from my baby's big day."

I promise her I will and silently hope for a miracle that she's lucid on our wedding day, too, but the chances of that are slim to none.

"What if..." Sage takes my hand. "We get married today?"

"What?" I look between her eyes, but she only smiles up at me.

"We all want her a part of the wedding and–" She turns to my mom. "–you're lucid right now. We don't know how long this miracle will last or if we'll get another one so we can get married right now."

My mom looks between the two of us before shaking her head. "I can't ask you to do that–"

"You didn't ask." Sage smiles at her, but I take her hand before turning her to me.

"Sage, you put so much work into the wedding. Are you really willing to sacrifice it for..."

"You?" She nods. "Of course I am." *How the hell did I become worthy of this woman?*

"Are you–"

"I'm sure! We can still have the big wedding in December. I'll still get to wear my big dress and take all of the pictures, it'll be a four-month late after-party for today."

I pull her in for a hug and nuzzle my face in her neck. "Thank you, Dory."

"This works perfectly."

I pull away, and she's still smiling as if she really wants to do this.

"Now you can get the private, intimate wedding you wanted, and I can still have my over-the-top princess wedding." She turns to my mom now. "And you won't miss a second of it."

I refuse to fucking cry, so I swallow the lump down my throat, and we get ready to go to the courthouse. Conveniently, Sage just got done with a photo shoot, so her hair and makeup are done, not that she needed it. I would've married her first thing in the morning with her in her pajamas and bonnet.

She has her agent pick her up a dress since she wanted to save her other dress for the bigger wedding, and her brother gets me a suit. Less than an hour later we're all in the courthouse and I'm genuinely shocked everyone dropped everything to be here. We kept it small. My mom, Sage's parents, and siblings, along with their partners. Moon, Capri, Jordan, and Mel also came.

It's more people than I wanted for *private* and if I could have it my way it'd just be our parents but Sage at least wanted our friends here. Especially her siblings so I walk down the aisle with my mom on my arm with a smile.

When we reach the alter, my mom kisses my cheek softly before taking a seat, and as I wait for Sage to walk through those doors, I realize what the fuck we're about to do, and my stomach is doing backflips, but I don't know why.

I'm not nervous to marry her. I've known for a while now that I wanted to marry this woman. I think the nerves settle because this is real. We're going to be *married*, and I cannot fuck it up.

I won't.

I pull in a deep breath, but then the doors swing open, and as everyone stands, I forget to breathe. When Sage said her agent was picking up a quick *little* backup dress, I should've known it'd still be over the fucking top.

She looks... stunning in her white gown. Her veil trails behind her for what seems like miles, and when my eyes meet hers, my vision starts to blur. I refuse to look away from her, but even if I wanted to, I couldn't. With every step closer she takes, my body screams louder to have her beside me.

Her dad clings to her arm as they make their way down the aisle, and when I notice her bouquet of blue peonies, I look over at my mom with a smile, and she must realize Sage intentionally chose her favorites.

Her dad kisses her forehead before letting me take her hand, and I immediately pull her in for a hug. "I love you so fucking much, Dory."

She laughs softly but when I hear it morphe into a soft cry I pull away and wipe her tears. "You're going to be upset if your makeup is ruined for the pictures."

She laughs harder, and I bring my lips to her.

Someone clears their throat from beside us, pulling Sage away. "People usually wait for me to say 'kiss the bride.'"

Everyone breaks into a laugh before we take a step away from each other. The officiant jokingly asks if we're ready, but before we can say yes, my mom makes her way to us.

I go still, silently fucking hoping she didn't check out on us again, but she apologizes quietly and turns to Sage. "I'm not sure if you have something borrowed, but–" She unclips her pin before handing it to Sage.

It's a lavender S with a white dove, and I immediately recognize it from the pins we gave out at Shanti's funeral.

"I was actually missing something borrowed, thank you."

My mom helps her pin it on the shoulder of her dress and I turn my head away from the crowd as the tears start coming.

"Shanti would have loved you." My mom's voice breaks before she goes on. "You take care of him for me, okay?"

I let my eyes fall shut as Sage promises that she will. I feel a soft kiss on my hand and force myself to look down at my mom. She gives me a small smile before kissing my hand again and making her way back to her seat before either of us can cry anymore.

"Ready?" Sage whispers before wiping my cheek.

"Yeah."

Sage and I don't tear our eyes apart from each other as the officiant starts the wedding, and it's as if we're the only ones in the room. By the time it's time to say our vows, it's clear Sage's excitement is traded for nerves.

"You go first." She whispers to me, and I shake my head at her as I bite back a smile. "Please?"

"No, you go first."

"No!" She whispers a bit louder, and I have to hold back a laugh as she nervously looks around the room.

"You forgot your vows, didn't you, Dory?"

"Of course not!" She looks offended that I even suggested that but a soft laugh still escapes her. "The wedding wasn't for another four months, I didn't get to write the end of mine." She looks like she feels horrible and I reassure her that it's fine before giving in and going first.

"Sage," My eyes start to sting again, and I mumble a curse at how fucking emotional I am. Her brothers are going to bully the shit out of me for this, but I genuinely couldn't care.

"You make me want to be a better person. I promise to always be and give you anything you want. I promise to support every choice you make. Whether it's to try to ride my bike and completely eat shit—"

Her pretty laugh reaches my ears, and I smile down at her at the reminder. She bought me a new bike and then begged me to let her ride it a *short distance*. Luckily she was fine when she fell since she fell before she even started the damn thing.

"–or to leave the country to model. I'll follow you even when you barely want to look at me."

She still smiles up at me, although a sadder smile touches her lips.

"I promise to never give up on us or you. I love you, Sage. I promise to love you forever. Death will not do us part because even in the afterlife, I'll find you and love you then."

There are a few awes from our family, but I keep my smile on Sage as I wipe her tears before she voices her vows to me.

"Leslie–" She barely starts before breaking into a hysterical laugh. I can't help but laugh beside her as I shove her hand away. I glance over at Moon, and he's dying of laughter. *I know this was his damn idea.*

"Liam—" She takes my hand again, pulling my gaze back to her. "—I once said you didn't meet my standards, and ever since, I've been eating my words. I hope we're partners in every life. You make me feel like I truly am without fault, and in return, I will remind you that you're *beyond* worthy of love."

I blink my tears away as she continues.

"You once wrote me a letter promising to give me all of your mornings, even though you hate them, but you have. You do what you say, and you always keep your promises, so I promise to keep this one; I promise to never leave your side. I promise to love you until my last breath, even when you lose your temper or threaten my cats after I refuse to give you what you want."

I let out a soft laugh but quickly clear my throat when a cry climbs up.

"I wanted to add more, but–"

"It's perfect, *you're* perfect."

When the officiant finally announces for us to kiss, I pull my perfect girl in, and I know for certain that marrying this woman was the best choice of my life.

Extended Epilogue

SAGE

Three years later

THE SOUND OF EVERYONE'S LAUGHTER and chattering slow-ly starts to fade as the second line appears on the test. I'm stuck in place for a beat before my heart feels like it's in my throat. My hands slowly start to shake, and I have to remind myself to breathe, but I don't think I remember how.

"Liam!" My voice comes out a bit more scared than I intended and I hear my family quiet down before my brothers tell Liam that I just called him.

"Dory? What's wrong?"

The door to the bathroom quickly opens, but he shuts it just as fast as he sees whatever look I'm wearing. His face slightly drops before his eyes scan me carefully. "What is it? Are you okay?" He grabs hold of my hand before touching me frantically, looking for something as if I'm physically harmed.

I can't seem to get the words out as I grab the pregnancy test and hand it to him. I watch for his reaction, and he brings it closer to him, but the second he realizes what this means, he only looks happy.

"You're pregnant?"

I nod slowly before breaking into a sob. He pulls me in and kisses me profusely. "Why are you crying like that?"

"I'm scared!" I break into another sob as I hold him tighter.

"Why are you scared, beloved?" He pulls away to look at me and he's just *smiling* as he brings his lips to mine.

"Because I'm *three* months postpartum, Lee!"

Our entire world was flipped upside down the first time I got pregnant, and motherhood has been amazing, but I can't imagine how we're going to manage another baby with our hands already so full.

"It's going to be okay." He takes hold of my shaking hands and kisses them softly. "We'll figure it out; you're *fine*, beloved." His words somehow drape a blanket of tranquility over me, and when I pull in another breath, I feel my panic die down.

"I don't understand how this could've happened."

A smirk grows on his face before his hands wrap around my waist. "I think I have some ideas as to how this happened." He kisses my neck, and I let out a laugh before shoving him away.

"This is all your fault."

He breaks into a laugh and pulls me back into him. "No one is at *fault*. This is good, right?"

I let out a breath before nodding because while I'm scared, I'm excited for another baby.

"Good," Liam nods before kissing my cheek twice. "And if anyone *was* at fault, then it'd be your horny ass."

I cover my face sheepishly before burying my face in his chest because he's right. After I was given the green light to have sex again, it's all I've been in the mood for. He *laughs* at me as if he just had the same thoughts, and I shake my head at myself.

"Hey, I'm not complaining."

"I bet you aren't!" I shove him again with a laugh before glancing down at my stomach. "My body is *never* going to look the way it was." I don't mean to sound so disappointed, but that's how it came out. I knew this was what came with being a mom, but it took a *long* time for me to accept the way my body changed.

"And that's fine," Liam reassures me, and I'm reminded of how supportive he's been in helping me accept my new body.

I let my eyes meet him, and he's watching me carefully as he rubs my stomach. "You are perfect the way you are, and you'll still be perfect with however my baby changes your body." He slowly drops to his knees, and I feel my eyes sting as he brings his lips to my stomach.

"I love you." My voice comes out just above a whisper, but when his eyes meet mine, I know he heard me just fine.

"I love you more." He kisses my stomach one more time before rising to his full height and kissing my cheek. "We're not naming this one after your brother."

I throw my head back with a laugh, and he smiles down at me, but I'm sure he's serious. When we announced our first pregnancy, August was very persistent that we name our baby after him since Sire didn't name their daughter after him, and that clearly wasn't going to work since she's a girl, but they said no before the gender reveal.

I hear my brothers laughing about something from the kitchen before the girls laugh, and a smile touches my lips.

"Can we tell them now since everyone's here?" I hear the excitement start to creep into my voice, and Liam smiles down at me before kissing my cheek again.

"Whatever you want." He looks between my eyes like he never wants to look away, and I'm so lucky that after all this time, we still feel like we're in that honeymoon phase. It shouldn't even be considered a phase anymore. This is my life.

I wipe my tears and grab the pregnancy test as I try to think of a quick way we can tell everyone. I tell Liam we should go with the basic bun in the oven so he gets it ready as I get my vlog camera and act like I'm recording for this week's vlog.

After a while, I hear a soft cry and look over at the baby in Liam's mom's arms on our couch. I walk over to tap a soft kiss on Jerzi's head. "Can I hold her?" I smile down at my baby, and she isn't too fussy, but I still want to comfort her.

I look over at Liam's mom, and when she looks up at me, I can see the confusion on her face as she holds my baby closer to her. I give her a small smile and Liam kisses our daughter before taking her from his mom.

"It's okay." He reassures her as I take our daughter from him.

"Shanti's been a bit fussy," She quickly stands. "You should let me hold her." She holds her hands out, but I take a small step back before offering her a smile, and I can see the way Liam tries to keep his small smile intact.

"Let my wife hold her for a while. You had her all morning."

I think she grows upset that I took the baby, but before she can voice a protest, Capri takes her hand and distracts her on the couch.

Ever since we've had the baby, Liam's mom has been wanting to visit more often, and I, of course, love having her around because momma's boy Liam is my favorite.

She thinks Jerzi is Shanti, and we don't correct her so she doesn't get upset or even more confused, but either way, I'm fine with her believing my baby is the daughter she lost. It brings her peace and doesn't negatively affect us. Except for when she gets a bit greedy and wants to hog my kid all day.

"Holy shit."

I turn on my heels at the shock in Sire's voice.

"Vid," He grabs her hand, and I walk over to see what's happening. "Vidia, look!"

I follow their line of sight and Mariana, their daughter, is standing with a smile and it's as if everyone holds their breath as she picks up her foot.

"Come on, princess." Sire holds his hand out to her, and I quickly grab my camera and turn it to her.

"Come to mommy." Vidia gets on the floor and holds a hand out.

"No, come to daddy."

I let out a soft laugh as they shove each other for their daughter's attention, but when she takes her first step, they go still, along with everyone else.

"Oh my goodness!" I quickly cover my mouth and rock Jerzi in my arms when she cries again.

"Here, beloved, let me take her." Liam kisses my cheek, and I smile up at him as he takes the baby and gives her a bottle.

When I glance back at my niece, she laughs softly before taking another step to her parents. They keep calling her while fighting for who she'll go to, and Mariana wobbles closer.

We all watch in shock as she takes her first steps all the way into Sire's arms. "Good job, baby!" He scoops her into her arms and we all cheer. Vidia looks happy but *not* about who she chose.

"You cheated."

I break into a laugh at how competitive she is, and my brother smiles down at his wife before kissing his daughter. "*How* did I cheat, Vid? She–"

"That's not fair. Give me my kid."

"You're such a sore loser!"

"*Give* me her."

The entire room is full of laughter as Sire walks away in a hurry, and Vidia quite literally tries to fight him for her baby.

I notice Liam shutting the oven, and when he turns to me, he gives me a soft nod. I feel my excitement grow as I set up my camera and sit at the kitchen counter with Liam as he feeds the baby.

August is looking through our cabinets, and I smile to myself. "August, can you check what's in the oven?"

He nods before turning to the oven. He looks confused at first glance, and takes the bun out. "It's just bread."

I laugh softly and cover my face because I probably should've told someone else but it'll be fun to watch him keep guessing.

"Where was it, though?"

He looks confused as he gestures to the oven. "Sage, you just saw me take it out of the oven." He laughs softly before closing the oven and putting the bread aside. I look over at Liam for help.

He shakes his head before turning to my twin. "August, this is a guessing game."

August turns back to us, and he immediately looks excited. "Okay, bread and an oven." He looks over at the bread again before glancing at the oven, probably for another hint.

I laugh softly, and Liam shakes his head before smiling down at his daughter as if everyone else in the room doesn't exist. I kiss the side of his face before turning around.

"Sire."

He and Vidia are taking pictures together in my mirror with their baby, but they both turn to me.

"Can you guys come help August with this guessing game we're playing?"

August says he doesn't need help, although he's been whispering to Hazel and Lisette for help.

Sire and Vidia walk over and look between the bun and August.

"I think I need a hint." August looks over at us but we don't offer any help so he turns to our brother. "Look–" He hands him the bun. "–it was in the oven."

I look between all of them, and when Vidia's eyes light up, I bring a finger to my mouth, and she nods discreetly before whispering to Hazel in Spanish. When she looks over at me, her eyes cut down to my stomach, and I nod, confirming their thoughts.

"Really?!" Lisette's jaw drops now but she covers her mouth as all of the girls walk over to me for a hug.

"Really what– wait did you guys figure it out already?"

I let out a laugh as I hug the girls, and they whisper their congratulations as the boys struggle in the kitchen.

"I'm confused!" August sounds like he's getting frustrated, but I know it's just because he doesn't like to be left out.

"Think about it, babe." Hazel helps him as she gestures to the oven. "What was in the oven?"

"A piece of bread?"

The girls laugh beside me, but Sire takes the bun from him and turns it in his hand. "I'm so fucking confused, it's just bread."

Vidia laughs softly, and when her daughter laughs in her arms, she kisses her head. "Tell Daddy it's a *bun* and not bread. Say *bun*."

"Bun, Daddy!"

We laugh at my niece, and Vidia pulls her closer before praising her for being so smart.

I see the realization set for Sire, and he looks between Liam and me. "Really?"

I nod slowly and blink my tears away.

"Really *what*?"

"There's a bun in the oven, August." Sire and Liam say at the same time, growing a bit impatient.

"What does that *mean*?"

"Oh my God," Liam mumbles beside me. "A *bun* in the *oven*. In reference to what have you heard that saying?" He gestures to Jerzi, then brings his hand to my stomach.

I can see the gears turning in August's head as he studies the two of us. "Wait..." His eyes drop down to my stomach as his smile grows. "Are you?"

I give him a nod before letting out a soft laugh. He rushes over to us, and I force my tears to stay at bay as he pulls me in for a hug. "Congratulations, guys!"

We thank him, and when August tries to hug Liam, he uses the excuse that he's holding the baby. He's warmed up to my brothers quite a bit these last few years but Liam doesn't like anyone touching him, it's not just my brothers.

"You two are *quick*." Lis teases and the girls laugh from beside her.

"That's because this one has been fucking like a rabbit recently."

"Liam Leslie!"

My brothers tell him they didn't need to know that and the entire room breaks into a laugh but I cover my face as I feel it heating in embarrassment. I hear Liam let out a deep laugh from beside me and I almost elbow him until I remember he's holding my baby.

I feel his warm breath by my ear before he even says anything. "I don't know why you're acting embarrassed. Horny Sage is my favorite."

"Stop it!" I bite back a laugh, and he smiles down at me before kissing me softly.

"I'm kidding." He pulls me closer and I melt into him as I look down at Jerzi, and she sleeps in his arms perfectly. "Mommy Sage is my favorite."

I look back up, and he's already watching me with a smile.

"And pregnant Sage." He rubs my stomach again. "Every version of you is my favorite. *You're* my favorite."

I bring my lips to his, and my worries from before seem so silly now. I know we'd be able to handle whatever is thrown our way as long as he's by my side.

"They'll be Irish twins!" I gasp at the sudden realization that both babies would be born within the same year. "What do you think it's going to be?"

"I want another girl." He answers so quickly, but it doesn't shock me. Liam wants all girls and while I said I don't care the gender, I secretly want at least one boy. I grew up with brothers, and I want my daughter to have that.

I look over at Hazel, and she's using Mariana's hand to flip off Sire. I break into a laugh before she says, "She actually meant to walk to Vidia. Look, she doesn't even like you."

"Stop teaching her that." Sire covers his daughter's hand before pulling her from Hazel's arms. "You're just mad she likes me more than you *and* your best friend."

Before they can bicker about this, *again,* I call Hazel over. "What was that thing you guys did to determine the gender of the baby?"

Vidia turns to us before Hazel can answer. "With the fork and spoon?"

"Yes! Can we try it?"

They agree, and I cover my eyes as they set up two chairs, each with a pillow on them, one with a fork under it, and the other with a spoon. When they tell me to uncover my eyes, everyone is standing around the chairs, and I look between the two of them.

"Don't think about it." Liam urges, but I don't look over at him because I'm sure he's looking at the one with the spoon under it. Without a second thought, I walk over to the chair on the right, and the whole room starts cheering.

"You owe me five hundred dollars." Lis voices, and I break into a laugh as Sire pulls out his wallet.

I quickly stand, and when I pick up the pillow, it reveals a fork under it. I pick it up before turning to Liam with a smile. "It's a boy!"

"We don't know that."

I tilt my head to the side as he lets August take the baby and closes the distance between us. "You believed it when I sat on the spoon for Jerzi."

He only shrugs, biting back a smile, and I narrow my eyes at him, "You secretly want a boy, don't you?"

He laughs softly as he pulls me in. "I have no idea what you're talking about. I want all girls."

I let out a laugh before he turns more serious.

"I don't care what it is as long as you're both healthy." He brings his lips to mine before I can respond, and I wrap my arms around his neck. In an instant, he lifts me, bringing my legs around his waist.

"Hey!" August's voice pulls us apart. "No PDA in front of the kids." He covers my daughter's eyes although she is sleeping, and Sire also covers his daughter's eyes.

I can't help but laugh at them, but Liam pulls me back in, and when his tongue slides into my mouth, I know it's just to mess with my brothers, but I kiss him back, and I'm *so* glad I get to call this man my husband and even happier he's the father of my kids.

Acknowledgments

Ash, words will never express how grateful I am for you! You helped with *so* much behind the scenes for this book, and I appreciate you so much for it.

Thank you to all of my beta readers, and *a huge* thank you to Lia and Marianne. You all helped me shape this book. This book was formed around a heavy topic, and I'm especially thankful to my strong beta readers who related to Sage and were able to help me represent her eating disorder the best way I could. I adore you all, remember you're perfect <3.

My readers. I LOVE you guys!! The love that I got from the amount I announced this book encouraged me to keep going every time I felt like giving up. I wrote The Plan for fun and for the girlies in my private story, but Without Fault was for you all. I love each and every one of you so much. Thank you for the support!

My content creator team, you all mean so much to me. The way you all helped me promote this book made me feel so special. Thank you for sharing this book every step of the way with me.

My parents! My number one supporter in everything I do. Thank you for supporting my dream and helping me make it a reality. I love you both so much !

About The Author

Janiah Benitez is a twenty-year-old hopeless romantic from New York City. When she's not writing, Janiah is trying to complete her neverending TBR. She's studying for her second passion, marine science, and between classes, she dreams of opening a bookstore.